Contact the author: brian@briangarrity.com

Or
Visit: www.briangarrity.com

Cover Design: Azlan Macleod
Author photo: Robert Ames
Illustrations: Brian D Garrity

For Father and Mother,
and all Brothers and Sisters of the river,
past, present, and future.

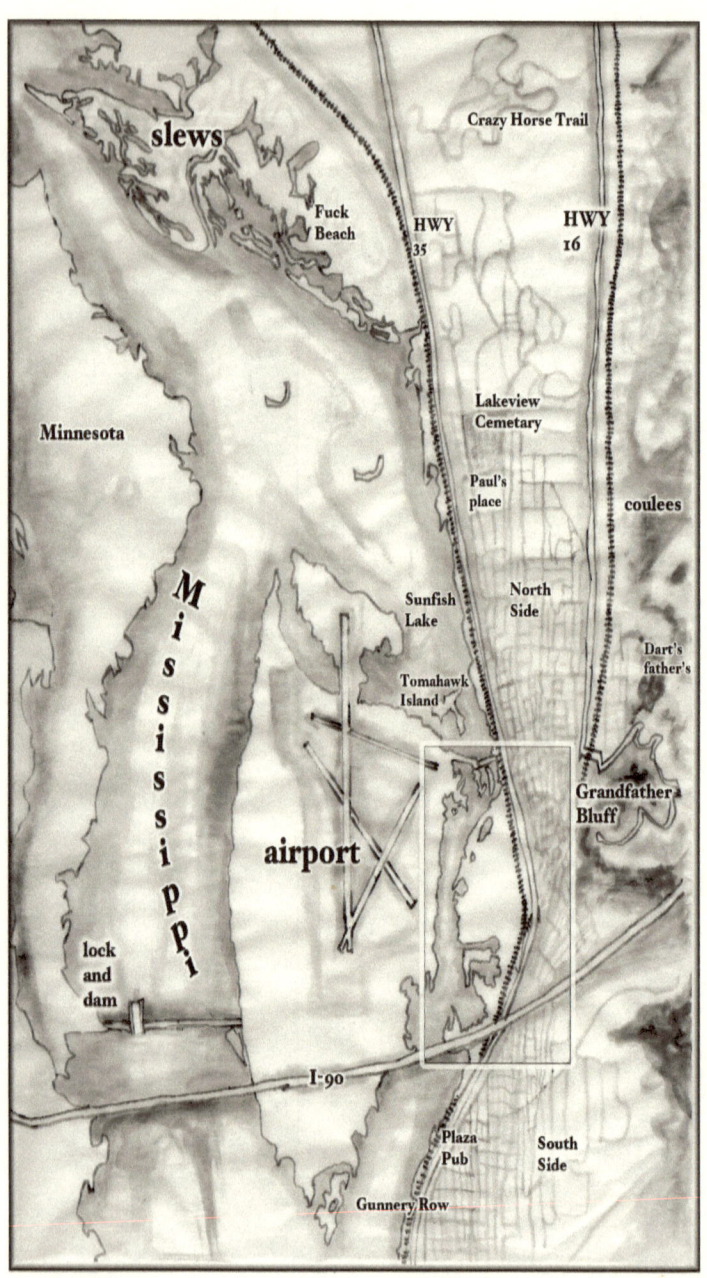

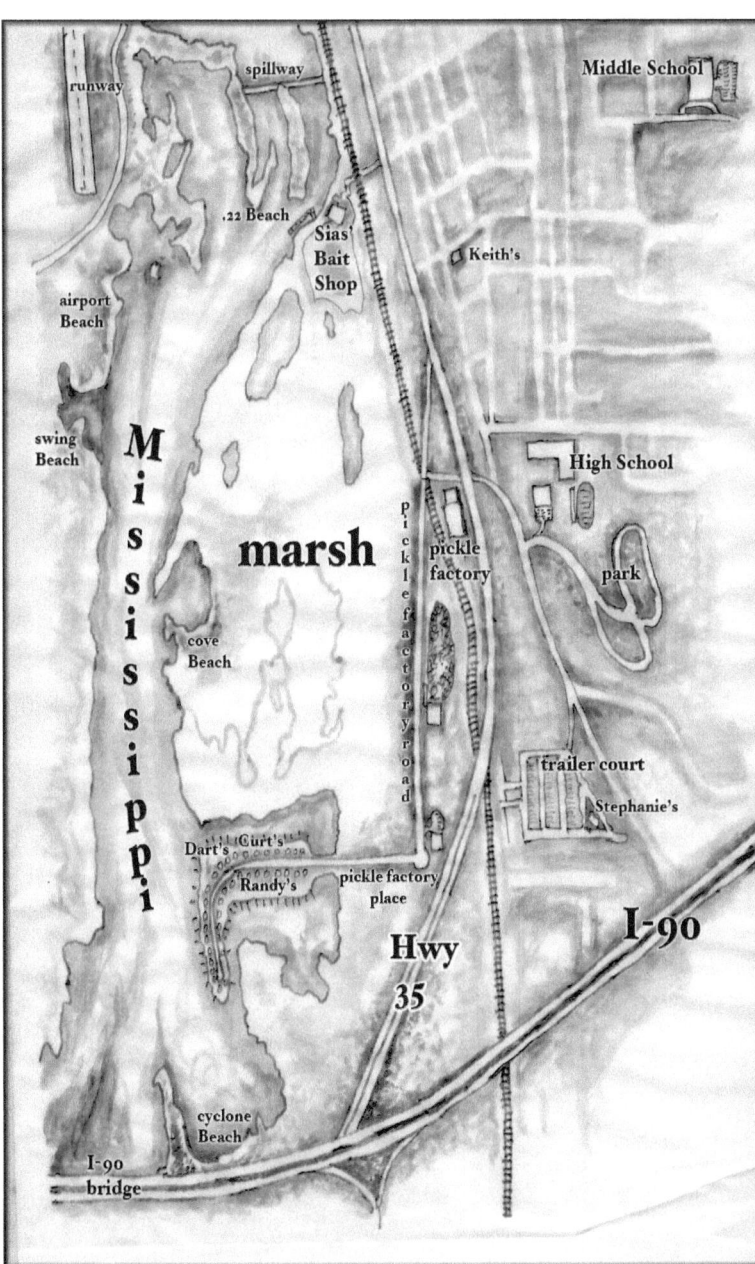

Still Waters Run Deep

1

AIRPORT BEACH

The bow of the small flat-bottom cut over the still waters of the canal like magic. *Like a diamond on glass,* thought Dart. He liked the feeling of his hand controlling the throttle, cut just back from full, saving that top-end for when you really needed it. The twenty-five horse Evinrude blared obediently, and sent a numbing vibration down his arm and throughout the craft. *It's a good motor,* he thought. *The hell with Curt and his damn Merc's.* Of course, everyone knew Curt's boat was faster, and if they didn't, Curt would be the first to correct that terrible oversight. Still, even *he* had been mesmerized into silence by the provocative beauty of the river on the verge of the summer evening.

It had taken awhile to plane the craft out with so many people aboard, and for one terrifying moment he thought that the old motor might fail him, might embarrass him in front of, no, not Curt; *Lynette.* A pleasant tingle shivered through him as he glanced up to the bow where she sat poised into the wind. His eyes crawled up her smooth, tanned thighs to her jeans, cut so short he could make the edge of her swimsuit peeking out. After that, nothing but the curve of spine and cut of shoulder-blade, interrupted by mere strap of bikini.

An older girl, in his boat.

She turned her head back, as if reading his mind, hair blown into a halo, and offered a serene smile of approval.

5

"Wing-dam!" Curt's voice in his ear.

Startled, he realized he was heading for a submerged run of rocks committed to memory since childhood. Expertly, he cut the throttle, swung rudder to port, slewing the hull violently from left to right, gunned the motor again, and swung the craft around the submerged menace.

Lynette scowled at him, now from the floor of the boat.

"Just about took out your lower unit, you did." Smugness radiated from Curt. "A Merc' could probably take a hit like that, but not that old 'Rude."

Randy shot him a glance from the center bench. *The hell with him, too.* Although they lived in the same neighborhood on the river, Randy's parents were too poor to afford even a rowboat. Randy was forever a tourist in his own backyard.

They left the peaceful little canal and howled into the main channel. The hull started a rhythmic slapping on the choppier waters, and each time it rose to meet another wave, the motor would let out a little yelp as the lower unit surfaced.

"Sounds like ya might be cavitating." Curt offered helpfully. "Might wanna' reset that tilt pin."

"It's set just fine." Dart twisted the throttle open and the small craft leaped forward. A surprised little bleat came from Lynette, and Curt let out a mighty whoop. Randy got a wider, tighter grip on the bench, but he was grinning like a fool.

Because this was it. This was the thing you just couldn't put into words, the thing you tried to explain to other people, to the town people. The sense of wholeness, of belonging to a small piece of perfection, shoreline slipping by and the water rushing to greet you, thunder of wind in your ears and hot sun on your body. Exhilaration of flying dangerously fast and close over the river with only a thin layer of aluminum between you and its surface, unforgiving as concrete at this speed. A nearly spiritual balance of all things, mechanical, human, and of nature. It was a bond no family, nation, or institution could impose or control. The river was their matriarch, and her judgments or rewards superceded any, and all authority.

The sun was a golden haze as they rounded the cove and spotted Airport Beach. The shoreline was checkered with the hulls of various craft, all carefully tied and anchored, and the beach itself was peppered with activity. *A high school party*, thought Dart, *and Lynette their ticket in*. He brought the craft in easy and fast, cutting the motor at the last moment. With practiced hand, he locked the outboard motor up and they slid smoothly to a stop on the calm shore.

*   *   *   *

Rip stood with his feet in the hot sand and observed the scene with detached interest. Lynette stepped lithely off the flat's bow and jiggled pleasantly up the beach to greet a cluster of the younger girls, mostly freshman and sophomores. He vaguely recognized the kids in the small boat as locals, the new generation of River Rats. The pilot, Dart was his name, was some sort of artist or something. The one next to him, Curt, he had seen leading the silhouette of an impressively fast little Mercury motor. Might be a tinkerer; probably just switched out the standard power to a speed prop. Third one he didn't recognize, was kind of scrunched up in the middle seat.

He surveyed his own vehicle, a battered silver Alumacraft V-hull, outfitted with an ancient Johnson thirty-five horsepower, contours suggesting art deco design. Plenty of power left in the old girl, but she just couldn't compete top-end with the newer, lighter speed models. He turned his attention back to the boys, who appeared unsure as to what to do next.

"*Hey! Hee-haa!* Shitly, Moe, look what we got here!" Voice like a bottle-cap pulled along a piano wire.

Here comes trouble.

The trio emerged from the crowd, strolling casually to the boy's boat, Paul, in customary pole position, his face and demeanor bearing an almost surreal resemblance to Popeye, if Popeye had had short shaggy red hair. There the resemblance ended. Paul's body was lanky, lean and tall, skin shot over with a good dose of freckles. In all the years Rip had known him, he had never seen Paul hurt anyone that didn't actually deserve it, but he seemed to get no end of pleasure in inflicting his particularly psychotic presence on the uninitiated.

"*She-ya*, what we got here?" Moe was 190 pounds of solid Scandinavian backwoods redneck, complete with workpants, wife-beater shirt, and meshback baseball cap, settled nearly to the tip of his nose. He also did a pretty good job as Paul's echo. Bringing up the rear was Shitly. The origin of his name an enigma, Shitly shared Moe's burly physique, and his taste in attire, always acting his silent understudy.

"Ain't no kids allowed at this party." Paul's cool blue eyes shone over crooked grin.

"She-ya, no kids." Moe trailed. Shitly just blinked dull, dark eyes.

Curt stood defiantly. "We got every right to be here. We gave Lynette a ride." Randy was frozen, walleyed, while Dart shifted uncomfortably back by the motor.

"Kids ain't got no rights." Paul had already started pushing them gently back out to the river. Moe joined him, unlit cigarette clamped between his teeth as they each gave a mighty shove, the boat slipping swiftly, silently, into the current. "And I'm sure Lynette thanks you for the ride. We can take it from here, boys."

Curt still stood as the boat was sucked downstream. All activity ceased, nobody moving or talking, until Curt's arms suddenly spasmed. "Man, this sucks!"

Paul's laughter rolled over the beach.

"*Rip*? Earth to Rip." Stephanie's voice reached him and he suppressed an urge to jump. Slowly, reluctantly, he turned his attention from the shrinking form on the river to meet her hazel eyes.

"Hey, Steph. What's happening?" He was leaning against the hull as she sauntered over and planted herself practically between his legs. He could smell the mix of coconut oil and sweat, an intoxicating aroma that went straight to his head.

"You all lost in thought up there?" A finger brushed his temple. "What you thinking about?" She smiled and there it was, that incredible space between her two front teeth. The tiny flaw on that most perfect pearl that renders it more mysterious and beautiful.

"Nothin' much, really."

"Say, I was just goin' in for a swim. Care to join?" Rip had finally managed to tear his eyes from hers only to realize that he was now staring at her breasts. He turned his attention to the party.

"Nah, I really should he helping to set things up. Where's Keith?" Her expression faltered slightly at the mention of his best friend and her boyfriend.

"Up there, ice'n the keg in." She stepped away and peeled off her shirt. String bikini. Figured. "Mind if I keep my clothes in your boat? Tents aren't up yet."

"Sure, no prob." He heard the pop of button-fly and saw the flash of silky abdomen and he was striding up the beach with purpose. Or perhaps, away from it.

*   *   *   *

"So now what we gonna' do?" With the threat of confrontation removed, Randy had come to life full of indignant anger. "Huh? Where we goin'?"

"Man, am I Pee Oh'd." Curt finally sat down. "Where *are* we going?"

Dart trolled through the darkening bayou, steering a zig-zagging course around submerged stumps and overhanging limbs. "To the party. I know a path that comes in around back."

"You mean we just gonna' sneak around?" Randy squeaked. "What fun is that?"

"Look. You wanna' turn around, go home and hang with the 'rents? I know I sure don't." Randy's eyes concurred his point.

"Hey, yeah, you know, …this could be pretty cool." Even in the growing darkness, Dart registered the familiar mischievous glint in Curt's eyes.

"Maybe some weird stuff'll happen after they get all drunk…" He inhaled sharply and grabbed Dart's shoulder. "…we could steal some beer!"

"See now? We're almost there." They passed through a light fog, perhaps smoke from a nearby campfire. Randy suddenly went into convulsions. The sound of a tiny drill screamed inside Dart's left ear. Involuntarily, he aped Randy's actions.

"Uh, …SKEETERS!" Curt was slapping his body and swatting the air. "Bug juice! Where's the BUG JUICE?"

The insects were everywhere now, a black blizzard, lighting, buzzing, biting.

"Randy! Bug juice! Bow hold!" Randy scrambled up to the front of the boat, Dart musing on how they must look to the mosquitoes, twitching, yelling, slapping at themselves. Smiling at this odd thought, he reflexively swatted himself hard enough in the nose to bring tears.

*   *   *   *

"Tapper. O.K. Who's got the tapper?" Keith's head whipped to and fro as he shook sand off his hands. Lynette walked up with Gaylene and Cheryl in tow, batting eyes.

"Hey, Keith, think we could get a brewski?" The other two stood back, fidgeting.

Keith leaned in close to her, smirking lecherously, voice low and menacing. "Not unless you've got a tapper hidden in those tiny cut-offs of yours, Lynn."

Her eyes popped. Her mouth rounded.

"Oh." The three of them backed down the beach, like a film run backwards.

His wolf's grin disappeared.

"Paul!" He barked, as Rip materialized out of the darkness. "Rip. Hey man, you seen Paul and his, ahh…"

"Entourage? Yeah. Just saw 'em down by the shore. Y'know, Steph's swimming out there alone. Might keep an eye on her."

"*Entourage...*"Keith seemed to taste the word. "I'm sure there's plenty of eyes on Stephanie." He shrugged. "Girl can take care of herself."

"*Heeyy... Keithiee...*" Paul's grin appeared from the darkness, Cheshire cat-like. Moe and Shitly emerged around him.

A battered and scraped axe hung from one hand, and he cradled a bundle of twigs in the other. "Just saw your woman takin' a dip down to-the-river. *She-Ya!*" Dried spittle was caked around his mouth. "Hotter 'an a *muskrat* in *July*."

Keith gave Rip a loaded glance. "Uh, ... thanks Paul. I think." He suddenly shifted into the courtroom demeanor that was surely an unconscious parody of his father. "Guys, what we have here is one sixteen-gallon keg of Wisconsin's finest, chilling to icy perfection. Problem is, the beer is in here ..." His knuckles chimed on the aluminum. "...and we want it to go here." He produced a plastic cup, holding it in front of Paul's eyes.

"Need a tapper." Moe's flat voice.

"Exactly!" Pleased at their deductive leap, murmurs of approval rippled through the trio. "And *who* was in charge of getting said *tapper*?" Keith shoved his hands in his pockets and balanced on his heels - a gesture of infinite patience. *Christ*, Rip thought, *he's actually enjoying this.*

Paul's face went blank, and a darkness seemed to settle over him. Suddenly he was alert and looked at Keith, who stared up into the sky. "Aw, ... Jeez, ... No worries. We was on our way ta' Sias' an ran into Glenn. He was headed over there anyway..."

"Glenn?" Hissed Keith. He gave a helpless gesture. "Jesus,... you gave,... Glenn?"

He seemed stuck, so Rip turned to Paul. "Guys, I gotta' go with Keith on this. Glenn's a real serious burnout case. I know he means well and all, but he hardly knows what day it is, ..."

"And now he's got our money." Keith dropped to the sand, back to them. "Tom fucking Terrific."

A furrow dug itself between Paul's eyebrows. His voice was soft. "Glenn's O.K. He'll come through."

Rip could only turn away, into a cooling breeze. The sun was down now, ambient twilight casting puffball clouds in brilliant hues of gold and red, contrasting the cold purple of the clean spaces between. Venus was a brilliant point pulling itself over the treeline, winking shards of color through the sky. Then it was there, the distant, but familiar growl of an outboard. He blew a sigh of relief.

"*There* he is."

Keith was up on his feet, gazing out over the water. "You sure?"

Paul's face was split by his familiar manic grin. "Know the sound of that 'ol Johnson anywhere. Fuckin-A!" He turned and exchanged fuckin-A's with Shitly and Moe, accentuated by knuckle and shoulder punches.

Glenn's boat faded in from the darkness of the river, sliding onto the shore. Puttering about the craft, deep in concentration, he never noticed the crowd of people surrounding him until, tap in hand, he prepared to step to shore. A spontaneous cheer arose, stopping him dead atop the bow. Windblown greasy hair hung over wet, deep-set eyes, poise suggesting he might bolt away at any moment. The crowd hushed, went still. Rip stood at the front of the group, not wanting to frighten him away, toes clenching the sand with a mind of their own.

Suddenly, Glenn's body relaxed, and a stoner-stupid smile stretched across his face. He brought his arms up, raising the tapper in a salute of triumph. People closed in with a large, warm noise, and greeted him, slapping his back.

Rip and Keith joined in with gusto.

* * * *

"It's perfect." Dart stood with hands on hips looking up at a tall dead Elm. "We build a two 'b four ladder up that side, and we put a jump platform there, and up there…" He ran over to a smaller tree that stretched out over the river. "…see? The rope is tied to this one and pulled up to the platform on the other tree by a guide line."

"I don't see nothin'." Randy was furiously scratching the bites on his arms and legs. "Christ it's dark. You sure we ain't lost?"

Oblivious to Randy's suffering, Curt warmed to the idea. "You know, if we lopped off the top, we'd have a perfect place for a platform. Thing is, who's gonna climb it?"

"Aw, I can climb that, no problem." Randy swatted at the darkness. "Hey, Dart, can I get some more of that bug juice? Getting eatin' alive here."

Curt grabbed the bottle out of Dart's hand, passed it over. "You? Climb that?"

"Sure, Randy's a regular monkey man." Dart tugged a large flashlight out of a pocket and snapped it on. The beam cut a swath of brilliance through the glade, and he turned to follow it. "The beach is through here, just over that last ridge. Rand, don't use all that up, man. It's the only bottle we got".

Reluctantly, Randy capped the bottle, shook it near his ear, and pursued the receding glow. Curt trailed, peeking frequently back over his shoulder.

A soft amber radiance pulsed through the trees as they approached the hillock. The sounds of voices and music appeared to be carried aloft by billowing clouds of phosphorescent sparks. Dart cut the light and they crawled, commando-style to the edge of the treeline. From there, the whole shore fell away, a wide crater, giving them an excellent view of the whole affair.

Surrounded by a sloping field of fine river-basin silt, a huge bonfire crackled with authority, stuttering light etching dimpled patterns of footprints from the people encircling it. A jerry-rigged sound system was set up on the far side, out of respect to the blowing smoke, and the flame's reach. The crowd's joyous cacophony mixed with the music as figures cavorted in and out of the water, bounding about the beach, mixing in random groups.

They lay there in silence, faces peeking out between the trees, taking it all in. There was something touching and innocent, Dart thought, about the way these people interacted in this, their one shared element. Most were social and economic outcasts, the products of poverty, broken homes, abusive, and alcoholic families. In most circles they were viewed as delinquents and miscreants, but here, together, they were accepted and mutually respected.

"Curt, ain't that Glenn, your brother?" Randy pointed to a figure occupied with the task of loading an outsized bong, small cluster of figures waiting anxiously around him.

"Awww… man. What's he doin' here?"

"Looks like he's smoking pot." Dart observed.

Curt groaned and rolled over on his back. "Jeez, just back from treatment and everything. Dad'll kill him if he finds out."

"You gonna' tell?"

"*Me*? No man. Glenn's been through enough. We *all* been through enough."

"He kinda' creeps me out. Why's he like that?"

Curt flipped back onto his stomach and looked at Randy, propping chin in hands. "Wasn't always that way. He usta' be… well, normal. Then, I don't know." His head shook "Won't say anything about it to me, but I hear the folks talkin'. Guess one time he mixed LSD and angel dust or something. Sorta' blew a fuse." His gaze went out and found his brother. "Ain't been the same since."

A somber silence followed, their attention turning back to the party. Randy jerked and pushed his way a little further through the bushes. "*Look*. There're those jerks that turned us away. They hangin' around your brother!"

"Yeah. That's Paul, Moe, and Shitly." Dart eyed the trio as they gathered around Glenn.

"What? You *know* em?"

"We see 'em around." Curt voiced. "They never been trouble before. Heck, Moe 'n Shitly even towed me in one time I ran the tank dry near Sias'." He let some sand fall between his fingers. "Maybe they were just showin' off for the chicks."

"Jerks like that never get no chicks." Randy mumbled, and Dart secretly agreed.

"Whoa, man. Speakin of ..." Curt hunkered up on his knees. "Check that blonde out."

Dart pushed Curt off to the side to get a look. "Oh yeah. Stephanie. She's a townie. So's her boyfriend, Keith, the guy next to her there. Old man's some big-shot lawyer in town. Whole family's rich. Had homeroom with his little brother last year."

"What they doin' hangin' around with the Rats." Randy squeaked.

"That guy there." Dart indicated a solitary figure hovering around a small silver V-bottom. "Rip. Guess he an' Keith must be pretty tight. See 'em around the slews sometimes."

"And Rip is a pretty major River Rat." Curt's tone held seldom heard respect.

Randy tugged at a piece of beach grass and stuck it in his mouth. "*We* River Rats, ain't we? I mean, we live on the river and all."

"Yeah." Dart sighed. "But to them, we're just kids." He followed the form of Lynette as she stepped up to the group gathered around Glenn, still flanked by Gaylene and Cheryl, her movements fluid and sensual, and he felt an impotent rage at the truth of his statement.

"We gotta' get closer." He turned to the other two. "Listen, the Rats are gonna' camp on the other side, the upwind ridge. Now, this treeline follows it all the way around, so we do the same. We come up under cover of the camp and the brush. Be close enough to touch 'em."

"Cool idea." Curt nodded.

Charged with a newfound mission, they set off to circumnavigate the sandy crater, although in retrospect, Dart realized he should have anticipated the explosive growth of sand-burrs that awaited them.

* * * *

Airport Beach lay at the end of the main runway of the small local airport, servicing everything from small personal craft, to medium-size turbo-props that flew in from hubs in the Twin Cities and Chicago.

Rip stood in the shallows, apart from the party, waves lapping at his feet, cool breeze tempering the fire's heat from his skin, watching as landing beacons flared above in the purple twilight.

The lights dipped and bobbed, mirrored by the flaccid river. They hovered drunkenly, two growing silver eyes joined by a flashing green nose, accompanied by a distant groan, rising in pitch, at odds with the serene way they drifted the air.

Then, in an abrupt detonation of light and sound, the aircraft thundered low overhead, splashing and flickering radiance, shadows pirouetting beneath his feet, the shiny fuselage reflecting liquid dollops of light as it dropped below the Isle's canopy, curtaining the beach in sudden silence.

All went dead still. No one spoke or moved. The ubiquitous background chatter of nature had ceased. Even the stereo had either ended its play or had succumbed to the enchantment of the moment. Only the fire still went merrily about its business, though it too was ominously silent.

The familiar *glurp* of a fish jump broke the spell, as a tearing banshee howl shrieked from beyond the treeline, Dopplering back to silence. The sound of the breaking turbo-props were a haunting thing at this proximity, bristling the little hairs at the base of Rip's neck.

There was an impromptu round of appreciate applause from the crowd, especially enthusiastic from the stoner's circle.

"Them turbo-props make the damndest racket." Paul was at his side, starting Rip. *How the hell did he do that?*

Paul twirled a finger. "Y'know, they flip their props 'round backwards an' throttle 'em up. Gives 'em air brakes. 'Cept they can only do it on the ground." This appeared to puzzle him.

He handed Rip a freshly filled cup.

"Thanks." Taking a long draw from the cup, he let the cool liquid slide down his throat. "Paul, why you give those kids such a hard time today? You know they're locals. You must've seen 'em around."

Paul cracked a grin. "She-ya, you just soft on 'em 'cause that one kid's a drawer like you usta' be."

Rip pinched the bridge of his nose and groaned. "Awww, ... drawer ain't even a word."

"Sure it is. Someone who draws is a drawer."

There was a rustle in the underbrush, and Moe and Shitly stumbled out.

"See that? I 'tol you." Moe's big ham of a hand pointed down the row of boats to his own. "Put 'er up a good three feet further 'n anyone else."

"What the *hell* you two talkin' about?" At the sound of Paul's voice, the two stopped and leaned into an invisible wind, their unsteady gaze finally finding them in the darkness.

"Paul, *she-ya!* Damn near scairt the willies outta' me." Shitly blinked in agreement. They weaved cautiously down the beach. Each were drinking two-fisted, Moe sporting an unlit cigarette tucked behind his ear, another glowing from the corner of his mouth, and a third, held in his right hand, was dropping ashes into his beer.

"Jus' showin' Shitly here my fine beachin' job."

"Fine my ass!" Paul's voice pitched back up manically, and he stepped over, leaning into Moe's face. "We wasn't con*test*'in it. We woulda', I'da been a whole boat-length in front of your sorry ass."

Moe drained his cup, let it drop, and leaned in so the bill of his cap kissed Paul's forehead. "The fuck you could." He snarled around the butt in his mouth.

"The fuck I *could*." Paul's hands shot up and gave Moe a mighty shove, sending him sprawling backwards in a shower of beer spray and sparks.

"God-*damn* it, Paul!" He stood up, brushing sand and embers off himself. Paul let loose a crazy cackle, and with a grunt from Moe the two launched at each other, locking bodies like a mismatched pair of sumo wrestlers. Shitly backed away, blinking his excitement.

This was nothing new to Rip. He'd seen them clash time and again, and knew these confrontations could last long. But not this time. This could be settled quickly enough.

He moved over to where the two grappled.

"I can beat you both."

Halting, each looked up, and they went down in a heap, Paul landing atop Moe.

"*Ha! ... Hee.*" Out of breath and struggling to get up, Paul chuckled gleefully. "Ain't no V-bottom ever gonna' out-beach my flat."

"Never happen." came Moe's winded voice from the ground. Paul offered a hand and hauled him up with a slap on the back.

"Well, *well* gentlemen, sounds like we've got a friendly wager goin' down here." Keith approached, arm slung around Stephanie. She leaned in and threw a glance at Paul and company. "Hi boys."

Shitly stared back as Paul and Moe mumbled greetings, brushing sand off their twisted clothing.

She hit Rip with a killer smile. "Hey, Rip."

"Hey Steph." He got real interested in his empty cup.

"Rip here thinks he can put that old V-bottom up on the shore further 'n our flats." Paul was talking to Keith but he was looking Stephanie up and down. "Damn 'V digs in too much. Ain't never gonna' happen."

"Never happen." Echoed Moe.

Keith caught Rip's eyes and Rip sent the barest hint of a nod back to him. He clapped his hands together. "Well, my bets on Rip. Any takers?"

Paul's tone was indignant. "She-ya, my bets on me."

"Right here buddy." Moe puffed around a newly lighted cigarette. Shitly's head bobbed some kind of affirmative.

"All right," Keith dug in his pockets and produced a crumpled bill. "How's about five bucks a head?"

The offer was greeted by a chorus of crickets.

Paul finally spoke. "She-ya Keith, I ain't got no money."

"No money." Backed Moe.

Rip cleared his throat, crossed his arms and sat on the bow of his boat. "Umm, ...Keith, we're not doing this for money. We're River Rats, dig? We just do it for the fuck of it."

"Fuckin-A-*right* for the fuck of it. Yeah!" Paul gave Rip a shot to the arm that almost took him off the bow.

Stephanie had her hands dug in her back pockets, breasts thrown out, hips nervously working back and forth. Rip kept catching coquettish glances from her that made him want to put his fist through the hull.

"O.K., rules are simple." He said, rubbing his sore shoulder. "We go out in formation, do one lap around the bay, and on the first pass, put 'er up on the beach as far as you can. One pass, one chance only. Measurement is made from a straight line through the center of the bow to the center of the stern, back to the water-line. Any questions?"

"We go out in formation, ..." Paul's voice cracked. " ...someone's gotta' take wake. I don't want to be that someone."

"*I'll* take third wake. You 'n Moe can settle who rides shotgun."

"Shotgun!" Paul's voice shrieked a fraction of a second before Moe's. The bigger guy shuffled off mumbling obscenities around his cigarette.

Giggling with delight, Paul carried his grin into the darkness. Rip pulled anchor from the beach and settled the transom into the water. He looked back and noticed that people were drawing together around Keith and Stephanie, who seemed to be explaining what was happening. *Well, if you're going to make a scene, be seen,* he thought as he pushed off, priming the carb.

Keith stuck two thumbs up into the night sky. "Good luck, Rip."

"Luck has nothing to do with it."

"God-*dammit* Shitly, get your fat ass outta' my boat," Moe's voice drifted out the darkness across the water. " ...you tryin' to make me loose?"

Rip was startled by hearty laughter until he realized it was his own.

The three craft roared into the still night, pulling out around the small bay, meeting the main channel briefly, and swinging back around to enter its opposite side.

Rip easily followed the other two, enjoying the buffeting night air and the swampy smells that it brought. The clean lines of the V-hull cut smoothly around the wakes of the two smaller flats, and he kept the more powerful motor cut to three-quarter throttle.

Up ahead, he could see Paul pull his boat out of its tight bank for a straight run up the beach. Moe followed suit and set himself to Paul's starboard, the cherry on his cigarette an eerie ruby beacon.

Rip continued to track the shoreline tightly as stumps and branches sailed dangerously close by. He watched Paul hit the beach, unconsciously praying that they would finish as far up as he had anticipated. As Moe's silhouette shot up the sand, Rip's bow finally caught up to their wake and gently sliced into it. In a nearly single motion, he jumped up on the seat and twisted the throttle open.

The motor barked, pushing him on top of the wake's crest, over the lip, gaining an additional little push as the shore rushed in at a sharp angle. He readied himself at the transom, making a final steering adjustment, cutting and locking up the motor where he intuited the shallows to begin.

There was a surreal moment of almost total silence as the shore slashed by with blurring speed.

Rip braced himself as the hull bit into the sand with a scraping roar, rocketing across the beach, nearly parallel to the shoreline. The wet, compacted silt offered almost no resistance, and he shot past the sterns of Moe and Paul so closely that he caught a fractured glance of them both diving for cover. Astonished faces sliced by, and he flashed that his trajectory was leading him up into the treeline quite a bit faster than he had anticipated. The boat jounced up into the softer dry sand still at an appreciable speed, when the bow buried itself in a cleft of young cottonwoods, yawing slightly, throwing him effortlessly through the air.

* * * *

"Would you be quiet, you big baby?"

"Got burrs all over my feet." Randy whispered hoarsely. He sat hunkered down between his knees, delicately pulling out the tiny barbed spheres that had stuck into his toes, uttering a pained yelp each time one was freed.

"Shoulda' worn shoes." Curt offered his for examination.

"Owww! Never worn shoes in summer."

"Guys. They're comin' back around." Dart carefully parted the thin shielding of branches before him. The crowd was close enough to touch the stragglers at the rear, but the din of the approaching boats easily concealed their conversation.

The first flat came snarling at the shore, voice cut abruptly to a strangled gurgle as its occupant killed the power and locked the outboard up. He slid an impressive distance, and came to a smooth stop amid scattered applause. The second boat attempted a similar approach, but was clearly hampered by the wake of the first. He ended up a good half-boat length short, obviously unhappy about it.

"Heck, that ain't nothing," Curt's voice a harsh whisper nearly inside Dart's ear. " ...one time, me an my Merc were ..."

"Shut up, will ya? Where's the other one? There were three ..." Then he heard it, the signature sound of an old Johnson being pushed, balls out, to its limit. " ...where is it?" He looked out to the mouth of the bay, the path of the first two, but there was nothing to be seen.

"Oh, hey." Curt grabbed his shoulder, half-spinning him. "Look, over there."

Seeing nothing at first, Dart noticed a small, reflected fleck of light, and an object separated from the treeline. He realized he was observing the craft bow-first.

"*Holy crap*. It's coming in along the shore-line. It's coming..." He suddenly locked eyes with Curt, his realization reflected there. " ...straight at us."

"Ouch." Randy bleated. "There. Got 'em all."

"Uh, Randy ..." Dart quick checked back and saw the hull booming and hissing up the sand, heard the noise of the crowd and swung back to Randy and yelled, "BOLT!" and he and Curt were moving as Randy just sat there on the ground staring stupidly at them, then Dart had a handful of his shirt, the sound of branches screeching and popping as they jumped behind an embankment, something landing heavily, close behind, and then it was quiet, except for Randy's small, sad voice ...

"Awww, more sandburs."

*   *   *   *

The stars were hard, bright gems, and they jeweled the night sky. Rip lay on his back, considering them, trying to catch his breath, wondering just how long he'd been here, like this, which, according to his scrambled time-sense, could have been an eternity. He was unable to recollect how he'd gotten there, or why he couldn't seem to breathe, but for the moment, these were small things compared to the vast celestial bouquet spread above.

A dark shape hovered into view and eclipsed the stars, carrying Keith's wide grin. "Hey bub, got all your parts?"

"Wh-whuff, ...?"

A second planetoid with a shock of red hair swung over him. "God-damndest thing I ever did see! *She-ya*! Crazy bastard, got to be a God-damned world record. Jeez-fucking Guinness!"

Then hands were reaching and pulling him up, and he doubled over as his breath finally got sucked back into his lungs.

"I ... uh ... the boat ..."

"A few more beauty marks." Keith gave him a light pat on the back. "Nothin' even you would notice. Come on, bub, this we got to celebrate."

They led him shakily down the slope, past the clump of trees where the stern of his craft stuck out at an odd angle, into the waiting crowd and the warm firelight.

"Beer this man!" Keith bellowed.

After a couple of friendly rounds and a round full of toasts, they all moved to the shoreline for the official measurement, forty-seven and-a-half paces, easily a record for this known stretch of the river. It took several extra-strong sets of hands to disentangle Rip's boat and place it on a more convenient swatch of beach. He carefully inspected the damage, concluded it was merely cosmetic, and turned attention back to the party.

Aerosmith's 'Season of Whither' poured plaintively from the speakers, and he spotted Keith and Stephanie sitting pow-wow with a group near the stereo. Keith was aggressively sucking on a very large joint and spotted Rip, waving him over.

"Eere, 'ave 'ome. 'S 'ood chit." Chest puffed out, his eyes bulged with the effort of holding the hit down, as he offered up the smoking spliff.

"Hey, no thanks man." He held up a full cup of beer. "I'm on a natural high."

The group broke up. Eyes glazed, Stephanie giggled and fell into Keith's lap. Keith made a kind of snorting sound, ejecting a great plume of blue smoke, went into a coughing fit that gave way to peals of laughter.

" … Natural … Jesus …you fuckin' slay me man."

Rip dropped to the sand, hearing the melancholy chords of the song drift away into the night. The cold brew tasted good and he could feel a slight buzz taking hold. Looking around the circle, he took in their faces, gently dappled by firelight, and felt an odd sense of deja vu. Actually, more a sense that he was seeing back in time, remembering things he was observing right now, a peculiar backward nostalgia. *Shit*, he thought, *I must've inhaled some second-hand smoke.* The thought put a grin on his face that he couldn't seem to get rid of.

Stephanie was grinning right back at him, and it was such a big, stupid, beautiful grin that he felt his lips stretch and a series of small chuckles escaped from deep inside. The word grin started bouncing around inside his head, *grin, grin, grin*, such an odd word, *grin*, that if you say it enough *grin* times it looses all its *grin*. Meaning.

A warm hand touched his shoulder, and he craned his neck to look back. "Grin?" he asked.

Lynette leaned overhead, face framed by a fan of dark hair. "Hey Rip. Saw that beaching you did back there. I mean, that was, like the coolest."

"Uhmm …" he managed.

"Mind if I sit here?" She indicated a patch of sand to his right that made up a small break in the circle.

"Uh, …*sure*. I mean, *no*. I mean, *yeah*, sit down."

As she slipped down next to him, he caught the interested glances of Stephanie and Keith, joint burning unnoticed in his hand as he waggled eyebrows suggestively. Stephanie gave Keith a hard slap to the shoulder and shot him a glance of her own, peppered with interest and maybe a hint of jealousy.

"Hey man, quit Bogart'n that joint." An irate voice quipped from the crowd.

Keith regarded the smoking roach as if he'd grown a sixth finger. "Oh, shit. Sorry." He passed it over to a girl who delicately maneuvered it between her fingernails, huffing the cherry back to life.

Rip felt the heat that Lynette brought from the fire radiating from her body, and he turned to see her gazing at him through a few strands of hair that had fallen over her face. Two years his junior, she would be a sophomore when school started in a couple of weeks. Technically, this put her into the 'too young' category, but she had matured early, and quite well at that.

She also had a reputation.

Suddenly, Rip felt a tremor of desire. Locked in her gaze, blood thrashing through his head, his mouth went dry. Her body emitted a thermal aura, encompassing them both. He felt a light sheen of sweat break out on his forehead and upper lip, and thought desperately of something, anything to say.

The moment was passing.

He cleared his throat. "So …"

The full-throated roar of a glass-packed V-8 broke the night as twin headlights peaked over the spine of the beach, followed by the shadowy outline of a monstrous four-wheel-drive. The vehicle topped the ridge, nosed down the steep embankment, and stopped just short of going end-over-end into the water. Then, with an angry blat, it roared down the bank, tires spraying sand high up into the air.

Lynette's head snapped in the direction of the approaching truck, and when it turned back, there was a knowing smile on her face.

"It's Slick." She chirped as she scrambled to her feet. "Slick's here." And she dashed off, leaving Rip, mouth agape, unspoken words still stuck in his throat.

Keith and Stephanie walked by, arm in arm, regarding him with exaggerated pity. Keith threw him a quick wink. "Smooth."

Rip sighed, sat up and brushed the sand off his ass. "As shit." He muttered and set off in the direction of the keg.

The four-wheel-drive locked its gigantic tires up and skidded to a stop near the bonfire, remarkably not running anybody over, and the drivers-side door cracked open with a loud, metallic *'gronk'*.

Lynette, Gaylene, and a few others gathered around the truck, as Slick leaned out brandishing a half-full bottle of Jack Daniels. His permanent grin beamed out from a sunburned face, beneath sun-bleached hair, as he raised the bottle in a sloppy salute.

"Happy fucking bicentennial!" He jumped to the ground and was instantly surrounded by the girls.

The passenger door gave a pained creak and snapped open. A shadowed figure roughly the size of an ox moved around and squeezed out the door. The heavy-duty suspension squeaked a sigh of relief as he stepped to the sand, the firelight finally catching him as he threw the door shut.

Larry Fisher stood six-foot-four and clocked in at around two hundred-eighty pounds, all solid bone and muscle. Even the baddest jocks at High School treated him with a fearful respect, and Rip had spent much of his formative years hiding from and being bullied by Larry. Given due course, none of this would have changed, but Larry did. As they grew up, Larry seemed to form a healing connection with the river and the characters that peopled it. This bond that tempered his naturally violent nature also left him oddly nurturing and protective of their peculiar enclave.

Two quarts of cheap vodka clinked together in one gigantic hand as he strode foreword and surveyed the gathering. "Buncha' wussies." He growled. "What the hell kinda' party is this? Somebody turn up the fuckin' music, will ya'?"

Obediently, the volume jumped up, and Black Sabbath's 'War Pigs' came pulsing through the speakers. Larry gave a satisfied snort and tipped back one of the bottles, draining it dry. "S'better." He muttered, tossing the empty into the fire, steering himself over to the keg where Rip was pouring a fresh one.

"Hey Rip!" He boomed, and with surprising speed faked a punch to his stomach. Some ingrained Pavlovian response made Rip jump back and double over, accurately spilling cold beer onto his crotch. Larry's big eyebrows scrunched together in confusion.

"A little jumpy tonight, aren't we?"

"Just reliving a little of the past, Larry." he said, trying to wipe away some of the embarrassing stain.

"Aww, … man." His eyes went soft, voice low, as one arm reached around to thump him on the back, two massive digits daintily plucking the cup from his hands. "You know it ain't like that no more. Let me get that for you."

He turned and bent over the keg, as Slick walked up with Lynette and Gaylene, each caught under an arm.

"Now, this is what I call a par-tee." He brayed infectiously, the girls giggling up at him, pointing. "Rip, what's goin' on, a little problem with the plumbing?" More laughter and giggles as Rip flushed.

Larry turned to Slick. "Don't give him no shit. My fault he spilt."

Slick went wisely silent.

Rip tried hard to ignore Lynette. "So Slick, how'd you get that thing over here? Last I looked, wasn't any road back there. Hell, didn't think there was even any land."

Larry hooked a thumb over his shoulder. "Crazy bastard found some kinda' access trail, trashed a cyclone fence, then we was cross'n some marsh shit. Thought we was gonna' sink." He shook his great head in admiration. "Fuckin' nutjob."

Rip regarded the battered and mud-splattered superstructure of the Blazer K-5. "Cool." was all he could think to say.

Slick laughed, the girls giggled, and Paul and Moe stumbled into the circle, each fighting their own personal battles with gravity.

"Larry fuckin' Fisher." Paul's glassy eyes swam over a twisted grin, in a sea of freckles. "She-ya, how they bitin' buddy?"

Larry's head bobbed atop a mountain of shoulders. "*Paul.* Ready for trappin' season?"

"Muskrats 'an beaver, *beware*!"

Moe began to sway in a slow counter-clockwise circle, becoming more top-heavy with each rotation, until he finally had to check himself, taking a clumsy step foreword. Larry's eyes locked on him.

"Jeez, Moe. You look like you could use a drink." He cracked open the remaining vodka bottle, pushing it into his hand. Moe regarded it dully for a moment, looked up at Larry with a mixture of confusion and awe.

"Uh, … thanks there, Larry." Then the bottle was up and he was taking a long pull. When it came down, a shiver ran through his body and he exhaled deeply. "Whooee …!" He handed the bottle back, scrunching the cap down tighter on his head. "Man, I needed that." He strode smartly off.

Larry gave a satisfied grunt and turned back to Paul. "Say, where's that other guy hangs around you two. What's his name, …?"

"You mean Shitly? *She-ya*, he passed out in the boat, …" Paul cupped his hands around his mouth and turned to the river. "…'*CAUS HE'S A BIG PUSSY!*" He shouted.

"What the hell's wrong with a big pussy, ya little dink?!" Came a shrill reply from the darkness. Paul leapt back in surprise as the others doubled over with laughter.

Stephanie stumbled into the light dragging Keith along and threw an arm around Paul. "Sorry, hon. Just couldn't let that one go."

Paul's ears turned an amazing shade of crimson as he shuffled his feet in the sand. "She-ya." he mumbled.

Keith gave a tug on her hand, freeing her from Paul and she fell into his arms. He finally noticed the newcomers, gaze settling on the truck.

"Slick. Larry. How the *hell* you get that death-trap over here?"

"Long story." Slick sniggered.

"Can I set you two up with a fresh one?" Larry was already pumping the tap and filling a glass.

Stephanie leaned unsteadily out from Keith's grasp, smiling up through tousled strands of hair. "Aw, Larry. You're so *sweeeet*."

Larry gave an unconcerned grunt and pretended to be busy with the tap, but his ears lit up like Paul's.

"Well, looks like the gangs all here." Rip announced. "I think this calls for a toast."

"Here, here."

"She-ya, *toast*."

Keith shifted Stephanie to his other arm. "Great idea, oh Sir beach-master. What'll we toast?"

Larry's eyebrows queried a silent question, but Rip gave a dismissive shrug. "Later."

"Let's toast the fuckin' bicentennial!" Slick offered.

"You already did that."

"She-ya, fuck the fuckin' bicentennial."

"Don't be badmouthin' the U.S. of fuckin' A, Paul." Larry grumbled.

Paul's eyes went as big as quarters, but he kept his mouth shut. Rip sighed, walked to the center of the group and raised his cup.

"To the river. To the Mississippi."

All hands came up and Larry leaned in with his bottle.

"To the Mississippi!" They chanted together.

And drank.

* * * *

"*Shhhh, …*"

"But, …"

Dart and Curt both clamped a hand around Randy's mouth, and he struggled to get free until they pointed out the shadow of Moe approaching their hiding spot in the brush. They were all still a bit jumpy since the incident with the truck, narrowly missing them as it came crashing through the forest.

Randy nodded wildly, and they released him to some very angry looks. The dark shape continued to advance, and Dart readied for a quick retreat, when Moe shuffled to a sudden stop. For the longest time he stood in place, a full cup in each hand, body weaving invisible patterns in the air, when an explosive belch erupted from his drooping mouth. Snapping out of his stupor, he carefully set the beers down one at a time in the sand next to him, and farted loudly.

By now, Curt and Randy were doubled over in spasms, bodies convulsing with the effort of trying not to laugh.

Moe slowly pulled himself upright, body swaying dangerously from side to side, as his hands sloppily worked open the large brass belt buckle that hung on the front of his work pants. It came free, and he pitched forward, face-first into the dirt.

Randy looked wide-eyed at Curt, Curt looked at Dart, and they all turned to Moe, who had begun snoring quietly. Slowly, silently they crept closer, weaving their way through the small saplings, reaching his inert form. Randy picked up a long stick and started in, but Dart snatched it away before he could do any poking.

Curt snagged the two glasses and they beat a stealthy retreat to a small clearing illuminated by a cool shaft of moonlight.

"Gaahh, …" Randy pulled the cup from his mouth, face screwing up into a grimace. "This tastes like crap."

"Id's dot so bad." Curt had the bridge of his nose pinched between thumb and forefinger, pinky waving daintily as he slugged down nearly half the contents of the cup in one gulp.

"Hey!" Randy yelped indignantly as Dart pulled the beer from his grasp, pinched his own nose closed, and tipped the cup up, carefully trying not to taste the cold, foamy liquid that poured down his throat. He gasped.

"I think I know now what they mean by acquired taste."

"What you got to acquire to like the taste of *that*?" Randy had his hand out and Dart passed over what remained.

"Prob'ly lots more beer." Dart belched and Curt sniggered. Randy plugged his nose and finished the cup, throwing it down in disgust. His eyes suddenly went wide and he looked up with deep concern.

"Hey guys, I'm not like, gonna' get wasted now, am I? I mean, my folks at home and all?"

And that, thought Dart, was Randy to a T. He'd leap first and consider the consequences after his leg was in a cast. Like him or not, at least you could give him one great thing; he was a man of action.

For some reason, this started him giggling, and Curt looked over. When he opened his mouth and all that came out was a tiny little hiccup, the expression on his face enough to make Dart totally lose it. Curt gave a snort, and they were both laughing hysterically, to Randy's great horror. He just sat there, shaking owl eyes back and forth, saying over and over …

"Oh, no … oh, no …"

* * * *

"Thass' what I was sayin'! Ya don't never lisson! No one never lissons!"

Rip's tongue was numb in his face and he was faintly aware that he was shouting. Keith just gave him a cool smile and spread his hands.

"Just 'caus you think I don't listen, don't mean I'm deaf."

"Oh. Yeah. Right. Sorry." Rip forced his attention to the background party blurs and willed them into focus. Some that he could make out were turned his way.

"What I mean when I say lisson', …I don't really mean lisson', … no, wait, …" He went on quietly, a more conspiratorial tone in his voice than he intended. " …I mean, like see. Hear. Understand." He focused out again.

"'S like, you're at a party. 'An you look 'cross 'th crowd 'an catch some chick lookin' back at you. Now, …you 'don know this chick, never seen her before, but there you are, starin' at each other through a shitload of other people, 'an even though it's only, maybe a fraction of a second, in your mind, you can go over to her, say hi, talk, get to know her, fuck, go steady, get married, divorce, die, all in that moment, ya' know? That one fuckin' moment 's so loaded. An' then some dickweed blocks the way, breaks the moment, and it's over." Rip let out a long baritone belch. "She's gone."

He felt a sharp spark at the back of his brain, the bright, tiny point of something much larger underneath. Something so huge his thoughts couldn't get around it. He mentally poked at the spark.

"Time, …"

"Time?" Keith regarded him with bored amusement.

"*Yeah*. What is it?" Rip leaned over for emphasis and his elbow buckled, dropping him to the ground.

"'Jus what 'th fuck *is* time, 'an wha'sit made of?" He struggled to sit back up.

"Made of?" Keith almost seemed interested.

"What? You a parrot?" Rip was having a little trouble focusing his eyes. "Stuff's made 'a stuff, ya' know? Ever'thin's made 'a somethin'. Sound got waves. Light got them, you know, foto-trons. I mean, here we are, stuck in the stuff. We can measure it with clocks an' watches, we ride in it an' it carries us from one end to the other, from life to death, like, … like the current of that river, but what *is* it? What's it fuckin' made of?"

Rip felt the spark dim, fade, and he was looking at Keith, who looked back with one of the strangest expressions he'd ever seen on his face.

"What I'd like to know, …" His eyes stayed on Rip's over the rim of his cup as he took a drink. " … is why some mid-west, white-trash, high-school, River Rat is rambling on about the composition of time-flow."

Rip blinked. "Izzat' what I wuz doin?"

Keith nodded a little gesture of acknowledgement over Rip's shoulder. Craning his neck, he saw Stephanie give a little curtsy and wave.

The stereo kicked out the sharp, staccato burst of a familiar guitar lick. People everywhere came to attention.

Keith stood up, brushing sand. "You, friend, need to get your head outta' the clouds for awhile, …" He leaned in, voice real low. " …*you*, … you need to get laid."

He gave Rip a little pat on the back and sauntered off in the general direction of Stephanie.

"'S easy for you to say." muttered Rip to himself.

The crowd was really getting into the song now, Rip recognizing The Sweet's 'Love is Like Oxygen'. Paul had jumped into the fray and was furiously playing air guitar, while Slick brandished an invisible mic and was pantomiming the lead vocals to Lynette and her circle of girlfriends.

More and more people began playing invisible instruments and the circle closed tighter around the fire, the flickering glow illuminating them from below. The ones who didn't play were dancing and stomping around in the sand, a strangely tribal interpretation of the song. Slick took center stage and crooned to the girls, who visibly swooned, and Rip smiled to himself.

Through the undulating mass of orange bodies and dark blue shadows, he spotted Keith step up to an expectant Stephanie and slide his hand deeply down the front of her shorts. She crumpled into him and her lips slid up to his ear. Keith half-nodded and they turned, leaning drunkenly into one another and vanished as the light from the campfire left them.

"Hey, you seen Moe around? I can't find him anywhere."

Startled, Rip turned around to see Shitly standing over him, full cup balanced between thick fingers.

"Shit, Shitly, you talked!"

Shitly blinked his coal eyes back at Rip.

*   *   *   *

Stephanie pulled Keith roughly by the belt buckle into a moon-washed clearing and rammed her tongue down his throat. Her body thrust against his as their hands rubbed, raked, and pawed over each other. Keith's mouth worked down her throat and with one quick motion he pulled her shirt up and off. For a moment she stood, arms over her head, suppliant, as her shirt wafted slowly to the ground, breasts quivering to her heavy breathing, nipples picked out large and hard by the cool light. Then his lips closed over one and her body bucked as she let out a sharp cry through clenched teeth.

"*Oh. My. God.*" It came out of Randy like a valve leaking air. "I can't believe I'm seeing this."

Curt put his index finger up to his lips, but he needn't have bothered. The party was getting way out of control. The music was turned up to speaker-splitting volume, people running and screaming, yelling, beneath the occasional concussive blast when some half-wit would toss an unopened bottle or can of bug-spray into the fire.

"Do you think they're, …uh, you know, gonna do it?" Randy looked back with eyes so large, Dart was sure they would just fall out of his head. "*Are* they doin it?"

"No, Randy. Not yet. Least I don't think so." Dart squirmed uneasily. "Look guys, I don't feel right about this."

Curt's eyes burned into him. "Are you freakin' kiddin? What's with you?"

"Yeah, what's with you, man?"

Curt's whisper was a harsh snarl. "I waited my whole life for this. Think of the stories we can tell. We'll be heroes."

Dart's gaze settled back on the couple.

Both were shirtless and glistening in the moonlight. Keith was snaking delicate panties off her bare rump and she was violently working an enormous bulge in his pants.

This wasn't like anything he'd seen in the movies, the gentle kissing and tender touching. This was something much more primal, animalistic. A sensation flowed through him, both alien and intimately familiar, and to his horror, his prick started throbbing in his shorts. He shuddered. He didn't know why, but he had to get away from there.

"Guys, I gotta' go. I don't feel so good." He lied. "Prob'ly something with the beer."

Curt turned his back. "Fine. I'm stayin' for the show."

"Me too." Randy mimicked Curt.

"Be at the boat." Dart backed off into the deeper brush, heart hammering hot blood through his skull. He got hopelessly lost for a time but eventually came upon the shoreline and followed it back to where he had docked.

* * * *

The rest of the evening washed over Rip in a series of events, disconnected and out of sequence.

Paul and Glenn, watery shadows before the fire, gravity very heavy on them now, threatening to pull them down to the earth anytime soon. Their thick slurred voices like another language.

"Now, ...where'd 'e go"

"Dunno. I'z lookin forum."

"Where?"

"Dunno. Why I'z lookin forum."

"She-ya."

Slick holding the hair out of Lynette's face as she lay doubled over a small fold-out picnic table puking her guts out, Cheryl and Gaylene flitting about, swooping in with words of consolation and then flying away when she convulsed with another gusher. Slick even managing a feel of her ripe, plum ass when he thought no one was watching, that good-natured smile never leaving his face.

The shocking taste of vodka making Rip gasp, pulling the bottle away from his lips. Two big brown watery eyes glittering with amusement floating in front of him.

He knows those eyes.

Larry Fisher's deep gravely voice.

"Forty-seven and a-half paces. Jesus, ..." His head shakes side to side. "Don't think nobody's tried a stunt like that since Billy Ray."

"No such person." Rip's lips said.

"Billy Ray?"

"Yeah ...Never ...Was ... One."

"Sure as fuck there was."

"You shittin?"

"No shit. Knew 'im." Larry snatched the bottle from Rip.

"Damn." Rip tried to sit up, sat back hard on the sand. "Damn, ..." He repeated. "...whereis'e? Whathappento'im?"

Around a mouthful of vodka Larry says. "No one knows for sure. Went fuckin' local, disappeared down some slew." He shrugs, end of story.

"Shit. Two weeks."

"Two weeks?"

"Wha'?"

"Two weeks. You just said two weeks. Shit Rip, you're hammered."

"Yeah, …" Rip stares at the dying fire, the embers spelling out some cryptic message in a long forgotten code. "Fuckin' school. Only two more weeks."

"Oh, right." Larry's voice is sympathetic. "Sorry."

"Sucks, …"

A roar crackles across the beach, Rip's head instinctively snaps up to see the airplane that isn't there, watching the thick blanket of stars double and triple with his vision. Larry Fisher, staring down the beach, a colossus of granite and sand towering over him, voice out of sync with his lips.

"Crazy bastard. Prob'ly gotta' do some damage control, …"

Stumbling down the shore, the sand a shifting and perilous hazard.

The moon, a majestic silver orb, its near-perfect twin reflected on the still river, drifting slowly down, inevitably bound for each other.

Crossed eyes of the cosmos.

The long familiar bite of the aluminum struts on the floor of his boat as he inches into his sleeping bag, and, curling up into a fetal position, pulls the zipper up, around, and over him.

Then, darkness, …and sinking.

* * * *

Dart was dangling his feet over the bow, pushing little ripples around when Curt and Randy emerged from an opaque curtain of foliage. He walked astern and primed the carb as Randy stepped in and Curt pushed off. The motor caught smoothly on the first pull and they set off down the main channel.

No one said a word on the journey back, and for that Dart was grateful. He was tired and confused from the long evening. The rip of the wind and the cool spray was a comforting thing, and he dropped off his passengers a few blocks down the canal from their homes. Even a silent motor was magnified by a calm, still body of water, and they were going to need more than their share of luck sneaking back in so late.

After a few mumbled goodbyes, he gunned the boat back around the tip of the peninsula and entered the channel on its opposite side, cutting the motor to glide smoothly up to his parents dock. He tied it off and tip-toed over the rotting boards to the steep, sandy embankment that led up to the backyard.

The dark, static shape of his stepfather seated on the deck stopped him with a sting of adrenaline. Making no concession to Dart's presence, he sat, attention out over the river. Beside him was a flimsy TV tray supporting the profiles of a saltshaker, beer can, and a half-full glass that threw blue and amber highlights into the shadows.

"Out late."

"Yeah." Dart felt sweat trickle from his underarms and tasted it on his lips, but he was magnetized in place, trying to anticipate where this could go.

The stepfather picked up the saltshaker and tipped three quick flicks into the beer glass. A cascade of foamy spirals made their way down to the bottom. As the head rose, he picked the glass off the table and took a foamy sip from it.

"Scorcher movin' in. Hot and humid."

Dart nodded in the dark. "Smelled it. Be here by morning."

There was an almost imperceptible nod of approval from his stepfather's silhouette. He carefully set the glass back on the TV tray.

"Better get inside before your 'ma finds you out so late."

"Right. Nite, Ted." Dart fumbled with the latch on the sliding door, finally finding the catch, letting himself into the darkened house.

*   *   *   *

The morning erupted around him with sticky green heat that left his lungs empty and a mouth so dry that his tongue felt fused to the roof of his palate. An insane cackling drove a hot spike of pain through his pounding head. Rip clawed around the inside of his sleeping bag, trying to find the small metal tab of the zipper. Once located, he carefully peeled himself free of the clinging thing, body covered in sweat. The open air brought little relief.

Although the sun couldn't have been up for more than an hour, the heat and humidity were already stifling. The manic laughter, much closer this time, shot another jolt through his cranium, and he raised himself on rubbery legs to behold a scene of such surreal carnage that it took a moment for all of it to filter in.

The beach itself resembled a scene from an old war documentary. Bodies and rubble were strewn around the central fire pit, which continued to belch out thick white smoke, and the charred remains of logs and branches suggested the bombed out husk of a city in miniature.

Paul lay convulsing on the ground, his face a sputtering mass of red veins as he tried to catch his breath, spastically pointing at a very pissed off Moe.

Every exposed area of his skin was covered by a matrix of bug bites, and it looked like he was trying to scratch them all at once. Moe seemed oblivious to Paul's taunting as he hopped from leg to leg, rubbing and scratching his limbs, muttering angrily around a cigarette. "Goddamn little motherfuckers… sneaky fuckin' little shits aint ya?"

Shitly stood up-shore and blinked condolences as Paul finally found his breath and let loose another screeching peal of laughter that got Rip out of his boat. He splashed unsteadily through the shallows, seeking solace to the explosions in his head through the cool waters of the bay.

A ruckus down the beach caught his attention and he squinted against the harsh sunlight. Slick's Blazer sat half-submerged in the water and a taught tether-line ran up the escarpment to an open-canopy Jeep that was struggling desperately to pull the larger vehicle free. Larry's mastodonic bulk sloshed around the sinking rear end, attempting to facilitate the extraction with a push from the back, surrounded by a flotilla of cans, bottles, and fast-food wrappers that cheerily bobbed out the rear window. Fortunately, Larry's harsh utterances were lost with distance.

A breeze parted the smoke briefly to reveal Glenn on the opposite side of the fire, busily sucking on a large purple bong. He caught Rip's glance, waving brightly as the curtain of smoke concealed him again.

"Ya'll look like something the cat jus' drug in, Rip."

Stephanie materialized out of the sun, barely clad in a string bikini, shining with sweat, looking him over through heavily-lidded eyes. She twirled a loose tie in her fingers, and he noticed the dark purple hickey at the base of her neck.

"Bad hair day." He grabbed at the bleach-blond scruff that stuck out the side of his head. "You know, …can't do a thing with it."

She gave him a sideways smile and then Keith had an arm curled around her shoulders. He was shirtless and Rip saw the hickies clustered around his neck. And the one next to his belt-buckle. The jackhammer working on his head went up another notch. Keith beamed and held forth a cup of beer glistening with condensation.

"Hair of the dog, bub?"

"Ugh, …" Rip's stomach did a slow turn, and in spite of the heat, a cold sweat broke out on his forehead. "…Christ, doesn't anyone drink water around here?"

Keith tipped the cup towards the river. "Water, water everywhere, …" He shrugged.

"Nice." He was aware of Stephanie's gaze as he pulled his shirt off, did a quick half-turn and dove into the water.

*   *   *   *

The heat had built to an oppressive pall, fusing the distant horizon to the shimmering gray sky. People wandered listlessly about the beach in a half-hearted attempt to clear away some of the refuse generated by the previous evening. There was an unspoken understanding that a beach was to be left as it was found, and nothing quite got Rip's temper up as when he'd discover one of his frequented sandbars trashed by the parties of pleasure cruisers. Whenever this happened, he would diligently pick the place clean, filling his boat with the garbage. Under cover of the night, he'd cruise up to one of the exclusive marinas in the wealthy districts, and dump the trash on their carefully manicured lawns.

He lay half-comatose on his boat's bench seat, unsuccessfully willing the heat to dry his soaked cut-offs, when an unfamiliar motor caught his ear. Determined to ignore it, he shrugged the sound off and tried to doze the rest of his hangover away. The sound continued to close in as it throttled down to idle, then he heard a clunk as the transmission was thrown into neutral, where it sat, a burbling annoyance.

He groaned. "Damn."

"Lynette!" Two voices piped in unison from the bay.

"*She-ya*! Moe. Shitly. Take a gander here!"

Rip sat up in irritation as the world spun. Idling just beyond depth was a craft he hadn't seen before. It appeared to be some sort of hybrid, the rear of a flat-bottom swooping to a V-hull bow, with the strange addition of a steering-wheel housing located at the middle bench-seat. Stranger still were the boat's occupants; identically dressed identical twins. The boy's owl eyes stared out through thick-lensed glasses that sat beneath protruding foreheads framed with wispy blond hair.

"Hey Lynette, ..." Repeated the one on the right.

"... we know you're there." Picked up the other.

"Ha! Heee-ya! Musta' had more ta' drink 'n I thought. *She-ya*, I'm seein' double." Paul's knobby fists squished his eyes as he waded into the water. Moe, his arms, legs, and face covered in dabs of white cream followed him in up to his knees.

Clunk, went the transmission, and the boat drifted back from their approach.

"Paul, you guys get back! Those're my brothers!" Lynette pranced down the beach, splashing into the shallows, pulling a shirt over her bikini. She swatted at Paul, driving him back to the shore still grinning and giggling. She set her hands on her hips and stared out defiantly at the twins.

"*Well*? What do you want?"

"Dad's real pissed, …" The one on the left pushed glasses up on his nose.

"… that you didn't come home last night." Finished the one on the right, and echoed the gesture.

"He sent us to find you." Together.

"*Oh God!*" Paul wailed and spun around on the sand. Moe barked a short laugh with Shitly his shadow.

Lynette turned and glared angrily back at them, exposing a glowing red hickey below her neck.

"Dammit Paul, knock it off!" She faced her brothers again. "Alright, *alright*, I'll come with you."

The twins regarded each other, sharing an invisible thought; then the one on the left palmed a lever. *Clunk*, went the transmission, and the craft crept forward to meet her. She boarded with a fluid movement and waved shoreward as Slick cut across the beach and stepped into the water.

"Don't forget these." He giggled and tossed shorts into her waiting arms. She flushed and flashed him a smile. As she sat she met the twin-lensed glare of her brothers.

"Trifton and Troy, don't you look at me like that."

Paul howled and sat back on the bank. "Trifton and Troy! She-ya! Fucking *faggot* twins!"

Lynette angrily flicked her hair and turned back to her brothers. *Clunk*, and they sped out to meet the open river.

Slick walked over and sat down next to Paul, picking up his laughter, as Larry's mammoth form loomed above them, one huge paw making quaint little bye-bye waves to the retreating craft.

Observing this, Rip felt a curious sense of voyeuristic detachment, an insubstantiality that bordered on the physical. The scene before him grew flickery and faint, with the graininess of an old film.

I'm not really here.

The thought shocked him; despite its impossibility, he felt a deep sense of truth at its core.

This is completely crazy. It's the heat and the hangover.

He watched himself pick up the anchor and set it on the floor of the bow. His actions seemed remotely guided, as if his body were being controlled a far distance from his mind. The light turned brackish and stuttered unevenly around him.

"I, … I'm taking off." He managed to croak, voice dim and washed, though no one appeared to hear.

It was only until he met up with the main channel that the aberrant perception finally left him, the satisfying smack of the hull against the waves bringing back light and clarity, wind pulling feverish heat away from his mind. Twisting the throttle fully open, the craft bolted forward and he was swallowed into the thick shadows of the shoreline.

Brian D Garrity

2

SWING BEACH

Brian D Garrity

Curt's garage was the only air-conditioned garage Dart had seen. He felt the cool humming thrush of it as he let himself into the side access door, and found him and Randy gathered around Curt's motor. The '73 twenty-horsepower Mercury outboard sat bolted to a sawhorse, its sleek black contours interrupted by the absence of a lower unit, which Curt had carefully laid out on the workbench. He proudly held up a shiny, black mandala for Dart to inspect.

"Lookit' this."

"It's a prop."

"It's a speed prop."

"So I see."

"Rebuilt." He set it down and picked up a chrome crescent wrench. "Just got it this morning." Lifting the lower-unit off the bench with his other hand, he squatted down, slipping it in place, carefully lining up bolt-holes.

"Got a great price on it." Sliding the bolts in, he quickly hand-tightened them. Dart jumped up and sat on the work counter near Randy, fingers playing over the little jars filled with various screws, nuts, and bolts that were suspended from the shelf by their lids. Above them sat a small radio that squelched out Al Stewart, singing 'Year Of The Cat'. The wrench flashed in Curt's hands as he expertly tightened them to some specific torque.

Randy spun the prop around on his finger and looked over it at Dart.

"So what was up with you last night? Why'd you split?"

"I dunno'," He sighed. "It just felt weird, you know? Like I was some kinda' peeping-tom, or pervert."

"Boy howdy, …" Chuckled up Curt's voice from under the motor. "… *we* wasn't the perverts there last night."

"Yeah, man." Randy's eyes were bright. "I never knew doin' it was like that. I thought they was killin' each other, the way she was yellin' and all, …"

Dart tried to push away the image of Stephanie poised and naked in the moonlight.

"… and he sure had a big prick."

Curt stood and pulled the propeller from Randy's finger, twirling it around his own. "Randy, he had a hard-on."

"A what?"

Curt locked eyes with Dart as the prop spun to a stop on his finger. They both burst into laughter, Curt shaking his head as he bent down again.

"What? …Guys?" Randy's face was a hot red question mark.

"Erection? …Boner? …Stiffy?" Dart offered to Curt's choked giggling from the floor.

Randy crossed his arms and scowled. "What? What is it? Just tell me."

Curt abruptly jumped up from the floor brandishing the wrench victoriously over his head.

"Done! …Finally! …Finished!" He beamed as he tossed it back on the bench, patting the cowling of the Mercury.

"All freakin' summer. Borrin' out the heads. Installin' new compression rings for the pistons. Findin' a freakin' TIG welder to reinforce the transom to handle the extra power." He was walking in circles around the motor.

"And now, a new speed prop, …"

"Rebuilt." reminded Dart.

"…that's gonna' make this the baddest machine on the Mississippi. C'mon man, help me haul it down to the boat." He was already loosening the transom screws.

Randy's arms stayed crossed. "Not until you tell me."

"I got it." Dart slid off the bench and the two of them lifted the heavy motor from the sawhorse, carrying it through the access door. Randy scuttled after them, hands buried deep in his pockets.

The tropical air wrapped around them like a hot, wet blanket as they shuffled their cargo around the back of Curt's house and down the sandy slope to where it met the water. Sweat squirted down Dart's forehead and pooled painfully in his eyes. Randy still skulked along behind them, bottom lip pooched out into a pout.

"Curt, this thing's getting heavy, and I can't see a thing." He tried to brush the sweat off on his sleeve, but since he was shirtless, succeeded only in pushing more into his eyes.

"Almost there." Curt panted. "Randy, a hand please?"

"Tell me."

"Ask your parents."

"I will. And then I'll tell them who told me to ask them."

"Kee-ryst." Curt rolled his eyes. "Never mind. Here we are." They splashed in the shallows up to the stern. "Whatever you do, don't let that lower-unit touch the sand."

"Yeah, Curt. Done this before, you know?"

It took just a few short minutes to bolt the motor down, connect the fuel line, and pump mixture into the carburetor. Curt adjusted the trim, gave them the thumbs up and braced himself between the transom and the rear bench. He palmed the grip on the handle and gave a mighty tug.

Nothing.

The smile still frozen on his face, he coiled his body and took another pull.

The outboard farted once and boiled out a puff of greasy-blue cloud.

Curt took his foot off the transom and placed it on top of the cowling. "Start, fer Chrissakes." He muttered, and yanked again on the flywheel cord.

The motor coughed, spat another ugly cloud, shuddered, spat again, and then rumbled to life, idling easily as the little pisshole squirted oily rainbows onto the water. Curt stepped down, proudly regarding his creation with a smile that threatened to split his skull.

"Me an' Randy was talkin' 'bout takin' a cruise to the barge lanes. Look for a rope to make that swing. C'mon along. My turn for a change."

"Nah, I can't." Dart kicked a pebble into the water where it disappeared with a musical *plook*. "Gotta' go pack. Dad's pickin' me up in a couple hours."

"You leavin' for the weekend again?" Randy had already climbed aboard. "Sister goin' too?"

"Stacey? Nah. She got plans or practice or something. Seems like she's always got plans. Truth, I think she's kinda' scared of him."

Curt's eyes narrowed. "He beat you two?"

"Nothin' like that." He kicked another pebble. "Just gets kinda' strange when he drinks."

Curt and Randy nodded in unison.

"Why you go then?"

"I dunno'. Guess it's like he needs me there. Like it's my responsibility."

Dart looked at his feet.

"When you comin' back?"

"Sunday, 'bout noon."

Curt threw back the gear lever and gave the handle a quick twist. The motor snarled obediently and the bow slid off the sand as the flat backed quickly into the channel.

"Pick you up then." Curt was beaming, finally at the helm of his own boat. He swung the bow around and snapped the transmission into drive. "Plenty to do, we want to get this done before school starts." Then he and Randy were trolling down the narrow channel, past rows of docks and their assorted watercraft, to meet the murky expanse of the Mississippi.

Dart watched them putter away and wiped the sweat from his forehead into his hair. Something glittered in the silt by his foot and he bent and extracted a small reddish-brown stone, washing it off in the river. When held up to the sun it became translucent, a ruby glow cut through with veins and circular whorls of ice-white quartz. An eye-agate. Very rare, and, if you were superstitious, very good luck.

He slipped it into his pocket and set off down the shore in the direction of his house.

* * * *

The heat had stirred up straight-line thermals from the south, and these oven-hot gusts had in turn churned up a pretty good chop of white-caps. Curt slowly let the throttle open, carefully listening for any inconsistencies in the tone that would indicate trouble. With the waves banging into the hull, the blast of the wind, and the din of the outboard, Randy couldn't hear a word Curt was shouting at him barely a foot away.

"What?" He felt the vibrations from his vocal cords on his lips but heard nothing as the word was torn away in the explosion of sound. He pointed to his ears and shrugged.

The boat was bucking pretty hard now, the bow rising off one wave high into the air, holding briefly aloft, then dropping down to smash into the next, throwing them back up again.

Curt pointed to the bow and Randy understood immediately. He waited till they hit the next wave, scrambled from the rear bench to the center one, dispersing their weight more evenly. They planed out quickly, the boat skipping easily from one crest to the other, picking up speed, vastly improving the ride. Curt gave him the OK symbol with his thumb and forefinger and cranked the throttle wide-open.

The Merc's wail climbed an octave as it pushed a rooster-tail plume of water off the stern. They shot foreword, the ride turning into a butt-numbing, tooth rattling barrage of vibration. Randy held himself white-knuckled to his seat, his attention fixated on one of the incandescent orange life preservers that lay on the floor. It seemed to be doing a ghostly dance by itself, jiggling and hopping around over the ribbing, until, with one final bounce it caught the wind and shot astern, where Curt plucked it easily out of the air with his free hand.

They were now going far faster than the manufacturer had intended. Curt could feel the craft threatening to launch into the air and flip with every tug of the wind, yet he kept the throttle buried, making minute adjustments to keep it on the water, savoring the edge. Randy was frozen with a deer-caught-in the-headlights look that made him want to pull off something to really spook the guy, when a glint in his peripheral vision caught his attention. He turned his head just in time to see the boat rocket past them, a greasy blur of light and sound that Curt recognized an instant before its wash cascaded over them.

It was the exact same model as his.

"Oh, fuck me." It was a phrase Curt's father used often, a phrase he'd used in his head but had never spoken aloud. He cut the throttle as they cracked against the other boat's wake and slowed to an idle as both boys, drenched and dripping, stared after the retreating plume of its own rooster-tail.

Up ahead, the Interstate spanned the river with two massive bridges, these in turn supported by groups of three squat concrete columns that rose from the riverbed. The mysterious craft was approaching these directly on edge, and without a hint of hesitation, it neatly zig-zagged between all six columns, materializing on the far side. It tore around an outcropping of trees and disappeared.

Curt and Randy sat back down, though neither could remember standing. The Merc's puttering was the only sound breaking the surrounding cocoon of silence.

"I didn't just see that."

"Who, …who *was* that?" Randy's voice a cracked whisper as he squeegeed water out of his eyes with a thumb.

"Only one person I can think of." Curt couldn't stop staring at the wake marks already drying away, disappearing from the surface of the concrete pillars.

"You don't mean, …"

"Had to be. Had to be Billy Ray."

*　*　*　*

The town lay nestled in the massive folds of the coulees from the bluff ridge that ran along the river. Highway 35 cut a swath that vaguely described its course, bridging marshes, clinging to sandstone cliffs, managing to create a significant physical barrier between the town, and the eclectic cluster of enclaves that populated the river's edge. Pickle-Factory Road crossed the highway and sloped steep down to the marshes. At the bottom, where it met the train tracks, stood an ancient stone warehouse that the street had been named after. According to local myth, during World War Two, German prisoners were incarcerated there, forced to can pickles for the Government. As a child, Dart used to scrutinize old war movies he saw on TV for clues regarding the importance of these pickles, but he never did catch a single reference.

From there, the road snaked past the lumberyard, bisecting an old junkyard, which sprawled mainly in the direction of the tracks, townside. Inevitably some of the wrecks found themselves in the shallow marshes on the road's opposite side. Squatting next to the ancient slatted fence that marked the end of the junkyard was the Black Knight Bar, a drab cinder-block cube frequented by local fishermen, neon lights flickering through the windows, a weathered Past Blue Ribbon sign jutting from its façade that looked like it had hung there since before the last, great war. Pickle Factory Road took a right angle there, and became Pickle Factory Place, the rutted and pot-holed strip of asphalt turning into a gravel road that straddled the narrow peninsula that Dart, Curt, and Randy called home.

He walked the road as he had done countless times before. To his right, looking south, was the sprawl of a great marsh, and through the wavering haze of heat he saw churning gray clouds of mosquito's hanging there like a living, poisonous fog. On his left a thick tangle of trees followed the curve of the channel, sweeping up to follow the highway, its progress beyond the undergrowth marked by the occasional flash of sunlight on metal. Before him the road rolled out straight for a quarter-mile, kissed the main drag of the river, then hooked south half that distance to a turnaround. One road in, one road out.

For cars.

He walked the road and thought about the invisible line that lay beneath his feet, the green-dashed demarcation he'd seen on a county map once that divided the homes lined along the north side from those on the south. That delineation meant that he and Curt would be attending school at Central High in a small northern suburb, and Randy would go to Logan, who, it so happened, were fierce rivals.

Dart walked the road and thought about that arbitrary line, a thing drawn for convenience sake by some county engineer flunky, most likely, and how it'd affected generations of school-children past, and others to follow. He thought about these things because that's what walking the road allowed him to do. To think. People of the neighborhood passed him in their comings and goings while he was on these frequent excursions and they usually got around to asking *why* they always saw him walking? Where did he go, what did he do? He read the suspicion in their eyes, especially adults, but he never understood. When trying to answer them, he was generally met with a perplexed dismissal that he failed to grasp as well. He could only conclude an overall disapproval of personal introspection, but this ran contrary to most he'd been taught.

The choking cough of a badly tuned engine grew behind him and a piss-yellow Montego pulled up, shuddering along beside him. Glenn's face poked out, watery blood-shot eyes peering from beneath greasy brown strands of hair that fell across them. A pale white claw pulled at the strands and tried to tuck them back behind his ears.

"Hey Dart. Whatcha' doin' man?"

"Just walkin'."

"Walkin'? Yeah? How's that goin'?"

"Uh, … pretty good."

"Cool." Glenn's head bobbed quickly and his eyes darted down the road and the hair fell back in his face. "Hey, you over at my place today? You know if the old man's at home?"

"Was with Curt this morning. Your parents took their boat up through the locks earlier. They prob'ly be gone till dark."

"Cool." His head bobbed loose more hair and the claw pulled and tucked it back. A vacant smile touched his face and he glanced back at Dart. "OK. Take it easy, man." The car snorted and popped, nearly stalled, then launched down the road trailing a blue-black tornado of exhaust.

Dart consulted the cheap Timex that was strapped to his wrist. *One forty-seven. Dad's late again.*

He flashed back to the time about a year ago that he'd waited all day, but his father never showed up. There had been no calls, no answers when they tried to reach him. He'd simply vanished. That evening he had gone to bed in a black cloud of fear and anguish, sure that something terrible had happened, and spent a restless night in a malaise of dark fantasies. Father materialized the next morning with a huge purple welt on his forehead, and a cheerily dismissive story about loosing control of the car and being knocked unconscious from the steering wheel, but Dart's illusions of security were shattered forever.

He really hated to wait.

A familiar drone reached his ears and secret relief flooded him. A tiny fire engine red British roadster pulled up with a full-throated purr and his father leaned over and popped the passenger door.

"Hey kiddo," He bellowed and Dart could smell the tart sting of gin as he peered over the leather and hardwood console. "Where's your sister?"

"Awww, … you know. She's got these plans."

For a moment, the amicable look left his father's face, and was replaced by a vacant desolation, a haunted look that Dart only passively recognized, and then the façade was up again, and he beamed up through the doorway.

"Will then," Affecting an Australian accent. " … et's jus you 'an me, laddie."

Dart managed to wriggle himself and his backpack into the miniscule but surprisingly comfortable passenger compartment and found himself again pondering the vagaries between his fathers opulent six-foot three frame and the size of this diminutive automobile. They pulled a tight U-turn and headed back down the road, through town, and up into the thickly wooded bluffs.

* * * *

Curt and Randy cruised south, following the river through town to a wide bay that served as the industrial section. The rows of docks lining the banks were dwarfed by towering metal skeletons of cranes, and the massive hulls of barge-trains waiting to be either filled or unloaded. They prowled the silent hulks for over half an hour until they found what they wanted, a rusting old tug with a superstructure that reminded Curt of one of those plastic models that Dart was always putting together. A battleship called the U.S.S. Arizona.

Curt pulled the boat in and bumped it against a bundle of age-graying ropes hanging along its side that cascaded over the deck, from far overhead.

"Well, they ain't gonna' miss one of these." The heavy hemp twines were as thick as his forearm and he struggled to pull the free end of one out of the water. The rope that came out was covered by thick, green mucilage that slid through Curt's hands.

"Ughh, … Randy, would you grab this? Slippery 'n heavy as all heck."

"I ain't touchin' that."

"C'mon man!" Curt commanded. "I almost got this. Just need a little help. We gotta' have this rope."

Randy squeamishly acquiesced, and between them, they pulled in fifteen feet of slimy rope that sat coiled and stinking on the floor of Curt's boat.

"That'll dry up quick there." Curt was washing his hands in the river and looking up at the remaining length of the cable where it disappeared twenty feet above them over the deck. "Think you can climb that?"

"Yeah, no problem, ..." Randy rubbed his hands together in the water. "...if I can get this crap off'a my hands. One thing first though."

"What's that?" Curt sniffed his fingers, made a face.

"Tell me."

"Jeez, Randy. I swear, you musta' grown up in a cave or something."

"C'mon Curt. Just tell me."

Curt sighed. He told him.

Randy's small, wiry frame pulled itself quickly up the fat cordage, the jack-saw from Curt's lockbox slung over one shoulder. There was a little difficulty at the top, but he managed to grab a rusty cleat and heave himself onto the deck. After a quick look around, he set to work with the saw, the sharp serrated teeth making quick work of the timeworn strands.

Randy peered over the edge as he cut. "Hey Curt."

"Yeah?" He squinted up.

"How you suppose Billy Ray got that boat to go so fast? Same make as yours, ain't it?"

"Yeah. Don't know. Looked like the same motor, too, but it was hard to make out, thing went by so fast."

"Think maybe it was a thirty-five or forty?" Randy was sweating, loosing his grip on the saw.

"Couldn't be. Fourteen footer is maxed out at twenty horsepower, 'an you saw how we were doing."

"What is it then?"

"Wish I knew."

"O.K. I'm just about through here. You might ..." The remaining strands snapped with a resonant bang and the cut end whip-shot over the deck, leaving a puffy gray cloud.

Luckily Curt had stepped back to the stern when the plummeting mass of rope, like the great tentacle of a dying sea-monster, slammed into the floor of his boat. He heard rivets pop as the small craft canted crazily to port, nearly capsizing, and as it righted itself he lost his footing and tumbled over the side.

"Curt! Hey Curt, you O.K.?" Randy scuttled down one of the remaining ropes and clamored over the loose pile in the boat, frantically searching the water around him. He heard a splash and breathed a sigh of relief as Curt's head bobbed up near the hull, spitting out a little fountain of river water.

"I think, …" He gasped as he grasped Randy's outstretched hand. "… we shoulda' thought that through a little better."

* * * *

Rip found himself following the curve of the airport's shoreline, heading south to downtown. The setting sun followed him, and as he rounded the bend he spotted two of the kids from the previous day on one of the small sandbars that marked the southern tip of the island. They had what appeared to be a considerable length of barge rope spread out on the sand, the smaller one about eight feet up a tree that hung out over the water. They'd both stopped what they were doing and regarded him with slack expressions. He tipped up his hand in a wave, the taller one on the shore returning it. Kid in the tree obviously had his hands full.

He cruised on, the sun a gentle orange orb that hung stationary off his shoulder as the islands and bluffs moved between them. Rip wanted to get downtown, to the Park, before it got dark.

* * * *

Dart's father rented the second-story of an ancient re-converted farmhouse that stood sentinel on the brink of the descent to the river valley. It anchored the intersection of two county roads that crossed each other; one that snaked down nearly a thousand feet to the fertile chasm that the town and river occupied, the other following the border of rolling pastures and meadows of the Great Plains.

The evening blew in with hot winds that billowed the grasslands hissing through the trees. Dart worked awhile on a sculpture of a Tyrannosaurus Rex that he'd molded out of modeling clay, then went into the backyard to practice throwing his father's old bayonet, flipping it into a stump. He watched the sun sink below the meadows, rendered a dull red blob through the intervening atmosphere. As it fragmented and dissolved it dawned on him how different the sunsets were up here. How mornings and evenings were extended significantly from the valley. It seemed an important distinction, though he couldn't exactly figure out why.

He practiced until it was almost too dark to see, his father leaning out the second story window, highball glass clattering in hand.

"Dart! Hamburger Helper venison-style is just about ready."

"All right, dad. Be right up."

"How's it going with that thing? You know it's from an old M-1. Not balanced for throwing."

"Actually, I think I'm getting pretty good."

His father chuckled. "Go get 'em, kiddo." The ice chimed as he disappeared into the orange glow of the window.

Dart had to brace himself with his right foot to pull the blade from the rotting wood. He wiped it on his jeans, picking his way up the perilous staircase that clung to the side of the old building. His thoughts swirled around a bright core of excitement over his plans for later that evening; from the tattered copy of T.V. Guide his father compulsively kept by the set, he'd learned that the late show, the often ill-named Shock Theater, was playing an honest-to-God monster movie tonight. The film, 'Equinox' had often been referenced and pictured in the various monster and fantasy magazines that he had to keep hidden from The Stepfather, and had grown to an almost mythical proportion in his mind.

He reached the top landing and pushed open the noisy screen door when he smelled the rich aroma of dinner. Dart realized that he'd forgotten how much he really liked his father's Venison Helper.

*   *   *   *

They called it Gunnery Row, and Rip stepped down a stretch of the circular Parkway that ran abreast the artificial shoreline of downtown.

The cars lining the Avenue cast hard monochrome reflections from sizzling sodium-vapor lamps hooking overhead. The mixed chorus of hot-rodded engines, souped-up sound systems, and excited chatter flurried past as he picked his way through the milling crowd.

A '55 Chevy encircled by jocks wearing letter jackets, clutching cheerleader girlfriends, were exchanging taunts with the greaser proprietors of a rough-and-tumble, heavily built '67 Camero. The greaser's girlfriends looked tough and sleazy, traits Rip admired, one of them offering him a wink as he passed.

…passed a racing orange GTO parked nose to nose with a Torino fastback, both on fat, wide meats mounted to deep dish chromes, both hoods popped, resembling battling dinosaurs.

Catching the fractured parlance of popular mechanics…

"Six-fifty double-pumper Holley and 'an Eidlebrock riser…"

"Four twenty-seven? Cobra, yeah, good engine, but it ain't shit up against the four-forty wedge…"

"Ford? Stands for Found On Road Dead. Fuck Chevy's. I tell you, …Mopar."

An El-Camino bed held kids propped on lawn chairs, passing out cans of beer from an overstocked cooler, while next to them a skunk-striped '69 Mach-1 drew the largest crowd of all.

The fragrance of marijuana and cigarette smoke mixed with the sweet sickly stench of decay that constantly permeated the concrete waterfront. As Rip picked his way past, he mused that these car enthusiasts regarded their creations in the same subjective way that a parent might view an unattractive child. They displayed these creative endeavors as shiny beacons of their individuality, whereas Rip saw a nearly homogenous line-up of patched-together junkyard refuse, made over with generous amounts of bondo and primer, distractedly ornamented with an occasional piece of new chrome. Except maybe for the Mach-1. That really was a showpiece.

He recognized the towering mass of Slick's Blazer ahead and cut in its direction, when he sensed and heard a ripple of excitement flow down the avenue. There was a noticeable change in the momentum of the crowd, and he watched with amusement as beer cans disappeared, sodas taking their place. Joints and pipes winked out of existence, accompanied by the telltale creak and slam of cooler lids, these in turn concealed by tarps and blankets.

Sure enough, glancing back down the street, he saw the police cruiser crawling along, its high intensity beam splashing over the hulks of the derelicts to the indignant cries of those frozen in the light. He continued his slow stroll as the cruiser rolled by, its pristine tires making crackle-popping sounds on the warm pavement, then it was past, turning the corner, heading back into town. Magically, the coolers, the beers, the pot, all reappeared.

"You know, if they were smart, they'd send another cruiser through about two minutes after the first one." Keith's voice came from around the front of the Blazer.

"I wouldn't give them any ideas if I were you." Rip announced, rounding the massive grill. "Unless you're taking your father's side now."

"Well, *there* he is." Slick had his hand in Lynette's back pocket, leaning against the hood, still covered in mud dried to the shape and texture of stucco. Keith faced them with Stephanie, Cheryl, and Gaylene, all crowded around Cheryl's dwarfed VW Bug.

"My old man is a lawyer, Rip. He's got no sides." Keith tipped up a can of soda.

"Yeah, you keep telling yourself that."

"Hey, Rip." Stephanie's eyes twinkled, the other girls cooing their greetings.

"Ladies." His attention went to the cans in their hands. "Mountain Dew? Jesus, Keith, drinking pop?"

"Mountain Do! Check this out." He peeled the label off the can, revealing a Pabst Blue Ribbon medallion. "Pretty cool, huh? Got these at Metamorphosis. You know, the head shop?"

"I'm drinkin' a Popsi!" Slick held his up with a giggle.

"Yeah, that *is* pretty cool."

"Want one Rip?" Cheryl held out a can with a label that resembled a popular root beer. He accepted it gratefully.

"Thanks Cheryl." She smiled up at him, stepping back, bumping into Gaylene. He cracked open the can, pulling off the tab, carefully bending it in half and dropping it into his pocket. He hated stepping on the damn things.

"So, what's on the agenda tonight?"

"*Agenda*?" Keith hooked his arms around Stephanie's shoulders, peeping around her head, back down the Avenue. "Yonder comes our *agenda*."

He heard it before he saw it.

The subsonic snarl of an unthinkably vicious beast rose, thundered closer, as the candied amber wash of fog-lamps crept over the pavement at his feet. Rip felt the syncopated thump of cylinders on a custom camshaft, heard the hiss of air being sucked into a manifold as the 'Cuda nosed down and crouched next to them, its sinister contours suggesting supersonic speed, even standing still. The matte-black paint job absorbed all highlights and reflections, with the bumpers and deep-dish rims somehow rendered in the same opaque tone. Abruptly, the thunder of the big engine ceased, releasing the grip it had on Rip's chest. The tinted window slid into the door and the driver slithered out, sat on the doorframe, elbows resting on the roof.

Everything about this guy said hardcore grease-monkey, from his short shock of oily black hair, to the washed-out black tee-shirt sporting a cigarette pack rolled into the sleeve. His dark, wide set eyes regarded them without expression as he freed a pack of Marlboros and lit one up with the clink of a Zippo.

"Keith, hey bro, what's your pleasure?"

"Hey Marlon, …" Keith exchanged glances with Slick as he stepped around Stephanie, who was looking at the 'Cuda with what appeared to be awe. "…uh, we're lookin for a lid?" It came out a question.

"No probleemo." He spread sinewy arms. "Step into my office."

The passenger door clacked open, and through a pall of smoke stepped a tall, thin brunette that resembled the driver so closely she could've passed for his sister. Her straight black hair was shoulder-length and she shared his light olive skin tone. Clad only in a tight black tube top that clung to her small, shapely breasts and short-cut Levis, she smiled at her captive audience and bent to collapse the front seat.

"That's my girl, Andrea, and her friend, Viv." Marlon spoke to the night sky. "She's from West Salem."

From the dual darkness of the car's doorway came a spectre that froze Rip's heart. She flowed from the back seat and stepped lightly to the asphalt, the very air around her rippling with energy. Pale hazel eyes held him captive, framed by a cascade of flaxen hair. Her sun-bronzed skin was luminous against the night.

"Hey. Who're you?"

Rip knew the question was directed at him, but he couldn't find the words. He was acutely aware of the group's eyes on him. Keith slipped behind her, giving a thumbs-up, and slid into the vacant passenger seat. The door closed.

Andrea nudged Viv. "You *do* have a name, don't you?"

"Well, yeah, ..." Rip scratched his head. "... my name's Rip."

"Rip, ..." Viv smiled, Rip registering her full lips, upper one slightly thicker than the lower. "... what a cool name."

"My name's Slick."

Viv shot an annoyed glance over Rip's shoulder. "What the hell kind of name is that?"

Laughter from behind him and Stephanie's voice; "*Oohh*, burn!"

The door of the 'Cuda clapped open again and Keith hopped out, stuffing a baggie into his pocket. Marlon leaned over the console, eyes working between the girls, settling on Rip.

"You Rip?"

"Yeah?"

"On the river, hear you *the man*."

"Well, ..."

"Let's take a ride. You might dig this." He leaned back and disappeared, disembodied voice floating out from the black hole of the interior. "Hop in, ladies."

Andrea folded the passenger seat forward and held it as Viv backed in, and Rip found himself following, hypnotized by magnificent opal eyes that never left his. He settled into the seat next to her, smelling the car's sharp reek of gas, pot, and exhaust, taking a quick look back.

Keith had retreated into Slick's truck and was busy with what Rip assumed was rolling a joint. Slick, Lynette, and the rest stared back, and the look of pure jealousy that radiated from Stephanie was a thing that warmed his heart. Then Andrea was in and the door closed.

Rip strained ahead. "Marlon, is it?"

"Yeah, kid."

"Where we goin?"

Andrea gave a little snort from the front seat.

"Don't matter where."

"No?"

"Nah." He magically produced another cigarette from his sleeve. "It's all about *how* you get there."

Chromed flash and snap of a Zippo, and Marlon's face was curled around the drivers seat bathed in amber, facing him. Chink of keys turning around the ignition and the world was filled with concussive thunder.

"You're about to experience the pure beauty of four-hundred forty cubic inches of precision-tuned Detroit steel!" Marlon shouted over the cacophony, face transformed to a demon mask by the cigarette's glow. "Man, … ain't nothing like it!"

Andrea gave a shriek and wrapped her arms around him, grinning back at Rip. "Marlon's king of the street! No one can touch him!"

Rip slowly settled back into his seat and glanced over at Viv. She watched him, slight smile touching her lips.

The 'Cuda snailed forward, engine protesting the pedestrian pace, as they followed the arc of the Avenue away from the park toward town. A stop sign glowed ahead and they growled to a stop, the car's body quavering against the torque. Marlon's face reappeared between the front seats, twisted grin spread from one fuzzy muttonchop to the other. Another snap-flash of chrome and he was holding one of the largest switchblades that Rip had ever seen.

Feeling a trickle of sweat slide down his temple, Rip cast a frantic glance over at Viv. She just smiled back and put a warm, dry hand over his. "Relax, Rip. This is fun."

And he did. It all melted away when she looked into him. He was fascinated by the way the tip of her tongue appeared between her teeth while she spoke.

"O.K. bro, this is a game we play!" Marlon slapped a ten-spot on the console between Andrea and him, buried the big blade into it, pinning down the bill. "You like rock-n-roll Rip?"

"I love rock-n-roll!"

"Good man!" He held out a cassette tape and tapped it on the wiggling butt of the switchblade.

"New group! Scorpions! They kick!" He turned, slipped the tape in the deck and palmed the stick-shift knob. Crunchy guitar chords crashed through the speakers.

"Rules are simple! When I tromp it, you try to grab the money! If you get to it before I hit third gear, it's yours! Got it?"

"Yeah, but …"

Marlon slipped the clutch, mashed the gas pedal, and the still night was rent by the unholy wail of the angry engine.

Tires screaming, the earth slid out from beneath them as the 'Cuda canted sideways. Rip was up before he realized what he was doing, and made a grab for the bill. A shudder ran through the frame as the full-posi locked traction bars to the pavement. The car launched forward, hurtling Rip heavily back into his seat, legs askew before him. Marlon speed-shifted into second, the tires chirped, grabbing, G-force throwing legs to the roof, tangling with his searching hands. The powerplant screamed to a crescendo, and when it dropped into third an invisible hand flipped Rip upside-down and placed his head gently on the floor-mat.

The deceleration dumped his body unceremoniously to the floor, and above the blatting-crackle of the vehicle down-shifting, he heard muffled laughter over the din of the sound-system.

"Fuck-a-duck." He muttered up at the springs of the passenger seat.

*　*　*　*

The late night was alive with the chorus of crickets and warm winds that pushed the tall meadow grasses into dizzying patterns. Silent fulminations of heat-lightning illuminated cumulonimbus mountains far out on the horizon.

It was very late, and Dart wandered in a daze to the bridging crest of the meadow, hypnotized by the rolling savanna, and iridescent swarms of fireflies that boiled above. The movie had been crude but inspiring, and within his head images and ideas swirled and merged. There was a light touch on his cheek that he instinctively swatted at. His fingers came away smeared with the fading green glow of a firefly's lifeblood. He watched, as the iridescence ebbed to darkness with the faint flickering of a heartbeat.

Did the bug die with the light?

Immediate and utter silence blanketed the hilltop. A soft, strange light moved over his hand, over the landscape, and sudden primal fear cemented him motionless. A wave of nausea cramped his bowels, the fine hairs on his neck bristling. With tremendous effort, he forced his gaze upward, hearing the strain of bone against adrenaline tightened muscle in the soundless night.

It was a nacreous smear on the night sky. A formless opalescence that sheared it's silent way across the heavens. It shimmered with crystalline phosphorescence, shedding and collecting prismatic little pieces of itself, traveling impossibly fast. Dart couldn't guess at the size of the thing, but he had the impression that it was very large. It raced to its rendezvous with the horizon, where it abruptly dropped below the treeline of the adjacent valley. For a brief instant he saw silhouettes of the forest projected by the eerie light, and braced for an impact that never came.

It had simply vanished.

The chirp of a cricket sounded loudly next to him, joined quickly by another, then more. Soon the meadow was in full chorus again and Dart remembered to breathe. He stood in the darkness a long time before heading back, knowing there wasn't going to be any sleep tonight.

*   *   *   *

"*Viv.* That for Vivian?"

"Nope." She absently twisted and spit-glued the joint. "It's for vivid." She smiled at his reaction. "My parents are hippies."

They were alone in the back seat of the 'Cuda. Marlon and Andrea had left to hang out with Keith and the gang after they'd returned to the park.

"Vivid." Rip gave a low whistle. "Now that's a cool name."

"Sometimes ..." She folded up the baggie, made it disappear, and placed the damp joint in his hand. She held out a lighter. "Here, ...I'll light you."

"Uh, ... well, I don't really smoke, ... pot."

"Really." In the dim light he could see a mischievous sparkle in her eyes and she threw a leg up and over, straddling his lap. She plucked the joint from his fingers and ran the lighter's flame over one of it's tapered ends, coaxing an even, orange cherry.

"Viv?" He managed a whisper. He didn't know what to do with his hands.

She took a long, slow drag and he could hear a faint sizzling as the cherry traveled its length. Slowly leaning into him, her soft lips were over his, wet tongue slipping through his teeth, sliding into his mouth. He gasped and she exhaled, emptying her lungs into his. Rip's arms went around her, crushing her sweet warmth into his, and he took it all and held her in.

When they finally separated they were still joined by a dewy strand of saliva she gently wiped from his lips. Breathing heavily, her glazed eyes searched his.

"What do you think about that?"

"I think a lot of that."

Around the battering of his heart he could feel a twisting something that circled his stomach, arcing outward, a bright core twining his spine, polishing it in cool chrome, bursting through his skin in a crashing epiphany. Peering back at her, a milky luminescence coursed her body, punctuating each strand of hair, traveling over the delicate planes of her face and mouth, burning into the back of her eyes. Her beauty and proximity stunned him. He ached for her, and the pain was pure joy.

She giggled and wriggled on his lap.

"You feel it?"

"Oh yeah."

His hands slipped under the back of her shirt tracing the smooth architecture of her ribs, caressing the perfect symmetry of her shoulder blades as her breath came out in short, hot gasps. He brought his hands slowly around to her breasts, fingers exploring the hard, twin orbs of her nipples. She exhaled a soft, low moan, thighs beginning a rhythmic gyration on his lap, heat growing there, burning. Their lips and bodies came fiercely together again as she clawed his shirt up, rasping bare breasts across his chest. When they finally came up for air, she leaned back, guiding his hand down her flat belly into her pants, beneath silky underwear, where he felt her burning, soft moisture.

The world spun, and nothing existed, nothing but them and the moment.

Vivid's body arched back and grew taught, head thrown, eyes closed, lips slightly parted as he slowly withdrew his hand and tasted her. Then her lips were over his again, fingers still in his mouth, tasting them both, her hands working down the zipper of his shorts, when there was an abrupt knocking on the window near his ear.

"Hey you two, get a room already, will ya'?"

Faces pressed in all around them, tongues lolling, eyes bugging, he quickly got his zipper back up. Vivid composed herself with a quiet dignity that eternally won her his admiration, and he ran a hand through her tousled hair.

"C'mon. Let's go back to my boat."

"Yeah." Her smile was genuine and unaffected.

They spilled out of the 'Cuda to a rally of catcalls, applause, and an acid glare from Stephanie. Marlon merely nodded and gave the hood an affectionate pat. Rip knew he had to play this cool.

"Guess I know how a fish in a fishbowl feels." He threw an arm around Vivid and they turned to walk away.

Slick's voice piped up from behind them. "Guess I just seen my first porn!"

Rip flipped him the bird high over his shoulder as they walked back down the avenue to where his V-hull was moored, back to the privacy and anonymity of the river.

*   *   *   *

"Dart."

No answer.

"Dart!"

No answer.

"Now where's that boy up and gone to?"

Dart's mother threw her hands up on her sharp hips and blew a sigh back into his empty room. "Out all weekend. Bed's still made. Boy can't even stick around long enough to say hello to his mother?"

"Boat's gone. He's out on the river." The Stepfather stood behind her in the dark hallway swirling a glass of Old Style, the Kent in his other hand chuffing gray trails of smoke over her shoulder.

"I don't understand. Just what the hell does he do out there all the time." Her eyes ran over the disorganized clutter of his room.

"He isn't meeting up with the football team, that's a given." A dark smirk crossed his lips. "Loner, just like his old man."

Dart's mother slowly turned to face him, voice level. "Funny, I seem to remember a certain time when his old man mopped the floor with your face."

The smile remained, a hard, angular thing.

*   *   *   *

Curt had naturally forgotten to pick him up.

Dart met up with them at the place his mind had already christened Swing Beach. Curt and Randy were busy knotting a monster rope that dangled from a tree leaning out over the river. They looked up from their work in the shadowed glade, as his boat scraped to a stop on the bank.

"Hey Curt, thanks for the ride."

"Huh? Oh, … *crap*. Sorry. Spaced it."

"No prob." He jumped down to the cool, wet sand. "See you got the rope. Good work. How'd it go?"

Curt and Randy anxiously traded off on the adventures of the past weekend, and about the near capsizing of his boat, Curt displaying the jagged holes in his hull where the rivets had popped clean and gone.

"Takes in water real slow." He crossed his arms, shook his head sadly. "Gotta keep a coffee can to bail with."

Dart followed the line of the swing high up into the canopy, where it was tied off.

"Nice job with the rope. You do that, Randy?"

Randy's thin chest stuck out. "Yup."

"He got stuck."

"What?"

"Got scared while he was up there and froze."

"I wasn't scared, …"

"Had to climb up and help him down."

"… just got a little freaked out. Hey, it's a lot higher'n it looks."

"For sure. Don't ever wanna' do *that* again."

Dart gave the rig an experimental tug. "Well, looks like it's tied off pretty ace."

Curt patted the rough bark of the old, dead oak. "Someone's gonna' need to cap this thing to build the jump platform." He produced the jack-saw, pointed it at Dart and grinned. "Who's up for the honors?"

They worked slowly up the massive trunk by nailing scrap pieces of two-by-fours into the tree with salvaged ten-penny nails that Randy would pound straight and hand up to them, forming a makeshift ladder. They proceeded this way until Dart met with a knobby fork in the tree.

Randy jangled the soup can far below. "We runnin' outta' fixable nails!"

"That's okay." Dart glanced down and immediately looked back up. *Bad idea.* "Let's cap it here. I think we're high enough." *Maybe too high,* he thought, redoubling his grip around one of the forked limbs.

"How tall *is* that?" Curt was climbing up below him.

"How would *I* know?"

"Here." Curt offered a length of twine that stretched up from the beach below. "Hold that up and we'll measure it."

"Uh, … sure Curt, whatever you say." He groped blindly behind him, found the thing, and held it to the intended cut. Randy tied a knot where it touched ground and Curt climbed down to measure it against his boat.

"'Bout thirty-six feet!"

"*That all?* Christ, seems like a hundred, at least!"

"Other one's a lot higher'n that!" Randy's voice chirped from below.

Dart glanced at the overhang and saw that this was true. "One problem here. This part of the fork grows in the way of the jump-off."

"Bringing the jack-saw up!" Curt announced, slipping it over his shoulder, climbing back up again.

Oh, crap, thought Dart.

They lassoed a line around one of the out-hanging branches of the troublesome limb. Dart tenuously straddled the crotch of the fork, hacking away as they tugged on the line, attempting a controlled fall of the heavy branch.

The wood was like rock, or the blade was very dull, because it was taking a hell of a long time to get through the thing, and Dart paused to rest his aching arms, readjusting his footing, wiping sweat from his eyes. He cautiously peered down, seeing Randy pull at shorts that had ridden up his butt, as Curt listlessly tugged the line.

"Hey, you guys ever see a, … um, … U.F.O.?"

Curt's eyes snapped up. "You mean a flying saucer?"

"Nah, ding-nut! A *U.F.O.*, … *unidentified flying object.*"

"I seen something once." Randy sniffed at his fingers. "Turned out it was just some 'ole weather balloon."

Dart described as best he could the strange lights he had seen the previous evening over the grassy meadow. And even though it was mid-afternoon on a hot summer day, his skin broke out in goosebumps as he finished the story. "Freakiest thing I ever saw. Didn't get a lick of sleep last night." He didn't mention balling like a baby while running back through the field to his father's place. Some things were just personal.

"Man, I never heard nothing like that. You say you saw it land behind the trees in the next coulee?"

Dart started back in on the limb.

"Sure looked that way. Even made the old man hike over there this morning." His father, grumbling every step of the way about a bad stomach, the heat of the sun, kid's overblown imagination, while Dart had a pretty good idea from the number of cocktails he'd thrown back that he was just in the throes of an old-fashioned hangover.

The saw was biting better now as it dug into the moister core of the dead limb, sending pulpy little trails down to his friends upturned faces.

"Well?"

"Well, … *nothing*. No crater, no saucer. Not even a broken branch." There was a hefty crack and the tree beneath him shuddered. He jerked the blade out of its track, inching away from the cut.

"I think that's got it. Give it a yank!"

Curt and Randy leaned back on the line and the bough uttered a high, piercing shriek, but stayed were it was.

"Try it again!"

They heaved hard, and there was a thunderous report as the limb broke free and came crashing down, sending each tumbling down the beach. For a terrifying instant Dart felt the rotted old trunk sway, certain it would topple in the opposite direction, carrying him with it to the forest floor. But the roots of the big, old tree must've run far and deep, for it trembled to a stop.

A cloud of insects boiled in the air, trying to locate their vanished purchase as he swatted them away, slowly peering back down.

"Hey, you guys all right?"

Curt pulled Randy up and they brushed away sand. "Yeah, …" He kicked at the smashed, fallen bough. "Dang!"

A warm breeze brought the shrill whine of an outboard unfamiliar to Dart's ear, and he spotted an odd-shaped craft coursing slowly across the main channel towards their beach.

"You hear that?" Randy's head batted around his neck trying to locate the source of the sound. "You see who it is?"

"See it, but don't know it. Looks like their comin' in, though."

Indeed, the craft seemed to be making a bee-line directly at them. As it grew in size Dart noticed the odd configuration of a steering column bolted to the center bench, when he realized that its occupants were all bikini –clad girls, all waving and calling his name.

Curt looked up, puzzled. "Popular guy."

"Hey, it's Lynette. And Cheryl. And Gaylene." And Dart's heart nearly leaped out of his throat as he recognized the remaining girl: Cheryl's younger sister.

The boat approached at an awkward angle, and as Lynette struggled with the steering wheel and throttle, she managed to kill the motor, allowing the current to grasp and pull them past the beach. She frantically keyed the ignition, ignoring the distressed cries of the other girls as Curt waded waist-deep in the water, yelling at them to toss a line. At the last moment, Cheryl's kid sister [*Sara, Dart remembered*] grabbed the bright yellow nylon cord and threw it bull's eye into Curt's hands. He shouldered it against the current and pulled them back to the beach, as they clapped and cheered for their rescuer.

"Think ya might've flooded it." Curt offered as they climbed past him to the beach, their bodies chocolate-brown from the long summer. Lynette padded beneath the tree, peering up quizzically.

"What'cha doin' up there, Dart?"

"Building a rope swing." The other girls gathered as he climbed down. "Weird boat. Is it yours?"

"My old man's." She sighed dramatically, bringing life to her breasts, trailing fingers through brunette hair. "Got pissed at me for stayin' out the other night and grounded me." She smiled. "So I stole his boat."

"Wow."

"Yeah. Look, sorry about that shit with Paul that other night. He can be a real jerk, but when you get to know him, he's all right."

"Still think he's a jerk." Randy mumbled in the background.

"Oh, hey, …" Her arms fluttered around behind her. "… does everybody know each other? This is Dart and Curt and, … uh,"

"*Randy*." Scowling, he crossed his arms over his thin chest.

"… yeah, and this is Gaylene, Cheryl, and that's her kid sister, Sara."

"I know Dart." She stepped forward, squinting up at him through the bright sunlight. "We both had Mr. Perch's homeroom last year. Who you got next year?"

"Mr. Ball."

"I got Mrs. Blank."

Dart swallowed dryly. "They sure got weird names."

Sara smiled. "*Yeah*, I never noticed before."

He felt a flush rush through his entire body and suppressed an overwhelming urge to squirm. He'd never shared this close a proximity to her before, noting the perfect lightning-bolt part created by her pig-tails, sun selecting blue highlights from raven black hair. With dark, olive skin and almond-shaped eyes, she bore almost no resemblance to her older sister's blond-haired blue-eyed Scandinavian features.

"Whatizzit?" She scowled, crossing tanned arms over her breasts. *Christ, had he been staring?*

"*Oohh*, I think he likes you." Lynette gave Sara a taunting shove towards Dart.

"Shut up!" She spun and faced the other girls, throwing up her hands. "*GOD!*" She spun again, stamping past Dart, angrily puffing away a strand of hair that had curled into her mouth.

"Hey, look, I was just, …"

"You too!" She yelled over her shoulder, tugging at the thin material barely covering her bottom as she marched to the far corner of the beach. Dart tore his gaze away and met the wide grin on Curt's mug. Randy made kissy-faces.

"Aw, c'mon guys, gimme' a break."

It dawned on him then that he might have a secret that he couldn't share with even his best friends. He realized that he might just possibly be in love.

The rest of the work went quickly. The platform itself was a scrap of three-quarter inch plywood, silvered with age. They framed it in with the remaining two-by-fours around the fork over, the newly cut cap. The girls hung around, their presence bolstering productivity. It certainly helped Dart brave the heights, and as they splashed about below, in and out of the water, he kept catching owlish little glances from Sara, as she remained a diplomatic distance from him and the tree.

Finally, with the last brace in place, it was time to test the swing's trajectory with an unmanned test. Dart sat on the platform, legs swung over the edge as he pulled the heavy barge rope up with a smaller nylon line, the weight of it threatening to pull him over the edge.

Now, to stand up.

He was frozen, one hand clutching the heavy knot, legs locked around the underside of the platform, his other arm clamped in a death-grip around the trunk. He became aware of an acute clarity in his perceptions. The breeze rolling through the trees became a roiling thunder, each leaf chattering a distinct overtone. The rough texture of the trunk. The bite of the plywood against his calves.

There's nothing to hold onto, he realized. *No handrails, no branches. What the hell were we thinking?* The square of plywood beneath him shrunk, perspective below yawing with dizzying vertigo.

A piercing buzz drove through his ears and he watched a wasp, hung, preserved in time inches from his face, wings stitching a mobius strip through the air, the bright bands of color on it's abdomen a pulsing semaphore. He blinked and it disappeared, the drone persisting.

"Hey, you fall asleep up there?"

They stood clustered around the base of the big oak. Levering his back against the trunk, he carefully pushed himself up on wobbly legs to a standing position, both hands gripping the rope tightly. A wave of nausea passed as he felt the slight give of the platform. The nausea made him dizzy, and he forced it away taking slow, deep breaths.

"Hey, what's taking so long?"

"Jeez Randy, give me a minute, will ya? Nobody's tried this thing out yet."

"You ain't chicken, are ya? C'mon down 'an I'll throw the rope."

"Randy, …" Dart stopped, spotting the origin of the continued buzzing sound.

Three small craft in tight formation cut foaming white wakes down the channel. Three craft that Dart knew all too well.

Don't, he thought desperately, *please don't look*; but at the last moment Rip's head snapped up and he locked eyes with Dart. Then his boat, tailing Paul and Moe's, disappeared behind the glade of leaves that otherwise obscured the beach. In a flash he realized the fragile nature of their situation, and his worst fears were confirmed when he heard the reverse Doppler of their turnaround.

"Shit!" It was the fist time he'd sworn aloud and the word seemed to jump from his mouth. From below he heard Randy's surprised gasp, as Sara stared up in concern.

"What is it Dart?"

"Look behind you, guys." The six of them all turned and Lynette let out a little squeal of delight.

"Hey, it's Rip and the boys."

Curt wilted into the sand. "Aw, crap."

Cheryl's eyes darted between Lynette and Curt. "Why? What's wrong?"

There would be no unmanned test swing of the rope. There was no time. He needed to jump, now, before the other River Rats came and tried it first. If that happened, they would loose all proprietary claims to the beach and the rope, despite all their hard work.

Curt looked up in despair. "Uh, … Dart?"

"I know."

He took another deep breath, smelling pollen in the leaves, the chalky scent of a faraway bonfire, the slight tang of gasoline from the cooling outboards, and beneath it all the deep murky aroma of the Mississippi.

"Everybody stand away from the tree!" They stepped back as the three boats reappeared, framed by the glade. Dart could see Paul gesticulating wildly between him and the people on the ground, He could only hope that they had sense enough to stay out of his way.

Dart balanced his weight on the platform, balanced the rope in front of him, and sensed the moment as a fulcrum. He took one last glance down and saw Sara peering up, silently mouthing the words *'be careful'*.

He stepped off into space.

3

FUCK BEACH

Brian D Garrity

He passed the window.

A simple wooden pane set into the side of a garage in the darkening alley that leaned drunkenly away from the dirt road, mullions describing a cross.

The striated accumulation of multiple paint layers, scabbed and pulled away, surrounded the aperture of the window. The interior was a greasy smear seen through the slippage of the ancient glass. Rip slowed his pace and glanced first left, than right, but he was alone in the gathering twilight.

Fist clenching and unclenching, he approached the window.

This time he would do it…

Sias' had been unusually quiet when he'd docked his boat at the pier near the bait shop. From there he'd climbed his way up the familiar path towards Keith's house, through the traileryard of campers and visiting fishermen, mostly black, mostly out-of-state. Crossing over two sets of railroad tracks to the switchback trail that climbed the steep embankment from the spillway to the highway, it was a good 150 feet of grunting vertical ascension, through brambles and blackberries. Clearing the overgrowth, thorns dragging and snagging at his legs and shorts, he'd finally parted a curtain of foliage to emerge on a small sloping meadow that humped over the berm of the interstate.

Keith's house, or rather his parents, rested on its opposite, a rambling Arts and Crafts from the turn of the century; legacy from the age of the lumber barons, standing sentinel over Highway 35 and the river valley.

Each time he took this junket to Keith's, the window beckoned him, speaking of long lean years in neglect and solitude, of purpose passed, and promises unfulfilled. A voice triggering something buried, lurking; an inexplicable desire to smash his fist through this sad, lonely pane of glass.

Was it really as fragile as it appeared? Or did the rotting mullions contain some hidden strength held together by sheer stubbornness of age?

Rip again curled his fingers into a fist, studied the ridge of knuckles, four fleshy bumps, and visualized punching them through the yielding solids of glass and wood. Saw the dagger slash of splintered crystal cut into soft tissue, dark crimson spray. The urge took flight, vanishing as it had each time before.

The porch light was an amber beacon. Keith's father answered the door dressed in the full regalia of a commander in the Coast Guard Reserves uniform. His thick eyebrows scrunched together in annoyance beneath a polished brim, deep-set eyes peering over braided gold epaulets and shining brass buttons that marched down starched white fabric. A phlemy harrumphing sound rumbled from somewhere in his chest.

"You're Keith's friend."

"Uh, yes sir." Rip coughed into his hand. He could hear overlapping voices from deep within the house.

Keith's father's eyes flickered into the room and back to Rip. "We're having an occasion here tonight. Lots of very important people." He stepped back, beckoning him inside with the hand that wasn't holding the door. Slipping past, Rip could smell the sour reek of alcohol on his breath. "Guys are in Keith's room. I'd like you boys to keep a low profile tonight, understand?"

"Yes sir." Rip started toward the back of the house as Keith's fathers voice bellowed from behind him.

"And stay out of the booze, fer Christ's sake!"

"Yes sir."

Keith's room was in the basement, ancient wooden stairs leaning at precarious angles, and negotiating his way down, Rip could hear Paul's voice cutting the air.

"…buck 'a carp, she-ya, can ya' believe that? Buck a fuckin' carp. Sold six of 'em."

He ducked under a low, thick header beam, turned the corner around an old lath and plaster partition and almost stepped on Slick, sprawled against the wall, sitting on the floor, iced drink in hand, permanent grin creased into his face.

"Rip buddy." He tipped the glass in mock salute.

"Hey man." Keith was kicked back on his bed in the corner, large bottle of booze in hand, beneath posters of Aerosmith, Black Sabbath, Jimmy Page with his crazy double-necked guitar, and a black and white still of a moody James Dean. He knocked back a big swallow of the clear liquid, capped it and tossed it across the room. Rip caught it one-handed and read the label. Philips Vodka. The bottle was warm.

"Keith, your old man, when he let me in, …"

"Told you 'Stay outta' the booze.' I know." He threw his arms out in a helpless gesture. "Too late. Can't be helped now. Might as well catch up."

A single bare bulb dangled from a ceramic fixture set into the low-hanging joists, illuminating the room from the corner that Paul occupied, sunk low into a Day-Glo green bean bag chair. Each time he shifted weight, a thin stream of tiny white beads pissed from a tear in the side and joined a small lake already on the floor.

"Jus' telling the guys how I sold a 'coupla niggers at Sias' some carp I caught today"

Rip paused, the bottle halfway to his lips. "Aw c'mon Paul. You know I don't like that word."

Paul's hand reflexively shot through his hair, porcupining it in bright red quills, catching light from the bulb, as more Styrofoam balls pumped onto the floor.

"Don't mean nuthin' by it. Call each other niggers, ya' know? First amendment 'an shit."

"Paul, when your ancestors have spent two hundred years in slavery, then you got the right to call yourself anything you want."

Paul gacked into the Hamburgler glass he'd been drinking from, sending spray over his knees and onto the bean bag. "She-ya, man. I'm a hundred percent Irish."

Slick's giggle quickly turned into braying laughter and Keith launched a finger into the air. "Touche'! I do believe that's one for Paul."

"OK. Alright." Rip sighed, tipped the neck of the bottle. "Point taken. But Paul?"

"Rip?"

"For me, OK? Just try 'an curb it around me."

"You got it. Sheesh, your such a pussy for a River Rat."

"Yeah, yeah, I'm a pussy." He poured a mouthful of vodka into his mouth and swallowed. It burned like warm acid and tasted something akin to paint thinner. Tears welled up in his eyes. "Jeez," He gasped, trying to keep it down. " ...coulda' at least chilled the shit."

"Beggars can't be choosy. You'll get used to it." Keith probed behind his pillows and produced a small tin stash-box. "'Sides, I got something here to make the evening flow a little smoother." Prying the lid open, he held up a joint the size of a small cigar.

"Fatty!" Paul pumped his fist in the air, further depleting the chair.

"Thought you couldn't smoke down here."

"Can't." He slid off the bed and pulled open a door on the back wall between him and Paul. "But in the labyrinth, anything is possible."

Slick lurched off the floor and stuck his head through the door. "Storage. Seen it before."

Producing a chromed flashlight from underneath the bed, Keith clicked the switch on the handle, playing the beam into the darkness. "House is friggin' old. Nooks and crannies back there my parents have no idea exist." He turned back to them, mischievous smile on his face, waggling the dube Groucho-Marx style. "Hope none of you are afraid of ghosts."

"She-ya."

"Let's get this party rolling."

Rip took another belt off the bottle. "Fuckin' shit, you were right."

"Uhn?" Keith looked confused.

"Getting used to it already."

They followed the cone of illumination through the crowded storage space that bordered Keith's room, sneaking between narrow cobwebbed corridors of furniture and cabinets. Fingering the hasp on a low slatted wooden door hidden behind a stack of chairs, Keith pushed it slowly out. The ancient hinge emitted a tortured groan, causing him to hunch his shoulders and push a finger up to his lips, but whether it was to shush them or the door, Rip couldn't tell.

Beyond ran a narrow corral of sorts that tracked first left, then right, the darkness punctuated by the stamp of footsteps and muted murmurings from the party above. Walking single-file, Rip could see Paul, up ahead, flinch at each whispery touch of spider web, and he managed to get his shirt snagged on a couple rusty nail-heads that had worked their way out of the wall. They made a final turn, and the din from above receded behind them.

Keith placed the flashlight on the floor, the ray raking ancient knotty textures up the wall. He turned and pulled a plastic lighter from his jeans. "Near as I can tell, we're beneath the pantry in the kitchen." Voice a hoarse whisper as he snicked flame from the lighter and touched it to the end of the joint. "Safe, but you gotta' be quiet."

They gathered around as he took a long hit, the cherry's radiance traveling its length. Passing it to Slick, Keith huffed in a fat finger of smoke curling from out his mouth, Slick passing to Paul after his turn. Ejecting a thin fog, Keith croaked; "Co-lumbian gold."

Slick was still holding. "No 'chit?"

"Com-press pack, man. Straight from South America."

Paul, holding his, passed it over to Rip.

"Kinda stemmy and seedy, but it's, …gold."

Rip considered the joint, and Paul took in his hesitation. "In 'er out?"

Plucking it from Paul's fingers, he took a cautious draw. The smoke was milder than expected, so he topped it off, sucking in a little more, handing it back to Keith, who watched him curiously, eyes visibly glazing over, even in the subdued light.

"Hey, ...man. So, like, ...what's up with you and that sweet little piece of ass Viv?"

Something was happening to his lungs. A burning, building pressure had started from the inside and was trying to force its way out. As a release valve, Rip slowly leaked some of the smoke from his mouth, but that only aggravated the problem. He blew the hit and his body convulsed with the searing pain of passing hot lava.

All eyes were on him. He took a gulp of air, found he couldn't hold it in, and barked a harsh, tearing cough that quickly led to a series of scorching hacks.

Keith jumped, stubbing out the stogie. "*Shit*. Back to the bedroom."

He grabbed the flashlight and they raced back through the darkness. Rip strained to see through tearing eyes, coughing uncontrollably, bounding off walls, a nervous giggle starting up ahead from Paul, turning to a raucous shriek of delight when Slick tumbled noisily over an upturned end table. They burst through the bedroom door accompanied by the sounds of unsteady footfalls overhead and dove to their respective corners. Keith latched the door behind them, throwing himself casually on his bed.

Rip was doubled over, trying to stifle the spasms renting his lungs when the door upstairs opened. Keith was mouthing something to them, but through the racking barbs of pain he couldn't make it out. He pointed wildly and Rip looked around, every thing appearing normal, except, of course for his wild coughing jag, and then he could read Keith's lips. They were saying 'BOOZE'. Suddenly all their drinks materialized, He shakily slid the bottle behind him, steps now resonating down the stairs, coming slower and slower, shoes visible, polished, starched cuff, and then Keith's dad was standing toad-like in his uniform before them, swaying, bell glass of cognac in one hand, lit cigarette in the other. "Alright. What you boys up to?"

Fascinated by the unfolding tableau, Rip forgot to cough.

Keith, lying back, tossed up a shirt and snatched it out of the air. "Nothin' much, dad. Rip here thought it might be interesting to drink pop with his lungs, but, as you can see, the experiment was not a success."

"You OK, boy?"

"Yessir." He managed, voice gravelly from the damage to his throat. "Just tryin' to catch my breath." It really was amazing how amphibian the man's face was becoming, bulbous saliva-covered lips beneath buggy, bloodshot eyeballs, and he was pretty positive that he could actually see a ghostly pall of alcohol floating about his weaving presence. The planes of perspective in the small room kept shifting as the froggy face beneath the cap slowly swiveled to look at each of them in turn. Rip felt dangerously close to the edge of hysterical laughter at the comic apparition, nearly loosing it when his nostrils quivered and poked the air a couple times, thick eyebrows furrowing in disapproval.

"What's that smell?"

Keith held up a small, dark cone. "Just burning incense, dad. With all the smoking going on up there, it's kinda' starting to reek down here."

His father considered the cigarette still smoldering between his own fingers, grunted, and executed a sloppy heel-turn. "As you were, gentlemen." He drifted back up the stairs.

The door closed.

Slick broke first, a pent chattering snicker escaping his sinus, then they all were out of control, Paul kicking at the chair, unleashing another avalanche of beads, Keith burying his head into a pillow, and Rip nearly tipping over the bottle behind him, falling back.

Sniffing back snot that he'd ejected, Rip gasped, "God, I think I'm gonna' puke."

Keith wiped at the tears running down his cheeks. "Fuck, that was close."

"Too funny." Slick shook his head

Paul's face was still buried in his hands, unable to stop, body convulsing uncontrollably.

"Hey." Keith rummaged around his shelves and produced a box of glow-sticks, little white plastic tubes that, when cracked, mixed certain chemicals and glowed for about fifteen minutes. "Hey, …what do you think we can do with these?"

He had that look in his eyes.

*   *   *   *

The stuffed bulb of a cattail sprung from beneath Curt's foot and whupped Randy full in the face, launching a wispy cloud of silver filaments into the air, sticking to his cheek and hair.

"Owww, …" He pawed the stuff from his eyes. "Dang, watch what 'cher doin'."

"Doin' nothin' but steppin'. Hang back a bit and you won't get hit."

Dredged from the silt of the bog, the banks of the lumberyard's back-lot loomed behind them as they dragged their payload across the marsh.

Randy carried a bundle of two-by-fours, six footers, and Curt struggled with a large slab of half-inch plywood, arms splayed to their widest reach, where his fingers were barely able to curl around the edges. Up ahead, breaking through dry and brittle clumps of tall marsh grass, Dart balanced two long planks of rough-cut two-by-sixes.

The heat of the day was dispersing in the oncoming twilight, the wide expanse of marshland pulsing a waning, golden hue, air stilled as it followed the sun. Normally, this region would be flooded with two or three feet of water, a vast swamp inaccessible by either foot or boat, but the summer had been abnormally hot and dry, allowing them approach to the unguarded flank of the mill. A whippoorwill cried from somewhere and Randy planted his feet, panting.

"Think we can take a break? Things're heavy."

Dart turned, nearly cracking Curt with a board. "Wanna' get that grove of trees up there between us 'an sightline of the yard."

"Keep movin." Curt grunted into the panel. "Feel like there's eyes all over my back."

"Wasn't nobody there."

"Guard could check anytime. Still light enough."

Huffing greasy bangs from his eyes, Randy chased through the brush after them. Reaching the darkening copse, they relinquished their burdens, collapsing into delicate banks of dried grass, trying to catch their breath.

"It's just over that next sandbar." Dart wiped sweat from his forehead. "More'n halfway there."

Curt sat on the plywood. "It's good 'an hidden, too. We can't let them Rats find our new tree fort." He lay back, fingers locked behind his head. "They just take it over like the rope swing."

"Ain't fair." Randy flopped back against a small bush. "That was our idea. We built it. Can't even get near it, no more, so many people."

"No good any more anyway." Dart eased back, resting his head against the weave of dry blades. "With all that traffic, the trees startin' to pull down into the river. Hey, check out the sky."

"Wow."

The sun had long since set, but its final rays reached over the world, shifted a vibrant scarlet by the intervening atmosphere. It raked the cloud's scalloped underbellies, creating a molten, airborne river of fire that illuminated the bayou, briefly, in a soft magenta glow. They watched as it faded to bruised purple.

"That, ..." But Dart couldn't find any words.

Curt sat up. "Rand?"

"Yeah, that was, ..."

"Randy, you might want to pull your ass outta' that buncha' weeds there. Think it might be poison oak."

Randy leaped like a spider from where he lay. "Jesus!" He danced a jitterbug, convulsively consulting his bare arms and thighs. "I'm allergic! Am I allergic?"

"Hey, wait." Dart pulled up, moved forward, drawn by the familiarity of the palm-shaped leaf and its serrations. "That's not, ..." He drew closer. "It is! It's, ...pot!"

"What?" Randy froze as Curt approached.

"Holy crap! It is! Here's another one. And another!"

"Rand' the *man*. Good score."

"Well, …"

"What you think all that's worth, Curt?"

"*Nothin'* till it's dried and cured." He probed about the base of the plant.

Randy began thrashing again. "You know how to do that?"

"Well, …" He got a grip on the collected stalks, pulling its roots free from the soft sand and mulch, holding it aloft. "…Glenn told me that you gotta' dry it upside down so's the resin flows into the leaves."

"What's resin?" Randy's fingers twitched over his elbows, jerking down to scratch at his knees.

"Stuff gets you high." His head snapped up. "Randy, it *ain't* poison oak!"

"Not that. Skeeters commin' out. Break out the bug-juice Dart."

They slathered themselves with insecticide and continued their crossing with the additional baggage of the three plants. Ahead was the island where Curt's boat was beached, where their tent was pitched beneath a stand of trees that held the skeletal framework of their new tree-fort.

*   *   *   *

'When the levee breaks' by Led Zepplin broke from Keith's speakers at an appreciable volume, but no one seemed to care, and the Blacklight was on, illuminating the vibrant warpaint daubs of goo from the glow-sticks that they'd smeared over their faces and naked torso's. The walls, too, throbbed with petroglyphs of light.

Judging from the transmissions coming from the ceiling, things upstairs were going pretty well, also.

They'd been back and forth to the secret room a few more times over the course of the evening to take hits from Keith's stogie, and to allow Paul and Slick to smoke their Marlboros. Rip's high was mellowing out, though his drunk seemed to have reached a tipping point.

The Blacklight had transformed their tanned skin a deep purple. Keith stood unsteadily before Rip, glowing green skeleton of slashes and curves smeared over his chest and skull, mouth working around radiant ivory teeth, but through the wash of guitar chords he couldn't make out a single word.

"Whas'sat?"

With a singular motion, Keith dropped to the bed and spun the stereo's dial to silence. "*Said*, that you can tell how a girl fucks by the way she walks."

"She-ya." Paul's red hair was a blaze of flame atop his head. The beanbag chair had spent most of its contents, so that his body was mostly consumed in the flaccid plastic.

"How so?" Rip tried wrapping his mind around the concept.

"See, ..." Keith pointed a finger into the air. "...it's all in the ass. The ass is key. You know how Anita walks, back straight, ass stuck out, kinda' bowlegged?"

"The cheerleader, yeah?"

"Doggie style. Even barks when she does it."

Slick pushed up from the floor. "Yeah?" He'd painted targets around his nipples and a smiley face on his stomach.

"And Cheryl, she's got that tight pooper, but really thin hips and walks with those little steps? Missionary only. Gaylene's got those long legs, really throws her hips into it. She likes it on top."

"Alright, *mister scientist*, ..." Slick leaned over and poured from the nearly empty bottle. "...how about *Lynette*. How does she fuck?"

Keith shook his head sadly. "Sorry, man. Dead-fish fuck. Just lies there. Pussy even smells like fish."

Slick slumped back to the floor. "*He's right.* How'd you know?"

"Experience, man." He picked the bottle up, sloshed the remaining contents. "All based on personal field experience."

"You fucked Lynette?"

"Who hasn't?"

This all was an amazing revelation to Rip. "That's *genius*, man. So, ...What about Stephanie?"

"Mmmm, …"He worked a mouthful of liquor down his throat and leaned on his side. "…you know how she struts around, rolls her ass, hips movin', shoulders and tits movin', everything movin', really." He implored, an open gesture. "Well, should tell you. Pretty much everything. Too bad she might be pregnant."

A needle skipped in Rip's mind. "Say *what?*"

"*Oh shit*, shouldn't 'a told you that. Yeah, she's like, late. But, mum's the word. Say nothing, right?"

"Right."

"Nothing."

"She-ya."

"Paul." Slick pointed with the leading edge of his glass. "You been kinda' quiet. Come clean, you a virgin, or what?"

"Ain't had but one woman, … Dawn." His voice drifted up from the folds of the chair. "Don't remember how she walked, but she played my balls with her stocking-foot under the table, while we was playing quarters at Slick's."

"Dawn Mumm?"

"Mum's the word."

"The *preacher's* daughter?"

"She-ya."

"Jesus."

"Oh, that's fucking rich." Keith turned to Rip. "And you, my friend. Fess up about that hottie butt-munch Viv."

Paul howled from the chair. "*Butt-munch!* Hee-ha!"

"Shit, I don't kiss and tell."

"Didn't ask about kissing. Talking 'bout fucking here."

"Maybe."

Paul's scrawny torso rose from the wreckage of the beanbag, the blacklight thickening the buckshot patterns of freckles beneath vibrant glow-stick hieroglyphics. "Hey, i'zat really true?" He looked earnestly curious. "Do you really munch them girls butts?"

"Uh, … no Paul. Just a figure of speech." But Rip could practically see the wheels starting to turn in his friend's mind. "So, …is Viv a *true* blond?"

He sighed. "Everywhere."

"Blond snatch is soft."

"Like a mink's pelt." Rip tipped his head back, recalling the night. "Not skanky either. Tastes like butter."

"Goddamn!" Keith launched off the bed and began pogoing about the room, showering it with vodka. *"I want a new hole!* I need to fuck a new hole!" He stopped, tipped over the bottle, displaying its lack of contents. "Booze's gone. What we do now?"

Paul snaked himself out from rubbery folds, and stood, momentarily slipping on a small glacier of blinding foam beads, pulling himself together with mock dignity. "Frickin' time for a joyride."

"Joyride, *fuck yeah.*" Slick's hand was in the air.

Keith pumped his fist. "Tits, man! Tits *and* boobs!"

Rip burped. "What the fuck's a joyride?"

Keith threw him an exasperated look, turned to the other two, then back. "We find a *car*, and then we take it for a *ride.*"

"You steal a car."

"No. We do *not* steal. We *find* a car, and take it for a *ride.* We do not *keep* the car."

"Uh, ... doesn't Sick have his blazer here?"

Slick pulled his shoulders up. "What's the fun with that?"

"It's, ...*legal?*"

"*Exactly!*'

"OK." Rip's mind was suddenly filled with crime drama scenarios from bad television cop shows. "OK, ...how *exactly* do we get outta' this basement, through that crowd, without bein' noticed."

"Sshhheeeeeiiiiit, ..." Keith somehow enunciated this with about four syllables. "... got that covered."

*   *   *   *

The bonfire had been set up in proper teepee fashion, bolstered by leanings of driftwood and kindling of dried windfalls scrounged from the dense center of the isle. Smoldering, it collapsed in on itself and burst back into life, illuminating the faces of Dart, Randy, and Curt.

The place was known as Tomahawk Island, and local legend held that it once was a gathering spot for various tribes of Native Americans. The myth was firmly supported by the fact that Dart had personally found two exquisitely chiseled quartz arrowheads on its sandy beaches. Geographically, it was quite near to where they lived, but because the island was located just north of the spillway, one had to circumnavigate the airport to the far end of the main channel and endure the time-consuming process of passing through the locks to reach it by boat. This suited their purposes ideally, as it was far enough off the main boating lanes as to be rendered practically non-existent to anybody but a true, dyed-in-the-wool River Rat, and during the winter, when the river had frozen, could be easily accessed on foot.

It was a rare late-summer evening, still and silent, broken occasionally by the distant trill of a bird or the hiss-pop of a branch being consumed by the fire, and once by the sepulchral drumming of a passing barge's engines, its spotlight a magnesium eye rushing with crazed velocity up and down the shoreline, holding them briefly in brilliant luminosity, before moving on. The moon pushed up over the treeline, bloated and orange, shedding color and mass as it rose, burning a path through the soft quilting of the Milky Way.

Skewered on sharpened twigs, three hot dogs hovered over the fire, spitting grease. Randy pulled his in and examined it. Satisfied, he trapped it in a bun. Reaching into a nearby Styrofoam cooler, he pulled out a bottle of ketchup.

"See, I heard one time, a guy tied off his boat at the lock, ..." He spread a thick finger of the condiment over the length of the dog. "...and the water level starts to drop. Don't know until the thing starts to tip what's goin' on, then, it's too late." Stuffing half the thing into his mouth, he bit down, juices exploding over his chin.

Dart heard this one before. "Hey didn't he, ..."

Somehow Randy spoke around the mouthful. "*Dang it.* My story." He chewed once, swallowed. "You *always* tellin' stories."

"Randy, ..." Curt blew on his hot dog. "...*everyone* knows that one. Ropes keep cinching tighter so he can't untie the knots. Thing keeps tippin' further against the wall, and he *knows* those two lines ain't gonna' hold the whole weight of the boat." He bit off one end, plain, right off the stick.

"So he pulls his knife, ..." Dart picked up the story, prepping his own; bun, ketchup, *and* mustard. "...dufus cuts it underhand, and when that line lets go its load, he stabs himself in the throat. Bleeds to death. Drowns."

"Yeah, ..." Randy squashed the remaining half in his mouth, went to work fixing another.

"My sister almost drowned when she was sucked out into the open river by the undertow of a passing barge."

Randy looked at Dart. "Stacey?"

"Yeah."

"Old man told me 'bout this one guy, pullin' a skier? Looses it but the driver don't see him for awhile." Curt bit off the hot dog's opposite end, balancing it. "Finally spot's he's pullin' nothin', turns around and cruises back the way he came but he can't see nobody, when his 'Merc, ...think it was a big old 95 horse, jumps like he rode a log."

Dart considered his meal. "Aww, man. I'm tryin to eat."

"Yeah. Opened up the back of his head. Brains 'an blood all over the river." He plucked off the remaining nub of the wiener and ate it.

"They probably just a bunch 'a old wives tales, anyway. Billy Ray's real though. We seen him." Randy eased the dog over the fire. "Right, Curt?"

"Well, can't be certain, but man, ..." He made two boats with his hands, and shot one past the other. "...dude was on us and past us before you could see anything."

"No way." Dart took a bite.

"Burned us with his rooster-tail, and then, ..." Curt squiggled a hand through the air. "...zig-zagged though the I-90 pylons." He breathed a sigh of reverence. "All of them."

"*What?*"

"Yeah, never saw nothin' like it. Didn't even slow down."

"Wait. You sayin' he stitched through all six supports?"

"Yup."

Dart considered the significance of this.

"Gotta' do that."

"You? With your 'Rude?"

"Why not?"

"Well, …you might bite it into a concrete pylon."

Dart chewed solemnly, finishing his hot dog. He absently started drawing patterns in the sand with his stick. "Isn't about the boat or the motor. It's the pilot."

"Gonna' get yourself killed." Randy fixed his second, again wolfing half of it down in a single bite.

"Billy Ray can do that with his hopped up rig, then *I* can do it."

Curt threw his skewer into the fire. "Well hell, if *you* can do it, then I can do it, too." He held out his hand. "Bet."

They shook on it.

Dart stood, stretched, and yawned. "Gonna' turn in. Lot to do tomorrow." He brushed the sand from his ass and started toward the tent, Curt following suite.

"Me too. Kinda' bushed from haulin' all that lumber."

Randy was still working on the second half of his hot dog. "I'll be right there. Gotta' pinch a loaf."

Pulling the zipper down the doorway, Dart glanced over his shoulder. "Just do your business where we won't be steppin' on it."

"And bury it deep." Curt followed him in.

The bright eye of the moon burned overhead through the tent's fabric as Dart lay in his sleeping bag, waiting to drift off. There was a muffled series of snickers beside him, then Curt was tapping his shoulder. Dart turned his head and was witness to a memorable scene.

Randy had positioned himself between the tent and the fire, so that the silhouette of his crouching form, shorts pooled around his ankles, was projected larger than life on the wall of the tent. From the curve of his bare buttocks a pointed turd grew, extending slowly, then dropping, followed by another.

Dart found himself choking laughter into his pillow when he heard Curt whisper: "Stupid fucker."

Initially, he was shocked. They'd never before used that kind of language, but then it dawned on him that this was what cussing was *for*. Only an obscene word could encapsulate what they were witnessing. And it was almost too funny to bear when the shadow Randy realized he'd forgotten the toilet paper in the tent, and began hopping around in earnest, looking for leaves to wipe his ass.

Stupid fucker.

*   *   *   *

"Thunderchicken!" Paul ran his hands over the vehicle's glossy quarter-panel.

Slick walked around to the front of the massive hood. "Sixty-nine. Got a big-block 429."

"That's our girl." Keith scrutinized their surroundings. "C'mon."

"Uhm, …guys?" Rip paused. "I'm not sure this is such a great idea. You really know how to break into that thing?"

The Ford Thunderbird sat parked on a darkened, and mostly deserted lane. Paul reached down to the driver's side door-handle and depressed the latch. It swung open with silent precision. "She-ya." He slid in.

"*Get in.*" Keith hissed, popping open the passenger door. "*C'mon, Rip.*"

He and Slick entered the backseat through the two rear suicide doors. Paul was doing something under the dash, and Keith spun to face them, grinning maniacally, the ghost of illumination still clinging to his face and arms. "See, these older cars are simple as shit to hot-wire."

On cue, the starter cranked over a couple times, then the big engine hummed smoothly to life. Paul rose from the driver's seat, slipped the transmission into drive, and they rolled slowly down the street for a half block before he queued the headlights to life, slowly accelerating to the center of town.

"Damn, that was easy." Rip was suitably impressed, rolling down the window, spilling fragrant night air through the cab.

"What a rush, huh?" Keith kept switch-backing from the road in front to the back seat.

"Didn't know you could drive, Paul."

"Don't 'zackly have ma' license, …"

"You don't, …'

"…but usta' drive tractor and the pickup at ma' Grampy's."

Rip considered their situation. "Uhm."

"Where I learned the hot-wiring, too."

"Soo, …" Rip watched as the tree lined boulevard rolled past, houses on both sides settled deep in their yards, windows pulsing amber jack-o-lantern faces. "…this is what you big city slickers do for kicks, huh?"

Slick swiveled in his seat. "Let's show this River Rat some real in-town action. Let's hit the *Plasma Pud.*"

"Plasma fucking *what?*"

"The Plaza Pub." Keith clarified. "A bar in the new mall. Primo idea. Dollar pitcher night, *and* Sandy's working tonight."

"Keith, you know I'm not eighteen yet."

"Said *Sandy* was working. Not a problem."

Plaza Pub was a vestibule located within the center of a strip mall that faced the highway, and subsequently, the river. The remainder of the mall was closed for the night, and access was barred on each side of the entryway by means of complicated gates that resembled the set of a science fiction movie. The wash of fluorescent lighting stuttered harshly against Rip's eyes, and he realized that he was having a little trouble walking straight. The dark cocoon of the bar's entrance was a welcoming sight.

"You really think it's a good idea to leave the car out there like that?"

"Relax, bub, …" Keith ushered him through the doorway. "…it's cool."

Inside, something by 38 Special was playing on the jukebox. A few old timers were curled over the bar, some younger groups clustered around tables in the back and on a raised platform that paralleled the bar. A woman approached, wiping hands with a rag. She was older, maybe twenty-five, but hot in a wiry, athletic kind of way, and she scanned them, eyes lighting first on Rip, then Keith.

"Hey boys. 'S it goin?"

"Evening Sandy." Keith leaned forward, straight-arming the bar. "I do believe that it's dollar pitcher night?"

"Yup." She worked a piece of gum and looked back at Rip. "Ya' gonna' introduce your new friend here?"

"Sandy, this is Rip. Rip, Sandy."

"Rip, welcome to The Plaza." He shook her extended hand, fingers thin and calloused, grip lingering slightly. "So why haven't I seen you in here before?"

Slick bent in. "Rip lives on the river. We're showin' him the town."

Interest flickered in her gaze. "So, you got a boat then?"

"Yeah, I got a boat." This woman was oozing sexuality, but one of a new nature, more predatory, and he was fairly buzzing with it. "It's kinda' 'a beater though, ..."

"She-ya!" Paul trumpeted. "Rip here's the king mother 'a all the River Rats. Crazy as a cornered 'coon."

"I dig the river." She tongued her gum, then snapped shoulder length hair and was all business. "Duane's out tonight, but I still want you boys ta' keep yer noses clean, OK? Don't wanna' get in trouble with management."

Keith held up a hand. "Scout's honor, Sand."

Turning over a plastic pitcher from the counter, she moved to the taps. "What'll it be? Old Style or Blatz?"

They looked around at each other and Keith shrugged. "Blatz?"

"Right." She worked the handle, filling the vessel with tawny liquid, set it out with four glasses.

Keith reached in his pocket. "I got first round." He set a dollar on the bar, and after some careful digging, dropped a quarter on top. "For you."

"Ooh, big spender." She smiled, took the cash and produced a plastic basket. "Free pretzels in the machine. Soak up some of that alcohol." They gathered their wares and she leaned back over the bar. "Nice ta' meet cha' Rip. Stop in again sometime, 'kay?"

"You too, Sandy. I will."

As they worked their way to a table on the riser near the entrance, Rip turned to Keith and whispered: "Jesus, she's hot."

"Yeah. Heard she strips over at Viner's Club. Bartends here on nights off."

"Man. Seen her?"

"Nah. They card there."

Three pitchers, two baskets of pretzels, and a half dozen trips to the bathroom later, found them pretty comfortable with their surroundings. Rip took in the paneled walls festooned with neon beer signs, mirrors silk-screened with replicate logos, oversized trout, bass, and muskies, frozen in time, mounted to whorled cross-sections of logs, and the occasional deer trophy. The lighting was low and cozy, the seats plush and comfortable, and 'Peter Frampton Live' played on the jukebox. It was his first time drinking in a bar, and he decided he could very much get used to this.

Slick emptied the last of the pitcher into his glass, producing a perfect head that foamed up just slightly over the top. "Lookit that!" He pointed, proudly. "TV beer!"

"You ever, …" Keith waved his around, sloshing it onto the table. "…you ever notice how the names of beers sound like the noise it makes when you open a can or bottle?" He held his glass aloft. "*Blatz.*"

Slick sipped at the head, leaving a creamy mustache around his mouth. "*Schlitz.*"

Rip thought. "*Pabst.*"

"She-ya, *Bush.*"

"See, it's all marketing. You say the name *Bush*, 'n your mind makes that connection, 'n you want a beer." He sniggered. "Well, *Bush* actually has a double meaning, but that's even more effective." He toasted the air. "Sex always sells."

'Barracuda' by Heart was playing on the juke, and beneath it, Rip heard a strangely familiar rumble from the parking lot.

"Wait a minute." Slick was elbowing the table now. "Just a sec. What about, …what about *Miller*?"

Paul straightened up. "*Hamms.*"

"*Special Export.*" Added Rip.

"Mmm, …" He tapped at his lower lip. "…mmm, …" Keith slapped the table a little too hard. "M' just saying that a *dis*proportionate amount of names sound like that."

The pub's doors opened and Rip was shocked to see Marlon, Andrea, and Viv, who was practically hanging off some musclebound ex-military type, enter the bar and pass directly before their table.

She caught his shocked glance and pouted out her lower lip; *Awww, don't cry.* Marlon hucked his shoulders; *Chicks, what you gonna' do?"* Then they moved back to a dark corner by the Pac Man and the Asteroid games.

"Awww, …*burn.*" Slick shook his head a little too smugly. Rip experienced twin poles of rage and humiliation.

"*What the fuck?* "He lurched to his feet.

"Easy, bub." Keith grabbed at his shoulders, pulling him back to the seat. "Cool it, man. She's just a run-around Sue."

"Yeah but, …*what the fuck?'*

"Not like you're girlfriend or anything. And he *is* my connection with, you know, …" He appealed to Rip. "*Plus* the fact that those two could probably stomp the shit outta' us." Keith looked around the table, then at him. "You want 'ta, … um, leave?"

Rip belched, sighed. "I want more fucking beer."

It was his turn anyway.

Sandy's farewell's echoed from a shimmering corridor as he passed through the blasting light of the entryway and then they were in the car, driving, cruising Gunnery Row, shouting at jocks in red letterman jackets clustered around a Corvette, *"Central High rules!, Logan sucks!"*; Paul laughing, yelling; *"buttmunch!"* as they flipped the bird, and he was puking through the open window into the slip-stream of the Thunderbird, jetting streams of Blatz mixed with clods of pretzel matter burning through mouth and nose, then they were on a picnic table in the park that overlooked the High School, toking the rest of Keith's joint, but then he was in the car, moving again and they were negotiating the hairpin turns of the park when a red light swipes through the cab followed by blue and the blare of a siren; Paul goes "Shit!" and punches it, but when the big engine kicks in, the rear end slides out, the road drops, and when they hit the tree the headlights briefly illuminate its shudder as the car shimmies sideways, and as Rip is launched over the front seat he strangely has time to consider his trajectory, that it will eventually lead him to the intersection of the window and the roof, and when it does everything ceases to exist.

*   *   *   *

Curt was talking in his sleep, strange words that made no sense.

"But the itsy-bitsy thing wouldn't take it."

Dredged from the depths of slumber, Dart opened bleary eyes on the camera obscura of the tent's wall.

His sleep-drugged mind had trouble processing the apparition that was projected from the dimming firelight, but it appeared large, moving about, searching, shifting shape, four-legged, then standing on two, exposing claws, talons, and he sensed a deep, primal revulsion, seeing the horned lupine head swivel through bristled mane atop its shoulders, and knew he should be afraid, hearing its thick panting, that he should do *something*, but sleep was claiming him again, drawing him down through dense, dark layers into shifting oblivion.

*   *   *   *

He was upside-down.

No, wait.

The person trying to talk to him was leaning over the wrong way, so he must be lying down. Painted lights played over the man's face and he had cheeks textured like moon craters and in his eyes was a curious mix of concern and contempt, and he wore a hat.

A policeman's hat.

Words were crashing in on waves. "How'ya feelin, Boy?"

Rip pulled up on his elbows and the world swam briefly as he painfully attempted to comprehend his surroundings. There was wetness on his forehead, running down his cheek, and a damper patch at his crotch. Keith, Slick, and Paul were lined in front of a cruiser, cherries alight, arms handcuffed behind them, and they were watching him with wide eyes.

Keith spat on the ground. "Welcome back, dead boy."

"She-ya, pissed yer pants, did." Paul was grinning like a skull.

"Shut the fuck up!" The cop barked back at them, and turned to Rip. "Can ya stand up, boy?"

"*Phoah*, gonna try." This he slowly did with the cop's assistance as a pale Lincoln Continental swept its headlights through the park and came to a rest next to the Thunderbird. The top of the young pine had snapped off and lay on its crumpled hood. Rip wilted unsteadily to the ground next to the other three, leaning against the patrol car. Keith's father, still in uniform, exited with authority from the vehicle. He surveyed the scene, pausing briefly to shake his head, message his jowls, and let loose a boozy sigh before walking up to the officer.

"Officer, …Karpinsky, …right?"

"That's right, Mr. Sturgeon."

"Oh, *jeez*, …" Paul shrieked. "…fucking *Carp!*"

Karpinski's movements were swift. The nightstick slammed into Paul's abdomen with a hollow drumbeat, pitching him face forward to the dirt, spluttering, still laughing. Slick, Keith, and Rip were all too shocked to even react. "I *said*, shut up, *punk*." He turned to Keith's father.

"I know who you are, counselor, but the truth is that your son and his, ah, …friends here have given me a pretty bad fucking night, here…"

Mr. Sturgeon was coolly unaffected. "Who was driving?"

"That punk puke, the carrot-top, Paul."

"Might I have a word in private with you, officer?"

"Of course, counselor."

They moved off, and Rip edged next to Paul, who was still gagging. "You OK, man?"

Paul retched into the gravel, slowly jerking up onto his knees between gasps. *"That carp fucking pig."*

Rip looked to the others. He fingered the blood on his head. "This is really fucked up, man."

"Lighten up, …" Keith adjusted the arms clasped behind his back. "…be cool. Which is some advice I would like to impart upon our friend Paul, here."

"Fucking carp."

He pointed with his head. "My old man's on it."

Keith's father was in deep negotiations with officer Karpinski, and when he pulled out his wallet, they stepped back, disappearing in the shadow of a tree.

"He shouldn'ta sticked Paul." Slick looked unusually pale. "Outta' fucking line."

"She-ya." Paul spat.

Keith started giggling.

"The fuck you laughing at?" Rip had managed to pull himself upright with the aid of the cruiser's doorhandle. "Really, if there *is* anything funny goin' on here, I would appreciate being let in on it."

"That cop's daughter?" Keith's voice went low. "She got called on for servicing the Logan Lacrosse team last year. Gangbanged the whole squad. Had ta' pump the slut's stomach, she swallowed so much jiz."

"No shit? What's her name?"

Keith regarded Slick. "I don't know *hosebag*, Thing is, the old man's the one that took care of that potentially damaging incident. Y'know, made it disappear."

"I don't know, ..." Rip went silent at the approach of the two adults.

Karpinsky went to work on Keith and Slick's handcuffs. "You three are off, on the recognizance of Mr. Sturgeon. You, ..." He jerked up on Paul's manacles, nearly dislocating his shoulder. "...are going for a ride."

"Ahh! Carp *motherfucker!*"

"Dad!"

"Shut up!" Keith's father commanded. "Somebody has to answer for this." He nodded towards the cop, who was guiding Paul's staggering form into the backseat of the cruiser. "Officer, we'll be in touch."

"Right, counselor." Karpinski tipped his hat, slipped in the driver's seat, and launched through the park, cherries on fire.

Keith's father turned, appraising them, whites of eyes swimming yellow, from a calm, dispassionate gaze behind which lurked a feral glint.

"Gentlemen, you are in a world of shit."

*   *   *   *

The river was leaden, and lay like glass, broken only occasionally by the shadow of a ripple or whorl. Dart watched two dragonflies scribble the air above a patch of swamp grass, skin rippling brilliant iridescent hues, mutually joined at abdomen's end, mating. The sun pulsed through a haze, echoing the stilted, dead air. It was Friday morning, the last weekend before he started 8th grade at the newly constructed middle school. His first and last year there, before graduating to the old High School.

Dart yawned, tilting his head to evaluate the progress on the tree fort. They'd finished the roof the previous evening, and spent their first night there, him and Curt, Randy being away on some family holiday. The basic construction was done, and Curt emerged, feet-first from an opening in the floor, backing down the row of two-by-fours nailed onto the trunk.

"Y'know, I got Glenn's old car stereo, …" Curt spat into the river, a whitish foam that congealed and spun down on the current. "…could set it up in there with a car battery. Ten band equalizer, too." He ran a hand through dark, oily hair. "It's a fifty watt booster."

Dart nodded, eyeing their boats beached side-by-side on the embankment, mind drifting downstream to the thick row of concrete pylons rising from the river beneath Interstate 90.

Today was perfect.

*　　*　　*　　*

Idling around the spillway, Rip watched water roll over the massive concrete retainer, spitting out the occasional fish and gnarled piece of deadfall, at the half dozen or so fishermen in heavy rubber waders throwing lines into the churning undertow. It spawned great whirlpools, spinning liquid galaxies, creating obscene sucking noises lolling about its base.

The susurrus was broken by the whine of twin outboards rounding the channel's bend, dropping to a low growl, as they appeared, surging past the no wake buoy. He recognized the battered hull of Paul's olive green flat, followed by Moe's lower, slightly wider boat, Shitley riding shotgun. They puttered up, nosing into formation beside him.

"Hey Rip. What'chya doin, man?" A big purple shiner surrounded Paul's right eye, above his grin.

"Just cruisin'. What you guys up to?"

Moe held up a couple of fishing rods, light catching the spoon of a daredevil hooked through an eyelet, and muttered around the butt of a cigarette. "Gonna' try to sell some carp." Normally, considering their distance and the engine noise his voice would have been lost, but for the river's crazy acoustics. Shitley nodded, blinking his consent.

"Got court next week." Paul practically vibrated with unspent energy in his seat. "Talkin' 'bout sendin' me to juvy up in Trempealeau."

"Shit, Paul, …" Rip dropped his head in his hand. "…I'm sorry…"

"She-ya, no big deal. Who needs High School. 'Sides, ..." He pointed at the swelling on his face. "...could use a vacation from the old man."

Pulling a pack of Marlboros from the pocket of a sleeveless work-shirt, Moe began tapping it upside-down on his palm. "Ain't Paul's first juvy duty." Shucking away cellophane and foil, he drew out a cigarette and lit it off the butt still in his mouth. "Prob'ly not the last."

Paul will be eighteen next year, Dart thought, *and next time he'll be tried as an adult. Next time, Paul will go to prison.* However, he felt no need to voice this sobering fact. "It's just not fair, Paul."

"Heh, heh, ..." He chuckled sadly. "...ain't nothin' fair, Rip. Git used to that shit, and you be a happier man for it."

Hand dropping from the throttle, slowing, Rip watched the two other craft crawl ahead. "Hey, I think you just stated a basic tenet there. Didn't know you were a philosopher, Paul."

"What the hell's a tenet? One of your *book* words?" He waved a hand dismissively in the air as they drifted away towards the shore. "Them carp ain't gonna' catch themselves. Later, man."

"See ya'." *Wouldn't wanna be ya,* his mind added, unbidden. Working the rudder around, turning downstream with the current, he glided along the overgrown shoreline, passing the dense tangle of foliage overhanging the river. He startled a cluster of painted turtles sunning themselves on a nearby log, their tiny bodies magically disappearing like a silent string of firecrackers. Moving out from the shadows of the bayou, sunlight reached out from the enshrouding canopy holding the boat in its radiance, and as he gunned the motor to meet the main channel, a solitary figure beckoned from a small sandbar. Pulling a tight arc, he guided the craft in, sliding ashore as Stephanie approached, clasping clothes and a small cooler, striped string bikini barely concealing the curves of her bronzed body.

"Hey Rip." Brushing a feathered strand of bangs from her face, she set her effects on the bow. "Fancy meetin' you here."

"OK, I give up, ..." It was virtually impossible to keep his eyes off the way her hips swayed to an unheard beat. "...how did you get all the way out here?"

"That? Easy, just walked over the spillway."

"You know how dangerous that is?"

"No. How?"

"Shit, Steph, every year some dumbass stumbles over that thing into the undertow and drowns." He nodded his head at the boat. "Let me give you a ride back."

She smiled, briefly exposing the gap between her teeth. "Don't wanna' go back. Take me for a ride, Rip. Show me something I haven't seen."

"Tall order." The roguish glint in her eyes was intimidating, and he was having a hard time meeting them. "Know of a couple places on the far side of the dam, but we'd have to pass through the locks. Got the time?"

"Nothing but." She sprung into the hull and dropped onto the bench beside him, then sprang back up again. "Fuck!"

"Might want to put those shorts back on. Aluminum gets hot cooking in the sun."

"Think I burnt my ass." She presented him the scarcely covered element of her anatomy that was legend amongst the local male population.

"Looks fine… to me."

The air was calm, the ride was smooth, and little was said between them most of the way. Rip could sense a subtle tension, something that had shifted away from their usual lighthearted flirting, and he wasn't quite sure he could identify its source yet. Luckily the colossal iron gates of the locks were swinging open as they arrived, releasing a half dozen pleasure craft to frolic on the main channel, eliminating a potentially long and awkward wait. They followed a small number of others idling into the mechanized canal to await the water's rise.

"This is unreal." Stephanie looked a little uneasy as the gates shut, silencing the warning klaxon, entombing them. "I never realized the things were so fucking big."

"Have to be." Rip cut the motor, reaching out to secure one of the knotted ropes that lined the walls. "Every barge that goes up or down the Mississippi has to pass through here. Might as well get comfortable. Takes about fifteen minutes to raise the raise the water.

"Well then, …" She covered the center bench with cushions, and oblivious to the obvious attentions of the surrounding boats, sluiced her shorts to the floor. "Ah guess ah gotta' get me some of that sun." She draped her body over the width of the hull.

Jesus, stay cool. Rip felt an uncomfortable pressure building. *Something's going on here, but don't loose it.* "Good idea."

Pulling his shirt off, he lay across the rear bench, settling beneath the throttle. The water rose, pushing them incrementally up the wall, and they absorbed the sun in respective silence.

The trill of the Klaxon broke into his slumber, and Rip scrambled to his feet, to find them adrift, the gates opening. "Mother, …" He pulled the start-cord and the motor purred to life with a blueish fog. Stephanie started briefly, body lifting from the cushions, seating herself to face him. "Wow." Fingered her eyes. "Drifted off." Watching as he dodged between craft, pushing past others toward the breach in the far wall, she reseated next to him on the stern, and in the brief silence before acceleration, turned to him and blurted: "Keith and I broke up."

Cool as a cucumber. He twisted the throttle and they roared out onto the tributary. *Cold as ice.*

*   *   *   *

They were running it full-out, and for the first time in his life, Dart was high.

They'd stripped the dried plants of their leaves, filling nearly half a garbage bag with the scraggly green stuff, and Curt produced a pipe he'd lifted from his brother's stash-box. The taste was harsh and raw, and bit at his throat, but they managed to smoke through a bowlful. He thought that all the negative propaganda and mystique surrounding the pot culture was pretty overblown. Truth be said, the effects were fairly mild, but he *definitely* felt something, and he was starting to notice certain things about the ride itself

As Curt pulled inevitably ahead, he realized he knew, instinctively, that running against the current *and* the wind, like this, he had slightly more control over the yoke. He could maneuver just a bit more tightly.

He could also see, as the I-90 overpass approached, that Curt was loosing his nerve. His craft hesitated slightly as the bridge and columns came on with alarming speed. Sure enough, he ducked between the first two before giving up, looping out through the main underpass in defeat as Dart charged straight in.

The motor's echo blasted off the hard planes of the bridge, enveloping him in sound as he swiveled through the first pylon, wake kicking a hard wash against the concrete. Yanking the rudder left, then right, throwing his weight into the movement, he stitched his way through the first set of columns, definitely *not* thinking about what happens when a flimsy kinetic force meets an immovable object, easily slaloming through the second set, feeling the maneuvers before they needed to be performed. Then he was through, and burst from the shadows and noise into the open channel.

The sunlight basked him in warm triumph, but he felt both elation and disappointment. Partly because the thing had just seemed so *damn easy,* and because he had only one witness to the event, but that shadowing vanished almost immediately when Curt swooped in to flank, frog-eyed with awe.

*   *   *   *

Stephanie freed two lukewarm twelve-ounce Blatz grenades with an ear-biting squelch from the Styrofoam cooler. Their resemblance to the classic pineapple grenade design from World War Two, and the green hue of the glass bottles ascribed as much to their nickname as Keith and Paul's penchant for pitching the empties onto the pavement from a moving vehicle. With the obvious satisfying results.

"Tell me, just what the fuck *was* that?" Rip accepted the beer, twisting off its top, taking a thirsty pull off the bottle.

"Petty boss, huh?" She settled next to him on the bow, bare thigh rubbing his leg. They'd beached on a tiny, obscured glade, barely enough sandbar to berth the boat and throw down a towel, but it was obviously virgin territory. The white sand rolling up the embankment in wind-blown dunes was unmarred by footprints. "Ever seen anything like that?"

"Nah. No" He shook his head. They'd witnessed Dart's run through the pylons from a distance on their way here, and the audacity of the move had floored Rip. "Kid must have balls of steel."

"Bet you could do it."

"Damn straight. Just never thought of it before."

There was tautness to the silence that followed.

Stephanie sighed. "He thought I was pregnant. Why he dumped me, *asshole.*" She absently twisted a strand of hair and stared out over the marsh. "I *know* he was screwing around. He fucked Lynette, but you probably already knew *that.*"

"Shit Steph, …" He stammered, "…Keith and I just hang out sometimes. Don't know half what he does. Only thing I really *know,* is the river."

"Yeah, …" Her eyes found him again. "…River Rat, …." She paused, ran a tongue over her lips. "I *wasn't,* y'know? Just *late,* but that fucking *coward* ran like a sissy from a fight."

"Umm, …"

"C'mon." Dropping off the bow, she moved down the beach to the towel. "Sit next to me, Rip."

He followed, and they sat quietly watching waves lap against the shore. A rippled disturbance broke the shallows nearby, dimpling the surface in a lazy arc towards deeper water, starting Stephanie. "What was that?"

"School of minnows." Rip washed back the final warm backwash of his beer with a grimace. "Smaller school of bigger fish feedin' on em'. Probably Northerns."

Head bowing slightly, she turned her back to him. "The ride must've tensed up my neck. Could you give it a rub, Rip?"

"Sure." His hands were huge against the delicate planes of her shoulders, and as he worked thumbs into the muscle surrounding her sinewy neck, he could feel a hot, beating pulse.

"Umm. *Yeah*. Nice." Settling into the rhythm, she pressed her body back, head hanging forward, spilling sun-bleached auburn locks nearly to her knees. "That feels *so* good."

 Feeling heat building beneath her skin, his fingers kept running interference on the neckstrap. "Is that in your way?' Before he could reply, she'd untied it, cupping breasts in her palms. His cut-off's felt like they were shrinking.

"I, ...I really don't know what I'm doing, here."

"*God,* you're doing great. Just don't stop."

Oh, Christ. Chemicals sluiced into his brain, realizing he'd passed over the seduction's threshold, shorts now barely concealing his reaction. His fingers dug in more savagely, orbiting her shoulders, and she swayed with the movement, suddenly breaking off.

"OK. *My* turn."

"*What?'*

"Turn *around,* silly." She skillfully retied the top. "I'm gonna' do you, now."

Shifting around on the blanket, making a half-hearted attempt to conceal what was happening in his pants, he presented his back to Stephanie.

"Take off your shirt." This he did, and her fine fingers played over the muscles of his back, their bodies touching once, twice, then coming together, skin slipping over his, breath paying out in shortening rasps nearer his ear, her whisper a detonation in his head. *"What you thinking about, Rip?"*

Fine tributaries of sweat forming in the space between them flowed, and rolled down into his cut-offs. "Thinking?" He had a ridiculous and overwhelming urge to belch, and swallowed hard. "Why does everyone ask me that? I don't know. A lot of things? If I thought about what I was thinking, ..." Words spilled uselessly out his mouth. "...I'd be thinking about, ...*thought?* And right now, I'm not really able to figure out what that means."

"*Why?*"

"A little distracted, maybe?"

"*Why?*"

A shivering reflection cut through Rip's field of vision, and then they were locked deeply, mouth to mouth, molars grinding as their tongues burrowed, her hands pushing him back onto the sand, nails raking up his chest, leaking low animal groans from somewhere deep inside her breast.

Breaking off, she leapt up, straddling his thighs, one hand kneading his groin, the other skillfully freeing the button-fly of his Levis.

"Let me see it." Skin rarely exposed was touched by the sun's heat as she harshly grasped his girth, teeth bared, stroking. "*So long. Wanted it for so long.*"

Her panting barely audible over the roaring in his head, she pulled them both upright, relinquishing her grip only as he slipped the bikini-bottom down, revealing a slash of tan-line and her thin, downy nape.

Grinding hard against his face, he ran a tongue between her legs, rolling in and over her bellybutton, ribcage, rooting beneath her top, to settle on her nipple, sucking an entire small breast into his mouth. They toppled back to the beach, he on top of her, guiding him, and despite the fact that she was quite ready, very wet, he was meeting a lot of resistance, realizing how much *tighter* than Viv she was, when she shuddered, opened, shrieking "*God! Oh God, yeah!*"

He was deep inside, the beach around them flickering with surreal intensity, bodies slapping a rhythm, her nails furrowing his back, when an aberrant thought freed itself from a troublesome corner of his mind; *Keith was right,* and then, immediately; *No,* but it was too late, the image of Keith doing exactly *this* to her stuck stubbornly in his mind. Keith and his numerous indiscretions and God knew how many possible infections flowing back into him from their shared bodily fluids, and *goddamn* if he didn't hear the run of an approaching motor, right here, right now, in the most remote location he could pick. Rip felt himself going soft, Stephanie kneading his bare buttocks in desperation, bucking beneath him, suddenly noticing sand creeping uncomfortably into unwanted crevices, as the boat spun by close enough to their most intimate moment to cover them in a fine mist of overspray, and he slipped from her, like a piece of shriveled, useless fruit.

*   *   *   *

Slew cruising.

Curt's boat slid smoothly over pathways between fields of water lilies, and coursed through narrow canals of the marsh's grass. Dart sat next to him, cross-braced against the stern, hanging on for dear life, and loving every second of it. This was unknown territory, but Curt was going balls-out blind, testing fate and his intuitive ability against alien waters, the prop throwing a high spray behind them, transom set to it's shallowest depth to discourage any unwanted entanglement with local underwater flora. They turned at a water-bound copse and had to duck immediately beneath a tree that leaned out over their path, it's thick, mossy trunk flying mere inches above their heads. Dart bellowed a nervously joyful *"Whooo!"*

He supposed this was some unstated celebration of his maneuver between the I-90 pylons, as Curt had insisted that they leave his boat back on Tomahawk Island to do some *serious exploring,* and after smoking another bowl-full of the harsh, green homegrown they'd set off for parts unknown.

Foliage slapped at the hull, then their arms and legs, occasionally depositing random insect passengers, and the canal narrowed. Curt kept the throttle buried, constantly checking their position against the sun. As they skewed around another corner, the waters opened up, revealing a small beach on which was berthed a very familiar craft, and something else.

The pathway was still relatively narrow, their speed high, so they scarcely had time to register the pale, naked ass stuttering between a tanned pair of slender, splayed legs, before they pulled past and around another outcropping. Dart turned to meet Curt's incredulous gaze with his own, breaking at the last second to bob beneath another approaching deadfall, shouting together over the blare of the motor as they sat back up;

"Fuck Beach!"

4

.22 BEACH

Brian D Garrity

Nearly two weeks into school, and still the heat clung to the valley, despite the calendar's insistence upon the change of seasons. Rip sat in the torpid classroom, doodling in his notebook, watching the ancient ceiling fans uselessly push dust motes and hot air around through tilting shafts of sunlight, half-listening to Mr. Pike drone on about manifest destiny. Keith's desk was conspicuously empty.

"Ethnocentrism, …" The teacher suddenly barked, jumping up from his chair for emphasis. His passive-aggressive demeanor had made itself apparent early on with the class, and he momentarily had their collective attention. ", …a large word, indeed, with an even larger meaning, as is another we will become acquainted with. *Xenophobia.*" He strolled out from behind the desk and paced, running fingers through a salt-and-pepper crew-cut, when the door burst open, rattling the window-glass.

Keith pulled into the room on rubbery legs, face flushed, crazed expression on his face as he regarded the eighteen sets of eyes suddenly locked on him. "Hi-ya, …"

Slowly folding arms in front of his chest, Mr. Pike scowled darkly. "Mr. Sturgeon, you're late."

Starting at the voice, Keith turned to the front desk, a growing chorus of nervous twitters trickling around the room. "Uh, …yeah, …couldn't be helped, y'know. Parents, little brother, uh, …things?"

"Would you take your seat and join the rest of the class, please?"

"*Groovy,* ...groovy." He picked his way with exaggerated care between rows of desks, shooting out a forefinger. "*Hey,* Gaylene." Catching Rip's eye, winking. "What's happenin', Rip." Reaching his desk, he leaned over and slapped the back of the student in front of him. "Tony, how'z it goin' man?" Tony's golden curls bobbed before darkened aviator glasses in a bare nod of acknowledgment, as Keith lowered into his chair with a loud sigh.

The teacher crossed the room, closing the open door, staring daggers the entire time in Keith's direction. "To continue, ..."

His monotone trolled Rip back into a stupor as he absently sketched google-eyed Don Martin characters cavorting between blue ruled lines of the spiral notebook pages. He daydreamed of the river, and his secret tryst with Stephanie, obsessively consulting the stalled hands of the clock on the wall. A commotion stirred somewhere behind him, followed by a wet hiccup, followed by uneasy whispering, and Keith's unmistakable but unusually manic laughter. Mr. Pike's voice stopped mid-sentence, leaving the room in an aural void.

Again, Keith brayed mirthfully, cutting the silence and drawing the teacher's predatory gaze. "*Mr. Sturgeon,* would you like to share with the class what you seem to find so humorous."

"Uhm, ...yeah, ...I mean, no sir."

"Oh *please,* Keith, I openly invite you to enlighten me as to any deficiencies that you may perceive in the lesson that I am currently trying to dispense."

"No disrespect at all, sir, ..." His voice had resumed trademark conciliatory, yet mocking tone. "...I find your subject *fascinating,* and your delivery *riveting.*"

Mr. Pike seethed. "Keith, I will have no *sarcasm* in this classroom."

"Yes, sir."

"See me after class."

"I know, sir."

Murmurs drifted about the room, abruptly silenced by the teacher's frustrated imperative. "To! Continue!" Rip finally glanced back to see Keith lurch suddenly from his seat, straight-arming the desk before him, pallor pale, and an alarming shade of green.

"*Sir?*" He gulped.

"Keith, I've given you your chance to have your say. No more interruptions, *please!*"

"Sir?"

"Dammit, boy, what is it?"

Expression eerily mirroring his father's on the night of the accident, a grotesque croaking sound issued from somewhere deep inside his diaphragm. Keith's bloodshot eyes bugged out over a distended mouth which dripped a singular silver strand of saliva, before an explosive torrent of bile was ejected, spewing onto his desk, cascading in a vile tsunami over Tony and other students before him, filling the classroom with the stench of vomit and alcohol.

*   *   *   *

He still couldn't get used to the smell of the new school.

A heavy industrial aroma permeated the recent construction, not unlike that of the plastic modeling cement he'd often used at home, but this was a reek of a whole different magnitude, cloying and sharp, stinging his sinus' to eye-watering irritation.

Since the building's opening, parents and teachers had been promoting the revolutionary and progressive 'open' design, where different grades were mixed and clustered into quadrants, known as 'pods'. These were divided by movable modular soundproof walls, color-coded in bright primaries to signify their respective pods, all floating within a sprawling single-story enclosure. Also touted by the community was its claim to address environmental issues, reflected by the almost complete lack of inefficient windows, and overhead banks of energy-saving fluorescent lights.

The overall effect of which was utterly at odds with the designer's original intentions.

Surrounded by the pea-green enclosures of pod three, Dart sat in Ms. [never to be addressed by the sexist formal Miss or Mrs.] Garr's ecology class, attention divided between the lecture at hand, and the distracting presence of Sara, three rows over. She was clad in a yellow skin-tight tube top today, presenting a definite recent growth-surge.

"The world population now stands at just over four billion. That is double the number of people that occupied the planet in nineteen-thirty." Ms. Garr paused, an odd figure to Dart, hair a brunette explosion of frizz hovering over large squared glasses that camouflaged half her face in an optic blur, body moving indistinguishably beneath folds of dyed fabric. Her voice raised an octave. "Now I know that the thirties must seem like *ancient* times to you, but that was less than fifty years ago." She leaned dramatically beneath the overhead. "It took the combined chance elements of the planet's evolution and the evolution of our species over four and a half billion years to produce two billion humans, yet merely two generations later, the population doubles. What does this tell you?"

This was getting interesting, and Dart took notice.

"Rain forests, the source of the most diverse plant and animal species on the planet, are disappearing by deforestation at a rate of 15,000 acres per day." She threw a hand up, and started ticking off digits with a cracked, lacquered fingernail. "*Pollution*, a world-wide epidemic, is killing lakes and rivers, contaminating land, contaminating air, poisoning drinking water, and creating acid rain. Over half of the animal species known to exist at the turn of the century are now either endangered or extinct. We have an energy crisis. We have smog. Disease epidemics. Drought. Famine. War. Genocide." Her lenses turned out to the room. "So. What do all these things have in common?"

The class was silent. Dart tried to turn this alarming information around in his head. He'd seen and sensed changes on the river in the last couple of years, the increased human traffic, waste, and pollution, the disappearance of the soft-shelled turtle, but assumed it was natural process: that some larger, unseen course was at work. What if it was merely the result of accident and ignorance? Could people really let this happen?

Sara's hand raised hesitantly, the sole one in the class. "Humans?"

"Very good, Sara. Nice to hear that someone is listening." The teacher moved around and settled in front of her desk.

"Humans, yes. More precisely, the *overpopulation* of humans. You see, when a species emerges that has no natural adversaries, it inherently overruns it's own environment, abusing the very substance of its support system. Science designates this a *weed species*. Unfortunately, it has recently become increasingly obvious that humankind has become exactly that, a weed species." Her hands came together in a light slap. "People, we are at a tipping point. Yours is the generation that will have to answer to the consequences of the follies of previous generations. Either we address these issues immediately, or suffer terrible corollary effects. Human overpopulation is a potentially terminal disease for the earth, and the key to our future survival is an awareness of population control. That is why we are here today. To learn how to take responsibility, and to take action." She picked some notes from off the desk, shuffled them. Dart's thoughts drifted again to the river, attention inevitably turning back to Sara.

His eyes were drawn to where she was sitting, absently chewing on a pencil's eraser. He recalled their shared time on the beach, her dark, trim body moving with athletic grace, and the slipped glances he'd caught from her. Surely, she must like him. At the very least she must be aware of his *own* presence in this class, though she'd yet to acknowledge it. Countless times he'd tried to muster the courage to approach her, just to drop a casual greeting, only to be paralyzed mute by an unknown and overwhelming terror.

These feelings were completely alien to Dart. They deepened daily, thoughts of Sara leaking into his mind from all sides, intruding even on his preferred form of escapism: drawing. Several sketches of her were secretly stashed in amongst his notes.

He had to break through this stumbling block.

He needed to be with her.

He …

He's cruising the Mississippi alone, feeling the power of the outboard, the freedom of the wind, the warmth of the sun, when he notices a disturbance in the water between him and the shore. Reacting quickly, he banks the boat and approaches a thinning stream of bubbles. Throwing the Evinrude into neutral, he grabs his trusty mushroom-anchor, tossing it over the side. Without hesitation, he dives into the river.

Through the green murkiness, he follows the thread of bubbles down to a sinking form, feeling the cold pressure of the depths. He finds an outstretched hand, grasping and pulling up, up with all his strength, lungs painfully pushed to their limit, tearing against his ribcage, before breaking the surface with her, with Sara. She's unresponsive, and he struggles to move her inert form to the flat-bottom.

While wresting her into the boat, he's shocked to discover that she's lost the top of her bikini, vulnerably exposing her nakedness to the world. He is forced in his struggles to grope her chest, feeling sharp nipples atop the yielding mounds of her breasts, before levering her over the side

She isn't breathing! Thank goodness for the Boating Safety Courses and the required class in CPR. Leaning over, propping her head back, he puts his mouth over her cold lips and blows, watching her bosom rise and fall.

Nothing.

This is serious! Placing two hands to the left of her sternum, he pushes sharply, counting one, two, guiltily relishing the feeling beneath his fingers. Pushing again, She gags, spitting up water, and he turns her sideways as the spasm passes. Lowering his mouth again to hers, he feels spreading warmth there, as a tongue is slipped into his. He hesitates briefly before pulling back, hearing a welcome gasp, as her eyes open, regarding him with reverence.

"Oh, Dart, what happened?"

"You went under. Jeez, Sara, I thought you were a goner."

"My hero."

"Your top, Sara, it was gone, …"

"It's OK." She guides his hands to her body, breathing faster now. "You can touch them. It's the least I can do for you for saving my life. I want you to feel me."

As his fingers come into contact, he registers a distant, escalating noise. Sara turns her head. "Dart, what is that sound?"

"Sound?" Confused, distracted, his hand travels down the concave of her stomach, strange noise building around them, his hand trailing lower, lower, and he looks up ...

From the look she shot back across the classroom, through the exiting students, he must have been staring at least through the duration of the recess bell, which halted with a resonant echo.

Ms. Garr's voice trilled. "Three words I want you to remember, people! *Zero! Population! Growth!*"

Joining the migration, Sara gave him a look of seething contempt before slipping out the door.

Sitting alone in abject humiliation, he gathered his books, placing them strategically, and limped his way past Ms. Garr, out into the hallway.

*   *   *   *

The High School's student parking was located behind the newly renovated gymnasium, which, by an apparent design oversight, completely obscured the lot's sightline from the rest of the school. The resulting determinism created a cross-nexus of interaction between the differing cadres populating the institution. Here, Greasers were Kings, Jocks hung with Stoners, Delinquents tolerated the Geeks, and River Rats chummed with Townies, the most notable exception being a conspicuous lack of straights. Drinking, smoking, and dealing were the main forum of exchange, these activities almost exclusively centering about the vehicles. One group after another would pile into a car or truck and roll off into the park to conduct business, passing others entering the lot, having completed theirs. This procession continued ceaselessly throughout the day, dominated, but not limited to the seniors, whose schedules were checkerboarded with frequent break-periods.

Slick lay back on the oversized hood of his Blazer, arms folded behind his head, leaning against the windshield, taking in the sun. He giggled uncontrollably, as the overture from Rush's ' 2112 ' detonated from the rear speakers. "You gotta' be fuckin' shittin' me, man."

"I shit you not. Puked all over Tony right there in the middle of class." Rip sat high up on the front fender.

Tony prowled back and forth before the grill, sniffing frequently at the Phys- Ed shirt liberated from his gym locker. "Haven't washed this in a real long time. Don't know what smells worse, …" He dejectedly shook a clasp of blond curls before the ubiquitous aviators shielding his eyes. "…this, or the one Keith barfed on."

"You serious, man?" Rip shook his head down at him. "Not like you got a choice. Can't get that reek outta' my head."

This set Slick off on another row. "Oh Keith, you bad, bad, boy." He whistled. "School's really gonna' be a drag without him or Paul around."

Tony sighed sadly. "Got nothing else but my mascot uniform for the pep rally today." He glanced up in earnest. "You guys coming?"

Slick froze, sat up. "You, …you're Billy Blufftopper?"

"Yeah." His posture straightened, proudly.

"God, that is so ga, …"

"That is so great, Tony." Rip interrupted. He eyed Slick. "Yeah, we'll be there."

"*Hey guys*. Heard about Keith." Stephanie sashayed into the small space between a vinyl-topped Cutlass and the Blazer. Gaylene and Anita followed, books clasped to their breasts. "Is it true?"

Tony backed off. Rip caught Stephanie's eyes as Slick jumped to his knees on the hood. "Afraid it is, ladies, and poor Tony here was the victim."

"Aww, poor Tony." Gaylene proffered condolences, Tony shrinking away, plucking self-consciously at his shirt. A shadow fell over him.

Tommy 'Nuts' Neitzel was quarterback of the Central High Blufftoppers, and would have cast a large shadow even hadn't he been flanked by the team's two star linebackers. His meaty hand smacked Tony's startled shoulder. "Tone, whatcha' doin' hangin' with these, …" He thrust out a pointed jaw. "…*stoners*."

"Lay off, Nuts. "Stephanie snorted. "These guys are friends."

He ignored her. "You too, Anita. You're first-string cheerleader."

A smile froze Anita's face, dark eyes darting beneath feathered brunette locks. She drifted back, gravitating toward the players. "Gotta' get to the rally early anyway." She clucked an embarrassed, nervous giggle. "See ya!"

"Guys, …" Slick spread his arms. "…that kinda' talk really hurts."

Nuts shook his head in disgust. "Losers." He guided Tony and Anita into his queue, herding the four of them off across the lawn. "Same bunch that got Keith kicked off the team."

Slick rolled eyes at Rip. "Oh, burn! *Burn!*"

Rounding the gym's wall, Rip watched Nuts turn to Tony, heard him mutter, "Tone, you smell B.O?"

"*Jesus*, I hate fucking straights." Slick slid off the hood. Lynette stepped forward.

Stephanie turned to Rip. "So, what you guys up to?"

Moe's head bobbed out the back seat window, spit-sealing a joint. "All ready. Let's go." Shitly's shadow hovered in the seat beside him.

"As you can see, …" Slick stepped around Lynette, cracked the door and jumped into the cab. "…we've got a full ride and pressing business at hand. You coming, Rip?"

Dropping off the fender, Rip met Stephanie's gaze. "Later?"

Her eyes burned. "Yeah, right." They slipped past, joining the throng working it's way into the gym. Rip turned and threw himself into the passenger seat. Slick spun the volume down and held up the joint. "OK. Yeah. We're *doin'* this."

"I still got class, Slick."

"*Cancelled*, due to *pep-rally*." Slick keyed the engine and hit reverse. "Think you can handle that with a buzz?"

Moe leaned between them over the front bench-seat pulling a black plastic lighter from his shirt pocket. "*She-ya*, can't handle class *without* a buzz."

"*Alright*." Rip waved his hands. "OK. Just hold on a second. I know this must seem weird to you, but I've only been high a few times, and never at school before."

"Easy, man, it's a *pep-rally*." Backing out the space, Slick lit up from Moe's flame. He guided the spluttering machine to the lot's exit, toed the brake, straight-arming the smoldering spliff over the cluttered bench seat. Ejecting a blue plume of smoke off the windshield's interior, he turned. "Which direction?"

Hesitantly accepting the joint, Rip shrugged his shoulders, eying a line of young pines along the roadway, one of which was snapped off halfway up. "I dunno. Straight?"

Slick giggled. "*Forward*, never straight."

* * * *

The red rubber kick-ball arced in from nowhere, impacting with sufficient force between where Dart and Curt stood to tear a divot from the newly laid sod. It ricocheted off the freshly painted wall behind them, leaving a greasy smear. Startled, Dart instinctively grabbed the ball out of the air on its rebound.

"Jeez, that was close."

Recess was almost over, and the kids were knotted into various gatherings scattered about the playground. Wind pushed through the trees, slipping down from the ridge of bluffs surrounding the school, bringing the autumnal fragrance of sumac and honeysuckle.

"*Hey!*" Three boys approached from the far side of the grounds.

"Aww, shit." Dart considered the ball balanced atop his notebook.

"*Hey, you!*"

"What? Whose that?" Curt squinted.

Dart felt a bending, mental vertigo.

"Brad Thornton. A bully. Got hemophilia, so he can't touch you, you can't touch him. His two friends there, Timmy Weasely and Duncan Wheat do the touching."

"They sick too?"

Dart stared at the ball. "They're psycho."

"*Hey fuzzy!*"

"Who's fuzzy?"

"Apparently, I am."

"*Fuzzy wuzzy was a bear*, …" As the trio drew near, it became apparent to Dart that in the intervening years, since he was transferred from his old school, out from under their previous tyranny, time had merely rendered them more malicious. Timmy had developed into an almost cartoonish caricature of his surname, body twisted and hard, shifty and rodent-like. Duncan had filled out to the stature of a lumberjack, freakishly large for the seventh grade, gaze sadistically hostile. Brad, surrounded by the two thugs, had simply *grown*, body rounded and soft, face fleshy and pale, holding droopy, dead eyes.

Curt shifted nervously. "Why they call you fuzzy?"

"'Cause of my hair, I think."

"…*Fuzzy wuzzy had no hair*, …" Brad smiled coldly.

Curt turned. "Y'know, your hair is kinda' fuzzy."

"Shut up."

"What'd you do to these guys?"

"Nothin'." Dart sighed and squared his shoulders. "Told you, they're psycho."

"…*Fuzzy wuzzy wasn't fuzzy*, …" Other students shrank at their approach.

The trio halted, encircling them, Brad holding hands up. "…*was he?*"

Timmy scurried in close. "Been along time, fuzzy."

"Not long enough."

Curt held out his hand. "I'm Curt."

Duncan turned to the others. "Squirt. What kinda' name's that, anyway?"

"I said *Curt*."

Brad ignored him. "You got our ball, fuzzy."

"Uh, yeah, … well, … you mean this." He held up the ball.

"Yeah, that."

"Just picked it up off the ground after it almost hit us. You throw it?"

Timmy twitched. "Don't get *smart*, fuzzy."

"Yeah, stupid." Duncan drawled.

"*Hey*, you know Sara, chick with the tits?" Brad's hands squeezed imaginary breasts before his flabby chest.

"Yeah, …she's in my eco class." Dart felt a rising spark of anger.

"Heard you were sweet on her." His thick lips set themselves in a parody of a grin.

"*What*?" The playground reeled before him. He looked at Curt, who was looking back with the same shock he felt. He turned back to Brad. "Who said that?"

"Is it true?"

"I have no idea what you're talking about."

Duncan leaned in. "She's off-limits, fuzzy."

"I really haven't the *slightest* clue as to what you're talking about." Dart replied with honest surprise. "Who told you this?"

A small crowd began to gather around them.

"Give me that ball." Brad made a grab, and because he knew that the slightest collision between their bodies could start an unstoppable bruise, the shallowest cut a major medical emergency, and definitely *not* because he was afraid, Dart jumped back. He dropped the ball and the notebook, it's contents scattering before them. A detailed rendering of Sara in her bikini settled to the ground at Brad's feet, for him and all to see.

The courtyard went silent and still. Brad's eyes worked back and forth between the drawing and Dart in utter disbelief, as Duncan moved in.

"You are *so* dead, fuzzy"

The punch came low and swift, and Dart didn't know he'd been hit until he found himself sitting on the grass, hiccupping for breath, dumbstruck, regarding his tormenters, as Mr. Ball appeared, leaning over, hands on hips. "The *hell* is goin' on here."

A recess bell sounded in the distance. He unsuccessfully tried to suck in enough breath for a reply, noticing Curt had somehow disappeared. The three bullies backed off, teacher turning to them. "What kinda' stunts are you and your bunch up to today, Bradley?"

"What you sayin', Mr. Ball?" Brad had stopped and looked back, expression devoid of emotion. "We haven't done 'nothing."

The teacher grinned slyly, tone lowering to a growl. "Do not, for a second, think I don't know your kind, Bradley, 'cause I do. Small minds are extremely easy to read."

Dart finally found his air, and gasped. " *It's OK, ...*" He picked up the red rubber sphere from where it lay near him and held it aloft. "*...didn't see it coming, ...*" Gasp. "*...knocked the wind outta' me. Here.*" Tossing it, Brad caught the ball. Dart noticed the drawing still beneath his foot.

"See? Just an accident."

Ignoring them, Mr. Ball bent and helped Dart up with his papers. "You sure you're alright?"

"Yeah, yes sir. Thanks."

The teacher turned to the trio. "I got my eye on you three. You try anything, I'll be on you so fast It'll make your head spin." He turned to the entrance and moved away, shouting over one shoulder. "Get back to class!"

Brad casually plucked the paper up from under his shoe and tore it into thin shreds as Mr. Ball disappeared through the doors.

The courtyard was hushed, empty. The surrounding planes of industrial architecture, beneath the bright, cloud-peppered sky somehow rendered ominous by the absence of any human activity.

Dart was confettied with the pieces of his creation.

"See you after school, fuzzy."

They left, and Dart felt time constrict itself around him.

*   *   *   *

His mouth and throat were a desert.

Trapped up in the crowded bleachers between Slick and Moe, conscious of their incriminating collective odor, Rip sat transfixed by the travesty unfolding before him.

The gymnasium reverberated with the concerted echoing of thundering feet, clapping hands, and screaming voices, drowning out 'We Are the Champions' that the P.A. system attempted to carry, as the pageantry below built to a bizarre crescendo.

The senior cheerleader squad rushed onto the floor in a series of coordinated gymnastics. Their short purple and white uniform skirts showed to best advantage matching purple panties, with one glaring pink exception, leading the frenzied crowd in a bolstering chant.

> *Bluff-toppers, Bluff-toppers, it's do or die!*
> *Logan, Logan's gonna' cry!*
> *Bluff-toppers, Bluff-toppers got the right stuff!*
> *Logan, Logan ain't got enough!*
> *Bluff-toppers, Bluff-toppers, make that score!*
> *Logan, Logan, oh so sore!*
> *Bluff-toppers, Bluff-toppers, crush their heads!*
> *Logan, Logan, you're so dead!*

They exited to a detonating ovation, Rip's mind cringing at the absurdity of the display. Thinking about the drinking fountain just outside the hallway, he tried to un-cement his tongue from his palette.

The football team churned out from between the bleachers, a purple and white blur led by Nuts, helmets in hand, chanting in unison to raucous applause. They burst through a paper barrier of the Bluff-toppers logo held by two cheerleaders, then systematically dismembered, in effigy, a uniformed dummy dressed in the Logan team colors. The twisted nature of the spectacle appeared lost to everyone but Rip.

He really needed to leave, to get that drink of cool, crisp water.

"Bubbler." He blurted.

His comment should have been lost beneath the pandemonium, but Moe turned, breathing a halitosis of stale dope and tobacco. "What'chew talkin' about?"

"Got to git to the bubbler." It was difficult to form words around the thick paste in his mouth.

"Yeah, that cottonmouth can be a bitch."

"Nawww!" Slick slapped his arm. "No way! You gotta' be shittin' me! Check it out!" He pointed.

Tony wheeled out onto the floor, following the team, riding a unicycle, and a hush fell over the assembly hall. Dressed in purple suede lederhosen over white-collared short-sleeved shirt, he was topped by a miniature Tyrolienne hat, accented by pheasant feathers. His bare legs furiously pumped balance, clad in purple striped athletic tube-socks, holding aloft a triangular Bluff-toppers banner. A wave of laughter started rolling down the bleachers as Tony pedaled out front and center, his aviators reflecting the crowd, a curious slack expression on his face, and a conspicuous bulge in the crotch of his lederhosen.

Rip bolted upright, stumbling over Moe and Shitly to reach the center isle, down the steps, to exit the auditorium, and into the hallway to find the drinking fountain.

*　　*　　*　　*

There had to be a word that meant what it felt like when someone was watching you and you could feel it but not see it. He'd been feeling it since recess. Maybe he'd ask a teacher.

Nobody ever really paid attention to him before. But now they were doing it in a very conspicuous way. He'd feel a creepy, crawling sensation over his neck and back, and turn, seeing multiple heads look away, suddenly interested in the familiar things surrounding them; the desk, the notebook, the ceiling, the lecture.

Time was pulling a trick too. The big wall-clock's hands would sit on a pair of numbers for an absurdly long time, then leap ahead each time he was jolted anew by thoughts of what would happen after school.

2:06 PM: Last class of the day, he ran into Randy exiting junior biology, the same cubicle his science class was held in. His face held a panicked expression, and Dart feared it had something to do with himself. Randy waved him over.

"Hey Dart!" He was fidgeting like he needed to pee. "You know what we just learned today in class?"

"*What?*" It was a statement of confusion, but Randy interpreted it as interest.

"You know what it means to smell something? Little pieces of it, of the thing you're smelling, go *up your nose.* Microbes. It goes in your body." His brown eyes burned beneath the straight-line bangs of a recent bowl-cut. "Just think, ... it's in your brain. You smell something like poo, you're actually inhaling actual poo into you're nose." His fingers cupped his face, turning his voice into a muffled quack. "I ain't never smellin" nothing again."

"You can't *not* smell anything, Randy." He sighed, glanced at the hallway clock. "I've got to get to class. Headin' home after school?"

"Yeah, ..." He quacked. "Meet'cha out front?"

"Yeah."

The subject of Mr. Ball's science class was nuclear war. On the development and deployment of the first and second nuclear weapon strikes on Hiroshima and Nagasaki, the subsequent damage, radiation, disease, burning, mutilation, and mutation. Of the fission weapons that were hundred's of times as powerful as their predecessors, being manufactured and stockpiled at an insane rate, the concept of Mutual Assured Destruction. There was a map of scalloped fallout patterns that looped graphically around strategic U.S. cities. There was a 16mm film showing a suburban tract of houses flowing as if under water, blossoming and flowering into flame, , before being blown into oblivion by the punch of an invisible wave. Pigs, staked to the ground in a group, were seized by sudden sunlight, fur crawling with fingers of smoke, simultaneously writhing against their restraints as skin was cooked to their living bodies.

The bell rang and Dart drifted out in a fog of fear. The hallway slipped past, an endless corridor of lockers, doorways, and coat-racks. Approaching with a dreadful inevitability, sunlight a dazzling super-nova beyond, the entryway drew closer.

The front courtyard teamed with the usual activity; yellow-orange busses stacked through the thoroughfare, butting up against a log-jam of late-model suburban vehicles holding awaiting parents, relatives, and older siblings, as the middle school students milled about the late afternoon sunshine after leaving the building. Dart willed himself anonymous, drifting through the gathering, seeking, but not finding any signs of his predators, which was good, but neither finding any trace of either Curt or Randy, a potential harbinger.

He'd gotten a block and-a-half beyond, turning a corner toward the river to pass a small open glade of greenery.

There, they'd waited for him.

"Hey fuzzy."

Brad, Timmy, and Duncan stood before a crowd of maybe a dozen kids, the number in his head multiplied by Dart's spiking dread. Curt stood back, apart from Randy, and Sara was there, eating from a small foil-packet of Old Dutch potato chips. Even though every part of his intuition insisted he flee this place, Dart's legs carried him toward the conflagration, lured against his will. "*Why?*, ...what do you want?"

Brad hitched a pair of pudgy knuckles up on his hips, spreading elbows. "You think you're so smart, *fuzzy*, runnin' around like furry little rat, makin' your stupid drawins'. You think anybody cares about that?" He stepped forward with his henchmen. "You River Rats think you're so cool. Think you're better'n the rest of us. I'm gonna' show everyone here, you're sweetie too, that you ain't."

"What?" He faced his audience, and fear dissolved into an unfamiliar indignation, a bright core of wrath igniting long dormant outrage. "You? *You're* not gonna' do anything!" He barked a bitter laugh. "You're sick! Why you got those goobers around you all the time! Why they *do* all you're dirty work, I have no idea! But if I hit you, or even if you hit me, you'll bruise up like a rotten tomato! Then your parents will sue my parents and take everything, just like what happened to *Jim Redwine!*"

The heady feeling of empowerment that had built during his brief tirade, collapsed within a single heartbeat as he beheld Brad's face undergoing a ghastly metamorphosis.

"Get him."

Timmy and Duncan jerked forward, but Dart was already moving, and he was fast. Dodging around a bush, he'd made it almost twenty feet to the sidewalk before Timmy hit him from behind, twisting ankles to bring him down hard on his back, impact expelling all air from his lungs. Timmy sat on his legs and Duncan held down his arms as Brad lowered his girth to the earth, the glazed, dead expression glued to his face. He pulled up two fat handfuls of field grass. Bound to the ground, hiccupping for air, Dart cast desperate glances to Curt and Randy, but they were already fading back, making for a get-away, as Brad straddled and settled onto his stomach.

"You got a real smart mouth for a fuzzy little rat. We got to do something about that." He mashed the two handfuls of grass down Dart's throat and leaned back. "Chew, fuzzy."

Duncan shifted knees painfully onto his hands, grabbing his nose and chin. He worked the jaw around the mess between his teeth, as Dart began convulsing from lack of oxygen.

"*Fuzzy wuzzy was a bear,* …wait, …" A perplexed expression crossed Brad's face, and still astride Dart's bucking body, he spread arms wide, palms down, mimicking a grand conductor. "Everybody! *Fuzzy wuzzy was a bear.*"

Timmy and Ducan's voices were joined by a few unsteady echo's.

"I *said* everybody. *Fuzzy wuzzy had no hair.*"

The chorus was strong now, Dart beginning to see spots.

"*Fuzzy wuzzy wasn't fuzzy,* …"He paused dramatically, looking down. "Was he?"

To Dart's further astonishment, Brad's fist came down on his stomach, ejecting a plume of wet mulch, which mostly landed back on his face, and when Brad stepped off and the other two set him free, he took in a great whoop of air and vegetable matter, coughing, curling on his side, watching the witnesses to his humiliation dissolve through a wet wash of tears. A choking sob escaped and snot shot down his lips.

"Go home, fuzzy."

Gasping, he wobbled up onto his legs, turned, and hobbled blindly away from the sounds, gradually gaining momentum until a hedge caught him in the thigh and spun him back to the ground. The sounds climbed in pitch as he rose, still gagging, and he ran all the way home, laughter following the entire two miles.

*   *   *   *

"Mandatory one-week expulsion from school? Off the team for three weeks? Demotion to second string?" Keith sighed sadly, drinking from a Blatz grenade, leaning against the K-5. "Grounded for a month. Old man's still pissed about that Thunderbird thing."

"Bummer." Slick offered from the hood.

"She-ya, *bullshit*." Paul popped the top of a grenade newly liberated from the cooler.

"Hey man, hold on a second." Rip pointed his beer. "I was there. You were fucking faced. Reap what you sow, y'know?"

Paul craned his neck. "Where the hell are Moe and Shitly?"

Slick belched. "Beatin' each other's meat, probably."

"I'm sure it's nothing nearly as intricate as that." Keith fingered his eyes.

"Still can't believe you drank a whole twelve-pack before first period."

"Fuck. Been hungover all day." He drained his drink, trashing it into a nearby 55-gallon drum that served as a waste container.

They were at a drive-out, off a hairpin turn on the slope of the park, overlooking the field, the school, the river, and the bluffs beyond, to where the sun was descending. From their vantage point, the floodlights of the football field burned against the early twilight, raking the gathering crowd dressed in coordinated hues of Logan red and gold, and the Blufftopper's purple on white. Muted drumbeats of a marching band echoed in asynchrony off buildings, up from the small valley.

"Hold the boat, I thought you said you were grounded."

Keith cast an annoyed glance at Rip. "*Game-night*? Old man don't know about the suspension from the team yet."

"Ah."

"Oh, hey, …" Slick skooched down to the grill. "…almost forgot. Havin' a little sendoff for Paul after the game, at .22 Beach."

"That's, …cool."

"Those two are probably getting the keg."

"Moe and Shitly?"

"Yup."

"She-ya, when you think you were gonna' tell *me*, butt-munch?"

"Just did. *Surprise*."

"She-ya."

A chorus of voices cheered above the basin as a formation of purple-white dots shifted over the field. "Shit." Rip reached into the cab and grabbed a cassette at random from a scattered pile lying on the seat. He slipped it into a deck hanging off a bracket from the underside of the dash, sprouting tentacles of wires snaking throughout the interior. Banks of LED lights blazed to life from the booster/equalizer, and AC/DC's 'T.N.T.' snarled from the speakers. A gold Trans Am pulled onto the hard-pack behind them, windows tinted nearly opaque above the screaming phoenix stenciled over the generous real estate of its hood.

"Well, this should be interesting." Keith armed himself with another bottle from the cooler.

The doors popped both open, spilling a thumping volume of unfamiliar music over Slick's system. It had a bubbly, danceable backbeat, the vocals sounding, to Rip's ears, like the frenzied yipping's of small, short-haired dogs. The driver and passenger rose from the front buckets, bobbing to the beat, flanking the car like gangsters in a prime-time private-eye melodrama. They were dressed oddly in similar light toned polyester suit-coats, over dark wing-collared shirts opened at the chest, exposing a shiny topography of gold colored chains and medallions. The slacks coordinated with the jackets, and were obscenely tight at the crotch and thigh, billowing down to a generous bell-bottom that shifted over polished pointed beetle-boots. The driver's suntanned face stuck out from beneath a globe of puffy, brown hair, eyes covered by oversized rimless sunglasses also favored by the passenger, slick-backed, finger waved hair, a fashionable counter-point to the driver's.

Paul horked beer-foam through his nose, spending the next several moments convulsively trying to catch his breath against uncontrollable laughter.

"What we got here, Joey?" The driver pulled a skinny comb from his back pocket, leisurely running it through his ample coiffure. "Looks like a bunch of burn-out Blufftoppers."

"What I'm seein' here, too, Todd." The passenger sneered.

"*Jesus,* …" Keith moved a little unsteadily from the bumper. "…what the fuck they teach you over at Logan?"

Slick slipped to the ground. "Yeah. Didn't know the circus was coming to town."

"That's good." Todd put the comb away. "Circus coming to town. Hear that, Joey?"

"Yeah, that's real good, Todd. Specially from a bunch of Central High rednecks." Joey slapped a bejeweled hand on the roof. Rip recognized a mood-ring.

"*Heyyy,* watch the paintjob there, Joey."

"*Wup,*… sorry Todd."

"Redneck?" Clad in worn, torn Levis, worker boots, sleeveless denim jacket over a wife-beater T-shirt, skin sprinkled with freckles, Paul, who'd finally recovered from his seizure, cocked elbows behind him. He took two menacing steps forward. "Who you callin' *redneck*?"

Rip felt a fight-or-flight surge of adrenaline. "Hey man, what's goin' on here?"

"*Pfft*! See, Joey? Besides the obvious, the redneck tip-off is the music. Hear what they're listenin' to?"

"AC/DC fucking rock!" Slick edged closer to the Trans Am.

Todd moved toward him. "Fucking *fag* music. What you think AC/DC means, anyway?"

"Alternating current? Direct current?" said Rip, trying to be helpful.

"Means, you go both ways." Joey drifted in. "*Means* you're a fucking *fag*."

Rip threw his hands up. "You gonna' fight about music? Thought you were going to fight about football teams."

"She-ya!" Paul rallied further up. "Then what the hell you call that shit?"

"This, ..." Todd swooped out his arms, a gesture that included his hair, apparel, the car, and the music. "...is *Disco!*"

"Well, if that's Disco, ..." Slick closed the circle. "... Disco *sucks!*"

Todd snapped fingers behind his back. Stephanie and Lynette tumbled out from behind the folded front buckets, each holding a bottle of Boone's Farm Strawberry Hill, giggling, eyes glassy, lips swollen and bruised.

"*What the fuck*?" Rip and Keith chanted together.

"Hey, boys." Lynette waved from where she sat on the ground, upending the bottle.

Keith pointed at Stephanie. "You fucking slut!"

"Takes one to know one!"

"Greg, ...Bobby!" Todd called, as two similarly attired and ornamented Disco dilettantes emerged from either side of the rear-seat.

"Greg? Bobby?" Keith belched, threw down his beer, stepping up to Todd, as the newcomers moved to flanking positions. "What is this? The fucking Brady Bunch?"

"Gettin' real tired of your lowlife, Blufftopper lip." Joey squared off to Slick.

"So this *is* about school. Or is this really about the chicks now?" Rip exasperated. "Guess I'm kinda' confused about the issues here. Maybe we should define, ..."

Joey jabbed with a hard right. Slick was smallish, but solid, and, as Rip knew from experience, fast as lightning. He sidestepped the swing, and almost casually backhanded Joey in the jaw, who went down hard.

The girls shrieked.

Todd took out a distracted Keith with a right roundabout, as Bobby stepped out from behind Slick and punched Paul in the teeth, who'd jerked back intuitively from the incoming blow, diffusing much of its impact. Greg leaped over Keith and tackled Rip onto his stomach, pinning, then raising him to his knees, arms locked in a wrestler's hold behind his back.

"*Hey*! Fuck!" Rip struggled painfully.

"Shut up dirtbag! Stay fucking put!"

Paul smiled redly, a rivulet of blood coursing down his chin. He spat out a tooth and in a blur of motion hit Bobby just below the sternum, collapsing him like a marionette.

"*Alright* Paul!" Stephanie toasted, still seated on the grass.

Todd reached into his back pocket, the playing field's lights briefly slashing over the chromed switchblade as it as it flipped open and locked.

"Hey! That's not playing fucking fair!" Slick backed off. He grabbed an empty from the trash, smashed it against the barrel, but true to its nature, the Blatz grenade shattered to nothing, leaving him with only the small, green rim. He threw it away in disgust.

"Let me the fuck *go*!"

"I said *stay put*, dirtball!" Greg hauled Rip up by his elbows, sending a scathing agony through his shoulder blades.

"*God*!"

Keith groaned from somewhere behind him as a cloaked shape trembled out from the shadows, snaking down the drive, murmuring a subsonic growl as it perched in their midst. The passenger door of the 'Cuda opened and from it rose the improbably large shape of Larry Fisher, who serenely considered the tableau.

"The fuck is goin' on here?"

The driver's window rolled down and Marlon slid out, sitting on the sill, pulling on a Marlboro. Slick pointed angrily to Todd.

"This Logan asswipe just pulled a blade on us!"

Larry pulled at his lower lip. "Why's he dressed like that?"

Todd shifted the knife unsteadily between Slick and Larry, genuinely perplexed. "This is *Disco!*"

Marlon spat. "Disco sucks."

"That's what *I* said!"

"Goddamn Blufftopper redneck lowlife's!" Bobby had somehow made his way back to the Trans Am, and was now advancing with a length of heavy-gauge chain, swinging it in a slow arc.

"OK, fuckwit." Larry strolled toward him as Keith sprang up from behind Todd and tackled him, the switchblade flying from his grip. Rip felt the tension on his arms momentarily slacken, and he snapped his head back, connecting with Greg's face hard enough to bring a painful flash of color before his eyes, then he was free. Bobby lunged with the chain as Larry stepped into the swing, the links wrapping harmlessly around his massive forearm. Keith delivered a series of well executed blows to the back of Todd's head as Larry jerked Bobby off the ground, through the air, bouncing his skull off the Blazer's chrome rim with a dim metallic gong. He rolled and curled into a ball of agony. Keith stood, breathing harshly, fingering his burst lip, surveying the prone Logan bodies before him.

"Fuckin '*A right!*" Paul stepped over Bobby's squirming form, plucking the blade from the ground, folding and stashing it in his pocket.

Rip felt at the back of his head the growing goose egg; turned and saw Greg crouched, snuffling, cradling his nose. Larry, still trailing the chain, scooped him up by the belt. He walked over to Bobby who was bleeding impressively from a scalp-wound, grabbed him by the scruff with the other hand, and dragged them to the Trans Am.

"You're no longer welcome here. Leave now." He tossed them to the spoiler of their vehicle.

Keith flipped Todd with a kick to the ribs. "Go home, *Logan.*"

Joey was up and Paul jerked at him. "Get yer' Disco *ass* outta' here." Joey flinched and staggered away.

Rip rolled out his traumatized neck and shoulders, watching the banished as they crawled into the car, closed the doors, and cranked up the engine.

Straight-arming the K-5's cab, Keith slapped a hand to his forehead. "Man, It's been a long fucking day."

"Hey, what about us!" Stephanie and Lynette pounded on the Trans Am's doors. It lurched backwards, narrowly missing them, shifting forward, spraying a long arc of gravel before it met the pavement with a shriek, disappearing down the hill.

"Pricks." Larry brushed off his soiled denims.

The girls strolled up to the Blazer, tossing empty wine bottles into the trashcan. "Everyone alright?"

"What the fuck do you care?" Keith pouted, rubbing at his jaw.

"Yeah, get lost, *scaggs*!" Slick reached for another beer.

Stephanie threw a look at Lynette.

Paul spat blood, fingering the new hole in his maw. "Yeah, what you doin' with those losers, anyway?"

"You!" She shot a venomous glare at the bunch. "Yeah! It's perfectly fine if a guy fucks any slut that spreads her legs! Oh no, you *slag's* are actually admired for your sleazy behavior, but if a *girl* wants to have some fun, even a little, she's a whore! " Her glaze burned to Rip. "*You*, are a tribe of Neanderthal hypocrites!"

A hysterical uproar arose from the valley below

"Aw, that's not fair, Steph." Larry finished uncoiling the length of chain, letting it drop with a metallic note. Patterned welts rose around his arm.

. "Ohh, Larry, Larry, *Larry*." Lynette tiptoed an unsteady approach. "We don't mean you."

"No Larry,…" Stephanie attempted to wrap arms around his chest, laying her head on a huge pectoral. "…we like *you*. You're not like these assholes."

Keith groaned.

"Uhmm…" Larry growled, ears burning, nearly throwing Stephanie off as he turned in embarrassment. She managed a fairly dignified recovery.

"C'mon, Lynette, let's go to the game."

"Yeah, exit already, will 'ya?"

Marlon barked a laugh from his perch on the 'Cuda's door.

Stephanie turned as Lynette shot the rest of the group the finger. She kissed it, waving it away from them. "Bye, *Larry.*"

"Jesus." Keith shook his head at the retreating figures.

A cheer came from the valley, and there was movement. A siren sounded.

"Game's over."

"Who won?"

"Who cares?"

"I'm home. Hang tough, Paul." Slapping him on the shoulder, Keith turned, ambling dejectedly down the slope.

"Hey!" Rip started. "What about .22 Beach?"

"*Grounded?*" Throwing arms up, still walking. "'Gotta' play it cool 'till the old man hears about the suspension."

"What's at .22?" Larry coiled the chain carefully behind the passenger seat of the 'Cuda.

Swallowing painfully, Paul smiled. "Shippin' me up to Trempealeau tomorrow. Guess the guys got a kegger on the beach."

"Trempealeau?" Marlin lit a fresh Marlboro, from the butt of his last. "Spent some time there. Not too bad."

"Shit, Paul. Gonna' miss trappin' season."

"She-ya, what's a guy gonna' do?"

"Sorry can't make the party, but Marlon and I got business in town," They shook, Paul's hand disappearing in Larry's. "See ya' when they ship ya' back down the river, buddy." He moved to the car, stopped, turned. "Try to stay out of trouble for the next twenty-four, OK?"

"She-ya."

"Thanks for the hand, Lar."

"Not a bother."

Marlon slipped through the window, the four-forty Hemi impacting the evening air. The vehicle crawled away with exaggerated care, merging with the thickening shadows of trees.

The squashed ball of the sun cut beneath the western bluff ridge and vanished. The field beneath them cleared and the park filled with the sound and movement of exiting athletic supporters.

"Well, hell, …" Rip trashed his last beer. "…let's get on to .22 Beach, then."

Like the bellow of a prehistoric beast, the sound of the Barracuda's engine opening up rose from the valley as it joined traffic on the Highway, each gear shift punctuated by the sharp chirp of rubber on asphalt.

*　　*　　*　　*

"What the hell happened to your face?" His stepfather eyed him with thinly veiled hostility.

They sat at the dining room table, Dart, his mother, stepfather, his younger sister, and their visiting older stepsister.

The room's view of the river was framed by sliding glass doors opening onto the back porch. The kitchen was adjacent, centrally located, and shared an identical view, the only room on the first floor that hadn't been covered in deep orange shag carpet. An open stairway switch-backed from the living room to the second story, bristling with identical shag. Dart fingered bruises around his mouth, attention drifting briefly to his weekly duty vacuuming the stubborn stuff.

Linda Ronstadt sang 'You're No Good' from the Magnavox cabinet in the living room. The song drifted into the psychedelic instrumental break that he actually thought was pretty cool.

"He was beat up at school."

Though she went to the elementary school, his sister Stacey had excellent access to the middle school's grapevine, as her best friend happened to be Sarah's younger sister. Through some moderate twist of fate, she was also named Stacey.

"You were *beat up*? Hell, that doesn't look too bad." Ted snorted, the blueblack panther tattoo rippling beneath a hairy bicep as he reached for a generic beer in a canary yellow. It was emblazoned simply with the word BEER, in black, stencil type. "'S,matter, can't take care of yourself?"

"There were three of them." He glared at Stacey.

"Oh dear, …" His mother took a nervous sip off her cocktail. "…can we please just enjoy this fondue? I saw it in Good Housekeeping."

"Good Housekeeping, huh?" Ellen, his stepsister drawled sarcastically. She was nineteen and had graduated Logan the previous year. "Now there's a magazine that really knows how to keep a woman in her place." Bearing a passing resemblance to Farrah Fawcett, she'd taken to styling and clothing herself after the famous actress, erect nipples projecting shockingly from the thin, tight fabric of a tank-top. Dart was having a difficult time not staring.

"Ellen, please try and show a little respect for your stepmother."

"Oh, we know all about respect, don't we *Dad-dee*?"

A ripple twitched along the panther tattoo.

Dart realized she was stoned.

"Oh, …" Picking up one of the delicate, color-coded skewers, his mother set down a plate arranged with various raw meats. She lanced a red cube. 'It's simple, really, just cook the meat in the oil, …" A raw cobalt flame from a tin of Sterno tickled the belly of an enameled ochre pot centered on the table. She dipped the skewer into its boiling contents with a hollow hissing. "…to whatever delicious, …*Ohh!*" She jerked away from the cauldron, grasping her hand.

"Three of them. Where the hell were your buddies?"

Dart experienced a rising tide of shame. "Buddies?"

"You do have friends, don't you?"

"I, …uh, think they ran off."

"See there, a man can't stand alone his whole life, …" Piercing a beige cube of chicken, Ted dropped it into the pot. "…there's strength in numbers, …*hell-fire!*" Twitched his hand back.

The rising drone of a turbo-jet passing overhead shook the house and conversation was muted temporarily, familiarly, as it passed. Their house was located beneath one of the busier air traffic lanes from the airport across the river. Ted held a glare over the length of the table as the wail of the airbrakes receded.

"I really don't want to talk about it." Dart secured the curl of a shrimp on his skewer.

"Yeah, leave him alone, daddy." Ellen shook her head in befuddlement at the plates before her.

Stacey kneeled up on her seat, pigtails swinging dangerously near the flame. She dropped her parcel into the oil.

"Oww! *Mom-ee,* …" she jumped back. "…it *burned* me!"

"Oh, honey, …" Cautiously retrieving her steaming scabbard, his mother examined it in confusion. "…I don't know what we're doing wrong. It's very popular." She scraped the blackened morsel off onto the edge of her plate poking it with a long fingernail.

"All I'm saying is that this country was founded on teamwork. You can't survive as a loner. In the Navy we had to count on our buddies."

"God daddy, not the war again." Ellen let her skewer drop and jumped back with a shriek. "*Goddamn!*"

"*Yes,* the war again!" Ted pulled the seared chicken out of the pot and pointed it around the table. "On the Intrepid, when those Kamikaze's started dropping, you better believe your buddy had your back. That's how we stayed alive."

"It's not the same." Dart submerged his shrimp and felt a sharp pain. "*Owww!*" He rubbed hot oil off his hand.

"That's what's wrong with you kids today. You think all your problems are *brand new* to the world. Well, they're not. It *is* the same. People have been having the same problems since God created them. And if you won't listen to the one's that have figured that out, then you're condemned to make the same, old mistakes."

Ellen rolled bloodshot eyes, and sighed deeply, sending delicious tremors through her breasts, and Dart felt a rising conflict of lust and anger as he unskewered his shrimp.

"It *isn't* the same." He fought to control his voice. "This isn't the war. I'm not fighting the Japanese, and this isn't an aircraft carrier. This is a small, backwater, river town, and these are psycho redneck retards who like to beat up on anyone not like them!" He hadn't realized he was shouting until he stopped.

His mother broke the brief silence. "Dart, don't raise your voice to your fa ..." stifled herself, but it was out, and she couldn't take it back.

"He's not my father."

"Oh, dear." His mother slipped from her chair into the kitchen, as Ellen giggled. Stacey held him with eyes wide, framed by her pigtails. Ted frozen, scowling, held a chunk of chicken rigid, upright on its tine, as the kitchen erupted with the passive aggressive din of dishes and cabinet doors.

"I'm out of here." Dart stood.

"Awww, don't leave, Dart." Elbows cinched together on the table, Ellen rested her face in her palms, gaze distant, distracted. "It's just getting interesting."

Ted blinked. "The boat tank's dry."

"I filled it yesterday. *Doggeth!*" The beagle bound out from beneath the table where she was begging for scraps. Originally named Lori, he'd begun calling the pet Doggeth after watching 'Monty Python and the Holy Grail'. The moniker had stuck, to the degree that she no longer responded to her original name. He tossed the shrimp, and she snapped it out of the air.

"Go then. Leave."

He exited through the sliding doors, onto the porch, followed by the clattering of cookware and Glen Campbell on the Magnavox crooning 'Wichita Lineman'.

Shadows gathered around the clusters of Cottonwoods punctuating the shoreline as he prepped the boat for departure. Stacey followed, sidling down the sand embankment, regarding him in silence. He checked the running lights, fore and aft, and pulled the anchor from its berth in the bank. He set it on the floor, took a seat on the bow, and turned to her.

"OK, what do you want?"

"Why don't you like daddy, Dart?"

"He's not our father, Stace." He sighed, leaned toward her. "Our *father* is, …our father."

She sat beside him, her weight slightly displacing the small craft. "Father scares me."

"That's because you're too young to remember. That why you won't see him?"

She wrapped hands around herself, nodded her pigtails.

"He loves you, you know?"

She snuffled.

"You should see him."

"Where are you going, Dart?"

"I don't know. Out there. Away."

"The river."

"Yeah."

"Why did those boys beat you up?"

He fingered a smooth, flat stone and sent it skipping off to the darkness of the opposite bank. "I wish I knew, Stace, but I don't. Guess they're just missing something."

"Like what?"

"Like, …empathy."

"What's enthapy?"

"It's like, …when you see someone that's hurt, or crying, you feel bad for them. You experience what they do."

"Oh." She was a silhouette against the rippling silvered surface of the water, waves lapping quietly around them. "Why do you always go out there?"

"Jeez, Stace, you sure got a lot of questions today."

"I'm just tryin' to, …enthapy you. It seems so lonely."

"Look." He reached under the gunwale's hold, pulled a ribbed, silver flashlight. He struck the beam offshore, through the shallows, illuminating ichthyoid silhouettes of slumbering crappies and perches, their pectoral fins oscillating stabilization to the current. A school of minnows drifted by in equidistant formation, lighting briefly at the passing of a submerged painted turtle. A couple water spiders scuttled overhead, dimpling the water minutely with their delicate control of surface tension. From the far shore came the wet warning slap of a beaver's tail. He played the light to the water's edge by their feet, where a fine silt had settled, the darker sediment scribed by a number of mysterious trails, each ending in leaden lumps. He plucked one up from the riverbed, displacing a swirling nimbus, and held it aloft, raking light off the knurled surface of the mollusk, overgrown with a fine fur of greenish slime. The pale mucoid flesh of its foot slowly retreated into it's shell. "See? We're surrounded out here. How could anybody be lonely?"

"*Yewww.*" She backed away, up the beach. "Groty."

From somewhere distant came the cry of a loon.

*   *   *   *

They'd left the Blazer at Sias' Bait Shop and forded the spillway to the island, the sole access without a boat, and only when the river level was low. The beach was on the southern tip, and they were following the well-worn pathway in near darkness when he heard the bullet snip through the brush ahead and ricochet off an oak to his left with a cartoonish whine. It fluffed the hair at his temple before nicking through the branches behind, and Rip found himself on the ground with the others, almost before he registered the flat crack of the pistol's report.

"Hey! Goddamn it! Stop shooting, fer Chrissakes!" Paul's exclamations ejected small plumes of debris from where his face was buried in the ground. "*We* back here!"

"Paul?" came an uncertain voice from beyond the thicket.

"Who the hell else? "

Rip's pulse raced as he lay there realizing what a close call it had been. "Moe, you better have that Ruger holstered!"

"She-ya, don't have a holster for this old thing. Come on out. I ain't gonna' shoot you."

"Damn." Slick pushed up off the ground, brushing off his shirt and pants. They made their way through the clearing, past two bottles hanging by their necks off twigs, to the open beach where Shitly and Moe stood before a blazing bonfire, vermillion against an amethyst sky. Shitly held two half-full plastic cups as Moe placed a cigarette to his lips, pointing the pistol over his shoulder.

"Get yerself a brew. Quarterbarrel's in the sand. Cups are on the cooler. What the hell happened to your face, Paul?"

"Long story." He and Slick moved around the fire as Rip stepped up.

"Think you put a new part in my hair with that thing." He held out his hand. "Let me see it."

Moe shrugged and dropped the gun into his palm, still warm. Checking the action, finding a round in the chamber, Rip nodded back at the bottles dangling before the clearing. "Trying to hit those?"

"Shoots a little to the left."

Straightarming down the sights, making minute adjustments, he squeezed the trigger. The small sidearm bucked in his hand, sound surprisingly loud, and one of the bottles burst into fragments leaving only the neck swinging down around the stick.

Moe grinned, squinting through the pall of smoke that had gathered up under the brim of his hat. "Deadeye."

At the keg, Slick worked the tap. "Hey, what you got in this thing, anyway?"

Shitly spoke. "Blatz."

There was a short but profound silence, as there was very little precedence as to how to frame a reply of any kind to Shitly, finally broken by a low whistle from Slick.

"Well, I'm just gonna' have to accept the fact that I'm facing a serious case of the Blatz splats in the morning."

They sat around the fire, Rip and Paul feeding it logs and branches, Shitly packing a small brass pipe from a good two-finger bag, The still evening was punctuated occasionally by sharp reports from Slick and Moe, target practicing with the .22.

"Don't know what those assholes were talkin' about AC/DC bein' fag music." Paul found a loose tooth and wobbled it, experimentally. "Ain't nobody rock out harder."

Pocketing the weed, Shitly ran a Bic over the bowl, coaxing a bright burn, huffing and holding before passing it to Paul.

"Obviously, …" Rip finished his beer. "…a classic case of the pot calling the kettle black."

There was a commotion up the beach. As Paul drew on the pipe, Slick and Moe returned to the ring of fire, Moe angrily fiddling with the pistol's action. "Goddamn thing's jammed up again."

"Told you those Ruger's were piece's of shit." Slick spotted Paul handing off the bowl to Rip and placed himself next in line. "Get a Colt. Get a Smith and Wesson. Do not get a Ruger." He took the handoff from Rip.

Ejecting and examining the clip, Moe slipped it back, shook his head. "Only five rounds left anyway." He threw it in the boat's seat hold and dropped the lid.

"She-ya, …" Paul released his hit. "…I think you're right. You see the way them Disco boys was dressed? Hear their music? Callin' us fags? AC/DC? Shit, *they* was the queer ones."

Accepting the pipe from Slick, Moe sat in the sand. "These them Logan boys you ass-kicked?"

"Yup."

"They call AC/DC queer?"

"Said it was fag music."

"Jesus, …" Moe shook his head again, sadly. "…might as well call Judas Priest queer."

Paul coughed. "What?"

Moe paused, pipe halfway to his lips. "Just sayin' that callin' AC/DC fags is just as stupid as callin' Judas Priest fags."

Slick started giggling.

"Moe, Judas Priest is as queer as a three dollar bill."

"Shut up, Paul."

"You see the way they dress? You ever listen to their words?"

"No way is Judas Priest queer. Guys?" He appealed to the rest, but Slick was too far gone, doubled up on the sand, Shitly was a cipher, and Rip just shrugged, not wanting to get involved.

Paul leaped to his feet, screeching in falsetto. "*Hell bent, hell bent for* lea-thaa!" He grabbed at his crotch, tugging it at Moe's eye level. "*Da da-da da da-da da da-da da da-da!*"

"Shut the fuck up, Paul!" He jumped up and back, throwing down the pipe.

"*I'm the green manalushi, with the two-pronged crown!*" Stuffing a hand down the front of his jeans, Paul popped a peace sign out the fly. "*Da da-da da-da da da-da!*"

"Said, shut the fuck up!" He lurched forward, Paul ducking back, braying like a hyena.

"*Stand by for ex*-citer!" Wriggling the fingers.

"Fuck you!"

"*Diamonds, dia-monds and rust!*"

Rip plucked the bowl from the sand, finding its contents intact. "Actually, I think that one's a Joan Baez cover."

That set Slick off fresh, and even Shitly was showing a smile, when Moe's club-like fist slammed into Paul's shoulder, shutting him down for a beat.

"Well, ...all-*right*! I accept the challenge!" His arm shot out and impacted with Moe's shoulder.

Putting the pipe to his lips, Rip caught something burning behind Shitly's eyes that wasn't the fire.

"Probably a good thing no one brought up Queen." he deadpanned.

Rip guffawed, ejecting the bowl's half-burned payload on and around him, as Slick hiccupped to a silence and pointed a finger to his own temple. "Still waters run deep." Then broke into new, more hysterical peals of laughter.

Moe was delivering skeleton rattling blows to Paul, who'd look back, squint a grin, and release a screeching crackle-laugh, whip-lashing with terrible speed a sinewy arm to strike his opponent's broad shoulder with a meaty 'crack', each time provoking a moan from the larger man. Rip sat observing the familiar scene as Slick settled in, became quiet, then bored, finally wandering off into the glade to gather more firewood.

After nearly ten straight minutes their movements were sluggish, fatigued, strained. Barely able to move their target arms, Paul and Moe stubbornly continued pummeling each other with harsh rasps of breath and grunts of pain, when Slick burst abruptly from the brush.

"*Cop!*"

Rip felt the tingle wash of adrenaline flush through his chest and mind as startled movement erupted from everyone on the beach.

"*A buzz!*" Slick pointed at them with hilarity. "Oh God. You should *see* your faces."

Gazing at Shitly, Rip just shook his head and sighed as Paul and Moe slumped to the ground. "Goddammit Slick, if I wasn't so bushed, I'd whomp you one upside the head."

"I *know*." He made his way back to the fire carrying an armload of sticks and an air of mischievous mirth. "That's almost the best part."

Time flowed as beer from the keg, the calm, clear evening waning, cooling.

Later, and he had no means of measuring exactly how much, Rip wandered up the beach towards the beacon of the bonfire after taking a leak. His feet were wet, and he hoped that it was because he'd pissed in the river. The sand was becoming more difficult to navigate, and the sound of an animated discussion nearby was vaguely audible. He found Paul alone before the blaze, smoking, oddly sentinel, attention cast out beyond the far shore. Squatting beside him, Rip tried to see what held his attention.

A small group of gulls were skirmishing for possession of either a fish, or a small dead animal. Something struck him as odd, but he couldn't quite put his finger on it.

"See how one of them gulls will take that fish 'n try to run with it. Then the others chase and peck at him 'till he drops the thing." Paul's voice was changed, reflective; older than his years. "Then a different bird will grab it, and the first will chase with the rest 'till *he* drops it, and another picks it up." He took a slow drag and sighed out a pale nimbus. "And then the whole thing starts over again. What the hell can ya' take away from that?"

Thoughts a bit muzzy, Rip couldn't think of a reply, so he grabbed a partially filled cup from the sand, hoping it was his. He sipped silently, watching the birds leap into the air, shrieking indignities.

"What I think, is that they just like people. Got something everyone else want, but don't know what they got 'till someone takes it from them." He flicked the butt into the coals. "Then they want it back even more."

Rip shook his head. "Shit Paul. I'm gonna' miss you."

"Now, don't get all queer on me here, boy."

"Really don't think you need to worry 'bout that. You're butt-ugly."

Paul grinned. "She-ya."

Belching wetly, Rip looked out at the night. "Think this Indian summer will hold out much longer?"

"Nah, could turn any time."

"So, how long they got you up the river?"

"'Bout six months. Should be back for Spring quarter."

"Place won't be the same 'till then."

"River still be here."

Rip nodded and he realized what was bothering him about the birds. He'd never before seen gulls feeding at night.

Voices trailed up the beach, followed by the unsteady figures of Moe, Slick, and Shitly as they de-cloaked from the darkness.

"Goddammit Rip, …" Moe fumbled with a pack of cigarettes that slipped from his grasp and fell to the ground. Belching loudly, he dropped to the sand, Shitly following suit. "…would you explain to these fuckers the difference between a houseboat and a boathouse?" Slick stood back, shifting restlessly.

"A houseboat and a, …boathouse?"

"She-ya." Locating the pack, he fished out a cigarette, placing it filter out, in his mouth. "I mean, …I *know* what it is, but, …shit's a little scrambled up in my head right now." Pulling a twig out of the fire, he touched its flame to the filter, inhaled deeply, coughed violently, and spat it out in disgust. "Shit, need to get my second wind."

"A houseboat is a house for, …wait, a *boathouse* is a boat, …no, …just a second." The meanings that had seemed so clear a second ago were log-jamming in his mind, loosing meaning, as if he were infected by proximity to Moe's befuddlement.

"Well?" Slick's fidgeting had increased to an obscene little jig, and Paul looked at him sharply.

"What the hell's your problem?"

"Gotta' piss!"

"What are you waiting for, permission?"

"Waiting to find out, which is which."

"Jesus, …" Rip rolled his eyes. " …a *houseboat* is a boat, …no, a boathouse, …hang on, I was right the first time. A houseboat is a *house* for a, …no, that can't be right…"

"Aaahh!" Slick sprinted up the beach and was swallowed by the night.

"Wait. I think I got it." He tossed his cup in the coals. "A boathouse is a, …*houseboat*? Shit, lost it again." Moe grabbed his head in frustration and moaned.

"A houseboat is a boat with a house on it. A boathouse is housing for a boat." Shitly stated.

"*Thank you!*" Moe pitched backwards onto the beach.

"Shitly!" Paul slapped him on the back.

"See?" Rip pointed.

Slick exploded from the thicket and tore back down the beach. *"Cops! Cops!"*

"Well, if it isn't the boy who cried wolf, again." Paul growled.

"Not kidding. Back there. Two of 'em. MOVE!" It was clear by the way he booked past, panic in his eyes, that he wasn't joking, and their movements became coordinated and choreographed. Moe followed Slick down the beach, pulled anchor, and pushed the boat off shore. Shitly and Rip pulled the keg from where it was buried and hauled it down to the boat. Paul dowsed the fire with sand, not completely extinguishing but dimming it considerably. Two scythes of light lanced the dark foliage from deep in the woods, disembodied spectral eyes bobbing an approach.

They encircled the craft as Shitly tossed the keg onto the floor, Moe bringing the motor to life with a tug at the flywheel.

Paul, Slick, Shitly, and Rip each made a move to get in the boat, and stopped.

"Shit!" Rip kicked at the shallows.

"What?" Slick jumped into the boat. "Let's *go!*"

Moe sat crouched on the transom, one hand on the throttle, other ready at the gear lever. "Ain't enough room for everyone."

"What?"

"Only place we're goin' with this load is straight to the bottom."

Shitly sighed sadly, Paul slapping a hand off the bow. "Fuck!"

"Well, what the hell we gonna' *do?*"

"Well, it's my damn boat, so the rest of you better figure it out, and *fast.*"

From up on the beachhead came the telltale crackling of bodies pushing through overgrowth and sputtered murmurings of walkie-talkies. Flashlight beams played over the glade's curtain of leaves.

"I'm swimmin' before I get hauled in again." Paul started tearing at his shoelaces.

"Wait! Just one sec." They leered back wild-eyed as Rip held up a hand, hearing it out on the river. "I know that motor."

*　*　*　*

The opaque banks of the channel framed a moonless firmament, creating a frail, exquisite Rorschach intertwined with its reflection. A meteor skated across the heavens and burst silently into luminous dust, mirrored by its twin. Dart trolled out from the spillway, lost in the celestial display, feeling more of a belonging here than anywhere else. The world people had built was so ignorant, arrogant, selfish, and just downright *mean*, in comparison. He realized, with a sad certainty, that humans would never, ever understand nature. They simply were not constructed that way.

Passing a flashing buoy signaling entrance to the river, he throttled up, pulling around the small island, past the point of .22 Beach.

Had he not just spent the last fifteen minutes in the darkened canal, eyes adjusting to the absence of light, he never would have seen it. On the beach a dim cloud of smoke hovered over fading coals of a bonfire, and barely visible down the shoreline, shadowy figures clustered around a boat, signaling frantically. He tightened his turn, pointing the bow at the beach, and at his approach, two of them broke off, as the three others climbed into the boat and launched. Lights materialized atop the beachhead, reached down, and locked on him in a blinding wash.

"*Police! Halt!*" The hairs on the back of his neck bristled at the authoritative tone of the voice and his hand slipped off the throttle. The other boat blared past in the opposite direction. His bow barely kissed the shore before two figures broke through the glare and clamored onboard, roughly pushing him back out.

"Do not leave this beach, *Goddammit!* This is the *police!*" He could see the two officers stumbling down the sand now, struggling, both overweight and unused to its surface, but rapidly closing distance.

Dart recognized the two in his boat, and Rip turned back to him with a crazed expression, sweeping an arm out at the river. "Go, go, GO!"

He threw the Evinrude in reverse and gunned it, noting with a perverse sense of pride, even through the confusion, that the other two had the sense to stay counterweight at the bow, maximizing their backup speed. Water slapped hard against the flat transom.

The cops reached the waterline, panting heavily, trying to steady the light's beams. The shorter one halted, larger man running straight into the river. He waded up to his thighs, nearly reaching the receding craft. "Police! I order you to *halt* this *second*!"

Paul leaned tauntingly over the bow. "See ya, Carp!"

Karpinski's face, grotesquely illuminated by the wash of red and green running lights, was warped with seething hatred, impotent rage. He stopped only as the water reached his belt, and they broke away, gaining speed and distance.

Rip tipped a drunken little salute off his forehead.

"So long, *suckers*!"

Reaching down, Karpinski withdrew his service revolver and pointed it at them.

Rip hit the deck and Dart ducked down low as possible, giving the throttle an extra turn, transom throwing a heavy spray. Paul leapt up onto the gunwale beating at his chest. "Do it! C'mon, you fucking chickenshit Carp! *Do it*!

The moment fractured into multiple images, etched clearly in Dart's mind; Paul perched on the bow, tearing open the front of his shirt, screaming obscenities, cords standing out thick on his neck; the wavering muzzle of the gun and the wrathful face behind it; confused, terrified look of the deputy on the beach; icy sting of river-water; Rip's glance finding him from the floor, raised hand making twirling motions with a forefinger.

He spun the motor hard to port, cut the power. Rip reached up to clasp Paul's belt as the bow swung about. He threw it into forward, burying the throttle, the flat-bottom leaping ahead, cutting rapidly out into the main channel, beach dwindling behind them.

Leaving Paul behind, laughing hysterically up at the stars from where he lay on the center bench, Rip worked his way to the stern, sitting next to Dart, clasping head in hands, rocking back and forth.

"Oh man. Oh man." He turned, extending a hand. "I'm Rip."

He grasped it and shook, feeling the slip-stream of air cooling the sweat covering his body, smelling a combination of beer, pot smoke, wood smoke, cigarette smoke, and fear radiate from the guy.

"Dart."

Rip chuckled to himself, shaking his head. "*Oh man.*" He repeated, and when he looked back, even in the muted starlight, Dart could see depth and humor reflected in his clear blue eyes. "Dart, that was fucking *dece'*."

*   *   *   *

He was standing in his backyard, back to the canal, on the sandy verge that dropped to meet the water, staring up at his house. His sister fed mallard ducks breadcrumbs off the porch as they bobbed iridescent green heads, and his first indication that it was a dream was that, despite the fact that it was the middle of the day, stars covered the sky. He could hear the familiar distant purr of an airplane approaching for a landing, and saw two craft drop out of the peculiar dark light sky. With mounting terror he realized that their trajectory would lead them on a collision course directly above his house. He tried to voice this to his sister, but nothing would come out. Because of the warped perspective of dreams, he was able to perceive his stepfather piloting one of the aircraft, the other, vacant.

Helplessly he watched them soundlessly couple in the atmosphere, shredding, tearing, shedding aerodynamic form; plummeting ungracefully, shearing wings, propellers, turbines spitting jet fuel. The fuselages split, disgorging seats, luggage, and passengers, like viscera from a disemboweled muskellunge, to rain on the earth. The first body hit his roof with the force of a bomb, the canal behind him coming alive with impacts. He glanced in alarm back at his sister, but she and the ducks seemed oblivious to the carnage. All about him dismembered remains slammed to the ground, surrounding him in a gruesome debris field, as jettisoned apparel wafted through the air. The severed tail-section from one of the planes windmilled past, rudder and ailerons a spinning guillotined dervish, carving ruts through the lawn. A body burst like ripe fruit on the ground directly before him, torso flopping grotesquely to a halt at his feet. Looking down, he stared into the cold, dead eyes of his father.

5

COVE BEACH

Brian D Garrity

Early one morning mid October, mid week, Dart was awakened by clock radio to his favorite morning show, "Chicken Man vs. the Earth Polluters', and to the recurring barb of dread that knotted his stomach the start of each school day. He lay back and tried to listen to the show, willing it to distract him from the anxiety that plagued his mind, but it was futile.

It wasn't that Brad, Timmy, or Duncan ever gave him any trouble anymore. They'd waged their damage, and like all of their kind, moved on to other unsoiled targets of opportunity, but he bore the stigma of the humiliation, and classmates, even his teachers had been treating him as persona non grata. His mere presence quelling conversations into embarrassed glances, dispersing social throngs in the hallway, and on the playground. His classroom interaction, sparse as it had been, became nonexistent, the unspoken aura of rejection he carried generating a force field of shame that he could practically visualize. Any thoughts of Sara induced a mental cringe so severe that his mind sort of skipped, like the needle on a badly scratched record, over the memory.

Almost worse was the wedge between him, Curt, and Randy. It had been over a month since that awful day, and he still hadn't spoken with either, which was awkward enough at school, but nearly impossible within the tiny, isolated neighborhood. Even on the river, they'd cross paths without a wave or nod of acknowledgement. His visits to the tree fort had also become a casualty of his social gulag.

Rallying against dread of the struggle through another long, dark day, he willed himself out of bed. Crossing the room, he noted with resigned pride, the balsa wood scale models he'd crafted of a Sopwith Camel and a Fokker DR-1 triplane, hanging from the ceiling. The poster of Neil Armstrong's lunar landing he considered for the thousandth time, staring out at the landscape of an actual alien world. He sighed, digging his feet into the soft give of the shag carpet.

The morning outside the dining room window was sharp with autumn color. Stacey was sitting at the table behind an empty bowl, spooning fluorescent orange Tang granules into a glass-full of water. He greeted her with a yawn.

"It's what the astronauts drink." She commented perkily, bonging a rhythm with the spoon on the glass.

"Don't believe everything they tell you."

"It's true."

"I doubt it."

"Why not?"

"Stace, you can't drink liquids in space. There's no gravity."

"Why not?"

"Because it just blobs into a ball." He dropped into the chair opposite her and picked sleet from his eyes. "And if you touch it, it pops into a million balls. Would get into the computers."

Pulling the spoon free, she took a long drink and smiled. "They drink it from tubes."

"Tubes."

"Yeah, like toothpaste tubes, only with a straw."

"Well, I suppose that would work. Still doesn't mean they drink Tang."

"Sez' on TV."

He stood, shuffling to the pantry door. "That brings me back to, don't believe everything they tell you."

"Hey Dart?"

"Stace?"

"Could you reach the cereal for me?"

"Sure." He rose, fingered a latch, and it sprung free of its magnetic clasp. "What do you want?"

"What we got?"

He eyed the boxes on the top shelf, placed there away from Stacey's grasp because of her compulsive tendency to obsess on a certain cereal, to eat a whole box at one go. "Let's see." Pulling the first box, he shook it. "We got half a box of Honey Combs."

"Yeah, Honey Combs! No wait. What else?"

Tipping the tops, he read off names. "Quisp."

"Uhm."

"Frosted Mini Wheats."

"Nah."

"Super Sugar Crisp."

"Uhm."

"Sugar Corn Pops."

"Well, ..."

"Life."

"Ugh. I hate Life."

He smiled at the unintended irony. "Yeah, so do I. Hold on." Behind the row, he found one snuck back sideways. "Hold on. I think mom's been hiding something." He pulled out an unopened box and held it out to her. "Freakies."

"Yeah! Freakies!"

"I agree."

He pulled milk from the fridge, a bowl from the cabinet, and a spoon from the drawer, setting a place for himself at the table. Stacey stared at the bright cartoon illustrations on the box with barely concealed excitement.

"I want the prize."

Dart snatched it away from her grasp. "Now just *wait*. I'll make you a deal, OK? If it's Boss Moss, Grumbles, or Snorkeldorf, I get the prize. But, if it's Goody Goody, Gargle, Hamhose, or Cowmumble, you get it."

"I like the Snorkeldorf too."

"Alright, I concede. Snorkeldorf is yours too. Deal?"

"Deal." She bounced in her seat as he broke the box's seal, tipping it over his bowl. A few meager yellow pellets tinkled in, and suddenly it was overflowing with small, clear capsules containing brightly colored figures. Shocked, he reached a hand inside and pulled out more. The cereal box was almost entirely filled with prizes.

"Jackpot."

Stacey's eyes boggled between her pigtails. "Are they, …?"

"They're all here." The phone rang in the kitchen. He was barely aware of his mother answering it. "Jesus."

"You just said a naughty word."

"It's not a, …just don't tell mom, OK? Here, have a Hamhose."

There was a gasp from the kitchen, and then their mother was standing in the dining room doorway. Beehived hair clasped in purple headscarf, a nervous hand fluttering over the breast of her pink and green flower print dress, her cheeks were flushed, shock in her eyes. "That was Curt's mother. She said, …" She looked at the cereal bowl full of prizes and stopped, lowering into a chair, confused.

"Ma? What is it?" Dart was becoming concerned.

She looked up at him. "Helen said the Middle School burnt down."

"What?"

"Last night. It burnt to the ground. All classes are cancelled. Indefinitely."

A wave of elation spread slowly, cautiously throughout his mind. "Are you sure?"

"She was. Curt's father is a volunteer fireman, and I guess he's been fighting it all night. Still, … " She stood. "This is too important. Get ready, kids. I'm taking you to school."

"But you never drive us."

"I have to see this for myself." She seized her purse from the counter and began picking through it.

"Do *I* still have to go to school?" Stacey freed a blue Snorkeldorf from its packaging.

"Of course you do, sweetie." Locating keys, she moved to the garage door. "Bring your wind breakers along. It's getting chilly out."

Throughout the ride there, Dart kept his feelings carefully in check. He knew that if it were a hoax, or even if the facts were embellished and the damage was minimal, it could potentially deal his psyche a crushing blow, but the scene that greeted their arrival at the Middle School exceeded even his wildest expectations.

The fire department had cordoned off the street with trucks, personnel, and yellow caution tape. Civilian vehicles of every variety were scattered and parked randomly. Teachers, students, parents, and curious bystanders milled aimlessly about, seeking a vantage point to what lay beyond.

They stopped and Dart rushed out the car, past his mother to the front of the fray. The air held a rancid scorched chemical scent. Reaching the tape, he peered between the clustered throng, past the grumbling body of a hook and ladder, witnessing a scene of almost Biblical devastation.

Where the school once stood was now a charred and blackened scar on the landscape. Almost nothing recognizable or vertical remained, just a blasted vista of humped, twisted, smoldering metal tri-beams poking from ashen piles, broken occasionally by the shattered form of a former load-bearing wall. He tried to pinpoint the location of pod three in the remains, but the destruction was so complete, there was no real point of reference.

Looking back to the crowd, he saw Ms. Garr dabbing swollen red eyes with a paisley handkerchief. At Mr. Ball's approach, she broke down into sobs, throwing arms around him as he muttered back reassurances. They stepped away, revealing Curt and Randy standing directly behind the teachers, and Dart suddenly found himself staring back at his estranged friends. Each in turn dropped their gaze in mutual embarrassment, before Curt looked back up, huge grin on his face, and Dart pressed through the mob, running to greet them.

"Can you freakin' believe it?"

"I know. It's like a wish come true."

"Yeah. I keep thinking I must be dreaming, but now all my dreams are nightmares, so this must be real. You hear how it happened?"

"Old man says that someone broke into the office and tried to burn the school records, but they built the thing with such flammable materials, fire just took off like a bomb."

Randy said in a low voice. "I heard some teachers talking. Said they thought it was Brad Thornton."

Dart whistled.

"Alright people! May I have your attention?"

Mr. Ball had his hands up before a queue of teachers and firefighters, the assembly quieting and gathering closer. "There is nothing more for you to see or do here. This is now a matter for the Police and Fire Department, and they request that you go back home and let them do their work." He paused, clearly struggling with his emotions. "All classes are canceled for now. We will have an emergency meeting of the education department tomorrow to determine our next course of action, and you all will be notified of the outcome. Until then, …" His chin and shoulders dropped. "…thank you."

Reading faces on the students there, Dart clearly wasn't alone in wanting to cheer, but considering the collective mood of the officials and their parents, he and the others wisely suppressed their delight.

The early fall briskness was rapidly being dispelled by the rising sun. The three friends made their way alongside train tracks skirting a large, well tended graveyard. It had taken very little persuasion for their parents to allow them to break away on this hike. Despite her statements to the contrary, Dart knew that his mother savored her private time when they were at school. Now, faced with an indefinite period of his presence, she more than willingly acquiesced, as did Randy and Curt's mother.

"I brought along some of that weed." Curt peeked the edge of a tightly rolled baggie from his front pocket.

Dart unzipped his windbreaker and stepped up onto the rail, walking balance. "Cool. How much is left?"

"A lot."

Randy hopped on the opposite rail. "Curt put a stove in the tree fort."

"Oh yeah?"

"Yeah. Works real good. Gonna' be great in the winter."

"Where'd you get that, Curt?"

"Snarfed it from Glenn's ice house. Not that he's gonna' miss it."

"How's he doin'?"

"Not too great." Curt kicked at a mound of taconite. "Back in treatment."

"Rough, man. Your parents taking it OK?"

"Well, you know, guess they're getting kinda' used to it. Actually, it's better with him gone. He was really starting to freak me out."

"Yeah? How?"

Randy lost his footing and jumped onto a tie. "Tell him about the three wheelers."

"Three wheelers?"

"Yeah, …" Curt scratched nervously at the back of his head. "…me and Randy came back from riding the Honda's out on the marsh, and Glenn was home, he looks at us all intense, and asks 'hey, what's it like, riding those three wheelers out there?' I say, 'I don't know Glenn, it's just like riding out in the marsh', but he won't let it go, sayin' about how three wheels are different, are an odd number, not like four wheels on a car or two wheels on a bike, how three is a sacred number, like the Holy Trinity, but can also be evil, 'cause bad things come in three's, and then he *really* starts freaking out, saying how the devil's number is 666, that it's three numbers that are all divisible by three, and by this time he's yelling so loud that the old man has to come in and haul him away."

"Whoa, weird."

"Really weird."

Randy shuddered. "Creepy, what it is."

They stopped at an intersection, between a pair of crossing signals holding candy stripped arms aloft. They eyed the road that snaked up and disappeared into the forest at the foot of the mammoth bluff that loomed above them.

"Well, there it is, Grandfather Bluff." Dart peered at the faceted limestone escarpment, surface trenched and pitted, rimmed with tiny trees, so that in the right light, or the right state of mind, it could appear to be the face of an ancient giant peering out over the valley. Suddenly, he was seized by a profound sense of deja vue.

"*Jesus*." Curt turned away from the cliff, shocked expression on his face. "I just had the strangest feeling."

"*No way*. So did I."

"What?' Randy's head see-sawed between them. "What is it?"

"You didn't feel anything just now?"

"Like what? I'm hungry. Does that count?"

"No. It's like, ...this has all happened before."

"And we were, ...*are* all doing exactly the same things, and talking the same, ...oh *fuck*, here it is again!"

Another wave broke over Dart, and he felt his skin crawling, the hairs all standing straight. "*Shit*, let's just get out of here! Up the path!"

They broke and ran, trailing a confused Randy.

It took nearly an hour to ascend the back trail to the summit. The worn path switched back through thick overgrowth at its base, broadening out into open glades guarded by towering sandstone rises near the peak. There, it guided through a narrow cleft, portal to the sheer face of the cliff.

Stepping out to the edge of the abyss, the entire river valley yawed out before them, town below nestled like a cluster of jewels against a twining Mississippi. It reached to each horizon, a sightline to both Minnesota, and Iowa, all aflame with turning fall colors, especially the surrounding coulees, blanketed in a quiltwork of vibrant tones; the fiery reds and fluorescent oranges of maples, poplars brilliant yellow, ashes offering white underbellies in the breeze, interspersed with the deep unchanging greens of conifers.

A cool, clean breeze slip up the precipice and played with their hair. They were temporarily struck speechless by the magnificence of the vista. Dart backed away from the edge, experiencing a tilting vertigo.

"It all looks so different from up here."

"No kidding." Randy moved closer, toeing the rim.

"Just take it easy, Rand." Curt crouched nervously toward him.

"Yeah, be careful."

"What? You both scared of heights?"

"No Rand, just that the rock is real soft and crumbly, ..." Curt crossed his arms. "...and every year some dumbass takes the big drop screwing around just like you are."

"Remember that U student last year?" Dart offered.

"Yeah, but he was drunk."

"True, but you never know when that sandstone is gonna' let go." Uncertainty crossed Randy's face, but he was far too stubborn to move. "I ain't afraid of falling."

"It's not the fall that kills you, Rand."

He looked back. "No?"

"No." Curt smacked his hands together. "It's the sudden stop."

"Aww, screw you guys." But he was laughing, moving away.

They wound their way around worn ledges, evidence of decades of trespass strewn everywhere. Cans and bottles littered the perimeters of burnt out fire pits, garneted by the occasional cast off condom. The soft stone walls were scribed with layers of graffiti; hearts branded with names, names with years, years with schools, and, of course, hieroglyphs depicting a variety of perverse deeds.

Dart shook his head. "Man, someone should clean this place up."

Randy kicked the peeled foil of a condom wrapper. "Good thing you can't see all this from down there."

They settled on a sheltered shelf of denser, compacted rock that offered a sweeping panoramic view, beneath a six-foot pot leaf meticulously carved into the cliff above. Curt withdrew the baggie from his pocket and rolled it open, dropping a pack of Zig Zags onto his lap. Pulling a leaf free he pinched a generous amount from the bag, and began twisting a joint with impressive ability.

"Hey, you see that movie, Bad News Bears?"

Dart dangled legs over the edge of the shelf, next to him. "Yeah, I saw it about a couple months ago with my father."

"What you think about that Tatum O'Neil chick was in it?"

"I dunno. She's OK."

"I think she's pretty hot."

"You do?"

"Yeah." He gave a final turn to the spliff and spit-sealed it.

Randy tossed rocks off the face. "You know who I think is foxy?"

"Who, Rand?"

"Kristy McNichol, from that TV show, Family."

"Yeah. She's all right. I like her hair." Curt blew on the joint, turned to Dart. "Who do you thinks hotter, Tatum O'Neil or Kristy McNichol?"

"Well, actually, I kind of like Jodie Foster."

Pausing in mid-toss, Randy scowled back. "Ain't she a prostitute?"

"She's an actress, Randy. Just played a prostitute in Taxi Driver. She played Becky Thatcher, too, but that doesn't mean she's Tom Sawyer's girlfriend."

"Hey, you know who kinda' looks like Jodi Foster?" Curt sparked up and sucked in.

"No, who?"

Blowing out the hit, he handed it to Randy. "Sara, from class."

Dart blinked. "Uh, ... you toking now, Rand?"

"Well, yeah. I like it." Puffing the joint, he rolled smoke around his mouth and expelled it.

"Hey, you didn't even inhale."

"Sure I did."

"Give me that. Damn waste." He sucked hard on the thing, almost immediately feeling razor blades dig into his lungs, and started hacking uncontrollably.

From around the corner drifted the sound of approaching voices.

Jerking around in panic, Curt grabbed the roach. "Quiet, man. Someone's coming."

But the harder Dart tried to stop, the harsher and more painful the coughs came, the other two weaving around with alarm, their only escape the way they'd came.

"Hey, what's going on here?" It was a female voice. They turned to see Lynette, Gaylene, and Stephanie rounding the corner, each dangling the remains of a six-pack from its ring-tab.

Dart retched again, loudly.

"Hey, look!" Lynette pointed. "It's the little River Rats!"

Stephanie stepped up, and as Dart caught his breath, he observed how striking she was at this proximity, especially her eyes. "They got weed."

"Weed?" Gaylene regarded the stub between Curt's fingers. "Where'd you guys get that? There's been a major drought for, like, a month."

"Got a bunch."

"So, *share*!" Stumbling over her own bell bottoms, Dart realized that though it was barely after lunch, Lynette was already more than a little bit tipsy. "A friend with weed, ..."

Curt offered, and she lit up, Stephanie freeing a can of Bud from its ring, handing it to Dart. "Gonna' need something for that cough."

"Thanks." He wheezed. Popping it open, he took a cool, soothing drink.

Lynette blew her hit out, made a face. "*Hey*, what the fuck is this?"

"Me try." Gaylene greedily sucked the cherry to life.

"Quit hot-boxing that thing." Stephanie scowled.

Curt showed them the bag. "Found a couple of big plants in the marsh."

"Ditch weed!" Lynette threw up her arms.

Smoke rolling out her nostrils, Gaylene nodded solemnly. Stephanie took a dainty taste. "Yep, Wisco green."

Randy glowered. "What's wrong with it?"

"What's right with it?" Pouting, settling on a boulder, Lynette cracked a beer. She sighed. "The great drought goes on."

"You mean this stuff isn't any good?"

Stephanie grabbed the sack from Curt, sniffed it, handed it back. "Smoke that whole bag and all you'd get is a headache."

"Damn, we got half a garbage bag of this stuff."

She laughed and sat next to Lynette, Gaylene joining them. "By the way, what brings you River Rats so far outta' the water? For that matter, why aren't you in school?"

Dart handed the beer over to Curt. "Our school burnt down. What's your excuse?"

The girls traded shocked glances and Gaylene shrieked. "Oh my God! For real?"

"To the ground."

"*Holy shit.*" Lynette stood, wobbled, dropped back down. "You guys must be psyched! I mean, it's like everyone's fantasy, right?"

Dart belched. "Best day of my life."

"*That* deserves a toast." Stephanie grabbed one of Gaylene's beers. "Hey!"

"Give it up, lightweight. This is something special." She lobbed it over, Dart snatched it from the air. "Cheers." He tipped to the girls, bouncing the rim off the can in Curt's hand.

"Cheers!" They echoed.

Dart was beginning to feel a heart- swelling serenity. He couldn't remember any time he'd been more at peace with the world.

Throwing down her empty, Lynette rose again, and began a cautious, calculated stroll toward the boys, rolling hips, her flushed face holding a mischievous grin.

"Hey, you know, Dart, you, …you're pretty cute, you know, for a younger guy." She stopped before him, foreign hunger in her eyes. "You wanna' see my tits?"

Dart could only swallow.

She pulled her top up exposing full, firm alabaster breasts, ghost of a tan line still surrounding them, topped by wide, flat nipples that she began pinching between her thumb and forefinger. He was transfixed by the way they began to rise and harden, hearing Randy and Curt breathing nearby, when Stephanie stepped up and yanked her shirt back down.

"C'mon Lynn, leave 'em alone."

Lynette giggled, flashing her bellybutton. "Relax, Steph. Just givin' the kids some jerkin' material."

Stephanie tugged it down again, pulling her back. "Show's over, boys."

Putting up a token struggle, Lynette thrashed around. "You *do* do that, don't you? Beat your meat?" She staggered, nearly bringing Stephanie down with her. "Got hair on your balls yet?"

They might as well been carved out of sandstone themselves, and could only stare back.

A sudden shadow crossed the sun, accompanied by a rapid rustling sound, and the prehistoric silhouette of a pterosaur dropped through the air before them.

"Whoa!"

"You see that?"

"What the fuck?"

Both groups were hurrying to the edge when a second monster flashed by. Peering down, Dart recognized the shape of the triangle sail, adorned with garish colored stripes, small figure hanging beneath, floating down into the valley, following its predecessor's glide path.

"Hang gliders!" Randy yelled reverently.

"Fucking boss!" Stephanie followed its flight. "Looks like they're landing on the golf course."

Lynette craned her head to peer up the escarpment. "Jesus, wonder what kind of balls it takes to step off that drop."

Gaylene nodded at her friends. "Well, the first one's just touching down. We get back to the car quick enough, maybe we can find out."

Laughing, Stephanie playfully slapped her arm. "Bore pig. *C'mon*, let's go."

The boys watched, half stunned, as the girls gathered their beer and purses, and retreated back down the trail. Turning the corner, Lynette glanced back, waggling her fingers.

"Toodle-oo, little River Rats."

"Bye." Dart waved, but they were already gone. He turned, standing next to his friends, and considered the world spread out before him.

"Best goddamned day of my life."

"Goddamn." Echoed Curt.

*   *   *   *

"Goddamn school split-schedule gonna' seriously fuck with muskrat season." Moe muttered around a cigarette as he wound a length of heavy gauge chain about the base of a small sapling. He considered two rusty padlocks in his palm, chose one, and cinched it through a couple links.

The early morning was chilly and damp. Their breath hung, drifting in the air like lost ghosts, gradually deliquescing into the surrounding bank of fog that obscured both the origin, and destination of the row of boxcars at rest on the tracks nearby. Rip turned to Shitly, who just shrugged, rattling traps draped over the shoulder of his jacket.

"Yeah, you'd think there'd be some kind of child labor laws against us starting class at six-thirty in the morning."

"Yeah you'd think. Barely gives me an hour of light to do my run. With Paul gone, Shitly an' I gotta' cover *his* rounds too."

"Well, we *do* get done at noon, now. Plenty of time after school to check the traps."

Moe looked up. "She-ya, an' give every other trapper a chance to clean out *my* traps? Cold day in hell 'fore I let that happen." He stood, walking to the nearest boxcar, paying out a length of chain.

It was mid November, the first day of trapping season, directly following the final day of duck hunting season. Coincidentally, it was also the first day of the new split schedule they shared with the Middle School students. The weather had turned decidedly winterish immediately after Halloween, although temperatures had generally stayed above freezing. The last couple of weeks had been unseasonably rainy, raising water levels in the marshes, making transit slow and difficult.

Ducking beneath the boxcar's undercarriage, Moe threaded the other end of the chain through an opening in its rusting chassis, securing it with the second padlock. He stood, wiping grime from hands onto his jeans.

"You know, we went up and saw Paul last week."

Rip flipped up the collar of his jean jacket, tried to rub warmth into his hands. "Yeah? How's that crazy fucker doing?"

Moe turned to Shitly, who dropped his eyes. He looked back. "Not sure. Seemed, …different."

"Different how?"

"I don't know. Crazy, but not the usual Paul kinda' crazy." He searched the pockets of his goose down vest. "He was all hyper, and his eyes were all spaced. Kept showing us these drawings he done of muskrats and beavers that looked like they were by a little kid." Extracting three cans of Special Export, he placed them at his feet, continued rifling the pockets of his flannel.

"What you think's goin' on?"

"Lotta' tough timers up there, y'know? Mighta' fallen in with the wrong crowd. *Goddamn* it Shitly, would you borrow me a smoke?"

Rip laughed to himself, as Moe accepted the Marlboro.

Lighting it. "What's so funny?"

"Well, guess I always figured that Paul *was* the wrong crowd."

From an invisible distance churned the thunder of a locomotive and Moe shot the sleeve of his flannel, consulting a silvered Timex concealed beneath. "Ole six-fifteen, right on time."

Far off began a muted rhythm, a deep metallic pulse of approaching concussions that swept past as the cars dominoed against one another, each coupling jerking its cargo with a solid detonation, loosing a cloud of frost and dust. The iron wheels turned hesitantly, screeching angry chromium tones.

The chain slithered, straitened, and pulled taught from the trunk, straining against the uncompromising momentum of the train. Vibrating with tension, it sung a thrumming tone of its own, biting into bark, and for an instant seemed ready to snap, but the earth beneath suddenly relinquished its hold, and the sapling burst from the ground with a boiling gout of roots and loose soil.

They watched it lurch along the tracks, tethered to the diminishing boxcar, tumbling and tearing itself apart, leaving a trail of branches and twigs.

Withdrawing a knife from a belt sheath, Moe grabbed a beer, flipped it over, punching a hole in the bottom, sealing it with a finger. Turning it upright, he popped the top, tipped it over his mouth and sucked till the sides dented in. Releasing his finger from the knifehole, the can relinquished its entire contents in less than two seconds. Moe belched loudly, handing the knife to Rip.

"Better shotgun your beer."

Rip watched the caboose roll past from out of the haze, reopening access from the river to town. "Why?"

"Don't want to be late for class, do you?"

They made it with time to spare.

Third period was open on his schedule, and Rip wandered through a hallway of dazed and sleep deprived students. Keith waited by his locker.

"Not going to study hall, bub?" He joked.

"Thought I'd hit the lot and see if anybody's holding."

"Right. Good luck. I haven't seen so much as a nickel-bag in, like, two months."

"Yeah, man, this drought sucks." Spinning the combination, he flipped open the door, dumping in books, pulling free his jean jacket. A large hand clapped down on Keith's shoulder, and Nuts stood behind him, football jersey draped over his blockhouse physique. Anita stood at his side, beaming a cheerleader smile in her cheerleader uniform, jaw working on a large gob of gum.

"Hey Keith! How's it goin' buddy?"

"Hey, Nuts. Doin' well, yourself?"

"Can't complain. Rip buddy, how you doin?"

"Great Nuts. Thanks for asking."

"Big game tomorrow Keith, eh?"

"Yeah, well, I hope they let me off the bench for this one."

" Been hearing rumors, Keith. Lotsa' rumors."

"Really. From who."

"Well, I'm not really at liberty to say, but the words 'first string' have been tossed around."

"Damn, Nuts. That's great news."

"Hey, not a problem. Just keep it under your hat for now, eh?"

"Oh, of course, I understand."

"Hey, while I got you here, …" His square jaw dipped down, and he unconsciously gathered them in a huddle. "…me an' the boys are having a little get-together after the game at my place. Like it if you could come."

"Wow. Yeah, Nuts. I'd love too."

"You too, Rip. Show us some of those Kung Fu moves. *Hi-ya*!" He thrust out a palm.

"Sure. Thanks Nuts. See you there."

"Great!" He clubbed them both on the shoulder. "*Go Blufftoppers!*" He hauled an arm around Anita, who cracked her gum. They turned and plowed down the hall.

Ever since their brawl with the Logan Disco boys, word had gotten around school. The gossip had spread, magnifying the incident into an outright bloody war for the pride and dignity of the team, earning the respect of all the jocks. While that simply wasn't true, none of them were above basking in its glory.

Keith stared after their retreat. "Fucking Barbie and Ken."

" Don't know how you do it." Rip shook his head.

"Just playing the game, my friend."

The parking lot was a blaze of activity, inevitable fallout from the scheduling confusion. People congregating in groups, around and inside cars, smoking, laughing, drinking, muted beats of conflicting stereos lapping over one another. They spotted Slick's Blazer and made a B-line for it.

He was asleep behind the wheel, stereo vibrating the closed cab. Keith slapped the door. Slick jumped, considered them with bleary eyes, and rolled the window down, releasing the chorus of Boston's 'More Than a Feeling'.

"Hey." Rubbing his face, he bent and turned the music down.

"What's happenin?" Keith leaned on the handle.

"Just catching a few Z's. This new schedule sucks."

"No doubt. Hey, you don't know where Rip and I could, maybe, score a bag, do you?"

"Well, that's on everyone's mind these days, isn't it? I haven't been high in so long, been dreaming again like crazy. Nightmares too." He yawned. "What I wouldn't do for a little smoke."

The rumble of a familiar subsonic downshift detonated from the driveway as Marlon's 'Cuda rolled into the lot, prompting a small crowd to gather around it. Slick turned to Keith, who turned to Rip.

"Our best bet yet." He sighed.

They picked their way through the gathering. Marlon, sporting mirrored aviators and a thin goatee, slid up onto the window-sill, Zippo'd a Marlboro, and held palms out to his audience.

"Please, people. While I respect your patronage, I must ask you to be patient. This terrible drought continues, and I'm afraid I'm empty handed today." A collective groan spread throughout the throng. "Just a social visit today. You have my word though, that when it does break, you will hear about it from me first."

Rip and Keith weaved their way to the car. Andrea poked her head out the passenger window. "Hey Keith. Hey Rip, how you doin'?"

"Great Andrea, how about you?"

"Same." She offered a wide smile.

Marlon pointed pistol fingers at them. "Just the two muchachos I wanted to see. Step up to my office." He slid back inside.

They worked their way around the wedge of the hood and Rip leaned over the driver's side door. "So, that speech you just delivered true?"

"Mostly, yeah. Big Federal crackdown at the border." He shook his head sadly. "Not a bud to be found between here and the Rio Grande. But fear not." Tipping the shades up, he cracked a smile, the whites of his eyes laced with tiny red veins. "Got a special treat for special customers."

He presented a partially unwrapped square of foil that held a small sand-colored cube in its center. "Blond Lebanese hash. *Suh-weeet.*"

"Hash?" Keith bowed closer.

"Yup. Got a brick. Seven bucks a gram."

"How much in a gram?"

"You're lookin' at one."

"Shit. That's all?" Rip frowned. "That'll hardly fill a bowl."

"It's *hash*, man. A little goes a long way." He held up a small wood pipe with a few crumbs of the stuff sitting on the blackened screen of the bowl. "Be my guest. Take a taste."

A wave of agitation rippled over the parking lot and Keith jumped up. "Christ! It's the principal!"

Marlon made the objects in his hands disappear, leaned across Andrea, levering his seat forward. "Get in!"

They dove into the rear seat. Rip relived a brief nostalgia of the time he'd spent back here with Viv, until his head was filled with the reverberation of the engine within the cab, then the great angry yowl of it as they spun a perfect one-eighty, launching off into the park.

Later, Rip followed Keith down the hill back to the parking lot, fingering the small package of foil in his pocket. He resigned himself to the fact that he might've been ripped off. They'd each taken two lung-searing hits of the strangely sweet substance, and despite Marlon's assurances that the effects were delayed, was having serious doubts, when he found himself in the grip of a brain spinning body rush. The carpet of fallen leaves beneath their feet became alarmingly phosphorescent, bare branches above writhing, reaching into a cobalt blue sky, flexing frondless skeleton fingers at passing underbellies of fat clouds. The school building beyond was transformed into a startling array of abstracted angular forms.

"Whoa, I didn't think, …I mean, I thought, …" He was cut short by the sight of Keith's face transforming into a frog-like creature.

"Trippy, man." Said the toad face. "Good shit."

"Aw, fuck, …" He tried to turn away, but was transfixed by his friend's visage. "…I still got art class."

"So?" An enmity shone behind those eyes, and panic ignited within Rip. Had Keith heard about him and Stephanie? It was only that one time, and he'd never alluded knowing anything about it before, but this was a truly shifty creature he was dealing with. Malicious like his father, he'd truly enjoy a protracted game of cat and mouse.

No, dammit! It was just the drugs.

"Shit Keith, I think I got The Fear."

"The fear?"

"Yeah man, I can't do this. I can't go to class like this."

"Hah!" The toad smacked rubbery lips. "It's just art class. Hell, you're the star pupil."

"Well, …"

"Jesus, …" The face leaned closer. "Your eyes are really wasted."

"What?" He cringed from the sight of Keith's own blasted orbs.

"Here." Pulling out a pair of sunglasses, he slipped them over Rip's ears. "Better."

The polarized glass was instantly soothing, like a filter to a quieter, saner world.

The hallway kept stretching out, increasing in depth. Identical doors and lockers rolled past, and it seemed like the students were starting to repeat themselves. He was becoming concerned about being late for class, when the doorway to the art studio appeared. It jerked open and Mr. Kelp, the instructor, stood looking out, along with the rest of the class.

With a full beard, mop of long brown hair, and the demeanor of an ex beatnik, Mr. Kelp was contrary to the rest of the faculty, the only teacher with whose relationship Rip was on a more or less informal basis.

"Well, *well*, mister Ripley, good of you to join us. Care to come in?"

"Ah, yeah, sorry Kelp. New schedule, you know."

"Yeah, yeah, get in." He beckoned. "And take those glasses off."

"Can't I just, …"

The teacher pulled them off his face and leaned in with alarm. "Oh, *Christ*. Great." He turned to the crowded room. "Well people, Rip has come to class high today."

"Aww, c'mon Ron, give me a break." The class came alive with giggles and whispers.

"No, no, sit down. That is, if you can find your seat."

Sighing, he slumped down into a chair next to Cheryl. She twirled a strand of blond hair, suddenly leaning into him with big blue eyes. "Wow, you *are* baked. Where you find it?"

"Later."

"Class, we'll have a little experiment today, that Rip can helpfully assist us with." Mr. Kelp strode to the center of the room, gesturing in his direction. "Drugs and art. Help or hindrance?"

Taking up his drawing pad, Rip twiddled the newly sharpened number-two pencil in his fingers and considered the blank page. It was impossible to concentrate at first, conscious of all the attention being paid him, but he was seized by a vision complete in clarity and detail, a scenario that came from somewhere deep without. His fingers flew over the paper, illustrating the figure of a destitute astronaut stranded on an alien world, alone in front of his ruined craft, extraordinary creatures frolicking in the air above, over strange mountain ranges, beneath unknown moons. Rip could see the play of light on folds of fabric, the texture of stone and metal, the graceful arc of a tail slipping through the air. He could see the desolation on the star traveler's face, and when he was finally finished, he was alone in class. Mr. Kelp stood behind him, arms crossed, shaking his head.

"Well shit. I guess *that* backfired on me."

*   *   *   *

The train rolled slowly, blocking their route to school.

"We're gonna' be late our first day back." Randy whined.

"It's not going that fast." Curt tossed a rock that banged off a passing flat-car.

"Think we can climb through it?" Dart looked at the squealing steel wheels and tried not to picture what they would do to his limbs.

"Sure. Thing could be miles long."

They walked up the tracks against its course for a few hundred feet before turning. Curt readied himself for a run at the nearest boxcar when Dart yanked him back.

"Lookout!"

The remains of a small tree cart-wheeled past on the end of a long chain, narrowly missing them.

"What the hell was that?" Curt watched its retreat.

"A tree? C'mon, let's go." Matching the train's speed, they grabbed the handrail and swung up onto the walkway, threaded through to the other side and dropped down in front of the flashing signals.

"Piece of cake." Wiping grime onto his jacket, Curt led them up the street. A bright noon sun burned the sky, and they walked beneath the looming portico of the old, abandoned Pickle Factory. The warehouse had been constructed like a castle, with massive blocks of limestone. Pondering the rows of boarded-over windows, Dart was reminded of the incarcerated German prisoners here, obliged to bottle pickles for their sworn enemies for the duration of World War Two. He imagined their ghosts still wandering the deserted hallways.

They climbed a steep feeder-road that brought them to the highway. Crossing it, they passed a Kwik Trip bustling with loitering students. Randy hungrily scrutinized the hot dogs, potato chips, sodas, and slushies that students were snacking on.

Cutting through the park, they approached the High School from the rear, pausing before the old building, a four-story red brick structure flanked by ancient gnarled oaks, towering over the grassy hill it sat upon. The architecture was traditional academia, wide stone steps leading up to big double doors beneath a granite arch archaically inscribed with the word 'Education'.

"Now that looks like a school." Dart shifted his book bag to the other shoulder.

"For sure, not like that rat-trap Middle School. Ever been inside?"

"Nope. You?"

"Nah." They turned to Randy, who shook his head.

"Well, …"Dart consulted a sheet of paper he pulled from his bag. "…it says that orientation is in the gymnasium at noon." He pointed to an adjacent building; newer, tall and blocky, lined with high windows beneath an arched roof. "That would be my guess."

"Mine too."

Crossing the sloping lawn, they rounded the rear corner of the gym building and stopped.

Randy blinked. "Wow."

Curt slapped Dart in the arm. "You ever see anything like that?"

"Not at a school."

The parking lot was pandemonium.

The day had ended early for the entire High School, and it was one big party. People were scattered everywhere, knotting in throngs, dressed in letter jackets, band uniforms, leather jackets, and cheerleader uniforms. The rattle of muscle car engines, pulse of music, prattle of laughter, and thrum of conversations created a susurrus that clung over the crowd, beneath a lazy haze from hundreds of simultaneous cigarettes.

One of the baddest cars Dart had ever seen, camouflaged completely in matte-black, opened up with an ear-splitting roar. It spun tires all the way out of the park, leaving a rolling blueblack cloud, and a cheering group gathered about a four-wheel-drive behind. Dart recognized three of them. Rip turned to Moe, pointing at them. They each looked back, waved, Rip rapidly hooking his arm, yelling.

"Hey Dart! Come on over!"

Randy took a half-step back. "Oh shit."

Dart waved. "It's cool, I know 'em. C'mon."

He led the other two through the labyrinth of bodies and automobiles, ducking once as a football came sailing overhead. He'd just reestablished a sightline with the elevated off-road vehicle, when their way was suddenly blocked by three large shadows.

"Well, hello there, fuzzy. Been a coon's age, eh?"

Ice water ran through his veins at the sound of Brad's voice.

Timmy stepped closer. "And this is, …I remember. Coitus!"

"Ha, ha!" Duncan sniggered. "More like coitus interruptus!"

Timmy yelped like a hyena.

Curt dropped his eyes. "It's *Curt*."

"Shut up." Brad shifted his dead gaze. "And who's this?"

"Ra, ra, ra, …"

"Ra, ra, …" Duncan imitated. "…retard!"

Timmy shrieked again. "Retard! That's your new name."

"Hey? What's going on here?"

Rip, Moe, and Slick were suddenly standing behind the bullies. Dart had a brief moment of hope, of a chance for rescue, but Brad merely half turned back in annoyance.

"This isn't any of your business." Though separated by four grades, Brad and his gang of troglodytes actually outsized the seniors, bolstering their arrogance.

"Yeah, this is Middle School business." Timmy barked.

Rip turned to Moe. "He says this is Middle School business."

Moe shifted to the right, tugged at the brim of his John Deere hat, and threw a cigarette butt onto the asphalt. "Last I looked, this here wasn't Middle School."

Slick giggled, flanking to the left as Rip crossed his arms. "True. And Dart there is a friend of ours. So any business of his is business of ours." He nodded at Dart. "These guys giving you shit?"

With Brad's hostile gaze boring into him, Dart glanced nervously around at his two friends. "We, ...we can take care of ourselves."

"See?" Duncan thrust his chest out, hands on hips.

"She-ya, ..." Moe stepped nose to nose with Brad. "...yer' all twice as big as them kids. Ain't a fair fight."

Sensing perhaps for the first time a real threat, Brad's breath started an audible rasping between his pudgy lips, but his glare never wavered from Moe's. Dart could see the way that Slick and Rip had covertly maneuvered themselves to advantageous offensive positions, the tension between them palpable enough to start drawing a small crowd.

Randy suddenly blurted out. "You can't hit him! He's got hemophilia!"

"Homo-*what*?"

"He's right!" Brad blubbered, taking an infuriated step backward. "You can't touch me! If you hurt me, I'll have to go to the hospital! And then you'll go to jail, and my parents will sue you and your parents for everything they'll ever have!"

"What? You mean like this?" Moe's fist shot out to his side and caught Duncan hard in the stomach, folding him instantly to the ground. A cheer of approval rose from the gathering.

Brad went a whiter shade of pale and took another step back. Slick grinned at Timmy, who shrank back. Rip clapped Moe on the shoulder.

"Real shame about that bleeding disease, lardass, but you probably shouldn't have told my friend here about it."

"Wh, …why not?"

"Yeah, you see, Moe here is kinda' like a big cat." Slick started a slow advance the others followed. "He's real curious."

Taking another step forward, Rip chuckled. "Hell, he'd just as soon beat you to watch you blow up like a balloon."

Lighting a cigarette, Moe considered this. "Might be kinda' fun." Then he stepped on Duncan's hand, who'd been attempting to pull himself off the pavement, causing him to shriek and stumble back to his friends as they withdrew through a parting in the crowd.

"You can't do this to me!" But Brad was crying, and real fear was in all their eyes.

"Done and done, asshole." Now Dart could detect sincere rage in Rip's voice. "And if I *ever* see or hear you picking on anyone or anything again, I will hunt you down, and I will make you wish that you were never fucking born. Do you fucking understand me?"

Dart, Curt, and Randy looked on with sheer wonder as Brad whinnied once like a horse, burying face in hands, and ran off trailing his defeated posse.

Slick laughed at their retreat, turning to Rip. "Damn. Didn't know you had it in you."

"Yeah." Moe scowled over his cigarette. "Almost had me scared."

" Just really hate fucking bullies." He turned. " You guys alright?"

"Uh, yeah." Dart was abruptly aware of the dispersing onlookers. "Thanks."

"No prob. Us River Rats gotta' watch out for each other." Rip spat.

"Well, that's my good deed for the day." Slick strolled back to the truck. "Gonna' give it a soundtrack." He disappeared into the cab, and Deep Purple's 'Space Truckin' erupted from a pair of speakers stacked on the roof.

""C'mon Rip." Moe jerked his head. "Got the whole day ahead of us. You know, I might just get used to this new schedule after all."

"Yeah, fuck, let's hit the river." He followed Moe, then turned back and spread his arms to Dart, Curt, and Randy.

"Welcome to Central High!"

*   *   *   *

That Saturday, he sat with a death grip on the passenger seat of the Jensen Healy, as his father maneuvered the hairpin turns that coiled up the steep slope of the bluff. Identifying the odor of alcohol on his breath, Dart nervously considered the sheer wooded drop into the abyss on their left, guarded only by a frail fence of timber that was interspersed with telltale gaps. His father worked the transmission up and down, tires audibly biting into the asphalt at each curve.

Possibly noticing his anxiety, he turned to Dart and laughed. "Relax, kiddo. The car was made for this. Besides, I can't wait to get back. Got a surprise for you."

They were returning from the library, his favorite place to visit aside from the river, and a frequent stop on their weekends together. Earlier that summer he had accidentally happened upon a book titled 'Make Your Own Animated Movies', and it concerned a class being taught to children on the east coast called the 'Yellow Ball Workshop'. The book outlined the basic principals of animation in terms that was not only understandable, but fascinating. Dart was hooked. He'd repeatedly checked the book out, memorizing facts, techniques, and even the pictures.

It was actually quite simple, when whittled down to the basics. Film was just a series of pictures, flashed one after the other, with incremental movements between each one. The real magic wasn't in the technology, but in the brain. A phenomenon known as persistence of vision, a coping mechanism the mind used to give the world around it continuity, stitched the images together into fluid movement. Pioneer filmmakers had studied this, determining that anything less than sixteen images per second resulted in unwanted flickering and stuttering, so a worldwide standard had been set at twenty-four frames a second, ensuring a smooth, realistic projection. Eighteen frames per second had been adopted for home movies, allowing the slight flicker as a trade-off for consumer cost savings.

There were three different categories; cell animation, basically of the cartoon variety; cut-out animation, of the Monty Python variety; and his favorite; three dimensional animation. This was the style that had brought to life the monsters in the film he'd seen the night of the UFO.

Breathing a secret sigh of relief as they topped the ridge and turned onto the straightaway, Dart pulled his backpack from the rear seat, feeling the book inside. They approached the forlorn profile of the old farmhouse, leaning over the meadow, pulling into the dirt lot. They were greeted by a pair of mangy, agitated mutts, yelping against the end of their chains.

"Goddamn noisy dogs." Pulling himself up and out of the tiny roadster, his father tracked an unsteady approach to the miniature trunk, dragging out two suspiciously clinking bags of groceries. "I keep complaining to the owner about them, but he does nothing. One of these days they might get accidentally shot."

Dart thought that shooting the landlord's dogs might be counterproductive in any number of ways, but refrained from saying anything that might provoke his old man, this far along on his drink.

Following his careful progress up the rickety staircase, they entered through the kitchen. His father placed the bags on the counter and pointed to the living room. "It's in there."

He saw it immediately in the corner, fastened to a tripod, surrounded by the yellow cones of two Smith Victor movie lights on stands. A Bolex super-8 movie camera. It looked just like one of the phasers from Star Trek on TV.

"Wow!"

"Now don't get the wrong idea." His father leaned in the doorway, a mix already in hand. "It's on extended loan from the Technical Institute, where I just got a part-time teaching job."

"Does it do single frame?"

"Supposed to."

"Wow." He approached the camera with reverence, touching its smooth metallic contours, bending to peer through the eyepiece. There were three knobs on the right side. Dart switched the first to 'on' and pulled the trigger. The camera purred like a kitten. The second said FPS, which he knew from the book to mean 'frames per second', and had stopping points at the numbers 24, 18, and 1. Turning the switch to single frame, he pressed the trigger. The camera produced a click. The third said exposure, and had a setting for automatic, thank God.

"You like it?"

"It's perfect. Thanks."

"Here's the instructions. Oh, and I got you a roll of film." He handed over a booklet and a small fluorescent yellow and red box, Kodak logo on the front. "It's Kodachrome. Will that work?"

"I, …I don't know. Probably. Thanks again, Dad. I'm going to make an animation today." Opening the box, he found a foil pack inside that issued a faint chemical odor as it was breeched. It held a black plastic magazine sealed against light, save for a small window that exposed a frail beige thread of film lined with delicate sprocket holes.

The door of the film compartment released smoothly and accepted the magazine snugly. He snapped it shut, looking up. "I guess I'm ready to shoot."

Chuckling to himself, his father moved through the room, swirling the glass, chattering the ice inside. He lowered into the worn, overstuffed folds of the Lay-Zee-Boy before the TV, playing the news. The sound was off and the stereo was on, Harry Chapin delivering the heart-wrenching chorus of 'Cat's in the Cradle'.

"Go get 'em, kiddo."

Finding the Tyrannosaur he'd sculpted the previous summer, he determined it sophisticated enough to be the movie's star. He picked it free of dust bunny's, smoothing over damaged nicks in its skin, and set about sculpting its nemesis, depicted so frequently in dinosaur art; the plant-eating Triceratops. This took about an hour, the most difficult detail being its three horns, which he finally decided to carve out of balsa wood, after his attempts in modeling clay failed to hold their form.

The sun was slanting low through the windows as he started on the set, the Carpenters crooning 'Close To You' over the stereo. Dart reflected on his old man's despondent concession to current pop music, as it dissolved into 'If You leave Me Now', by Chicago. Between mixes, his father would stop by to check on the progress, but as the day, then the evening wore on, he withdrew into his routine stupor.

The base of the diorama was a sheet of leftover Styrofoam with sand appliqué via a liberal smearing of Elmer's Glue. The forest consisted of parts of a plastic plant pushed into the foam, abstractly bolstered by pieces of wax fruit his father kept in a bowl on the dining room table. The background was a green curtain he hung from the ceiling. Placing star and co-star in their respective spots on the stage, Dart framed the shot through the viewfinder, locked down the tripod, set up the lights, plugged them in, turned them on, and blew a fuse.

The TV, stereo, and all the lights in the living room died, but his father had passed out and didn't stir. The wiring in the place was old, and he knew the routine. He grabbed a fuse from a box in the kitchen cabinet, the flashlight beside it, and exited out into a night filled with the chorus of crickets. Picking his way down the staircase to the basement, he located the fuse box and replaced the blown one, remembering to bring up an extra extension cord to split power to another circuit.

The appliances came back to life, bathing the scene in mock daylight. Dart positioned the two Plasticine figures facing each other, the opening showdown of an epic battle that resonated throughout prehistory and through his mind, as he lowered the angle, repositioned the tri-pod, fine-tuned the focus, and pulled the trigger.

The camera clicked, capturing one eighteenth of a second.

Now what?

He tried to imagine the two creatures as alive, moving on their own, the T-rex balancing on two legs, Triceratops on four, the curl of their tails, necks craning, jaws snapping, all moving at once, but all at different speeds.

This was going to be quite a bit more complicated than he'd anticipated.

Pantomiming the movements he wanted to create, he'd try timing them in his head, kneel down, push and bend limbs into place, and expose a frame. After an hour he noticed that the figures had started melting from the heat of the lights, and had to kill them for about ten minutes to cool down the combatants sufficiently to work with again. Accepting this as part of the process, he kept the routine up for the next eight hours, until daylight began showing in the east. He was right back at it after breakfast. By the end of the weekend he had taken ninety-six frames.

A little over five seconds.

*   *   *   *

That Sunday Rip was back out on the river, due to a freakish heat wave, unusual for the end of November. It was nearly sixty degrees, and because most boats had already been stored for the winter, he practically had the waterway to himself. The wind was out, kicking up a hard chop that snapped at the Alumacraft's hull with a booming drumbeat. He spotted a small beach in the back sweep of a cove that bordered some broad marshland, steering for it, seeking shelter from the breeze.

Running the nose up onto the shore, he shut down, plucked a small, chambered pipe from the bow hold, and jumped to the sun-warmed sand.

He wasn't surprised to find it empty. The hash hadn't lasted long, but the chamber was still full from when he'd first bought it last summer, loaded with a small portion of his virginal dope purchase. If chamber-weed was the holy grail of stoner heaven, then this stuff was definitely Holy Trinity territory, having been super-charged by the hash.

He'd been saving it for a special occasion, and this fine, warm evening on the edge of winter seemed to merit its consumption. It took two pair of pliers to break the seal. He carefully extracted a compacted clump of resin-coated mulch, pinching out just enough for a couple of hits, the remainder prudently stored in a sinker-box

Re-assembling the pipe, he heard Dart's motor and saw the small flat jumping white-caps, driver's arm up in greeting. Rip waved back, motioned him in. The small John Boat swung to and rolled in, settling its bow onto the beach. Dart, his hair blown into tumbleweed snarls, gave the motor an extra boost, pushing further up-shore.

"Ahoy there, River Rat." Rip held up the pipe. "Just in time."

Smiling, Dart dropped off the gunwale. "Perfect. My brain could use a rest. After this weekend, it feels like it's about to explode."

"Yeah?" Rip searched his pockets for a lighter, found one. "What's blowin' your fuse?"

Dart watched him carefully draw flame over the bowl, cap it with the lighter against the breeze, and hand it over. "Actually, I was making my first animated movie. Or at least starting one. Barely."

"No 'chit?" He appeared genuinely surprised. Smoke leaked out his nostrils.

Dart mimicked Rip's actions. Nodding, handing back the pipe, he was thinking how much smoother and better tasting this weed was when it suddenly tore into his lungs, not burning like the ditch-weed, but expanding greatly, causing a searing series of coughs. His eyes leaked.

Releasing his hit in a faint plume, Rip leaned over. "You all right there? Gotta' cough to get off, y'know?" he giggled. "Guess I shoulda' warned you that this is some kickin' chamber weed."

"Chamber weed?" Dart hacked. "What the hell is that?"

"You'll find out. Tell me about this movie you're making."

So Dart started talking about finding the book, the camera, and how his father had accessed it, of sculpting the tyrannosaur, when he started detecting a subtle but growing shift in all things around him. Trailing off, he observed the strange way the setting sun cut from the south in its low winter arc, raking coulees wrinkling into the bluffs beyond the far shoreline. How it ignited swirling airborne flotsam, a flowing ghost river above the river, molding clouds, constantly shifting ephemera. He started to feel a blossoming euphoria, a primal joy he hadn't felt since he was very young.

"It's like Christmas day." He heard himself say.

Rip let out a hearty laugh. "Yeah, this is good. This is very good."

But when Dart looked back at Rip, he felt shock, shook his head. *No way.* He looked back and rubbed his eyes, but the illusion remained.

No friggin' way.

Pointing feebly, Dart croaked. "You're transparent."

"Whaaat?" The smile was still on Rip's face, but through it, Dart could see the naked limbs of the woods and sky beyond.

"I can see right through you."

"You are fucking high."

"No... Well, yeah I am, but, ..." Circling slowly, he watched the bluffs, then the river, move through Rip's body. " *This*, ...this is not going away."

"Man, you are wasted."

"It's really starting to freak me out."

"*You're* starting to freak me out." Rip's pallor had gone ashen, but that could have been his own boat, now shining through him.

"No man, you gotta' see this. You got a mirror?"

"A mirror? We're on the river!"

They each paused a beat, then raced to the shoreline to peer down at their reflections. The water in the cove was very calm.

"*Oh, fuck*. You seeing this?"

Dart couldn't breathe. "I only see myself."

"I'm only seeing you, too."

"Where are you?"

"I'm right fucking here!"

"But you're not there."

"I know! It's impossible!"

"This is so Twilight Zone."

"*Fuck*! What's it mean!" Kicking at the reflection, he and Dart were drenched in the backsplash, and as it coalesced, two shocked and dripping faces looked back up from the water.

Dart took in a grateful breath. "Good. You're back."

"Jesus." Slapping away the moisture on his face, Rip trudged back up the bank and sat in the sand. "The power of suggestion."

"Sorry." Dart moved up and leaned against his bow. "I've never really been this high before."

"No prob." Chuckling, Rip shook his head. "Still somewhat of an amateur myself. *Hey*, y'know, I saw that run you did between the I-90 pylons."

"Oh yeah? *Cool*. Glad somebody beside Curt checked it."

"Your buddy who chickened out?"

"Yup."

"Man, that was ballsy. Was it easy?"

"Actually, it was."

"Thought so."

"Well, I *was* high." He shook his head. "Or thought I was."

"That where you got the idea?"

"Hmm? Oh, nah… my friends saw Billy Ray pull it off this summer. We dared each other to try it."

"Billy Ray?"

"Yeah."

"You saw Billy Ray?"

"Not me. My friends were the ones that saw him."

"Billy Ray. Jesus." Rip pulled two beers from the Styrofoam cooler in his boat. "Adult beverage?"

"Please. My mouth feels all pasty."

"To the rescue. Special Ex will cut right through that cotton mouth."

Dart braced for a harsh, unpleasant flavor, but was surprised to find the beer actually complemented the pot's aftertaste. He thirstily gulped half it down.

"Yeah... better!" He belched, giggled, feeling far more in tune with the situation now, mind beginning to meander. "Hey ...Rip...you believe in UFO's?"

Rip considered. "You mean like, flying saucers, aliens, abductions, Chariots of the Gods, that kind of shit?"

"Well, ...yeah, I guess."

"I suppose anything's possible." Pausing for another drink. "Though, you know, technically a UFO is unidentified. Just means they don't know what it is. Only thing I'm sure of is that there's a lot of nut cases out there that'll say or do anything for attention."

Dart thought of Brad and his psycho crew. "No doubt about that. What about Bigfoot? The Loch Ness Monster?"

"Yeti? The Abominable Snow Man?" Rip sighed. The last reddened rays of the sun caught him in profile. "You know, I guess I'd like to believe in all those things. It seems like he world used to be such an infinite place. It had so many secrets, magic, mystery, and myth. But the crappy truth is that there are people everywhere now, all connected by satellites, phones, planes, ships, submarines, and if there was a Lost World, a forgotten tribe of missing links, a surviving deep sea dinosaur, or even a squadron of aliens cruising the stratosphere, someone woulda' filmed it, shot it, caught it, killed it, stuffed it, blown it up, or built a Holiday Inn on it. That's what I think."

Dart nodded and caught another thought. "What about the soft-shelled turtle?"

"Soft-shelled turtles?"

"Yeah."

"Freaky things. Had one bite me once. I was used to picking turtles up from the ass, but when I did this one, he twisted that beaky head of his all around, bent that rubbery shell, nipped me in the finger."

"Well...when's the last time you saw one?"

"I don't know. Been awhile, I guess."

"Remember how they used to be everywhere, especially on hot, sunny days? Always sunning on the beaches, but they were really hard to see, 'cause they were colored exactly like the sand."

"Yeah, you'd be walking along, and all of a sudden, part of the beach just gets up and wades into the water. Their eggs, too. Used to find nests of 'em everywhere."

"I don't think I've seen a single one in over two years."

Rip stood and scratched his head. "You know, I think you might be right."

"Was afraid of that."

"Why. What do you think happened to them?"

"Pollution."

Nodding, Rip started pacing. "Yeah, that's definitely getting worse. You see that foamy shit that's started to form on the back eddies? Toxic runoff. Also heard the Twin Cities is dumping raw sewage into the Mississippi now."

Dart was shocked. "They can't *do* that!"

"Can and do. Wish we could turn the river in reverse and run all that shit right back up their assholes. " He paused. "But I still see snappers and painters everywhere. Why wouldn't *they* be affected?"

"I think maybe that the soft-shell is specialized. Probably more sensitive to environment changes."

"Huh." The sun had dropped below the bluff range. The wind slacked, light of the golden hour shimmering briefly, fading. "You know, if you're right, then it's just fucking sad."

"I know. And it's only the beginning."

"Shit." Turning to the darkened marsh, Rip frowned. "Hey, you know if it's a full moon tonight?"

"Can't be. Was one a week ago."

"Then tell me what the hell that is?" Rip pointed to a soft pulse of illumination coming from beyond the woods. Something about the sight made the hair on Dart's hackles quill.

Approaching slowly, they topped the gradient of the small sandbar, and were struck into dumbfounded silence and immobility by the sight that greeted them. For over a full minute, neither could process a coherent thought adequately to orate or ambulate, until Rip just managed to mutter; "You've gotta' be fucking shitting me."

Hovering, *floating* really, above the darkening reaches of the marshland, burning with a soft opalescent radiation, was a vast and silent disk, a flying saucer, straight out of pulp science fiction.

* * * *

Early the following morning, Dart walked the road, escorting his sister and her two friends to the school bus stop a quarter mile away, down on the corner. It was still unusually warm, in the upper forties, and they were dressed in light jackets, hats, and gloves. The air was absolutely still, practically pressurized. Had he looked up, Dart might have witnessed something that would have pulled him from his thoughts, but his mind was churning.

Sleep last night had not been an option.

Not the greatest way to begin a school week, but he kept seeing the UFO, no, *flying saucer*, lifting, deliberate and magnificent, as if acknowledging their presence, drifting up soundlessly, dwindling to become another star in the evening sky. He couldn't help snickering to himself in disbelief at the memory.

"What'cha laughing at, Dart?"

"Huh?" Gazing down, he saw that Stacey was trading Wacky Packages with her friend Sheila from across the street, a Pell Mell sticker for a Weakies. Not a bad deal, a distant part of his mind related.

"Are you laughing at the funny clouds?"

Looking up to where she was pointing, he stopped. Overhead, wispy cirrus were racing with uncanny speed, nearly impossible considering that particular phenomenon resided in the upper reaches of the atmosphere. Even stranger still, when you considered the fact that there wasn't a breath of wind in the air.

An eerie foreboding crept over him, followed by thoughts redolent of last night; am I hallucinating this?

He turned in time to see the bluff range across the river disappear. Some sort of fog bank was moving in, except now he could see that it wasn't fog and it was coming in fast, boiling like a tidal wave, stretching from the north horizon to the south. As he watched, the airport evaporated.

He didn't like the look of this at all.

They were out in the open, exposed, on a thin peninsula of land surrounded by canals, the houses behind them, the bus stop ahead. The kids were stopped with him, oblivious, arguing over a Mountain Goo card. The words 'point of no return' flashed in his head.

"OK guys, listen up." They stopped and turned, responding to his grown-up tone. "We're all going to turn around and go back home."

Sheila and the little boy squealed with delight, but Stacey scowled, confused. "What about the bus and school?"

"Never mind that, Stace, we got to get moving. C'mon!"

They turned and witnessed the far shore vanish.

A collective gasp escaped the kids, Stacey's frightened voice crying. "What's that cloud coming, Dart?"

"Run! Run to your houses! Go!" He pushed Stacey, Sheila, and the little boy, Everett ahead of him, and they ran as in a nightmare, the street stretching out ahead of them like an elastic band. The children were whimpering now, instinctively sensing peril. As the debris cloud rose over the neighborhood, they reached Everett's house, Dart basically wrenching the door open, shoving him in, slamming it shut, and running back down the street.

He and Stacey were dashing from Sheila's porch to their home, only half a block away, when the Bradley house at the end of the street was gobbled up.

"Hold my hand!"

They were heading straight into the thing, dull roar finally reaching his ears. He watched in terror as houses were swallowed like vanishing domino's, and when theirs disappeared Stacey shrieked, so he picked her up into his arms, telling her to shut her eyes, and they were struck by a wall of wind so fierce that if not for their collective weight they'd probably have been thrown back. They were sandblasted by grit, branches, and other shrapnel it bore, but far worse was the cold, a cold he'd never experienced before, the cold of deep space. It burned painfully from the wind as Stacey bawled into his ear and he staggered down the street holding her, the cold biting into his eyes, his nose and his fingers.

Reaching the front door, his hands were almost too numb to work the knob. Their mother nearly dropped the glass of sherry she was holding as they burst into the living room. Gordon Lightfoot mourned the 'Edmond Fitzgerald' from the Magnavox in the corner.

"Why aren't you at sch, …?" But then her eyes went wild as Stacey wailed and held up fingers that were nearly blue, and Dart started uncontrollably shivering, eyes and nose running freely.

Rushing them to the bathroom, filling the tub with lukewarm water, she had them remove gloves, shoes, and socks, and immerse their hands and feet, a tried and true folk remedy. Dart felt the painful pins and needles of circulation returning to his extremities. His sister continued to blubber uncontrollably. They'd each endured worse cases of frostbite in the past, so he guessed she was reacting to the frightening force of nature that they had just been witness to. When finally she'd settled down, his mother stood, relief and concern on her face.

"I'll go call your schools. You two are staying home today."

The furnace growled to life. Dart dried up, went downstairs and peered out the sliding glass doors at a clear, bright, sunny morning. However impossible, it appeared that the unseasonable weather had returned. Then he heard his mother's gasp come from the kitchen.

"Oh my God."

"What is it?" He ran to her side.

"The thermometer, …"

Leaning over the counter, he peered out the window at the gauge that was mounted outside, and was amazed that the mercury stood below zero, *Fahrenheit*, and further shocked to actually see it still dropping. The sill near his face sighed a chilly breath.

"It's gonna' freeze fast. I've got to get the boat out of the river."

"Dress for deep winter."

"I know, Ma." Digging into the far reaches of the hallway closet, he unearthed his blue snowmobile suit with the hood, moon boots, and snowmobile gloves.

It was with the odd sensation of an astronaut breeching an airlock that he stepped back out the front door into the peculiarly bright sunlight. The first breath he took in froze his lungs, and he remembered to warm it over his tongue first, exhaling a white cumulous cloud that hung in the cryogenic morning. An approaching turbojet passed overhead, crackling thunderously loud and close. Dart heard every aural detail the engines emitted, recalling this was because in such extremely cold air, molecules were packed closer together, acting more as a liquid at relaying sounds. After the plane had touched-down, and the terrifying atmospheric shredding of the air-brakes had faded, a hush cocooned the neighborhood, frozen from the familiar sounds of the river and trees. The air about him glowed, refracting swirling little prismatic crystals. Incredibly, it seemed, as the temperature had bottomed out, dropping at least sixty degrees in less than ten minutes, the relative humidity in the atmosphere had flash frozen.

Turning the corner to the back of the house, and the river, he stepped onto the lawn. It crackled and broke, like a pointed latticework of ice. No stranger to extreme cold, he still was mystified by how severely out of context it was without the snow covering of deep winter.

Dart wandered over the terrain of an alien planet.

6

CHRYSTAL BEACH

The 'Rogue Alberta Clipper', as the local Channel 8 meteorologists had christened it, held the tri-state area in its icy grasp for nearly a week, and was talk of the region for far longer. It had claimed a total of seven known fatalities, most of them elderly, lured out by the promising warmth, underdressed and unaware, but the true and uncounted casualties were the wildlife and livestock.

The arctic front had poured down from Canada, a dry sub-zero air mass that had stagnated long enough to lock the Mississippi in a rare phenomenon known as Black Ice. Without winds to stir, or snow to cover or mar it, the still, frigid air continued its freeze, and the surface of the entire river solidified as smooth as a mirror, and clear as glass.

On his ice skates, Dart stood in the center of the frozen waterway looking back at his house, feeling a bizarre dislocation at being here without being in his boat. He was glad it was Saturday. The school's split shift had seemed a sweet deal at first, being able to sleep in until almost noon, but with the waning winter sunlight, it was already dark long before six, when they finished, and the routine of coming home at night had become a bit of a depressing burden.

Weekends, he was usually at his father's, but he'd called earlier to cancel. While he was anxious to finish work on his animation, Dart found being home a welcome break.

Glancing down, he saw a sunfish that had been trapped belly-up near the surface. He chipped through the ice with the back of his blade, chopping a little hole in its stomach, exposing frosty pink intestines.

The ice was remarkably deep, nearly three feet, and held all host of curiosities in its invisible grip. He'd seen birds, a turtle, and even a cat trapped in their transparent tombs. The day following the Big Freeze, he'd spotted an extremely rare bald eagle diving repeatedly at a patch of thickening ice that held an unfortunate trio of mallards, still alive but trapped.

A low rumbling rolled beneath the river, accompanied by a warbling musical note, bizarrely similar to a whale song. A crack snapped a frosty blade through the ice before Dart with a gunshot report. The Mississippi had frozen high, and as the level dropped, its frozen surface was forced to constantly adjust. There was really no danger of breaking through, but the first time Dart had heard that unearthly sound, he'd nearly shit his pants. Now, he relished it.

The temperatures had gradually climbed back up into the more comfortable twenties, with it the promise of approaching snow, yielding a strong southern wind. Feeling the tug of it on his parka, he had an idea. Turning back to the breeze, he unzipped his coat, holding it wide open. The wind filled it like a sail, and he started to slip over the frictionless surface without needing to work the skates, gradually gaining momentum, until he was zipping along, riding smoothly within a capsule of the moving air.

It was just like boating without the boat, completely silent, except for the faint sluice of the blades as they cut over the silvery surface. Dart laughed to himself, giddy at the sensation, watching the channels and sandbars slide by like an over cranked movie reel. Rolling thunder rumbled beneath him again, and a ragged lip of ice popped up and caught the serrated tips of his figure skates, unceremoniously throwing Dart onto his stomach, where he slowly spun to a stop.

Falling on ice could be serious business. He carefully checked for cuts, sprains, or breaks. Finding none, he counted himself lucky, and deployed the sail-skate once again.

The wooded peninsula that bridged the spillway and .22 Beach to the north end of the airport was a curious sight. It had flooded over in the November rains, frozen over in the Big Freeze. When the river level had dropped, the ice followed suit, leaving neat, circular ice collars around every tree trunk and sapling that reached up through the water.

With a whoop, Dart charged into the organic labyrinth. Lapsing temporarily back to childhood, pretending he was a Mustang fighter plane in pursuit of its quarry, he zig-zagged his way through the obstacle course, skates slapping and rebounding off the ice's odd angles at reckless and dangerous speeds. He crouched to slip beneath large overhanging branches, sprung over lower ones, adrenaline and endorphins pumping a primitive pleasure. Rounding a final tree, he rasped to a side-stop, blades throwing up plumes of rime, and stood at the edge of Sunfish Lake's expanse, a vast mirrored dish, overlooked by the highway and train tracks. In its center stood the rise of Tomahawk Island.

Sail-skating towards it across the small lake, he could identify the boxy construction of their tree fort nestled in the upper limbs of a thick copse of cottonwoods, and something else as well; the tin tube of a smoke stack and the feathery plume of smoke it was venting. The overcast sky had gone dark and thick, and the first fat snowflakes of the year started to drift by, aloft on the wind.

He sailed to the island.

"Check out what Randy found in a ditch on Pickle Factory Road." Curt pointed to the battered stack of Playboy and Penthouse magazines that stood in a corner of the fort.

"The Playboy chicks are hot, but I like the ones in Penthouse." Randy hungrily licked his lips. "They got their beavers spread wide open."

Dart had his skates off and was comfortably warming his feet in front of the small tin stove. It gave off a pleasant amber glow that warmly illuminated the interior, a single room of about eight by twelve, and roughly five feet high, just low enough to prevent him from standing up. It was nearly bare, except for the stove in the center, a small stack of kindling in one corner, and the nudie magazines in the other. Someone, probably Curt, had insulated the cracks by stapling the walls floor-to-ceiling with newspapers.

Listening to the crackle-pop of the burning branches that sporadically spat sparks out mouth of the tiny stove, he mused that there might be a potential problem with that choice of material.

"Here, check one out." Randy tossed a Playboy in his lap as Curt busied himself with rolling a joint from the huge bag of ditchweed. Having had the real thing, Dart wasn't sure he wanted to go back to smoking the Wisco green, but he wasn't really sure that he wanted to be seeing any more flying saucers anytime soon either.

He thumbed through the magazine, gazing at the glossy pictures of the women. They were completely naked, provocatively baring those hidden parts that he so achingly wished to see beneath Sara's bikini. He felt a tingling in the back of his head, and a familiar stirring in his upper thighs. Turning the pages he came upon the image of a woman wearing only a yellow construction hat, her nude body slathered and shining in grease. She grasped an air-hammer between her legs, head thrown back, body arched in ecstasy, and some special effect, maybe a multiple exposure, had been applied to make it seem as if she were rapidly vibrating.

Within his long johns, he felt himself spring suddenly rock-hard. He was flooded with a sensation similar to when he witnessed Stephanie and Keith on the beach, but a hundred times more intense, and, thank God for the thermals, felt like he might've peed a little. Suppressing a gasp, his foot gave a little involuntary kick. He glanced up in panic, but no one had noticed; Curt busy spit-sealing the Zig Zag; Randy feeding twigs into the fire.

Swallowing, trying to control his breathing, wondering what had just happened, he threw the magazine back onto the pile. "Nice."

"Check out the Penthouse." Randy nodded into the fire. "Open beavers."

"Later maybe. Let me start that." Snatching the joint from Curt's fingers, he torched it with a burning twig, running the cherry a quarter way along its length before handing it back, to the astonishment of the other two. Holding it in, he really noticed how this stuff just tasted like burnt weeds compared to what Rip had shared, but it was a suitable distraction to the spot of dampness in his pants.

When it was spent, they all sat back against the walls, and Dart could swear he felt *something*, if not just a little mellower.

Randy turned suddenly to Dart. "Hey, why ain't you at you dad's? It's Saturday right?"

"He's sick or something. Cancelled."

Now Curt was looking at him. "What's the deal with your parents, anyway? Why'd they get divorced?"

"Yeah. They're the only ones I ever heard of being divorced. My old man says it's against our religion to get divorced."

Wincing a little every time the D word was uttered, he sighed. "I don't know. Long story. I guess Ted used to be my father's best friend."

Curt whistled. "No shit?"

Dart nodded.

"Harsh, man."

"Yeah." This was not mellowing at all. He needed to change the subject. "Hey, you guys going to the Christmas dance?"

"I thought they moved it to the roller skating rink cause of, you know, no school to hold it in?" Curt's eyes were red and squinty, and Dart thought of the phrase Rip had uttered: the power of suggestion.

"I know, but you can't really call it a Christmas skate, or a Christmas roll, can you?"

Randy started giggling in a whiny falsetto. "Christmas roll?"

"Christmas roll!" Curt barked laughter, and Dart joined in, helplessly, and it gained momentum until they were all in tears, bent over, holding sides, and when it passed, Curt snuffled, wiping his eyes. "Hell no. You?"

"Not me. What about you, Rand?"

"No to the roll." That got them going again for another few minutes. After finally lapsing into silence, Randy started feeding more twigs into the stove. Curt acquired a wistful expression.

"If you got the chance to wish for one single thing, anything you want, what would you wish for?"

"Only one?" Dart baited.

"Just one."

"I'd wish for a million more wishes."

Randy applauded, but Curt shook his head. "No fair."

"No? I don't know, what would you want?"

"I'd want to fly."

"Fly? Like in an airplane?"

"Nah, like a bird. Or better yet, like Superman. Just point your body, and PLOW! Like a rocket."

"Yeah, that's a good one."

Randy sat back. "I know what I'd wish for."

"What's that?"

"To be rich."

"That's a shocker." Dart scratched at a tangle in his hair. "I guess if I could have any single thing I wanted, right now I'd wish for a time machine."

Curt looked perplexed. "Why?"

"A million and one uses. Think about it."

"Yeah!" Randy snapped a finger. "You could win any bet by going back and placing it on something you already know."

"Or you could make a million inventing something by traveling into the future and swiping somebody's idea. Or, like, kick ass at the stock market." Curt warmed to the idea.

"And you could be famous predicting disasters. Could save presidents from assassination." Dart laughed. "Hell, you could see which girls would say yes and which would say no if you asked them out."

"I think I want your time machine."

"Me too." Randy squeaked.

"Wait a minute." Dart held his hand up. "There might be a problem."

"What?"

"Paradox. I read this story once, …"

A groan went up from both Curt and Randy.

"…no, hold on. It was called 'A Sound of Thunder', and it was about these guys that went back in time on a safari to hunt a tyranna, …a dinosaur, and there were all these rules, like they can't interact with anything, and have to stay on this path; but this one guy freaks out and steps off the path, so when they get back to the present, everything's changed, the president is different and all, and when they check on it, they find out that the guy stepped on a butterfly."

The other two stared back, dumfounded.

"Don't you see? When the butterfly died so far in the past, it had a chain reaction to the present, like, some animal that was supposed to evolve might have starved because it couldn't eat the butterfly, and, …and, …"

They just looked on in silence. He noticed it was getting darker. He yawned, thought about his animation.

"I guess it'd just be cool to go back and see the dinosaurs."

When he finally left for home, a blizzard had started, and he had to fight the wind, and fat, wet snowflakes that lapped at his face, the entire way back.

*　　*　　*　　*

"It's really snowing now." Slick hit a control on the dash. The wipers stuttered back and forth, smearing the slushy mess on the windshield, rendering it slightly less opaque.

"Radio says its gonna' be a blizzard." Moe rolled down the window and threw his butt out. A chilly, snow-filled current blasted into the back seat where Rip and Shitly sat.

"Goddamnit Moe, use the ashtray!" The cold, wet kiss of the flakes were like a slap to Rip's face.

He turned back. "Sorry." Then laughed at the sight of them.

The Blazer was rolling along old Highway 16, a thin two-way, single lane strip of pavement that hugged the lower slopes of the bluffs, bordering the broad marshes far below. They were headed to the north side of town to meet up with Keith, and allegedly hooking up with a dealer that he claimed had a quarter pound of pot at a substantial discount. They'd all pooled their resources, and with Keith doubling the money, had just enough to afford it, with the understanding, of course, that if they dealt half, it would generate more than enough income for them to indulge the other half for free.

Secretly, Rip knew that this was dealer's logic. That in reality, it would never go down that way.

"This deal better be on the up and up." Headlights skewed on the windshield and flashed by Slick's face. "It's been so long, I think I actually got a hard-on for this weed."

"Just keep your eyes on the road." Rip nervously eyed the gathering darkness outside.

"Hey, just remembered, I got a letter in the mail from Paul today." Pulling an envelope from his jacket, Moe tossed it back to Rip.

Inside were two folded sheets of paper. The first was covered with Paul's juvenile script:

Hey Moe,

Say hi to Shitly and Rip and Slick and Keith. Its reely fun here I wish you guys could all come up here and party like old tymes. Howz the trapin? Howz Sias?

Got lots of new frends here and sonthin else new I cant say but its reely fun yull like it a lot.

Ill see you all soon cus they say they will spring me in spring. Ha ha.

Paul

PS. If you shoe the pikshers to Rip say Im sorry cus Im not a drawer like him.

The second page held doodles, child-like representations of the river's fauna. There were mallards, recognizable only because he'd colored their heads green, a pair of carp, turtles, a fat beaver with a flat, cross-hatched cartoon tail, and a thin, slinky mink. Dominating the center of the mural was a muskrat, who for some reason wore a golden crown.

The sight of these dismal little creatures cluttering the page tore open something beneath Rip's heart, and he was suddenly flooded with an inexplicable sadness so profound he felt a knot grow in his throat. The drawings before him began to blur. Taking a deep breath, he folded the papers and slipped them back into the envelope.

"Well?" Moe was twisted in the seat to face him. Ahead, Rip could see that they were rounding a corner and he started to say something when the world outside the windshield skewed sideways.

The big truck had become unstuck from the road by a patch of hidden ice, and it lazily spun through both lanes until it was completely backwards. All Rip could think of was the drop on the right and the cliff on the left, not forgetting the oncoming traffic in the other lane. He could see that all this was passing through Moe's mind as well, and though it all happened in less than half a second, he thought it extremely odd that he was able to have so many thoughts in such a short amount of time, then he remembered that the same thing happened in dreams, so that this must be a dream too, and as the truck started spinning back around, he kept waiting for them to launch over the ledge; to feel the weightlessness of the fatal drop into the marsh, when the road slipped back into view outside the windshield, the big tires chirruped briefly, locking back onto the asphalt, and they were once again rolling back down Highway 16 as if nothing had happened.

Slick rolled the truck to a stop on the shoulder. Nobody moved or spoke. Then they simultaneously ejected from each of the four doors into the blowing snow, converging in the red wash of the taillights. The evening sky held an eerie glow, light from the town absorbed and reflected by the enveloping flurry.

"Christ." Both Moe and Shitly were attempting to light cigarettes, each having difficulty because of the wind and the shaking of their hands. Rip's body was shuddering uncontrollably, as Slick paced back and forth between them, pulling at his hair.

"Did that just fuckin' happen? Jesus fuck!"

"I think I'm having a heart attack." Rip leaned against the tailgate and stuck a hand beneath his coat, checking to see if it was beating correctly, but the throb of the Blazer's idling V-8 obscured any aberrant vibrations.

"Ain't nobody gonna' believe this." Moe puffed manically.

"Hell, I don't believe it!" Slick was still pacing.

Eyes like saucers, Shitly lowered down on his haunches and blew smoke into the snowflakes. "Gotta' get off the highway."

Stopping, Slick snapped his finger. "Yes! The Crazy Horse Trail is just up the road. We can take it to County D, and then into town."

"Holy shit." Rip exhaled.

Moe launched his butt out on the blacktop, now covered in an icing of snow, turned to Rip. "How's your heart?"

"Still there, I guess."

At the trail's entrance, Slick jumped out and locked the front hubs, as Moe rifled through the pile of cassettes that lay on the front seat. Stopping at one, he chuckled to himself, holding it up for the benefit of the back seat occupants. He slipped it into the player, and right on cue, BTO broke into the night with 'Four Wheel Drive'.

Sliding back in, Slick grinned his approval, threw a lever from the drive column on the floor. They lurched forward, jouncing along the winding dirt and snow path, as branches drummed and scraped at the fenders, windshield, and roof. They followed the floating cones of headlights boring a hypnotizing tunnel through the drifting veil of blown snow.

The Blazer's reinforced suspension bucked like a bronco, and they braced arms against the ceiling, legs comically bouncing off the seats, moving deeper into the darkening marshlands. The trail would split frequently, and it was evident that Slick had spent previous time here, as he would choose one branch or another without hesitation. Rip marveled at the sound system, as there had not been a single warbled or skipped note during the course of this punishing ride, when the headlights picked out a steep incline directly ahead of them.

"Hold on!"

Slick floored the accelerator. They pitched nose-up so suddenly he was certain they would tip over backwards, but the truck bellowed and clawed its way up, rolling over the hump at top, then pitched down at an alarming angle, the powerplant now working to slow their descent.

"The first is the worst," declared Slick as they rolled out of the trough up a less severe gradient, topped it, and hurtled down the decline.

The path had turned into a series of humpbacks, each slightly milder, their speed increasing. Approaching the fourth rise, Moe shouted; "Take air!"

Which is exactly what they did. Only in mid descent, as the headlights panned down the other side, did they reveal a vehicle inexplicably parked across the trail directly before them. Rip had time to register that it was Cheryl's VW Bug, and that Cheryl and a guy he didn't recognize were standing behind it staring in shock at their approach. The Blazer bounced once and shot forward, even though Slick was now standing on the brake pedal, and T-boned the small car. Because the truck was so much heavier, and because they'd hit it on a decline, the impact was far less than Rip was prepared for, *spongy*, his traumatized conscious flashed, and the Bug flipped easily over into the air and landed on top of Cheryl, the Blazer skidding to a halt before nearly colliding with it again.

For the second time that evening there was an astonished pause of silence, and Rip realized that Slick's stereo had finally given up the ghost. When he looked back at him from the driver's seat, he saw absolute terror in those eyes.

Slowly exiting in tandem, Rip walked with Slick, Moe and Shitly through the dream-like swirl of snow to the overturned Beetle captured in the truck's lights, thinking crazily, that it looked more like an overturned turtle than a Beatle. He could hear something, a song he recognized, the car's stereo still playing "Shake Some Action' by the Flamin Groovies, suddenly pierced by a scream of exquisite pain, and Rip felt his legs turn to rubber as Slick croaked; "Oh God."

Rounding the car, they saw the guy holding a beer can, just staring down at Cheryl, the lower half of her body pinned beneath the roof, blood starting to run from her mouth and nose. She drew a ragged breath in and loosed another agonized peal. The guy stepped back a little. Shitly kneeled down beside her, grasping her hand, as Moe's hands went involuntarily to his head.

"Oh man, this is *so* fucked up."

"What were they doin' there?" Slick started hyperventilating.

Cheryl screamed again as Rip pointed to the truck. "Go get help."

"But what were they doin' there?"

"You and Moe go get help. Now!"

They scrambled back to the Blazer, which bore no discernable damage from the collision, and it tore around the wreckage, towards town, leaving them in near total darkness. The sole illumination was the Beetle's dome, which now pulsed up from beneath. Cheryl screamed again and Shitly burst into silent tears as Rip took off his coat and tried to cover what of her he could, secretly hating the part of him that was thinking about the missed dope deal.

The sound of her screaming over that song would be one of three things that would mark, and haunt him forever.

*　　*　　*　　*

The storm had dumped nearly three feet of snow onto the river valley, shutting down the town, and the schools, for a rare snow-day. One of Dart's duties on his roster of chores was snow removal, and he was now grateful for the purchase of a snow blower that his mother had contested last year, a massive orange mechanical monster. Gassed, oiled, and primed, it made short work of the job, until encountering drifts over five feet high at the end of the driveway; wind sculpted dunes like waves frozen in time. There it became an exercise in creative engineering.

When finished, he met up with Curt, and they combined efforts to transform their backyards into epic sled trails. The unbroken slope of the beach dropping to the frozen river was an ideal location, and because of the snow's depth, they were able to add special flourishes, like jumps over the retaining walls, and high banks that would switch course and cross trails, adding the crucial element of collision for multiple participants. Randy joined them later, after finishing his own chores.

As the encroaching twilight threatened to put an end to their activities, Dart, legs sore from kneeling all day in the plastic tub sleds, had the brilliant idea of bracing feet at the front and rear of the sled, making the run standing up. He somehow made it all the way down, thinking of that surfer guy on the opening of Hawaii Five-O, and got a round of applause from Curt and Randy. They pronounced it the most original use of a sled they'd seen in years.

The days passed as the advent of Christmas approached, and the weather manifested itself in all its winterized forms, switching gears from warm, gray and snowy to clear, crisp, and subzero, and Dart, Curt, and Randy reverted to their winter routine of activities; an annual defense against the onset of cabin fever. They built snow-forts, having great mock snow battles. They burrowed an intricate, and elaborate labyrinth of tunnels beneath the drifts connecting their yards, featuring a central room with a vaulted ceiling, nearly tall enough to stand in. A place where they could sneak the occasional beer, and smoke ditchweed joints. A place, Dart fantasized, to take girls to make out with, although this never happened.

They shoveled out a complex maze on the icy surface of the river to play dog-a-deer, a game Curt had invented. Basically it was touch-tag on skates, but far more challenging because of the intertwined paths, and, of course, the requisite skill in ice skating.

All these things he participated in with enthusiasm, and really did enjoy them as he had in years past, but Dart had started to notice a change in his attitude, a tarnishing of interest, a sense of needing to move on, with nothing to move on to. Part of this vacuum was fulfilled working on the animation at his father's house, which was nearly completed, but he still felt like something important was missing.

School, an activity that had metamorphosed from acute anxiety, to non-existence, to acute anarchy, had faded again to dull routine. He was a descent enough student to score better than passing grades without really needing to apply himself, but the isolation and repetition of the season triggered a lethargy. Dart yearned for the return of warmer weather to open the river back up to him.

"Dart!" His mother hung the handset of the telephone in its wall-cradle with an answering chime.

"Yeah, Mom." He'd been staring out the sliding glass doors of the dining room at the pewter-gray morning, ignoring breakfast. Doggeth was at her routine station beneath the table, tail batting rhythmically at his knees.

"You're going to the Christmas dance tonight."

"What?"

"You heard me."

"Why?"

"I just spoke with Curt's mother, who will be chaperoning tonight, and she told me that Curt said you two were not going." She crossed arms over her breasts. Her mind was set.

"Well, no, …"

"Helen and I both think that you two need to go to this event, …socialize a little. Your stepfather has a point, you know. All you ever do is spend time on that river, with those two friends. When you grow up, you'll realize how important it is to get along with different groups of people."

"But Ma, I really don't want, ..."

Uncrossing her arms, she threw them up beside her head.

"You're going. The. End."

It was a good thing his sister was already at school. Had she witnessed this exchange, the taunting would have been merciless.

With proper permission slips, students were able to bus directly from school after final class. It was well after dark when Dart and Curt filed out of the battered old vehicle with the other students, who promptly queued before the front door in the frigid air.

The River City Roller Rink was on the north side of town, bordering an older industrial section near the train yard, and had the appearance of an old aircraft hanger.

Curt signaled and they snuck away to the back of the building, behind a fenced in area for the trash. Dart slipped the small joint of ditchweed out of a shirt pocket from inside his coat he'd rolled in the boy's room after class. It was an early effort of his, but not too bad, holding together as they smoked it down to the roach. Curt was ready with a stick of gum when they were finished, Juicy Fruit, to kill the smell and conceal their breath. They walked back through the doors of the skating rink feeling pretty bad-assed.

The first thing that hit Dart was the music. It was loud, the beat resonating deep within his chest. He'd never heard sound at such a magnitude before. It was so clear that he could perceive tonal nuances he hadn't believed existed.

They followed the entryway as it opened up to a long counter. Behind it stood a pigeonholed wall holding hundreds of pairs of roller-skates, each assigned a size number. They were promptly waited on by a wrinkled old man with a swollen, veined nose, who returned with their skates, spraying the insides with an industrial smelling propellant.

"What the hell is that?" Dart wrinkled his nose.

"Kills toe-jam, right?" Curt winked at the geezer, who, instead of acknowledging the joke, merely shook his head in the affirmative.

"Jeez." They took the procured pairs in their fingertips, walking with them daintily held away from their bodies. To their left appeared a small café counter flanked by stools filled with students busily eating, drinking, and talking, and on the right the aircraft hanger opened out to a cavernous, darkened room. There Dart finally noticed the light show, prompting unbidden memories of the UFO, but this was far more garish and theatrical, the wheeling and pulsing rainbow hues tracking the beat of the music, as the skaters beneath rolled around a vast reflective floor in a giant spiraling oval. Tucked away in one of the far corners was a booth where a man lurked behind a rack of equipment, browsing music albums, presumably controlling the light and sound.

This was a completely new experience, total sensory saturation, and Dart turned to Curt and caught his child-like smile, the one he used to flash when they were younger, brand new friends.

"Curtis! There you are. And Dart, too."

"Hi Ma."

"Hey, Mrs. C."

Curt's mother was a severe, serious looking woman, whose conservative wardrobe appeared to have been culled from a time warp in the mid fifties, an absolute counter point to the contemporary styles Dart's mother favored. She had index fingers pushed tightly into her ears, jiggling golden icicles that dangled beneath her lobes.

"Where have you two been? Why do they have to play this trash so loud?"

"Just talking to some friends, ma. It's cool. I like the music like this."

Helen scowled her disapproval, bobbing the beak of her nose at the cargo in their hands. "Well? You boys going to skate, or not?"

"Yeah, Ma. Give us a chance here, OK?"

"All right, Curtis." She relaxed slightly, fingers falling from her ears, winced, stuck them back in place. "You both have a nice time, and *do* try to mingle with some of the other kids."

Then she was off, legs scissoring in a military manner, the crack of her heels audible even above the music. Dart turned to his friend.

"All right, Curtis."

"Shut up." Rolling his eyes. "Let's get these things on and show these people how it's done."

"You ever roller-skate before?"

"No. You?"

"Nah, but it can't be that much different from ice skating, can it?"

"What I'm thinking."

A low wall, lined with benches, divided the rink from the rest of the building. There, kids were clustered in groups, trading out shoes for skates, and about midway down Dart spotted an empty space next to Sara. Taking a deep breath, he set off in her direction.

"C'mon. Over here."

"But that's, ..."

"I know."

At his approach she looked up and gave the slightest of smiles. No pigtails tonight, but the lightning bolt of a part was there. Curt coughed nervously, but Dart spoke up boldly.

"Hey Sara, mind if we sit here?"

"Sure. Go right ahead."

"Thanks." He took the spot beside her, doffing moon boots, pausing as he reached for the skates. She seemed to read his mind, turning serious hazel eyes to him.

"Did you see that stuff they squirted in these?"

"Yeah. Makes you think, doesn't it?"

Head shaking. "I'm trying not to."

They both laughed. *So far, so good. Now for a little small talk.*

"This place is pretty cool. You ever been here before?"

"Yeah, a couple of times, with my sister." And suddenly Sara seemed to deflate, expelling a long, sad sigh.

Shit. "I'm sorry. I heard about Cheryl. How is she doing?"

Sniffling. "She was hurt pretty bad. Broken pelvis and a broken foot. They say she'll be OK, but it'll take awhile."

"God."

"Just a stupid accident. Wasn't even those guys fault that hit her car. Was that *A-hole* she was with that night parked her car in the middle of the trail. She really hates him."

"Harsh."

"Yeah."

"You know, I think your younger sister and mine are friends."

"Yeah, … her name's Stacey too, right?"

"Right. Weird, huh?"

"Yeah, really weird."

"She swims at our place on the river a lot. You should come with sometime. It's a lot of fun. Especially on a really hot day."

"That sounds pretty cool. Yeah, maybe I will. When, you know, it gets warmer."

"Well, yeah, right."

He'd just finished lacing the second pair of skates when something caught his attention. He glanced up to see Duncan and Timmy walking in their direction, Brad noticeably absent. Dart took delight in contemplating the sheer terror a hemophiliac like Brad would find in a place like this, where cuts, bruises, sprains, and even broken bones were not only possible, but frequent. Definitely a Brad-free zone.

Picking up on where his attention was focused, Sara started. "Look out, there's those bullies."

"Oh, don't worry about them." To her surprise, and Curt's amusement, he actually waved as they passed. "Hey Duncan. How's it goin', Timmy?"

Timmy sneered back, and Duncan popped him the bird, but their hearts really weren't in it. He and Curt shared a laugh as Sara offered a full smile.

"What was that about?"

"Nothing, really."

The music faded, revealing an undercurrent of aural clutter, suddenly buried in the opening chords of "Dancing Queen' by Abba. Sara rose abruptly, glancing out at the rink. "Oh…I love this song. See you out there." She tottered a little unsteadily and joined the stream of skaters.

Curt just sat there staring at him, laces still half threaded.

"What?"

"You like her, don't you?"

"Well, yeah, maybe I do. So what?"

"I don't know." He bent back down, finishing the job. "Maybe you could find out if she has a friend, or something?"

"Shit." He looked out at the surging tide of color and motion. "Randy doesn't know what he's missing."

Curt jumped up, testing the wheels. "His own fault for not wanting to cough up the seventy-five cents."

As it turned out, roller-skating *was* a lot like ice-skating, except for the stopping part, and it only took Dart a few minutes to really get the hang of it before he and Curt were slicing past the others on the rink. A mirror-ball hung from the ceiling, spinning hypnotic shards of colors around the floor that he tried to chase, but the effect was sometimes so disorienting he had to stop after a few near-misses with other skaters. He tried going backwards, and found that easy as well, but unlike on the open river, he had to constantly glance behind him to avoid collisions, finally giving it up out of frustration.

The students were starting to pair off, and Dart scanned the crowd for Sara, which was nearly impossible within the turmoil of the swirling crowd. He settled for simply passing everyone up, checking as he went by, not really sure what he'd do about finding her holding hands with another boy. Finally, he recognized her serrated hair-part a few skaters ahead, still by herself.

Psyching himself up for an approach, the music shifted abruptly from KC and the Sunshine Band to 'Evil Woman'. He immediately backed off, not wanting even an unconscious negative association to mar the tenuous run of good luck he was having tonight.

Biding time, he hung back, coasting with the crowd, watching her graceful movements. He felt like he was caught in a tractor beam, magnetically tethered to her, and when ELO segued to 'Dream Weaver', he knew that the decisive moment had arrived, action was required, and he threaded through bodies to her side, smiled and held out his hand.

She took it without hesitation, leaning up a little against him, her hand warm and dry, a conduit through which flowed a potential force, the sum of a million disparate elements assembling here, in this instant. As they coursed, hand in hand within the rolling throng, he felt the void start to fill.

*   *   *   *

Rip watched as the tiny drab shape of Keith drew closer over the unbroken plain of the snow covered Mississippi. The sky was blank, gray, and overcast, darker that the surrounding terrain. As the shape drew nearer, he saw that Keith was pulling a sled, the old rail type, its singular passenger a blocky Styrofoam cooler.

"Way the fuck out here, isn't he?" Keith's breaths puffed little choo-choo trains of clouds that chased themselves downriver.

"Blame the fish. Or at least Moe's sense of where they are. Nice sled."

"Kid brother's. Where is this again?"

Rip nodded his tasseled cap. "Other side of the Interstate Bridge."

"Shit. Not sure I'm really getting any of this."

"Me either, but Moe swears by it. Something he likes to do every winter."

"I think he just misses Paul."

"Probably."

"Taking it out on us."

 "Probably."

They passed beneath the towering double-decks of the I-90 Bridge, the passing traffic hammering out a syncopated metallic beat far above them. Rip corkscrewed his way through the line of thick concrete support pylons, Keith fixing him with a questioning look.

"What the hell you doing?"

"Plotting a course."

Clearing the far side, they spotted Moe's ice shanty, a lone structure punctuating the white tundra, pieced together from different source materials, in a sort of geometric multi-hued anti-camouflage. On one wall was painted a large cartoon skull and crossbones underscored by the words 'Keep Out', that actually had the opposite effect, making the place appear more inviting. Rip stepped up, rapped on the door, and it swung unevenly out on loose hinges.

"She-ya, 'bout time you guys got here." Moe stepped unsteadily out and belched loudly. "Damn near out of beer." He eyed the cooler on the sled.

"Jesus, Moe, it's , …" Keith shucked a coat sleeve and checked his watch. "…two in the afternoon. How many have you had?"

"Just the six-pack. C'mon, let's get you guys set up." He led them into the darkened cubicle that smelled of stale cigarettes, spilled beer, and trapped farts. Illumination came from two small slit windows near the top, breaks between boards, and a Coleman gas lantern hanging from the ceiling. Assorted fishing ordnance hung from the walls and was stacked into the corners, and a slush filled hole surrounded by folding canvas stools and empty beer cans dominated the center of the space. A small AM radio sat on an overturned bucket, tinily broadcasting the Ozark Mountain Daredevils hit, 'Jackie Blue'.

"Cozy." Keith looked doubtful.

"Fucking right." Firing up a Marlboro, Moe quickly filled the room with an eye stinging haze. "First things first." He pulled in the sled, shut the door, opened the cooler, and extracted three beers, quickly passing them around.

"The first most important tool for ice fishing," he pronounced, popping the tab.

An hour later, after Moe had demonstrated the use of the ice auger, they each sat in front of their own respective ice-holes, miniature pole in hand, staring at a bobber that surged sluggishly on top of a dollop of slush.

Rip squashed an empty. "I think I'm missing the point of this, Moe."

"Yeah, I'm fucking freezing."

"Have another beer. It'll warm you up."

"No. Like, what do you *do*?"

"You *fish*. Just like in summer, but on the ice."

"Yeah, but isn't part of the point of fishing in the summer about getting out and enjoying the weather?"

"I thought it was about catching fish."

"Not exactly doing that here, either."

Sighing heavily, Moe squashed his empty. "Paul and Shitly like it."

Rip handed him a fresh one from the cooler. "Well, Paul's gone, and Shitly's, …still dealing with shit."

Keith nudged his bobber with the tip of a boot. "And Slick, Slick's totally changed. I've never seen him like he is now." gazed up at Rip. "Was it that bad?"

"Yeah." A chill rippled through his body.

Setting his pole down, Moe stood slowly, deliberately. "Yeah, it was bad. But it was an accident. Wasn't nobody's fault. Shit happens. You deal with it."

He lumbered out the door and they heard the splash of urine on snow. Keith turned to Rip.

"Or you don't."

Two hours later they were over halfway through the case Keith had brought. Rip stood out in the tarnished twilight, emptying his bladder, adding to the impressionistic yellow piss-patterns surrounding the small structure, noticing that Moe had pissed his name in surprisingly neat cursive. He tottered back through the door and heard snoring over the radio's fading battery, which was whispering 'Billy Don't Be A Hero'.

"Moe's out." Keith hiccupped and hooked a thumb at the radio. "Song's about 'Nam."

Sitting back down on the uncomfortable band of stretched canvas, Rip stared forlornly at his inanimate bobber. "That was fucked up. Glad we're out of it now."

"Out of what?"

"The war."

"Old man says it was the liberals fault."

"Liberals? How?"

"That they prevented us from using any real force to kick their ass. That we should have nuked them."

"Shit, man, your father's nuts. You *are* both familiar with the concept of Mutual Assured Destruction, are you not?"

"Nobody would've retaliated for the Vietcong."

"You fucking kidding? They were backed by Russia *and* China. People like your father gonna' get this world blown up. People like that crook Nixon. Good riddance."

"Oh, look who's being naive now." Leaning forward, Keith slipped on the ice, nearly falling into his own hole. "You think Nixon was the only corrupt president? Or any politician, for that matter? Nah, he's just the only one that was caught."

"Well, …yeah, you're probably right there."

"Bank on it."

"It's just that, you'd think after thousands of years of civilization, philosophy, science, and technology, they'd figure out how to eliminate something so basic and wrong as war."

"Who's they?"

"I don't know. World leaders?"

"Corrupt." Keith countered. "I think it's just in our nature."

"War?"

"Conflict. Competition."

"You saying, as long as we exist, war will exist?"

"In some form or another, yup."

"Well then it's all bullshit and we're doomed." Rip threw his empty down in disgust, prompting a grunt from Moe. "Because war will eventually destroy us."

"Unless we learn to live with it." Keith pointed out.

"You can't live with self destruction. That's an oxymoron."

"It's a paradox."

"Whatever. I just think that if we're going to survive, the future is gonna' have to be something like Star Trek."

Keith hiccupped. "Star Trek? You mean, like, we all have to live in spaceships and on other planets, and fuck foxy green alien chicks?"

"No, …well, yeah to the green chick, but I mean the idea of the Federation of Planets, except here on earth, where all the different counties and nations work together to end starvation, greed, overpopulation, pollution, and all the other problems to make life in general more pleasant rather than, … furthering its misery."

Keith considered Rip from across his ice hole, reached into the cooler. "Keep dreaming, Bub."

"She-ya, just what the *fuck* you guys goin' on about?" Moe yawned, wiped some drool from his chin.

"Chicks." said Keith.

"Green alien chicks." added Rip.

"Nutjobs, the both of you." Moe's bobber dropped below the slush with a musical note, his pole bobbed, and his line payed out from the reel with a ratcheting whine. Pawing at the spinning handle, he locked it, the tip bending at a violent angle.

"Got one! A big one!"

Rip and Keith jumped up and gathered around.

"Grab the ladle! Skim off some of this slush so I can see!" Moe was pulling the delicate little pole almost double over his head, reeling it back down to the ice. Rip scooped away at the hole as Keith unhooked the lantern and held it overhead. Something flashed by in the depths beneath the opening.

"Holy shit, it is big!" Keith jumped back a little.

"Come here, you motherfucker." Moe mumbled, continuing the pull-reel combination with effort. "You are *not* getting away from me."

"C'mon Moe, you can get bring it in!" Rip cheered.

"Almost here." Panting with exertion, he reeled down to the ice and pulled, stopping halfway up.

"*Shit!*"

"What?" Keith moved back in with the lantern.

"*No way! Fuck! No fuckin' way!*" Tugging ineffectually against the resistance, Moe stomped his feet in the snow.

"What is it?" Rip asked, alarmed.

"Too small!"

"What?"

"The *hole*!" Moe howled. "*The hole's too small!*"

Rip squatted down with Keith holding the lantern over the well. Pressed up against the underside of the ice, at the end of the luminous crystal cave, was the mouth of a monstrous catfish, its beard of barbels wavering in the water like a nest of worms, Moe's treble-hook puncturing its great lips.

Keith started giggling, and Rip caught it too, the irony being too obvious. Moe continued to strain on the pole.

"*Goddamn* it, it's not funny!"

"Sorry, Moe, but you're gonna' have one hell of a fish story to tell."

Growling in frustration and rage, he tugged angrily, breaking the line, toppling him backwards into the wall, sending Rip and Keith into peals of uncontrollable laughter.

When they finally left, empty-handed, it was night, and had begun to snow. The airport's searchlight scythed through the flurries above, alternating turquoise to white, far bank aglow from the landing strip's lights. The cloud's underbelly held the town's illumination over the nearer bank, where they steered, pulling the little sled behind them, the cooler now filled with empties.

"It's snowing again."

"Really." Keith deadpanned.

"I'm starting to get real sick of snow."

"Why'n'cha go build yerself a snowman." Moe slurred around a cigarette.

"What?" Rip stopped.

Stumbling to a halt, Moe turned back. "Said build a snowman."

Kneeling, Rip scooped together a handful of snow and packed it together into a ball. The consistency was perfect, and he held it aloft. "Keith, your place is near the High School. Think we can sneak a ladder out of your garage?"

"If we can be quiet about it." He looked back at Rip. "I'm assuming we don't want to be answering questions about it from my father."

"You assume correct."

"What's this about?"

"Got an idea." Rip turned his face to the heavens feeling the cold caress of snowflakes. "Got a *great* idea."

*   *   *   *

They'd gotten into the habit of arriving early to school, partly out of boredom and the need to leave home, to the relief of their mothers, and partly because they dug hanging out with Rip and his friends before they left for the day.

Walking through the parking lot this morning, Dart could feel a current of excitement he thought unusual for mid-week in the middle of February. From the way Curt and Randy looked, they'd caught it too.

Spotting the superstructure of Slick's truck standing over the rows of cars in the lot, the three cut a course for it, and found the usual suspects gathered around in a curiously ecstatic mood. Even Slick, who after the accident with Cheryl had become moody and melancholic, seemed buoyed, back to his normal carefree self. He raised a hand.

"Mini River Rats, welcome."

"Hey guys. What's all the excitement?"

Slick looked to Moe, who looked to Shitly, who nodded to Keith, who turned to Rip, who shrugged, and then they all burst into laughter. Rip got it under control first.

"Apparently some *delinquents*, ..." Quote marks with his fingers. "...got up to some *shenanigans* last night and *defaced* school property." They all lost it again and Keith just waved his arm in the general direction of the school.

"Go around front. But hurry, or you might miss history."

There was a crowd around the main entrance, of both exiting high school and arriving middle school students. A throng of teachers unsuccessfully tried to keep them at bay, but it was easy to see what was attracting so much attention, even through the unbroken crowd.

"Holy crap." Randy stared wide-eyed and started to snigger.

"Unbelievable." Curt said, shaking his head.

"Brilliant," nodded Dart, in admiration.

Standing above the student's and teacher's heads, thrusting up nearly sixteen feet from the front courtyard, beneath the flapping American flag, was a giant and very realistically rendered erect penis, sculpted in snow. The helmet of its circumcised head pointed almost backward from the thick, arched shaft that rippled with ropy veins, the entire structure either painted or dyed Bluff-topper purple. Apparently the artisans had taken further pains to preserve their project by pouring cold water over it to freeze to ice over night, judging by the difficulty the custodian and his assistants were having destroying the object. One of the older students had a camera, and was taking pictures.

Dart spotted Sara nearby, talking to her sister, Cheryl, in a neck-brace and on crutches, surrounded by Lynette and a couple other friends. She broke off and walked up to him, wide grin beneath flushed cheeks.

"Well, what do you think?"

"Of the ice dong?"

She nodded, giggling, covering her mouth with her mittens.

"Snow prick?" Curt added.

"Cold cock?" offered Randy.

Nearly in tears now, she hiccupped back laughter, and to Dart she radiated perfection.

"I think that I'm glad that crappy middle school burnt down, 'cause this school kicks ass."

The sun had begun its slow seasonal return, and there was still a little light left in the sky when he got back home. His mother was in the kitchen, preparing a hot-dish, from the smell of it, stepfather in the den drinking beer, watching news, his sister nowhere to be seen. Somehow sensing his thoughts, his mother appeared from the kitchen, drying hands on a small patterned towel.

"Your sister is at Stacey's for dinner, and Ellen and her friend Mary are coming over later."

Dart finished hanging his winter gear. "Why?"

Sighing. "I guess they're going to some *rock* concert tonight. Stopping by for a few drinks beforehand." Pronouncing the word 'rock' like it was a sexually transmitted disease.

"That's cool."

"Heard there was some commotion at your school today. Do you know anything about that?"

"Really wasn't anything, Ma. Someone just made a perverse snow sculpture."

"A what?"

"Um, ...well, ...you know, ..."

She held up a hand. "Never mind. I don't want to know. Honestly, ..." She disappeared into the kitchen, but her head popped right back out the doorway.

"Oh, almost forgot, something came for you at Walgreen's today." She smiled. "Something you've been waiting for."

She held out a small green and white envelope covered in his careful script, and Dart's heart nearly stopped.

"My film!" He ran up, taking it from her, feeling the small circular reel within.

"The projector is in the hallway closet. Maybe you could treat us to a screening of your epic after supper, Mister De Mille."

"All right! Thanks Ma."

If his stepsister bore a passing resemblance to Farrah Fawcett, then her friend Mary bore a definite likeness to the brunette in 'Three's Company'. Both wore sweaters that, despite being winter wear, still retained the surprising ability to reveal every subtle nuance of their breasts and nipples. They sat together on the couch, full wineglasses in hand, flanked by his stepfather in the Lay-Z-boy, his mother seated on one of the dining room chairs he'd moved into the living room for the screening. Dart knelt behind the coffee table next to the projector, threading the film leader through spinning sprockets as Captain and Tennille sang 'Muskrat Love' over the Magnavox.

"So, you made this by yourself, Dart?" Mary batted broad lashes over her China doll eyes.

"Yeah, but it's my first, and I haven't seen it before, so it might not be very good." He caught the leader as it slinked out the rear and looped it onto the takeup reel. "Also, there's no sound."

"Oh, I'm sure it'll be just wonderful." Smiling warmly, his mother sipped at a cocktail.

"Of course." Ellen clapped and bounced on the couch.

"How long did you say this took you to make?" Ted picked a raw radish from a small dishful in his lap, salted it, biting into it with a crack. He chased it with a sip of generic beer.

"Well, about three months."

Murmurs of appreciation went around the room.

"Here goes." He turned off the table lamp, cloaking the room in darkness and switched the projector to forward. A knife of white light cut to the far wall, etching a luminous rectangle there that flickered briefly, then became a stuttering series of colored anamorphic blobs. They suddenly gave way to his impressionist forest of plastic plants and wax fruit, through which strode his Tyrannosaurus Rex, stopping to mouth a silent Plasticine roar of rage, prompting hushed gasps from the darkness. The Triceratops entered the frame to rush an attack on the carnivore, sticking its horned head into his adversary's belly, drawing pink beads of clay blood. It was crude and pretty herky-jerky, but it *worked*, they moved. He'd brought them to life, and Dart sat rapt, hardly breathing through the five short film vignettes, ending with a gigantic blue squid attacking a scale model railroad house nestled in cotton snow, pulling a kicking miniature modeling-clay man from a window, stuffing him into its mouth.

The frame washed white again as the takeup reel freewheeled, tick-ticking the tail-leader off the table, and Dart shut it down, turning on the light.

"Wow, Dart, …" Mary played with her dark bangs. "…that was really cool."

Ellen clapped. "Yeah. Freaky. Totally trippy."

Ted's face was unreadable. "That's it? Three months?" He picked up the radishes, the beer, and the salt shaker, stood, and walked to the den. "Good luck finding someone to pay you to do that."

"I thought it was very nice, dear," said his mother, patting his arm, trying to mask her confusion. She followed Ted.

"Don't listen to my father, the grumpy old perv." The girls were up, standing around him, too close. He could smell lip-gloss, feel their body heat.

"Yeah, I think your movie was amazing." Putting hands on her hips, Mary stared sincerely into his eyes. "You're very talented."

"Thanks."

"Are you staring at my tits?"

Startled, he pulled his eyes back to hers. "No!"

"Why not?" She massaged them through her sweater. "Don't you like them?"

"Yeah. OK. I *was* staring at them. They're very nice."

Mary smiled. "Thank you." Licking glossed lips. "You know, Ellen, your stepbrother is pretty cute."

Ellen blew a feathered blond lock from her face. "Jesus, Mary, he's only thirteen years old."

"I, … just turned fourteen."

"Awww, …" Pouting her lips, Mary gently stroked his chin. "Maybe in a couple of years."

Sweating and blushing heavily now, Dart ran interference on the subject. "Uh, … heard you were going to a concert tonight. Who you gonna' see?"

Turning to each other, the two inhaled as one, and shrieked together, like the little girls they no longer were:

"*Ted Nugent!*"

"Quiet out there!" Ted, from the den.

*　　*　　*　　*

"*The Nuge!*"

"*Cat Scratch Fever!*"

"*Wang Dang Sweet Poontang!*" Slick pounded on the roof of the Blazer in time to the music as Keith passed a bottle of Jack Daniels from the shotgun seat back to Moe, who took a hit and handed it over to Rip, taking his own searing helping before passing it on to Shitly. They were cruising through town, awakening streetlamps strobing to life overhead.

"This is so Boss!" Rip wiped away whiskey induced tears. "How did you get the tickets?"

Keith accepted the bottle again. "Well you know my old man's president of the local NRA chapter, right?"

"Didn't know, but it's pretty much a given."

"Well, as it turns out, Ted Nugent's a lifetime member of the NRA. Total gun nut." He upended the bottle. "Ah! Damn, that shit burns. Anyway, he turned over like, ten tickets to the chapter. Old man asks me if I know who this Nugent guy is. I'm like, *fuck yeah!*" Keith pulled out a guilded stack of tickets and passed them around.

"*The Nuge!*" Moe repeated, receiving his.

"We got good seats?" Rip squinted at the fine print.

"Seats? The stands are for losers. We got general admission. The *floor!*"

Spinning the wheel for a hard right, Slick turned to Keith. "Hey, quit Bogart'n that Daniels, man. Hand it over."

Traffic started to thicken as the art deco hump of the Civic Center's roof approached over the tops of Main Street's ancient brick warehouses, and as they pulled into the parking lot it was compounded by heavy foot traffic. The place resembled Gunnery Row to the tenth power. It seemed as though every freak, hippie, and metal-head from the tri-county area had jumped in their muscle cars and converged on this one street. They found a small space in the very back of the lot, pulled in, and took stock.

"OK. Everybody got all your shit?" Slick pulled a cap over his head.

"Wish ta' fuck we had some weed." Moe mourned.

"Never know. We might find some at the show." Keith pulled on his gloves.

"Yeah, right."

They tumbled from the truck and worked their way through the parked cars, the cold, and the snow.

"Hey, you smell that?" Slick sniffed at the night.

"Pot!" Moe's nose was working at it, too.

Shitly pointed to a battered old VW van packed with shadows, emitting a soft haze. They turned in its direction. The odor grew at their approach, and Slick walked up to the driver's window, rapping lightly on it. A rolling nimbus poured out as the window rolled down, bearded, droopy eyed face materializing as it dispersed, shoulder length hair held in check by a tie-dyed headband. He gazed at them vacantly, expectantly.

"Uh, hi there. I ah, … couldn't help, …" Slick fidgeted nervously with his coat zipper. "Um, you think you could sell us a little of that weed?"

"Sell? Far out. Ah, sorry, no can do."

A groan rose from the group behind Slick.

"Ah, yeah man, all I got is my personal stash, …" He held up a large baggie that contained nearly an ounce of what looked to be high grade buds. "…but I'd be happy to share with you guys."

Turning, Slick pumped his fist at his friends, mouthed the word 'yes', and turned back to the hippie. "Why thank you, sir. That would be very kind."

"Right on." Bobbing his head, smiling, he pulled a leaf from a pack of Zig-Zag's. "A friend with weed, is a friend indeed, right?"

"You are *so* right."

The line was long, and progressing slowly, but Rip didn't mind. There was an endless succession of things to hold his attention. The variety of people, the smells, even the lights from downtown seemed to hold a new significance. Every so often a bottle would make its rounds from either the front or rear, and each time he took a sip it seemed to be something different; beer, wine, vodka, whisky, gin, but he didn't mind. In fact, he rather enjoyed the diversity of flavors, and his mind treated it as a game. They shuffled through the cold of the outer doors into a large entrance hall festooned with posters for tonight's event. Keith elbowed him from ahead.

"Check it out." Pointing to a poster. "Head East is the opening act."

"Who's Head East?" Asked Moe from behind him.

Shitly shrugged behind Moe.

"They got that one song," said Slick from in front of Keith.

An image came to Rip's mind. "They got that album called 'Flat as a Pancake', with a picture of, …a pancake on it."

"Is that the song?" Moe.

"No. I think it's just the album."

"Well then, what's the song?" Keith.

"You'll know it when you hear it." Slick passed the Jack back to Keith.

"What's taking so long?"

Slick tried peeking around the bodies ahead of him. "I think they're searching people."

Keith glared at the bottle in his hand, still quarter full. "Searching? For what?"

"Probably booze, drugs."

"Shit! We gotta' drink this, fast!" Taking a deep tear, he handed it to Rip, who did likewise and handed it back to Moe. The bottle was passed rapidly up and down the line until it ended at Shitly, who drained and promptly tossed it far down the hall, where it exploded with a resounding crash that echoed throughout the atrium.

Thick-necked security guards barked at each other and into walkie-talkies, running about, but no one paid them any real attention. Moe chuckled and gave Shitly a chummy punch in the arm.

Nearing the main entrance, Rip heard an approaching susurrus, like waves on the river during a storm, and they were promptly waved through the doors by two uniformed security guards, no stops or searches.

"Holy mother, …" Keith had halted and Rip stepped next to him.

It was like being on the bottom of a giant roofed cereal bowl, the entire surface of which was overrun with a layer of seething humanity. People filled tiers and walkways, flowing out onto the floor, thousands of them. The place appeared to have generated its own climate, glaring sodium lights far overhead illuminating a vast boiling cloudbank generated by countless snaky threads of smoke drifting up from the body of the assemblage, the smell of marijuana pervasive, as beach balls bounced and Frisbee's lofted freely through the air. Rip followed the trajectory of one as it was hurtled by a chunky blonde woman from one side of the center, to connect violently with the back of an unsuspecting man's head on the other, causing him to spill a beer over the front of another woman's blouse. At the far end of the building stood a massive raised stage, framed by huge black stacks of speakers, surrounded with metallic grids from which were suspended hundreds of colored lights, occasionally flashing a chromatic wink as a technician tested a channel.

Rip's mind seemed to be fragmented, going simultaneously in several directions as he and his friends threaded between bodies, drawn magnetically to the stage. Part of him was marveling how this environment was a complete contrary to the river, man-made, artificial, a complete simulacrum of actual sensation, while another boggled at the construct of shared experience it generated, as he was helplessly, but euphorically pulled along by the tide of mass consciousness.

Without warning the overhead lights disappeared, shrouding the center in darkness. A collective gasp issued from the audience as they surged forward, dragging Rip along with them, while a dazzling slice of light cut to the stage, illuminating the singular form of a man behind a microphone. His arms were aloft, a ringmaster tasking his spectators, voice booming loud, clear, and concise.

"Ladies and gentlemen, *Head East!*"

A silent detonation of incandescence highlighted five figures upon the stage. A kick drum measured out a steady backbeat, sound signature so low Rip felt it resonate in his guts, shirt and hair pulsing in time. Suddenly the band moved as one, filling the auditorium with music as the crowd roared, Rip part of them, absolutely entrenched, reaching up with the rest to caress the sound with their fingertips. He saw Slick, Keith, Moe, and Shitly doing the same, and somehow they all found themselves right before the stage.

While the applause died down from their first song, a woman near him pulled her blouse up, flashing breasts to the band. The guitarist noticed, pointing her out to the bass player, and she held up a joint. He accepted it, holding it up for all to see, taking a huge drag, to the crowd's utter delight. He handed it back with a dopey smile. This seemed to prompt something in the gathering, for suddenly things were being passed around. The music started up again, and Rip took an offered bottle of Boone's Farm, passed it back down, and felt a tap on his back.

Turning, he saw Glenn, holding up a smoking glass bowl, flanked by two women that looked like the chicks from 'Three's Company'. The brunette fluttered her lashes over big blue eyes. As Rip tried to pull a hit from the overpacked pipe, he decided that the blonde actually looked more like Farrah Fawcett. He made to hand it back, but Glenn gave little shooing motions to pass it on, so he saluted him and the girls, received a sloppy peace sign in return, and turned it over to Keith, wondering how he'd ever get the thing back, deciding it wasn't his problem.

By the end of the set, the floor had started a slow tilt, and Rip realized he was starting to get on the wrong side of drunk. The band had reemerged from the curtain for their final encore to thundering applause. Moe stuck two fingers in his mouth, painfully wolf-whistling into his ear, and as they started through the first chords, Keith grabbed him by the arm and yelled.

"That's the *song*!"

Rip recognized it almost immediately, 'Never Been Any Reason', and so, it seemed, did the rest of the audience. The air around them caught fire with a galaxy of flickering lighters, and when they hit the chorus, acappella and in harmony, the crowd sang along.

The applause lasted well after the house lights had come up, dispelling the dream-like quality of the stage, but Rip was beyond caring at this point, anxious to see Ted Nugent play. The crowd had begun to disperse for the break, clearing a little more elbow-room up front. Slick drunkenly body checked him.

"That was the *shit!*"

"Fucking rocked!" His voice sounded under-water over the ringing in his ears.

"Bring on *The Nuge!*" Moe howled.

Keith consulted his wallet. "I'm gonna' see if I can get anyone to buy some beer. Bring some back if I can."

He staggered off into the crowd. Rip started to speculate on how Keith was going to find them again when someone handed him a joint, then a bottle, then a can, and those troubling little thoughts were chased to a far corner of his mind. The lights went down, and he drifted back with the flood of people to the edge of the stage.

Ted Nugent materialized beneath the lights brandishing his electric hollow-body guitar, signature mane of hair a firey corona orbiting head and shoulders. The crowd went hysterical, deafening, and he had to hold arms in the air for several minutes before they settled down sufficiently for him to speak.

Plucking the mike from its stand, he screamed. "Hey *Tomah!*"

Confused murmurs spread throughout the crowd. Slick leaned in and whispered:

"He got the wrong town."

Ted didn't notice. "Are you ready to *rock?*"

A lukewarm cheer rose that he clearly did not like.

"I *said!* Are you ready to *ROCK?!*"

The reply this time was thunderous. Pleased, Ted led his band into a rousing version of 'Stranglehold' so excessively loud, it actually hurt Rip's ears, but in a good way that he didn't mind. Finishing to frenzied approval from the audience, the band started into the opening riffs of 'Cat Scratch Fever', when something flew up onto the stage, Rip swore it was a Frisbee, and struck Ted Nugent in the face.

"Who the fuck threw that?" He screamed through the mike, music dwindling to a stop, as a nervous ripple ran through the assembly. He un-shouldered his guitar. The silence in the hall percolated with tension as he manically paced the stage, jabbing the Gibson out repeatedly, voice suddenly very small minus the amplification.

"Show me the motherfucker that threw that!"

From in front of Rip, Moe raised a fist and pierced the silence.

"The *Noooge*!"

Nugent's head snapped at the sound, and he moved suddenly before them, eyes wild with rage, and there was a meaty smack as Moe jerked back into Rip and slumped to the ground, Ted already crossing back over the stage, pausing briefly to yell into the mike.

"Fuck you, Tomah!"

He flipped them the bird, then he and the band walked out the wings. A rising murmur rose from the auditorium, punctuated by cries of outrage. Moe clawed his way back to a standing position, rubbing at a bloody lower lip.

"I got punched by Ted Nugent." Moe's eyes were filled with something close to adoration.

"Is that it? They're fucking done?"

Slick had a look Rip didn't like.

"Where the fuck is Keith?"

Shitly shook his head back, shrugged.

"This place is gonna' go sideways if, …"

The house lights came up and the voice of the crowd doubled.

"Shit."

A scream came from somewhere and a chair flew overhead and smashed into the drumkit.

Like an invisible switch was thrown, the entire place erupted into violence, air suddenly filled with projectiles large and small, stage rushed by an angry mob, overwhelming security and demolishing instruments and amplifiers. Fights broke out spontaneously, churning the mob's mass, as bodies thrashed against one another, Rip being pushed one way, pulled another, when a white flash of light exploded simultaneously in front of his eyes and in the back of his head. The floor tipped up to slap him in the face, boots and shoes grinding painfully into his hands, feet, and body, a removed faction of his mind curious that this was how it felt to be trampled to death. He was finally able to get an arm up, where it was grasped, and he was pulled from the grimy, sticky, slushy surface to stare into the calm, and utterly intoxicated smile of Stephanie. She regarded him hungrily and ran a tongue over her lips, still holding his hand.

"C'mon, Rip. Let's get out of here."

They were riding in the back seat of Gaylene's green vinyl-topped Maverick, a fact he was only intermittently conscious of as Stephanie was astride his lap, pushing her tongue as far down his throat as she could, dry-humping his uncomfortably displaced erection through both their jeans. Every once in a while her searching hands would painfully brush the spot on the back of his head that had been the target of something harder earlier that evening, and he would resurface inside the moving compartment to the glares of Lynette over the front seat, and the eyes of Gaylene in the rear view mirror.

"Jesus, guys, get a room." Lynette snapped in disgust, continuing to stare.

Retracting her tongue, Stephanie panted. "We wouldn't have to if you'd get us to my place."

"*You* told us to never talk about your place. *You're* the one said never to bring boys there." Gaylene's eyes from the mirror.

Stephanie groaned, reaching between his legs, gripping his crotch. "Get us there *now*, or I'll fuck him right here, in front of you two."

"All right. OK. Just keep your pants on."

"Yeah, don't think I'm gonna' go all lesbo for you, Steph." Lynette looked to where her hand was working. "I like cock way too much for that."

"You all want me." Stephanie whispered, slipping tongue back into his mouth. Rip submerged beneath some primordial blackout, Lynette still staring.

When next he came to, Stephanie was dismounting, pulling him out the door into the cold. The small Ford pulled away without a word of goodbye, and Rip found that they were standing in a snow-covered courtyard surrounded by a confusing cluster of single and twelve-wides bathed in murky orange sodium light.

"You live in a trailer park?"

"Kind of." Her eyes went instantly hard. "Why? You got a problem with that?"

"No. Fuck, just as long as it's warm, it's home."

"Good." Jerking his arm. "Let's go! Freezin' my tits off."

"I can help with that."

Slipping over snow and ice, they dashed drunkenly through the maze of prefabricated structures. She led them to a squat rectangle of cinderblock that looked as though it had once served as custodial center for the community, except for the empty flower boxes beneath gun-slit windows, and a mailbox posted out front.

He resisted an urge to comment as she unlocked the door, the interior greeting them with warmth, and a potpourri of old cigarettes, stale fry grease, and mildew. The entire space just basically a single open room, illuminated at one end by the unflattering wash of a hanging fluorescent shop fixture, crisscrossed by nylon lines from which hung drape partitions forming fundamental and very non-private rooms. She yanked him past a cluttered retro-fitted kitchen, towards a curtain bearing the images of playful kittens. Pulling it aside revealed a small fabric cubicle containing a single mattress sitting on the floor, a dresser behind, and a free standing set of shelves, holding an AM/FM radio, jewelry, makeup, and a mirror. Buzzed and horny as he was, Rip needed a minute to absorb the shock of this environment. Plus he needed to pee.

"You got a bathroom? I really gotta' go."

"Sure." She pointed proudly to a short cinderblock wall, shucking mittens and tearing down the zipper of her coat. "Just hurry."

There wasn't even a door. Just a corner around which confirmed his suspicions about the industrial nature of the building, including, as it did, both a urinal and an enclosed toilet stall, with an improvised shower in the corner. The room reeked of mold and the sharp tang of ancient urine. He chose to do his business in the urinal, splashing cold water from the sink on his face.

She was down to a thin T-shirt and jeans, pulling him into her space, sliding the cat-curtain shut, dimming the room.

"At least take your coat off." He worked open his buttons as she switched the radio on to 10cc singing 'I'm Not In Love' and pulled off her top.

"You know why they call themselves 10cc?"

"Who?" Rip dropped his coat, staring at her breasts.

"This band. 10cc. You know why?"

"No, why?"

Reaching out, she traced the swelling in his pants with a forefinger, smiling hazily. "It's how much you guys shoot when you cum. 10cc's of pud."

Her touch had him on fire. "Oh."

With a single swift feline move she removed her jeans, revealing no underwear and a fresh shave, everywhere. Fingers trailing up from her stomach over ribs, eyes glassing over, she whispered in a little singsong voice to herself.

"Mustache rides, …"

Swallowing heavily, Rip controlled his breathing. "What?"

Seeming to notice him again, she suddenly pushed him back, off his feet, onto her bed, jumping on top, pinning his arms down with sharp knees, gazing down from a waterfall of hair.

"I'm gonna' sit on your face."

Then his head was clamped between her naked thighs, pelvis grinding into his mouth, nearly suffocating him, the stubble from her recent shave chafing his lips and chin, her motions coming quicker as he gripped her buttocks and tried to follow with his tongue and fingers. She reached around and freed him from his open fly, holding on like some bizarre bronco rider, bucking and thrashing so wildly now that Rip was sure his neck would snap, trying to take little breaths between jolts, as she gave one final head spinning thrust, letting out a long, shuddering breath. Dampness spread over his lips.

Pulling off with a wet smack, gasping, he watched her flushed body glossy with sex sweat crawling backwards, lifting up, guiding him in, settling down until they were joined deeply. Her motions now slower, less frenzied, more methodical, she was whispering what he first thought were instructions of things she wanted him to do, Rip finally recognizing she was singing along to the radio. Somewhere far back in the receding world was the sound of a door, but they were really building now, sliding in, out, her singing starting to adopt a desperate tone, rhythm intensifying, and she gave a sharp cry as fluorescent light flooded the room to the sound of the curtain whipping aside and a deep angry voice.

"What the *fuck* is this, Steph?"

A shadow rose and she was pulled off, freeing his taut shaft to slap painfully onto his stomach.

"Tommy, go away!" She gathered a sheet around her on the floor. "This isn't any of you business."

"Bullshit." The shadow pointed at Rip, who was still humiliatingly exposed. "You the prick who got my sister pregnant?"

"What?" Tried to sit up, but the shadow pushed him back. "No. I didn't."

The shadow appeared to cross its arms. "Well what the fuck you doin' just now, prick?"

"Well, uh, …"

"Right! You're outta' here!" He was pulled with surprising force from the bed, left arm twisted behind his back, and bum-rushed through the room, followed by Stephanie's cries.

"Goddammit Tommy, stop! Bring him back!"

The front door hit Rip in the face, burst open, and he was propelled out into the night, his still rigid member bitten by the chilly air, as he tried to retain balance and button his fly over its girth. Turning, he saw the shadow reappear in the doorway.

"If I ever see you again, Keith, I swear, I'll kill you."

"I'm not, ..." Reply cut short by his coat that came twisting through the air, wrapping around his face. The door shut and he sighed deeply, disentangling himself, threading arms through sleeves, hearing muted shouts coming from inside.

At least he still had his boots on.

*　　*　　*　　*

The powdered pack of snow squeaked loudly beneath their boots, not unlike the sound of a Styrofoam cooler, but different too, sharper and more surreal. It was frigidly cold for a late March evening, at least ten below, probably the final arctic front for the winter season. Dart led Curt and Randy over the bluish snow-covered palette of Sunfish Lake, the three of them carefully duck-walking over it's slippery surface, beneath a still moonless night, bejeweled by countless hard points of stars. They crossed through the center, heading towards the opposite shoreline, towards home.

"Why does snow make that sound when it's so cold?" Randy emphasized his query with an extra foot crunch.

"Don't know. Curt?"

"Search me. Always squeaks in the cold. Squeaky snow."

"Squeaky snow."

"Yup."

"Guys, What's that?"

They searched in the direction that Randy was pointing, spotting the flickering barb of orange brilliance that appeared to hover above the frozen lake's surface. Dart felt the instant onset of UFO flashback.

Curt squinted into the distance, shielding eyes with a gloved hand, a gesture completely unnecessary in the darkness.

"I think it's, ...it's a fire."

Panic fled Dart's mind, replaced by confusion. "A fire in the middle of the lake?"

"That's what it looks like."

"What could be burning?"

"Search me. Let's take a look."

Figures of people surrounding the fire materialized as they neared, some standing, some sitting on folding canvas stools, encircled by a dimpling of footprints, and several parked sleds burdened with cargos of coolers and firewood. The boisterous, good-natured tone of their voices was barely audible.

They stopped, Curt scratching at his woolen hat.

"It's a bonfire."

"On the ice?" Dart was having a little trouble with the concept.

Randy was too. "Why doesn't it burn through?"

"Search me."

The distant voices had taken a more urgent tone, and they could tell from the waving arms, and come-hither gestures, they'd been spotted, and were being invited over.

Dart looked back at the other two.

"Well, c'mon then."

Bundled up for sub-zero weather they were unrecognizable, but when a hearty cheer rose from the group at their advance, and a familiar voice piped out; "Hail, mini River Rats." Dart realized that he should have known all along who would be crazy enough to initiate an event like this.

Moe was the only one not properly dressed against the conditions, wearing only his goose-down vest over a long sleeve shirt. Shivers vibrating his body caused the cherry from his cigarette to sketch glowing squiggles in the night air.

"She-ya, what the hell you'se doin' out here on a night like tonight."

Randy stepped out front. "Just comin' back from the tree-fort we built on Tomahawk Island."

He yelped when Curt kicked him in the leg.

They didn't seem to catch the slip, Dart parrying to cover. "Could ask you the same question."

"Celebrating." Keith held aloft a pillow-sized plastic bag filled with large buds of marijuana. "Quarter pound of Panama Red. The drought is officially over!"

The five of them cheered, toasting the chilly night with upraised cans.

"Well come on then, warm up by the fire." Rip waved them over.

Stepping into the circle, they felt its welcome heat. Curt held out a mitten.

"How come it doesn't burn through?"

Rip's eyes were drowsy and very red, and he smiled at the question. "I don't know, something to do with vapor lock. Never does, though."

Slick tore the lid off one of the coolers, producing a simulacrum of the squeaky snow sound. "Grab a 'sconnie, boys. Join the party."

Helping themselves each to an Old Style, Dart tabbed his can and turned it up over his mouth. Nothing came out.

"I think mine's frozen solid."

"Mine, too."

"Help." Squeaked Randy. "Stuck to my lip."

"That's the bitch about beer cans below zero." Rip stared in curiosity as Randy stretched his lip pulling the can away. "It's imperative to find the perfection zone around the fire. Too far away, your beer freezes. Too close, it boils." Clapped him on the shoulder. "Here guy, kneel closer to the fire. Warm it up, that tin will let your lip go."

"Why I stick to whiskey." Moe held up a bottle of Jack.

Shitly produced the long tube of a bong from his parka, handed it to Moe and nodded at his drink.

"Fuck yeah, Shitly. Great idea." Kneeling, he scooped up snow, packing the water chamber of the bong half full, tipping a generous amount of whisky into it.

"Jack pack." Breaking seal on the bag, Keith stuffed buds into a wooden bowl the size of his fist. "Best of both worlds. Tonight men, we live as kings."

"Aahh!" Randy fingered the rim of his can. "Think it pulled some skin away."

"Yeah, that'll happen." Slick giggled from his seat on the far side of the fire.

"So I'm banging this chick, Susan, from Logan, right?" Handing the filled bowl over to Moe, Keith zippered the baggie, stashing it in his coat.

Slick leaned around the blaze. "That the one with the tits?"

"*Definitely* the one with the tits. Anyway, she's knob-jobbing me, when she starts to go down below my balls, and the next thing I know, bitch's sticking her tongue in my asshole."

Slick launched a mouthful of beer, as groans of disgust rose from around the fire. Dart, Curt, and Randy considered each other with wide, shocked eyes.

Rip tipped him a can. "Conclusive evidence that the existence of the much contested butt-munch does *indeed* exist."

"She-ya." Moe shook his head at Shitly. "My ears feel dirty."

Slick leaned. "Did she really do that? What did it feel like? Did you like it?"

"Easy there, he-whore. Think I'm still working it out."

"Yeah, but would you let her do it again?"

"Fuck yeah."

Curt burst out laughing, Rip regarding him with a glassy expression. "Hey, you guys don't think we're corrupting the kids here, do you?"

Dart finished sucking a trickle of melt off from his beer cube. "You can't corrupt us. We're River Rats."

"Well spoken." He accepted the bong from Shitly, smoke billowing from the bowl and tube. Covering the carb with a finger, he drew in a burbling hit, holding, then ejecting a steady plume of smoke and steam vapor. "Smooth and sweet." Tipped it in their direction. "You don't have to if you don't want."

Dart grabbed the base of the paraphernalia and followed Rip's example, placing a finger over the carburetor, sucking in as smoky bubbles filled the chamber, releasing the carb, watching as the contents of the tube slid up into his lungs. He anticipated a harsh burning, but experienced only cool air with a sweet, slightly medicinal taste as he exhaled.

"That's real good." Dart watched the world before him start to contract like a Shrinky- Dink in an oven. Curt plucked the bong from his grasp and took a turn.

"Wow. That's so much better than our stash."

"You guys got weed?"

"Half a garbage bag full."

"Really?"

"We found two big plants in the marsh." Dart clarified.

Moe grunted. "Ditch weed."

"Yeah."

"Hey, It's my turn." Randy grabbed the bong from Curt.

"Randy, I don't know if you should, …"

Curt was met with a cold glare.

"I mean, it's a lot stronger than our, …"

Colder glare.

"Fucking go ahead then, it's your funeral."

After a prolonged fit of the giggles, during which, they were tolerated by the more experienced stoners, the three younger boys became eminently enamored with the fire, fascinated by its endless complexity and forms. They stared into its glowing depths, occasionally sighing with awe when the popping of a log loosed a nimbus of embers aloft.

Keith adjusted the proximity of the cooler to the fire. "My old man just got us a subscription to Home Box Office."

Slick belched. "Yeah? What the hell is that?"

"It's cable TV. You got this box with a bunch of channels on it, and you can watch whole movies, no commercials. Even got R rated ones."

"No shit?" Rip spit out a mouthful of hot beer, emptied it, helped himself to a fresh one.

"Yeah. Play some pretty twisted shit late at night."

Moe freed two Marlboros from a pack, handed one to Shitly, snapped his Bic. "Like what?"

"Came in on the middle of this scene the other night, don't even know what movie it was, guy sticks a shotgun up a chick's pussy and blows her insides out."

"Jesus." Rip mentally shoved the image from his mind.

"That's fucked up." Slick shook his head.

Dart, Curt, and Randy continued to gape at the licking flames.

"We're all becoming connected."

"What's that, bub?" Keith turned to Rip.

"Cables, satellites, everyone's being hooked together."

Moe belched. "That's a good thing, isn't it?"

Slick snapped a finger. "I saw on the news about this new company called Apple, that they were going to make something called personal home computers."

Keith scowled. "You mean the Beatles record company?"

"No, I think this is something different."

"Are you talking about those new calculator things?" Rip watched the younger River Rats stare into the bonfire.

"No, real computers, like the ones NASA uses on the Apollo."

Keith leaned forward. "What, these guys come in and build a whole new room in your house? Those things are huge."

"I don't know." Slick shook his head. "They showed something that looked like a big wooden typewriter. Said by the year two-thousand, everyone would have one, and that they could all communicate with each other."

"You mean like Star Trek?"

"I dunno'. I guess."

"That's a good thing, isn't it?" Moe repeated.

"Well, yeah." Keith started pacing in the snow. "I mean, you could correspond with anyone anywhere, and besides being able to do all the complicated calculations that computers can do, you could exchange all that information, not just talk, like on a phone." He stopped. "Yeah, just think of it, everyone having instant access to all the exact same knowledge. A new age of information, that's what needs to happen. It's the future!"

"Cool." Slick eased off his stool and stepped to the cooler.

"Except, …" Dark thoughts crossed Rip's mind.

Keith spat. "What?"

"Except what if the information was corrupted?"

"What do you mean?"

"Well, what if whoever's in charge of collecting the facts, the data, either made errors in ignorance, or deliberately manipulated it to their advantage? This universal fountain of information of yours would be infected, like a disease, a virus. And then everyone would be fucked."

"But don't you see, that's the beauty of it. There *is* no one in charge. It's gathered from everyone everywhere."

Rip laughed. "Even worse! Can you imagine the amount of mis- and disinformation, and just pure stupidity that would be generated by the sheer numbers of ignoramuses, retards, and psychos out there? You'd have a humanity unified by idiocy."

Shitly looked to Rip. "Lemmings." He moved to the cooler.

"*Exactly!*"

They all turned to the sound of the new voice. Dart faced them, wild eyes over a crooked grin.

"See, I read this short story once, ..." Curt and Randy groaned. "...called the 'Reptile Enclosure'. It's about this couple sitting in a huge crowd at the beach, and they're all listening to the radio about the last satellite being positioned to complete a global grid, and they all keep edging nearer to the water, listening to the reports, and when the satellite is finally in place, all the people march into the ocean."

The crackling of the fire punctuated the silence that followed.

"The fuck does that have to do with lizards?" Moe drawled.

"No! No, I get it." Rip paced over to Dart. "Once we all become connected, we lose our individuality. Our information becomes shared, our thoughts diluted, our personalities, society become homogenized, completely stagnant and mechanical, hive-mind, nineteen-eighty four, spying on each other, and we all end up mass produced robots, all doing the same, thinking the same."

The fire popped sharply, twice.

"Nutjobs, the three of you." Moe turned into the darkness. "I'm draining the dragon."

"*You're all robots.*"

They turned to watch Randy backing away, spastically waving his hands before bugging eyes. "All of you."

Curt laughed. "Give it a rest, Rand."

Slick pointed. "Yeah guy, chill out."

Keith snorted. "Good one, Slick."

Rip sniffled. "'Caus it's like, cold."

Dart grinned. "Right."

Shitly said. "Beep."

Randy leaped. "See?" His voice started climbing. "I'm the only real person left. You were sent to spy on me. To see what real people are like. All of you are robots, even my mom and pop."

"Randy, we are *not* robots." Dart took a step as Randy cringed back around the fire.

"You are too! You're *evil* robots."

"Rand, come on." Curt tried to move around the other side, but Randy let out a keening whine and scrabbled back the opposite way.

Something surged within Dart's brain, like jet fuel, and before realizing what he was doing, he was roaring at the top of his lungs, leaping over the fire to land directly in front of Randy's face.

"I'm EEEVIL!"

Utter stupefaction showed there momentarily, then Randy was howling, tearing away across the snow covered plain at an inhuman speed as Dart tried to give chase.

"Randy! Come back! I was just kidding!"

Randy quickly outdistanced him and disappeared into the treeline. The little bastard was faster than a spooked rabbit, and right now he pretty much was exactly that.

Slowing to a halt, Dart gulped at the glacial air, abruptly aware of a soft radiation of colors pulsing about him, and with growing dread, raised his head.

The entire firmament above was awash with a mind bending display of Aurora Borealis, great ribbons of shifting polychrome shimmering in silent incandescence throughout the heavens, a pulsing celestial curtain of liquid gemstones; emerald, ruby, sapphire. He followed cascading colors down to the horizon, where they flowed behind the naked trees of the forest, to the shoreline where the wind had sculpted huge snow dunes, catching and refracting rainbows in a thousand billion trapped snowflakes, rippling opalescent highlights over an ephemeral crystal beach.

*   *   *   *

The phone woke Dart early the following morning because it sounded wrong.

He sat up, strangely alert from having come directly out of deep sleep. He heard his mother's answering voice, and she too, sounded wrong. Then, Ted, and silence.

He drifted back to a dream where he was traveling down a road at terrific speed, veering out of control into a brick wall that zoomed in out of nowhere, and jerked awake to footsteps on the stairs. They appeared in his doorway, his mother's face ashen, eyes shocked, an alien look of compassion on Ted's. They just stood there for a few moments, contemplating each other across the space of his bedroom. His mother cleared her throat.

"It was those narrow roads and the ice." She blinked, like she was surprised at what she spoke. "That stupid little car of his. I could never understand that."

Dart looked at his mother as she swooned in the doorway.

"He went through the rail. Over the side. Near the top."

She turned briefly to Ted, then looked at Dart with naked grief. "It's your father, Dart. He, ...he's dead."

She fainted, and Ted caught her before she hit the floor.

7

CYCLONE BEACH

Brian D Garrity

He passed the window.

Walking through the alley dressed in his jean jacket, the air around him smelled sweetly of decay and moisture, a combination of odors he always attributed to the arrival of Spring. Flanked by the darkened humps of what remained of the melting snow drifts, surrounded by twin streams of runoff that trickled downhill, he stood before the dilapidated garage, strangely compelled by the simple sectioned pane of glass set into its wall.

Birds trilled persistently, mirthfully celebrating the arrival of the first truly warm day of the year. He walked slowly up to his distorted reflection, recalling that technically glass was considered a liquid, just not noticeable in a human timescale, as it took millennia to flow. In its reflection, he watched his features ripple and warp, transforming from ridiculous to monstrous. There was a sharp but diminutive crash, and Dart withdrew his fist, already starting to wheal with blood, from where the window had just been.

*   *   *   *

"I ran into Paul yesterday."
"You what?"

"Saw Paul. He's back." Moe pushed the mini-glacier of ice with the tip of an oar, leaning dangerously out over the edge of Sias' boat dock.

"You're shitting me." Rip turned to Shitly. "He shitting me?"

Shitly shook his head in the negative.

Sending the berg on its way out to the channel, Moe fired up a Marlboro. "Might not've recognized him if not for that carrot top of his. Real fuckin' skinny now."

"How long has he been back?"

"Said about a week."

"A week?" Rip worked his oar to free another chunk of ice from the dock. "When the fuck was he gonna' to tell us?"

"Said he's been busy. Moved out from his Pap's house. Say, what you think that is?"

They gazed out over the rolling, ice-packed, debris-choked river to where a fleshy, bloated corpse moved by on the current, four sticky legs pointing straight into the air.

"Looks like a pig." Shitly helped him steer his iceberg out to meet the flowing exodus. "Isn't Paul too young to be moving out? Wouldn't it be a violation of his probation?"

"Dunno. He done it, though." Pressing down on a larger unbroken section, his oar suddenly slipped, and Moe dropped onto the honeycombed surface of half-melted ice that canted dangerously toward the open section of freezing water.

"Grab my oar!" Rip and Shitly extended theirs as Moe scrabbled to grip them, hauling himself back onto the dock, managing to dunk only a single boot in his escape.

"Damn, that shit's cold." He sat on the dock, pulled off his boot and poured water out.

Lighting a cigarette, Shitly shook his head. "Fucking lucky."

"Now don't get all preachy on me, Shitly." Moe nodded down to the shrouded shapes on the dock. "Can't wait to get 'em back out."

Rip looked to where his Alumacraft sat next to Moe's johnboat, both beneath tarps, lined up with a dozen others atop the decking. "Preaching to the choir there, brother."

"Anyway, he's having a party tonight."

"Paul?"

"Yeah, at his new place. Said to invite everyone."

"Where is it?"

"Got the address right here." Wiggling a piece of paper from his pocket.

"Gonna' need beer."

Moe hooked a thumb back at the bait shop. "Stock up on our way out. Good ole' Sias' is back open for the season. Only one in this town that cares enough to serve us minors." Pointing. "Just what the hell is that?"

They turned to witness a grotesquely ballooned brownish corpse drift close by, fur matted and slashed, four thin hoof-tipped legs jutting out at various angles.

"Think it's a whitetail."

Moe stuck out an oar.

"Wait, don't, …"

But it was too late. The wooden blade cleaved the decomposed flesh like butter. With an obscene farting sound, the body expelled putrid trapped gasses around them in a rancid cloud that was so rank and vile, they were instantly retching, stumbling over one another to exit the dock.

That evening, Rip located the address Moe had given him.

Paul's new apartment was a small two-bedroom unit directly above the Blufftopper Bar, an ancient, seedy neighborhood dive located on the far northern boarder of town, adjacent to the old Lakeview Cemetery. Its singular access was from the rear, through a garbage strewn potholed parking lot, up a rickety staircase, to a dangerously rotting wood landing, illuminated solely against the twilight by a naked hanging bulb. He could hear the muted din of voices and music behind the door as he knocked.

It was pulled open by a tall man with unruly short black hair, acne ravaged skin, and a wide smile that held no warmth. From within, a stereo blasted 'Feels Like The First Time' by Foreigner, and voices bellowed to be heard above it.

"You must be one of Paul's friends."

"Yeah, I'm Rip."

"Charlie."

He shook the procured hand, sweaty and soft.

"C'mon in, Rip. You probably know more people here than I do."

He followed, stepping into a living room paneled in oak veneer, jam-packed with the shifting bodies of revelers, soft yellow lighting illuminating a dense drifting atmosphere of cigarette smoke. Steering the six-pack of Special Export before him, he twisted through the crowd, recognizing no one, until he spotted another room beyond a hallway. Entering the equally congested kitchen, he saw Slick, Moe, and Shitly playing quarters around the table. An apparition stepped before him.

"Rip buddy! She-ya, good to see you again!"

Paul had indeed changed. He was a living skeleton. The skin stretched over his jaw and cheekbones like thin freckled parchment, blazing eyes sunken into bruised sockets, shocks of crimson hair tousled in varying directions, but the smile was real, familiar, albeit missing a few teeth.

"Paul! Goddamn! Welcome back."

"She-ya, come here buddy." Paul gripped him in a bear hug. Rip felt bones poke through his shirt, grip surprisingly strong, body odor stronger.

Breaking off, Rip took in the room. "So, you got your own place."

"Share it with Charlie. Like it?"

"Yeah, It's great."

Paul bounced up and down on the balls of his feet, noticing the sixer in his hand. "She-ya, didn't need to bring that. Got a half-barrel right over here." Pulling the cans from his grasp, he slammed them into a refrigerator already half-filled with beer. He led him to a corner of the room, where people crowded around a tapper poking up from the center of a large aluminum cylinder, sitting in a growing wet stain on the floor.

"See? All the comforts of home. Hey Shelly?"

A spacey looking girl turned dopey eyes from the ceiling to him. "Yeah, Paul?"

"Cup for my friend Rip here."

"That'll be a buck."

258

"Said Rip's a friend. Just give him one."

She sighed, pulled one from the stack, and handed it over to Rip.

"Thanks."

Her eyes returned to the ceiling.

"So how you been, Paul?"

"Great, ..." Grinding teeth, he nodded a chin at something behind Rip's shoulder, snapping it back. "Gotta' go take care of something, but stick around. Fun's just starting." Working his way back through the crowd, he turned, grin now eerily sardonic. "*She-ya*, good ta' see you again, Rip."

He was absent most of the evening

An undetermined amount of time later, Rip sat at the kitchen table with Slick, Moe, and Shitly, playing quarters with them, losing badly. The party around them had begun to soften at the edges, and he was barely lucid enough to recognize this as a symptom of point of no return, when he heard the quarter rattle into the bottom of the glass again.

"Drink up!"

Not even sure whose voice it even belonged to, he obliged, draining the glass, refilling it from one of the pitchers on the table. He belched, esophagus filling with foam that shot out his mouth onto his chin.

Laughter. Looking up, his friends pointed at him in drunken hysterics, Slick pounding the table.

"Rip's got beer fangs!"

He smiled back at them across the table, swabbing his face with a sleeve. Paul squeezed through the crowd and stepped up to the table.

"Follow me guys, got a surprise."

Weaving through the small spaces between bodies, pinballing off walls, Rip kept staggering into Moe before him, and falling back into Shitly, who both did their best to give support. He suddenly found himself with them in a disheveled bedroom, party sounds muted through the closed door, looking down at a large mirror covered with small lines of white powder, Paul's skull-like face reflected beneath.

"Go ahead, try it."

"What is it?" Moe rubbed the back of his neck.

"That's cocaine, isn't it?" Slick looked to Paul.

"She-ya, pure Bolivian flake." Grinding teeth. "Best in town. Screw pot, shit's kid's stuff. This'll make you feel like a God."

"Where you get this?"

"Charlie gets it. I help him deal it." Nervous giggles. "Make killer cash money. How we can afford this place."

"How you, … do it?"

"Ya' snort it."

"Up your nose?"

"She-ya."

Rip was having a hard time keeping up. "Hey, isn't that the, …the Disco drug?"

"Fuck Disco!" Paul threw out stick-thin arms. "*She-ya*! Just watch."

He pulled out a twenty-dollar bill, the largest denomination he'd ever seen Paul possess, and rolled it into a tight tube, bent over the mirror. Sticking the bill in his nose, he vacuumed up two of the lines, one for each nostril.

"*Ahhh, Yeahhh*!" He yelled, sniffing repeatedly, handing the bill off to Slick.

"It doesn't hurt?"

"Fuck no!" Paul started boxing the air with bony fists. "Just the opposite!"

Slick bent and snorted his two lines, passed the bill to Moe who did his. Shitly made his disappear and passed the rolled twenty to Rip.

He bent slowly, the room's reflection slightly unbalancing. He twisted the bill tighter, stuck the tube in his nose, and inhaled.

The first thing he noticed was the flavor, like nothing he'd ever tasted before, then the back of his sinus' went numb, and the room jumped before him into startling clarity. He felt the drowsy drunkenness peel away, heart hammering charged blood throughout his body, and his mind launched, accelerating. He sniffed back a trickle of snot that leaked out his nose, and got an additional supercharge.

"Whoa, …" Slick was pinching the bridge of his nose.

Moe blinked. "*Shit* Paul, this is fucking great!"

Shitly wore a manic grin.

"Well?" Paul's legs drummed the floor.

Rip felt a tide of euphoria and confidence well up over his soul. "I feel like I could kick the world's ass."

"Ah-ha!" Racing around the room, clapping everyone on the their shoulders and backs, Paul tore open the door, admitting Kiss' 'Calling Doctor Love', and a drunken couple that had been leaning against it. "Let's get out there and *par-tee!*"

Stitching through the crowd with a new sizzling perception, Rip considered them from a fresh perspective. Slouchy, sloppy, slurry, he sized up each male as a potential adversary, deciding that in their current state, he could probably take anyone in the room.

Standing in line for a beer, he carried on a conversation with the guy in front of him, all the while a separate section of his mind tracking others in the kitchen, not really paying attention to what he was saying. When his turn came, he managed to over-pump the tap so it coughed foam, and he had to take several tries, pouring half out, tapping more in, till his glass was full, then draining it in one gulp and getting back in line.

He was noticing something else as well. Wandering the party, scanning the celebrants, he would linger on each girl there, summoning a growing desire. He would study their faces, lips, chests, the shape of their asses, thinking about what it would be like to touch them, to strip them naked, to enter them, and his libido flared. Looking from one to the other, his mind became host to a variety of fantasies and perversions, and he was panting, sweating, nostrils flaring, a hunter seeking prey. This wasn't mere desire or passing horniness; it was an atavistic hunger, and needed to be fed.

"Hey, Rip!"

He nearly knocked the cup out of Stephanie's glass when he turned. "Stephanie."

"You OK Rip? You look a little, …crazed."

"Yeah, I'm better than fine." Pulse hammering at his temples. "Who you here with?"

She pointed to the blond with a neck brace, on crutches. "Cheryl can't drive yet, so I drove her."

"Cool." He had to make a conscious effort to stop his foot from tapping.

She swirled her beer. "Say, I'm sorry about that time with my brother."

"Uh, …yeah, that's alright, …it's just, …"

"What?"

He swallowed. "Uh, …you know, …"

"No, what?"

Eyes crawling down her body. "Wish we could have finished what we started."

"Why, Rip." She smiled, fingered her hair. "That's uncharacteristically forward of you."

"Well, don't you?"

She met his eyes. "Of course."

"Well?"

"Well, what?"

"Wanna' duck outta' here for a while?"

She giggled. "Now?"

"Why not?"

Holding her glass up. "Well at least let a girl have another beer."

The earth was still spongy from the melted snow in the graveyard when they climbed through a gap in the ancient wrought iron fence. They'd just entered the first tier of headstones when Rip grabbed Stephanie by the waist, crushing her body against his, ramming a tongue down her throat. She gyrated, grinding hips, kissing back as they ran hands over each other's bodies, parting only to come up for air.

"Christ, Rip." She stroked his erection. "Let me help you with that."

Dropping to her knees, she unbuckled his belt, unbuttoned his fly, and pulled him free.

"Jesus, don't remember it being that big."

He felt the warmth of her lips close over him, grasping at her hair head bobbing up and down, but he was only getting harder, not any closer to release, when he had an idea.

"My balls, suck on my balls." he panted.

Feeling her tongue move down, a sudden sharp pain stabbed at his abdomen.

"Ow! Don't. Don't suck my balls."

Then she was back working on his head, tongue lapping furiously, but he wasn't coming, needing to go deeper, thrusting, back of her head connecting with the gravestone, and she pulled him out.

"*Stop* it, Rip."

But bloodthunder roared like a tsunami in his head, and he effortlessly pulled her from the ground, bending her over the gravestone, savagely pantsing her, pushing himself between the exposed pale hillocks of her buttocks, her voice lost as he ground his teeth and drove harder, each thrust faster and deeper, grasping her hips to piston against him, feeling her tightness, heat, friction, the surge building as their bodies rammed violently against each other and off the headstone, and when he finally came with a bolt of blinding white lightning, he roared over her screams, the first he was aware of them.

Pulling free, he backed away, gasping, dripping sweat, staring in horror as Stephanie slid to the base of the headstone, burying her head in the wet mulch, silently weeping, jeans and panties pooled around her ankles.

"Stephanie?"

"*Just leave me alone!*" She screamed, reaching back at her underwear, not turning.

Realization of what he'd just done struck him with nightmare dread, and Rip started hyperventilating. "Oh *God*, Stephanie, I'm sorry, ...I, ..."

"*Get away from me, Rip! Just fuck off and die!*"

Rip backed slowly away between rows of gravestones, letting the murky shadows of the cemetery swallow him into their depths.

*   *   *   *

The day was more like summer than late spring, and he walked the road.

The countless cottonwoods along the river valley had simultaneously bloomed, filling the air with drifting white balls of fuzz, swirling about like a temperate blizzard. They gathered in growing downy drifts upon lawns and along curbs in a benign mirage of the long winter season that had recently passed.

Every so often Dart would unexpectedly catch himself hearing the familiar sound of his father's approaching car, then it would all come back. His heart would plummet back into an abyss of sorrow and grief, but by now the feelings had become more blunted, like a memory, lingering less and less each day.

He spotted a familiar piss-yellow car draw near, pulling a blueish cloud along down the road, and Glenn pulled the Montego to a shuddery crawl alongside. To Dart's surprise, his stepsister leaned out from the passenger seat, face framed by Farrah feathered hair.

"Hi'ya Dart. What'cha doin'?"

"Just walkin'."

"Walkin'?"

Glenn smiled, bobbed his head, and clawed away a greasy strand of hair. "Yeah, man. He does that."

She wrinkled her nose. "Well, you want a ride?"

"Nah, I'm cool."

"You sure? You all right?"

"I'm fine. I just like walkin'."

"All right, then. See ya." She ducked back in as Glenn popped him the peace sign.

"Stay groovy, Dart."

"Peace."

The car backfired explosively and juttered down the street trailing its smokescreen.

He stepped up the curb to stand over a bank leading down to the channel, pausing to pick up a handful of smooth river-polished rocks, pitching them at the far shoreline for accuracy and distance, when a familiar voice from the road made him jump.

"Hey Dart!"

He turned to see Sara leaning out the window of Cheryl's VW Bug, its roof dimpled from having been hammered out, sporting a new discolored front quarterpanel. He walked up, seeing Cheryl in the driver's seat, and their little sister, Stacey, in back.

"Hey girls, what you doing in my neck of the woods?"

"Headin' to your place to go swimming." Cheryl pointed to her neck brace. "Well, they are, anyway."

"Yeah, your sister invited mine over." Her pigtails were back, but Sara's part was covered by a Brewers baseball cap. "So, …I thought I'd take *you* up on *your* invitation. If that's alright?"

"Sure. Yeah. That's great." He waved to Stacey in the rear seat, who smiled back.

Sara tilted her head. "Do you need a ride?"

"Nah, that's cool, I'll just meet you there."

"Alright, see ya." The Bug rolled ahead, its engine sounding like a souped-up sewing machine.

He switched direction and headed for home.

Dart rounded the corner of his house to the back yard, saw the two Stacey's splashing around in the shallows near the boat dock, his mother on the deck, wine glass in hand, talking to Cheryl and Sara. She turned, The Hollies crooning 'The Air That I Breathe' from a combination AM/FM CB band radio that sat nearby on a patio table.

"Well, there he is." Tipping her glass. "You never told me you were in the same class as Stacey's sister Sara, here."

"Uhm, yeah." He scratched nervously at his hair. "Just found out. Different homerooms, but we got Ecology together."

"Well isn't that nice. Maybe you can show her around the beach a little. Dart here is quite the River Rat."

"Really now." Cheryl gave him a sly grin.

"Oh my, yes. He's out there all the time. We can't keep him away."

"Perfect, then. Why don't you kids go have fun." Indicating her neck brace. "It'll be another month before this comes off."

His mother shook her head. "That's so sad. Can I get you a drink, Cheryl?"

"Yes, ma'am, a wine would be great."

"Please, call me Mary Jane." She slid open the glass door, stopped. "You *are* old enough, aren't you?"

Cheryl straightened. "I'll be eighteen this fall ma'am, …uh, Mary Jane."

His mother offered a conspiratorial wink. "Close enough."

Grasping beach towels, Dart led Sara down the lawn and over the retaining wall to the sandy slope that met the river. Squinting up at warmth radiating from the sunlight, she removed the cap from her head, revealing the jagged slash of her part.

"Just so you know, this is my first time on the beach this year." She considered him shyly. "So don't make fun of my super-white skin."

He laughed. "Mine too. So I won't if you won't."

Feigning nonchalance, he kicked off tennis shoes and doffed his shirt, as she stripped down to a striped string bikini, body coltish and athletic, breasts appearing to have doubled in stature since last summer.

"Hey, Stacey!" she called down the beach.

"What?" Two voices.

They traded smiles. "How's the water?"

"Fine!" His sister.

"Freezing!" Sara's Stacey.

She stepped down to the river, his mind drinking in every move she took. She pointed a toe into the shallows, eyes widening.

"It's cold."

"It always seems cold when you first get in." Shaking his head. "You'll get used to it."

Wading ankle-deep, she wrapped arms around her breasts. "*Still* cold."

"Aww, that's not how you do it." Darting suddenly down the beach, he ran up the gangway over the dock and launched himself off the edge, doing a complete flip into the river, his best move.

The water was a complete shock, numbing and knocking his breath out in a stream of bubbles, and he broke the surface with a roar.

"*RRAAHH*! That's really refreshing!"

The Staceys squealed.

"Liar!" His stepsister jiggled down the beach from next door in her two-piece, trailing a dopey, but happy looking Glenn, and then Curt raced past them already stripped down to his cut-offs.

"Swim party!"

He galloped across the dock and dove, disappearing below the surface with barely a ripple, coming up with his own cry.

"*GHHAA*! You weren't kidding! It *is* refreshing!"

Ellen splashed up to her thighs, stopped and shrieked.

"Jesus! You *are* lying. I'm totally nipping."

Sara caught his eye, looked away and blushed. If there were a hard nipple contest, she would have won, hands down, over Ellen.

Eventually, they all ended up in the water, and, like he'd promised, they got used to the temperature, to the point that it became more comfortable to stay submerged. Cheryl and his mother kept watch from the deck above, talking and listening to the radio. Eventually, they were joined by Helen, at which point cocktails substituted the wine.

They swam for most of the day. When Ellen, Glenn, and Curt finally left with their mother it was getting late, the sun low and amber. By then, even the Staceys endless resources of energy were starting to exhibit signs of weakening. They both sat on the bank sculpting sand castles, murmuring about princesses, kings, and dragons. By the tone of his mother's voice carrying down from the deck, Dart guessed that she was half in the bag already, and Cheryl didn't sound that much farther behind. The radio's volume was boosted, Hot Chocolate melancholically lamenting the tragic fate of 'Emma'.

Sara and Dart were the last ones in the river.

"Here, let me show you something." He swam toward the boat dock.

"What is it?" She followed, smoothing back her hair.

Reaching the far side, they grasped the decking, treading water. Most of the boat docks in the area were simple wood planking held afloat by a succession of fifty-five gallon drums, which were susceptible to puncture. His parents had decided to go a high tech route for theirs, opting for blocky lengths of bright orange nautical Styrofoam paralleling its length, leaving an open center isle. This was where he guided Sara, into the secret spot beneath the dock, cut off from all overhead light save for bright dashes of sunlight from between planks. The river beneath became luminous, a liquid emerald radiance rippling waves of light along the ceiling and walls, revealing all it held beneath; infinite flecks of spinning algae, passing schools of flickering minnows, both their treading bodies, warped and distorted.

He waited for a boat to pass out on the channel. "Hold your breath under water with me for a minute. Listen."

They each sucked in a breath and sank beneath the surface. He opened his eyes to see her weightless before him, hair a dark corona, the sun's rays pirouetting behind her body. The snarl of the boat faded to silence, revealing a subtle but ubiquitous background noise, thousands, millions of tiny clicks. He saw that she heard it too, a querulous expression crossing her face, until she could hold her breath no longer, letting loose a long string of bubbles as they surfaced.

"What was that sound?"

"Guess."

"I couldn't even begin to."

"Rocks. Stones. All of them, in the river, rolling against each other. The current is like a giant tumbler, smoothing them out forever."

Sara's eyes widened in wonder. Her lips parted in a slight smile, the light from beneath illuminating moisture beading her skin, heightening her nearly surreal beauty. She glanced down and uttered a startled squeak.

"What are those?" Her voice a hoarse whisper.

Looking down through the water, he laughed. "Don't worry, just sunfish. They can't hurt you. They're attracted to the salt on your skin."

They watched as silhouettes of the small creatures curiously approached, kiss their legs or arms with little fish lips, then dart away into the murk as another would draw near.

"It tickles." She giggled, pointing over his shoulder. "So, …uh, what's that?"

He poked at a gelatinous blob of slime that clung in the corner, wedged between foam and wood. "Huh. Looks like a cluster of frog eggs."

"That's pretty gross."

"I guess. Can't hurt you, though. Here, …" He reached up, fitting fingers through the boards, holding himself in place. "…do this. You won't have to tread."

She followed his example, and they faced each other less than a foot apart, immersed to the shoulders in the warm womb of the river. An uncomfortable silence grew, and she looked away, then back, holding his gaze.

"You really love the river, don't you?"

"It's, …special. To me. Right now, I guess, it's the only thing that makes sense."

Sara inhaled slowly, exhaled.

"I heard about your father, Dart. I'm so sorry."

Something deep within him stirred, unlocked.

"Sara, I've always liked you. I, …I think about you all the time. You're the coolest, prettiest girl I've ever seen. So I wonder, …if you, …ever, maybe, …felt kinda', …like that, sometime. About me."

Her arms wound around his neck, wet, warm body pressing against his skin, lips slipping over his, the barest hint of a tongue flickering over teeth, and he drowned in the moment as it echoed back and forth through time, finishing finally an eternity later to her curious smile.

"Dart, what is that?"

Turning slowly, he confronted the distinctive shape of a turd floating mere inches away, overgrown with a mossy cilia of waving green algae, recalling the raw sewage the Twin Cities were reported to have been dumping.

"Nothing. I think it's time to get out of the water."

*   *   *   *

It was the far side of nighttime, just before daybreak, and he stood
on his silent boat in the center of the Mississippi drifting with the
current and half- thoughts, a somnambulate traveler caught between
night and day, sleep and dreams. Further upstream than he'd ever
before ventured, Rip figured he was probably the only human on the
river at this time for a hundred miles. He stared at the apparition of
Twin Bluffs looming up out of the gloaming, two identical breast-like
peaks fringed in forest, their faces to the river sheared raw, revealing
sandstone interiors, sheer cliffs that dropped to the basin. He watched
as the approaching dawn drove a thick draping of fog down their
backs, a dense wraith-like soup that flowed in slow-motion through
paths of least resistance, its leading edge extending ropy tendrils to
weave through valleys and glades, slowly obscuring the lowlands,
eventually reaching down to touch the river itself.

As sole witness to this sublime natural phenomenon, he wondered
where these memories would go if he were to disappear.

When the sun peaked over the horizon, it found Rip sitting on an
abandoned Airport Beach, watching the flight paths of landing and
outgoing aircraft, attempting to stave off the inevitable.

His head throbbed with a hangover, his body and mind craved
more coke, and his lungs were raw from smoking it. His thoughts
would switch rapidly between willful determination, to dark suicidal
tracks, and he was aware that it was the drug, or maybe specifically
the lack of it that was doing this to him. But awareness didn't help.
Nothing but more of the drug seemed to, a relentless tailspin that
kept tightening.

He only had about a quarter gram left, in a fold in his pocket.
Powder, not freebase, not nearly enough to last until tonight, when
Charlie would return with a fresh supply.

At times, he was able to step outside himself and see what he had become, and marvel at how quickly and completely it had happened, but those moments of lucidity and self awareness were becoming increasingly rare, quelled by constant blitzkriegs of guilt and self loathing, demanding the instant gratification of self medication.

Rip pulled a lukewarm can of Old Style from the bench hold and gulped it down, watching the sunrise, feeling only slightly more numb. Catching a whiff of body odor, he stripped and dove into the river, drying naked on the beach in the warming sun.

Hearing the signature whine of a twenty-five horse Evinrude, he slipped on his cut-offs and waited as Dart approached, beaching the small flat-bottom next to the battered Alumacraft.

"Hey Rip. You look like shit."

Rip smiled sadly. "That's funny. That's exactly how I feel."

"No, I mean it. You alright?"

"Alright." Rip nodded mechanically. "That has relative subjectivity."

"Uh huh." Dart watched a Piper Cub roll in overhead, landing gear extended, engine blaring. "Been out on the river awhile?"

"Three days, two nights."

"Camping?"

"Riding."

"Where?"

"Everywhere."

"Guess that's why I haven't seen you at school."

Rip's answering gaze was both possessed and apathetic.

A drumming resonated from the river as the red-rusted prow of a barge's cargo tanker nudged out from the north end of the beach. It rode along the main channel with implacable momentum, full, judging from what little remained of the freeboard. It passed, and they watched the number of tanker's grow, sound of the massive diesel engines rising and dropping in tempo, echoing throughout the valley, barge slowly spanning the river from horizon to horizon.

They counted an incredible twelve tankers before the tug driving them rolled out from the treeline, except there were two.

Dart and Rip turned to one another, knowing the extra tug meant a whole additional row of tankers, hidden behind the ones they could see, doubling their number.

"Jesus, …" Rip scurried around to the bow of his boat. "…that thing must be displacing half the fucking Mississippi! Get these up on the beach, fast!"

They muscled the hulls of the small craft as far up the sand as they could. The waterline began to slowly recede, disclosing a glistening, hidden world of clay banks, kelp clusters, and clam beds. It quickened, suddenly reversing, pushing a tide two feet up over the high water mark. Sucking back farther, revealing the strangely obscene maw of a drop-off, it surged back again, higher this time, withdrawing, exposing a greater expanse of the river's naked bottom, silvery comma's of fish bodies flopping around in surprise, swelling back again and again, higher and higher around their ankles and calves. They held fast to their bobbing and dipping boats, the deluge nearly cresting the island, before slowly abating with the barge's passing, to its previous level.

Rip and Dart stood in the cool, wet sand. They listened to the receding pulse of the tug's twin engines.

"Well, I'll be damned." Rip shielded eyes against the sun with a shaky hand. The ship slipped behind the line of trees.

"There's *got* to be a restriction against that." Kicking a beached clamshell down the shore, Dart sat in the sand. "Somebody could drown from that undertow."

"Restrict, …" Lurching down to the shoreline, Rip pumped a fist into the air and shouted. "Restrict the undertow!"

He pulled a can from his boat, cracked the tab, greedily guzzling it. Belching loudly, Rip turned a demented gaze on him, laughing mirthlessly, pointing.

"You ever hear of Heisenberg's Uncertainty Principle?"

"Heisenberg?"

"Nah… No. Sorry." Waving a hand before him. "How would you? You're not even in High School. Hell, I don't even know why *I* know it."

"Why, what is it?"

"It,…it's this thing they discovered studying quantum particles. Freakishly small shit, man. Sub-atomic level. Anyway, this guy Heisenberg can't get any consistent results with these things, they're behaving very strangely, and he finds out this is because he is *watching* them, get it? That observing a phenomenon changes its outcome. Can you wrap your head around that shit? Like you'll never know how this thing really works, 'cause every time you try to measure or record it, it alters its behavior. Kinda' like that Zen, tree falling in the forest thing, right?" He shrugged. "Course, this is all happening on a quantum level, but, hell, I think that it reflects a fucked up sort of universal truth. Crazy shit, huh?"

"That's, …pretty crazy." Rip's erratic behavior was starting to make him uneasy.

"Right." Nodding to himself. "Know what else is weird? The Milky Way."

"The galaxy?"

"Yes!" He stretched arms up to the heavens. "Why is our galaxy named after a candy bar? I mean… does the Mars Corporation have some kind of mandate on the known universe? Oh, …Mars Corporation. Ha! I get it!"

"Well, …um, now that you mention it, …"

Rip turned, and he was the same old River Rat that had rescued him from Brad's gang. He was calm, confident, voice subdued.

"What kind of a name is Dart, anyway? That a nickname?"

"Uh, … no, it's my real name. Guess it runs in the family, 'cause it was my father's middle name." He tried to make a joke. "What about Rip? What's it stand for? Rest in peace?"

"Hardly." Gazing off downstream to where the barge had disappeared, Rip spoke softly. "Dart, I think it's about time you took off. I'll help you down with your boat."

The Evinrude purred to life on the first pull. Rip gave him a push-off from the bow, standing in the shallows.

"I always liked those old 'Rudes." Pointing to his motor. "Like my Johnson there, solid, trustworthy. Not like those cranky Mercury's. High maintenance. Who needs that?"

The current grabbed Dart's boat and pulled him out, but still he stood, watching the dwindling form of Rip disappear into the sweep of Airport Beach until it vanished, drifting around a bend. He sat at the transom, throttled up, and hydroplaned over the waters.

Swing Beach was a scene of utter disrepair and abandonment when he arrived, the rope hanging gray and fraying from a tree leaning precariously over the riverbank. The platform was a ruinous splintering of vandalized wood, the ladder of two-by-fours leading up to it missing half its rungs, the trunk they were attached to bearing the scorched scars of burn marks in the bark around its base.

Dart briefly relived the terrifying exhilaration of his first jump, the ground rushing up to greet him, the rope pulling out with bone-crushing gravity, faces of Curt, Randy, Lynette, Cheryl, Gaylene, and Sara tearing by with impossible speed before he was pitched up and out, the river below diminishing to a thin vein, a hopeless target to hit, hanging weightless, suspended, before dropping down, plummeting a stomach churning distance to strike the water with a jarring impact, plunging down, deep and dark, to the cooler current below, feeling pressure build, feet finally sinking into the mucky river bottom, thankful for the absence of any sharp, hidden debris, kicking up toward the light to break the surface for a grateful breath of air, to the cheers of his audience on the beach and the arriving flotilla of River Rats.

Holding out a hand, he gave the rope a gentle tug, and it seemed to unravel, disintegrate, dropping into the shallows to drift like the broken corpse of a snake.

He rode far upstream, taking time to pass through the locks, emerging as the titanic iron gates drew open to see a graying smudge hanging in the air directly to the north. Feeling an ominous foreboding, he steered in its direction.

Approaching Tomahawk Island, Dart could see the fire-blackened remains of the tree fort clinging to the trunks and limbs of the ravaged copse of trees, still spouting wispy threads of smoke.

The ground was warm and some of the branches still popped angrily with cooling embers as he moved through swirling eddies of ash to survey the remains. The blaze had obviously started with the stove. It lay on the ground in a melted heap of slag, beneath a huge charred hole through the flooring. The fort itself appeared to have been bombed. Little remained of the walls and ceiling, save for jagged carbonized sections of the frame clinging to the corners, defying gravity, still holding fast to their berthing. Strewn about the area was half-burnt debris of a telling nature: empty beer cans and smashed bottles, melted lawn chair, the broken half of a Styrofoam cooler, fused blobs of used condoms and their torn foil wrappers. The pages of Playboy and Penthouse were scattered everywhere, and he even happened upon a skimpy pair of white cotton panties, rusted spot of dried blood smeared onto the crotch.

When he finally arrived back home, the sun was slipping behind the bluffs, and his sister beckoned urgently from the shoreline as he docked the boat.

"Hurry Dart! She's gonna' kill it!" Her voice shrieked with panic.

"What's going on, Stace? Who's gonna' kill who?"

"The mother! She's killing her baby!" Stacey raced up and grabbed his hand, pulling him out to the beach. Stopping, she pointed, blubbering pathetically.

He heard a sound, a soft peep, and saw the hen mallard astraddle the sprawled form of a small duckling, wings ruffled, fluttering in agitation as it pecked violently at the tiny body.

"Hey!" He ran up. "*Yahh*! Get off!"

But the mother ignored him, striking repeatedly.

Not wanting to touch the creature, he grabbed a small rock and bounced it off her back with a hollow thud. Quacking angrily, she fluttered backward, revealing the baby's broken body, as it started a desperate cheeping.

"*Ohh*, Dart." His sister sobbed again. "What are we gonna' to do?"

"I don't know." He bent closer.

"I'm going to get Mom." Her footsteps went up the bank.

Curling his fingers around the delicate bundle of broken bones, he lifted the thing. Light as a feather, it radiated terrific heat for a being of its stature. He felt the fragile flutter of its heartbeat, saw the glistening, broken shards of brittle bird bones poking through torn flesh, eye turning up to him in abject terror, cheeping hysterically now.

"Here!" His sister's voice pronounced, and Dart turned, seeing his mother pulled to a stop by Stacey, staring at what he held in his hands.

"Ahh, …shit."

"Please, *Momeee*! We have to get it to the hospital!"

She shook her head sadly. "*Sweetee*, it's too late."

"But *MOM*!" She wailed. "They can make it better!"

"I'm sorry honey. The poor thing's going to die."

"But I don't want it to die!"

"Please, …" Dart held it up to her. "Isn't there anything we can do?"

She knelt in the sand and looked up at her two children. "It's probably the runt of the litter. The mother knew it wouldn't survive, and she had to put it out of its misery so she could take care of her other babies." She gently touched Stacey's quivering chin. "Now I know its very sad, but that's the way nature works."

"But, …*Momeee*, …" His sister began to blubber, tears streaming down her cheeks.

In his hand, the duckling gave a feeble peep and drew a single, tiny, unbroken webbed foot into the fine down of its breast, rolled its eyes back to white, shuddered, and died.

Dart felt profound anguish at a world so cruelly punitive to something merely born so helpless and innocent. Holding back his own tears, he gazed out over the far riverbank and witnessed a wraith-like cloud lift itself from the marshes and rise into the gathering twilight.

*   *   *   *

Paul was talking too fast for him to hear.

Or maybe it was the other way around. Maybe he was thinking so far ahead of what Paul was saying that he was missing his meaning. Either way, he couldn't make out a word, watching as his teeth clacked staccato against each other in his shrinking skull, emitting alien sounds, glass pipe smoking in one hand, the other waving a burning propane torch around like a blazing scimitar.

Then the rush was leaving him, tunnel vision receding, apartment rematerializing in all its slovenly glory. Nilsson, on the Hi-fi, lamented putting the lime in the 'Coconut', shrieking for a doctor.

He was standing in the living room watching Charlie, Paul's roommate, work small piles of white powder from a large mound centered on a mirror, atop a coffee table, into the tray of a double-beamed scale. He slid weights, adding or subtracting until the pointer rested on zero, pouring the contents into little folds of wax paper, pre-made, in a pile of their own on the couch. He noticed Rip's gaze, smiling coldly in return, face a roadmap of festering acne, similar to what had begun to appear on Paul's skin.

Paul dodged out the room, nearly tripping on a pizza box that lay amid other scattered trash. He dashed into the kitchen, with its sink stacked high in dishes covered with rotting matter, where Slick and Moe prepared another round of freebase on the gas stove. Shitly, the only one who didn't base, sat in a small chair against the wall, chopping rock on a hand-held mirror with a razor blade.

Drawing a finger over a nearby shelf revealed the entire room was coated with a fine, white dust.

The oncoming rush from basing the cocaine was an enchantment that Rip had never expected to experience in his life, a wave of pure contentment and clarity, but he was finding that it was subject to the harsh laws of diminishing returns, the heavenly highs quickly abating, giving way to longer and lower lows.

Bolting back into the room, torch thankfully extinguished, Paul pulled up in front of Charlie, admiring the bounty on the table before him.

"Y' ever see so much scratch?" He vibrated. "*She-ya,* we gonna' be rich."

"Careful around the shit, Paul." Charlie muttered, concentrating on his efforts. "You're higher 'n a kite, and I don't want you spilling any."

"*She-ya!*" Paul thrashed, teeth grinding, eyes rolling, breaking into braying, maniacal laughter.

Rip nodded at the table. "That's, … a lot of money there. You guys aren't worried about getting ripped off?"

"Hell no!" Lunging behind the couch, Paul produced a twelve gauge, pump action shotgun, and began waving it around.

"Jesus!"

Slick and Moe turned from their places before the stove.

"Whoa!"

"Yeah, cool it, Paul."

Shitly looked up from the chair and chuckled.

"Quit playing with the gun, Paul." Charlie muttered, patiently.

"Relax, pussies! It ain't loaded." He cleared the breech, showing it empty. "It's just fer' looks. And, …" He ratcheted the action. "…the *sound*. You doin' sometin' yer' not s'pose ta' be? You hear that sound? You shit your pants."

The firing pin clacked against the empty chamber.

Slick nodded his head. "Great, now we got that to worry about."

"Here's your shit." Paul tossed over a fold to Rip. "Ready to go. Wanna' cook up here?"

Rip considered the room. "Should probably get goin', Paul."

"All right then." Laying the gun back on the floor, he jerked forward, clammy hand grabbing his in a pistoning shake. "Good doin' business with you, buddy. *She-ya*, you and I go back a way, eh? "

"Yeah, we do."

"Been through the shit."

"Been through the shit, Paul."

"We'll get through this."

"Sure, Paul."

"See ya' later, buddy."

"See ya', Paul."

Shitly was giggling to himself as he passed on the way out.

"Something funny?"

Turning to him, Shitly's face was beaded with sweat beneath a mop of brown hair, depraved look in eyes Rip realized he'd never really witnessed before. He chopped obsessively at the mirror, crooked smile on his face.

"Ever hear the one about Gomer Pyle and his girlfriend?"

"Er, …what?"

"It's a joke." Tapping out a rolled bill, Shitly quickly twisted it and snorted two lines. "See, he's out with his girl, Lou Ann Poovie, …Ha! I can't believe they got away with that on TV, …Poovie! Can ya' believe it? Anyway, they're out on their first date, see, and when they finally get back to her place Gomer asks, 'Miss Poovie, would you let me put my finger in your bellybutton?"

He chopped out two more lines, snorting them. Rip looked on, galvanized. "Miss Poovie says, 'Why Gomer, it's only our first date. I would never let you do anything like that 'till after the third date'. So they go out again, …"

He drew out two more lines.

"And after, when they get back again to her place again, he asks, 'Miss Poovie, can I stick my finger in your bellybutton now?'" The lines disappeared. "And she says, 'Gomer, I told you, nothing like that 'till the third date.'

Chopping the last. "So they go out a third time, and they get back to her place, and Gomer says to her 'Miss Poovie, you told me that on our third date, you'd let me put my finger in your bellybutton."

He Hoovered the remaining residue, continuing. "And she says 'I made you a promise, Gomer, so go ahead'. And so he does, only she yells, and he asks what's wrong."

Jaws clenching, Shitly drew in a long breath through gritted teeth.

"And she says, 'Gomer, that's not my bellybutton!' and he says 'Surprise, surprise, surprise, that's not my finger either!' Ha! Get it?"

Rip stared down at his sardonic smile. "I think you better take it easy on that stuff, Shitly."

"Easy?" Thumbing dregs from the mirror, he ran them over his gums. "You think growing up with a name like Shitly is easy?"

Glancing about the room, Rip confirmed that he was the sole witness to this conversation.

"Think anybody's gonna' want to listen to something a guy named *Shitly's* got to say? Think anybody will take a *Shitly* seriously? Think a *Shitly* would ever get laid? *Jesus*."

Very quietly, Rip asked. "Then. What's your real name?"

The eyes that met his were haunted. He chuckled sadly. "Ahart. Don't that beat the fuck-all? *Ahart*. Only thing probably *worse* than Shitly. And I got my old man to blame for both."

He leaped up suddenly, grabbing at his stomach. "Goddamn. Gotta' run to the can, man. Shit fucks with my guts."

He vanished down the hallway.

Stepping outside onto the second floor landing, Rip noticed a hissing sonance present in the air. It appeared to be snowing, except it was far too warm for that, and the precipitate seemed to have life, fluttering, flowing like a school of fish around streetlights. All hard angles around him were strangely softened, blurred somehow, when he recognized what was happening.

Mayfly hatch. Millions upon millions of the newly hatched insects, choking the very air with their presence, alighting every surface with their growing number, a biblical plague, abruptly illuminated by the blue/red strobing of police bars chasing themselves around the back alley from a half-dozen cruiser's that were parked there.

Suddenly surrounded by moving bodies, Rip's hands were painfully bound behind his back, and he was forced down the rickety stairway, slithering dangerously over the fly's crushed bodies.

"Come with me, boy." Voice in his ear. "You're under arrest."

Reaching the bottom, the police officer face-planted him onto the pavement, forcing a knee into his back, smashing his face into the living biomass. He struggled to keep the things out of his mouth and eyes.

"You just stay right there while we round up your friends."

Rip strained his neck to see four officers on the landing kick open the door. After a brief pause there was a loud crash, followed by excited shouting, and they re-emerged, each escorting a bound figure, Paul's screaming voice following him out the door.

"Goddamned fucking Carp! Let me go!"

"I told you to shut up, you punk puke." Karpinski growled, pushing Paul at the rear of the queue.

Slick was leading the group, and when his captor slipped on the aggregation of insect bodies, toppling sloppily down the stairs, he wasted no time, sprinting to the bottom and across the alley, chased by cheers from his friends, hands still clasped behind his back.

"Goddammit! Grab him!" Karpinski bawled.

Rip struggled on the ground to keep the officer restraining him from following pursuit, receiving a knee to the neck for his trouble.

Slick darted by, out to the street, and disappeared.

"We'll get him later." Karpinski swatted disgustedly at the encroaching nimbus of insects. "Fucking bugs."

They marched their subjects down to the awaiting cars. Rip watched them pass, from his vantage point on the ground. Charlie, being led vacant and distant, Moe, still somehow smoking a cigarette despite the fact that his hands were manacled behind his back, Paul, screeching indignantly.

"Nothin' but a carp, motherfucker. Nothin' but a carp!"

Karpinski checked him in the back of the head with the stock of the shotgun he was holding, bringing him to his knees, groaning in anguish.

"Keep it up carrot-top, and you'll get more of the same."

Then there was a sound.

Recognizing its sinister tone, they all turned to see the figure of Shitly on the porch, framed in the lighted doorway, wielding the twelve-gauge.

"Let them go!" He started down the stairs.

The cops all reacted, throwing their quarry to the ground, reaching for their side arms.

Karpinski shouldered his shotgun and shouted. "Freeze! Drop that weapon immediately!"

"Shitly! Stop!" Moe cried, ejecting his smoldering butt onto a few startled Mayflies.

The shadowed form continued moving down the staircase.

"I mean it, son! Freeze right there and drop the weapon!" Karpinski chambered a round.

"I said, let them go!"

"Don't shoot, goddammit!" Paul pleaded from the ground. "The gun ain't even loaded!"

"For Christ sake, Shitly, stop!" Rip yelled.

Shitly stepped into the reeling blaze of light, alternating between aqua blue, and deep blood red, sheepish grin beneath hard eyes, wreathed in the cascading swarm of insects.

"That's far *enough*!" Karpinski's voice carried a hysterical edge.

"Who the fuck, are you to tell me what to do?"

A chorus of clicks came from the other cops cocking their hammers.

"I'm the man with the gun, son."

Shitly looked down and chuckled. "Well, you're not the only one, …"

He raised the weapon.

The flat report of the revolvers sounded like firecrackers in the alley, and Rip screamed seeing the holes punch into his friend's body, but he hardly seemed to notice, sighting down the barrel as Karpinski's shotgun roared, sounding like a cannon. Shitly jerked comically backward, landing like a broken doll in a lifting plume of Mayflies.

The smell of cordite, and the gentle hissing of insect wings filled the space, everything else frozen in time, until officer Karpinski, face stricken, dropped to his knees and started retching.

A wave of pure rage surged through Rip, and he spun, kicking out and connecting with something hard. Lurching awkwardly to his feet, he ran to where his friend lay, already accumulating a thin fringe of Mayfly's, trying not to see the torn, leaking maw where his legs should have been joined.

"*Jesus, Shitly.*"

Shitly looked back with naked terror, drawing shuddering breaths through chattering teeth stained by a dark, viscous liquid.

"*I didn't think it would hurt so bad.*"

Bright comets erupted with piercing pain in Rip's head before all went dark.

*   *   *   *

In the dream, Dart stood in the schoolyard of the Middle School.

It was a warm, bright day, and puffy white cauliflowers of cumulous skimmed over a clean cobalt sky.

The school was nestled squarely in the river valley, monolithic runs of the bluffs framing the east and western horizons. The cragged peak of Grandfather's Bluff loomed impossibly close to the cinder-block building, which was warped strangely out of proportion from its real-life counterpart.

Giving a cursory glance around, he noticed that the place was peculiarly quiet. Swings and jungle gyms stood still and empty, the football field stretching far away from the silent row of bleachers. Hard sunlight glanced off burnished metal surfaces, highlights burning into his eyes, somehow rendering the stillness even more ominous. There was a curious deadness to the air, as if the whole valley had been encapsulated with a mounting pressure.

The cry of an air raid siren cut through the day and he was compelled to peer up at Grandfather's Buff, towering majestically overhead, scraping the bottoms of clouds.

There was a sub-sonic thump, felt more than heard. A pinpoint of blinding white light from on the peak flared painfully bright over his field of vision. Instinctively turning away, he cautiously looked back, seeing through the building with a bizarre X-ray vision; infrastructure visible, revealing layers and levels of classrooms, structural supports and anchor points.

A dark, icy claw of terror clutched his heart as the top of the bluff disintegrated. It rose above in a deadly plume of fire and super-heated gasses. Heart jack-hammering within his ribcage, he sought shelter against the school wall, bracing for a shockwave he was sure to come.

Its shadow was thrown over the playground. He saw with alarm, that the shadow was shrinking, as the intensity of the surrounding light escalated.

Quiet. He thought. *It's just too quiet.*

Then he heard it.

Like the shush of an incoming wake, it announced its approach, a great tidal wave of white noise. The light around him magnified, shifting to a glaring yellow, shadow closing in on the wall like twin wands of a divining wand seeking their mark, sound building, a billion pool balls crashing and tearing into one another.

He crushed himself to the cinderblocks, feeling the first wave of heat, breath catching in his chest, light shifting to an angry red. The swings and jungle gyms all gave a silent breath of smoke, sinking in on themselves, bleachers pouring molten quicksilver onto the smoking field.

The wall shielding him was dissolving, disintegrating from each side, him in the middle. He realized that the terrible cacophony was the cataclysmic collisions of molecules, the structure of reality tearing itself apart, the noise growing to a deafening crescendo, light burning everything away, leaving only him and the diminishing shadow of the wall.

This was the end, the end of it all, and he willed time to stop, *please God stop*, the bricks around him pulverizing into heat and energy and sound impossibly loud, clattering, smashing, clobbering, then the wall pie-sliced into non-existence; he was going, dissipating, a million, billion, trillion, subatomic events tearing him apart, ripping away at his very fractal being,

His soul went out like a light bulb.

He screamed.

*   *   *   *

The air on the peak of Grandfather's Bluff was warm and unusually still.

It was the last day of school, and tradition mandated a ceremonial gathering here. Rip sat on a picnic table near the scenic overlook, swilling beer, watching people arrive and the light fade.

A dozen or so jocks had turned up early, and not having the wasters experience of pacing themselves, were already loudly and obnoxiously inebriated, their cheerleader groupies caterwauling and stumbling drunkenly about the small park. Tony wandered aimlessly by, clutching a plastic cup of flat beer. His mascot's Tyrolienne hat was clamped over golden locks of his curls, pheasant feathers pointing phallically into the air, ubiquitous aviators shielding his eyes despite the encroaching twilight.

Lynette was here with Cheryl, Gaylene, and her twin brothers Trifton and Troy, but like the rest of the revelers, they ignored his presence. Rip guessed that this social ostracism was at least in some part due to his connection with Shitly's death.

Stephanie was absent. He hadn't seen her since that terrible night in the graveyard, which wasn't really that remarkable considering he hadn't been back to school since then, either.

He watched the darkness accrue in the valley spread out below, lights of the town winking on to reveal the hidden matrix of its grid, terminating more organically in a long swoop at the river's bend.

Slick's Blazer pulled up around the corner, sporting a displaced front bumper, another winter's worth of rust, and newer dents in the front and rear quarterpanels. It strode through the parking lot, jumped the curb, swerved around a small maple, and shuddered to a stop before his table, ripping Alice Cooper's 'School's Out' into the evening.

The night of Shitly's death, Rip had gone cold turkey off the drug, five torturous nights and days. He considered himself clean, albeit a small overcompensation of the alcohol abuse, staying away from *that place*. Observing his friends now with the benefit of a fresh perspective, he could well meter the level of deprivation to which they had fallen.

"Howdy, stranger." Slick leaped from the cab, looking shriveled, like he somehow shrunk.

Paul was a bag of bones, clothes tented loosely around his body. "Hey, Rip buddy. Where you been? Didn't see ya' at Shitly's funeral."

"Ahart." He muttered.

"What's that?" Moe had aged about ten years, thinner, with the addition of a beer gut that hung over his belt buckle.

"His real name was Ahart."

"Really." Sucking on a cigarette, Moe stopped to consider this.

"So, what say, buddy?" Paul clambered onto the picnic table, sitting next to him. "Care for a little bump to get the night started?"

"Nah, thanks." Shaking his head. "I'm not doing that anymore."

"*She-ya*, don't know what you're missing."

"I think I do, Paul."

A belligerent bellow sounded above the raised voices from the group of jocks, followed by others.

Slick sneered. "Fuckin' straights. Shouldn't be allowed to drink if they can't handle it." He turned and yelled in their direction. "Yeah, I remember my first beer!"

This merely encouraged another long round of excited whoops.

"Ha! Fuckin' jocks." Paul slapped him on the shoulder with a bony fist. "So this is it, eh? The end?"

"I suppose." Rip didn't know if he meant High School, but with his recent string of absentees, there was no way he would be graduating.

"No more pencils, no more books, no more teachers dirty looks." Paul sang dismally off key, along with the refrain, jumping up on top of the table. "School's *out*! For summer! School's *out*! Forever! "He leaped to the ground. "Our whole lives ahead of us, an shit!"

"Right."

Lynette lead Cheryl and Gaylene from behind the truck.

"Hey guys, where the hell have you all been? I haven't seen you in, …aah!"

Rip wondered how she would have reacted without the forgiving cloak of darkness.

"Hey Lynette, how you been?" Slick's attempt at savoir-faire was practically grotesque.

"Hi, uh, …Slick?"

"Great party tonight, eh?"

"Sure." She tried to ignore his lecherous gaze.

Gaylene shuffled out from behind, nervously fingering her cup. She looked at each of them.

"I just wanted to say, …uh, how sorry I am about what happened to Shitly. I didn't know him very well, but I know he was a good friend of yours."

"Ahh, Shitly was a good ole' boy!" Moe wailed.

"Yeah, he was. Thanks, Gaylene." Paul nodded somberly.

"How about you, Rip?" Cheryl moved up and sat where Paul had been. "How have you been?"

"Oh, I've been better. How you feeing? All healed?"

"All healed." She smiled, cocking her head in a way that he found unexpectedly beautiful. "I always wanted to thank you for being with me on that, …on that night."

"Aw shit Cheryl, I felt so bad, …"

"No, I mean it. No one else would, …and you know poor Shitly, …just that, you were a kind of an angel to me that night. I just wanted you to know that."

"Thanks Cheryl." He tried to look grateful. "That helps."

Thunder from the four-forty wedge preceded the 'Cuda as it nosed into the parking lot and shut down. Larry pulled his bulk from the passenger door as Marlon slipped out the driver's side, followed by Andrea and Viv from the back seat.

"Just put a Corvette to fucking shame!" Marlon greeted as they joined the growing throng.

"And that was with my fat ass along for the ride." Grunted Larry. "Pure testament to the power behind Motor City."

"*Hey*, Larry." Lynette chirped.

"Ladies." He waved. "Gentleman, …" Stopping, thick fingers pulled unconsciously at his lower lip. "…Paul?"

"She-ya, how ya' been, big guy?"

"Hey Rip." Viv twirled a strand of platinum hair, giving Cheryl sitting next to him a catty appraisal.

"Viv." He nodded. "Hey Andrea."

She blinked almond eyes back at him.

"Ah, Rip, can I have a word? 'Scuse us folks." Nearly pulling him off the table, Larry led him out to the lookout railing, the town beneath them blazing like Christmas tree lights. He bent down to Rip's level.

"Just what the fuck is wrong with Paul and his crew? I mean, I know Shitly getting killed is a hard thing and all, ..."

"It's the cocaine, Larry." He broke out. "They're dealing it, snorting it, smoking it. They're addicted to it."

"The Disco drug?"

"It's not just Disco. I was hooked too. It's bad, Larry, really bad."

"Disco's bad enough, but Jesus fuck." He magically produced a bottle of vodka from somewhere on his person and took a deep swill. "It looks like they're getting eaten alive."

"It killed Shitly. It's killing them." He shook his head. "I don't know what to do."

"Do?" Exhaling sadly, he shook his head, draping his gigantic proportions over the railing, staring out into the night. "Nothing *to* do. Social Darwinism, man. Only the strong and adaptable survive."

"That's kinda' harsh."

"Life's harsh."

"You been reading Nietzsche, Larry?"

"Who's Nietzsche?"

A bonfire was started in one of the fire-pits, and the party gathered around its cheerful glow. The number of jocks thinned and finally disappeared, prematurely spent, staggering off into the darkness, cheerleaders in tow. Rip sat drinking with the group, yet apart from them, sensing a growing distance. At some point a toast was raised to Shitly, after which Lynette led the group in a drinking song.

> *Here's to brother Shitly, brother Shitly, brother Shitly,*
> *Oh here's to brother Shitly, so drink chug-alugga drink,*
> *Drink, chug-alugga, drink chug-alugga,*
> *Drink chug-alugga, drink chug-alugga,*
> *Here's to brother Shitly, so drink chug-alugga, drink.*

Rip was disgusted. It was a pointless pathetic song for a pointless pathetic death.

He was returning from the keg with a new beer, watching Paul, Moe, and Slick work their way back to the truck, presumably to do drugs, when an orange Pontiac Firebird pulled into the lot. Nuts stepped out with his girlfriend, Anita, followed by Keith and Stephanie.

Rip paused, listening as the crowd greeted their arrival, Nuts chanting '*Blufftoppers*'. He watched Keith drape an arm around Stephanie's shoulders, finally spotting him, a funny expression surfacing on his face.

"Well, hey there, *bub*."

Seeing him, Stephanie shook her head as Keith pulled his arm free and stepped up.

"Been awhile, eh? What'cha' been up to, *bub*?"

He never saw the fist, but the world jogged, his nose cracked, and agony exploded over the front of his face as he lay splayed out on the grass.

"Hey!" Paul shouted from the Blazer.

"*Fuck my girl, HUH!?*"

Kicking him in the ribs, Rip thought he heard another crack.

"*You practically raped her! She told me what you did!*"

Another punt, definitely a crack this time.

"Kick his ass, Keith!" Bawled Nuts.

"Keith, stop! It wasn't like that!" Stephanie ran up, but suddenly he wasn't there anymore, only a large, dark shadow.

"Alright. Enough of this. You OK, Rip?"

He tried to nod, wasn't sure he succeeded.

"Hey! No interference. He was kicking his ass!"

Larry turned to Nuts. "Nobody's kicking anybody's ass tonight but me."

Nuts shrunk back, seeming to really see him for the first time. "Right. Live and let live. That shit."

"Aww, c'mon, Larry!" yelled Keith from somewhere behind him.

"Not now." Placing hands on hips, he seemed to inflate. "We'll sort things out later. Emotions are runnin' kinda' high right now."

"She-ya." Paul stood over him. "The fuck, Rip?"

Larry turned. "Get him outta' here, OK? We'll be right with you."

"Leavin' anyhow. Don't need no escort."

"Getting one anyway, Paul."

Then Slick and Moe were scooping him up, dragging him to the truck as Paul leaned around Larry.

"Hey Keith! Thank your old man for me for being drunk at the disposition. His fuck-up got us all off on a technicality! Ha!"

"Fuck you, you freak! Just get your River Rats asses outta' here!"

They threw Rip in the passenger's seat. He painfully tried to quell the flow of blood from his nose with a sleeve of his shirt, tasting it in his mouth, still somehow able to smell the chemical after-burn of freebase in the cab. Slick jumped in and keyed the ignition, turning to him with a frightening grin that split his face, revealing receding gums surrounding his ruined bridgework.

"I'd offer you a bump for the pain, but I think your bumper's broken. Ha! Ha! Ha!"

His friends were all coked to the gills.

Slick played a dangerous game of cat and mouse, following Marlon down the steep, narrow switchback road, at one point passing him in the blind oncoming lane around a hairpin turn, the very curve that Dart's father lost his life on. Rip actually felt the tires on the passenger side briefly leave the road, as Paul and Moe shrieked maniacally from the back seat.

They made it down to the foot of the bluff, the grade finally leveling out. Rolling past the golf course, the train signal came alive, blinking angry red eyes at the night, klaxon clanging a rhythm, slowly lowering a flashing, candy-striped arm to restrain their progress.

Slick braked at the barrier, throwing the shift lever up to park in disgust, on the steering column.

"Fuck!"

From the backseat, Paul screeched. "Goddamnit, just go! These things can take fifteen, twenty minutes!"

The 'Cuda pulled up behind them and roared.

"The gate's down, Paul, I can't go."

"Shit, then at least get some tuneage going."

Clawing at the cassettes scattered over the seat, he found one and held it up. "Blue Oyster Cult!"

Rip watched as the trains headlamp winked at them out of the darkness.

"Play 'Godzilla!'" Moe yelled.

"It's a *tape*, Moe, not an album. You'll take what comes." He fed it into the slot, launching the opening chords of 'Don't Fear the Reaper'.

The train's light started to fill the cab, its horn trumpeting.

From behind, Marlon's engine answered with a blare of its own.

Giggling spastically, Slick tromped down on the accelerator, the Blazer snorting back.

From all the light, the noise, and the pain in his face and ribs, Rip felt like his head was going supernova.

"Slick, could you please not do that?"

"What? *This*?" Slick kicked repeatedly at the gas pedal, the Chevy's V-8 blaring, glass-packs crackling, the 'Cuda behind them answering contrapuntally. The train whistle shrieked, riding over the cacophony, light expanding, the ground beginning to tremble at the diesel's approach.

"Don't fear the reaper, Rip."

Epileptically breaking into air guitar, stomping at the accelerator like a kick-drum, Slick thrashed about in his seat, singing to the song, and Rip was suddenly struck by a crystal-clear certainty of all things to come.

He concentrated on Slick's hand, now transformed into an object of extreme portent. It flailed about, mimicking guitar chords, backlit by the flashing warning lights, burning vividly, washing out in the headlamp's glare, as it struck the gear shift on the steering column.

There was a brief pause, time enough for Slick to turn and trade him a look, as if to say, *are you fucking shitting me*; as his foot hit the gas in perfect synchronization for the transmission to catch. The truck lurched forward, splintering through the guard-rail.

The locomotive towered over them as it bore down, horn blaring, earth rumbling, white light scorching the cab, and as they hurtled through the space of a perfect union, Rip stared back at his fate, and knew now that time was energy, energy was matter, matter was time, all in absolute concert, everything connected, from the gravity warping pulse of the largest quasar, to the smallest subatomic quantum event, each moment living in harmony within its own universe, and when twenty-thousand tons of kinetic momentum traveling well over sixty miles an hour intersected the Blazer crossing the tracks, iron cleaved steel, shredding aluminum, shattering bone into muscle, crushing organs into tissue, merging blood with hydraulic fluids, fusing organic to synthetic, pile-driving again and again, spinning the hapless machine forty-seven times for almost a half-mile, leaving a horrific wake of debris along the tracks, finally coming to a rest, the leaking bio-mechanical mass still attached to the forward coupling, and even as Rip's corporeal body was violently torn from existence, his final thought held briefly in the aether:

I live here forever.

*   *   *   *

"Hey, anybody checked the weather forecast?"

Randy craned his head from where he hung, upside down, atop the railroad trestle. His sweat dripped down between Dart and Curt's boats below, where they idled against the current. "Yeah. It's really freakin' hot."

He shook the can of spray paint in his hand, clattering the ball inside, and added an extra flourish to the side of the bridge. He stood up on the track, extending arms.

"Well, what you think?"

Dart considered the orange Day-Glo words.

RIVER RATS

4-EVER

"Very nice, Rand."

"You see how I used the number four instead of the word?"

"Yeah, good touch. It's creative."

Curt looked up impatiently. "C'mon, Rand, let's get going."

Taking care to prop the aerosol can on top of the rail, Randy dropped off the bridge into the channel, between the two boats, scissor-style. He climbed aboard with Curt and they cruised out to an oppressing heat, passing torrid air barely a relief. Sliding over the glassy, dead surface of the water, Dart pulled a curve around the Interstate Bridge so tight the hull of his flat actually skipped through the turn, motor barking angrily at the brief cavitations.

Curt had rigged his boat with a makeshift stereo from a used car system. He'd fashioned homemade plywood speaker cabinets, powered by a stolen car battery, and was playing it now, stubbornly ignoring the fact that it was impossible to hear over the motor.

I-90 Beach was named for its obvious proximity to the Interstate Highway, separated from it by a thicket of young cottonwood willows, a chain-link fence, and a rise of limestone boulders covered with an overgrowth of sandburs. The sandbar itself was large, a long slope of fine, clean silicate, dredged from the river bottom for the construction of the highway, popular with swimmers because of its gradual drop-off. When they pulled up and anchored, it was curiously deserted.

In the stagnant air, Dart broke out into a heavy sweat. "I don't ever remember this kind of heat. How hot do you think it is?"

"Ain't the heat. It's the humidity." Randy pulled the front of his shirt over the back of his head, exposing a belly curiously skinny and distended.

"And they're both at about one-hundred, I bet." Curt mopped his brow with the tail of his shirt, thought better, and removed it. "So, you wanna' set up now, or wait 'till it cools off."

"Do it now." Dart tore off his own T-shirt. "Don't want to do anything later but chill out."

They pitched the tent beneath a tropical sun, pounding stakes, threading tubes, raising the framework upright into the sand, rolling out sleeping bags, perspiring profusely within the sauna-like interior. Curt reconstructed the boat stereo in a far corner. Seeking refuge in the relatively cooler forest, they followed a trail through the adjacent wooded peninsula, gathering fuel for a bonfire.

The sun was a squat orange fireball fusing low with the zinc haze when they found their way back to the beach. The air was more temperate, though the sand still radiated a searing fever-heat. Cooling off in the river, they swam for about an hour under the darkening sky, reemerging to dry off and take stock of their supplies.

Hearing of a drink he thought sounded interesting, Dart had pinched a quart of Slo-Gin that had sat untouched for over a year from his parents liquor cabinet. Randy, at his suggestion, provided the orange juice mixer, which lay wedged in the ice at the bottom of the cooler, along with the requisite packages of hot dogs, buns, marshmallows, and condiments. Curt had a nickel-bag of pot, something called sinsemilla, that he'd bought from a dealer at school.

Mixing the Slow Screws into Styrofoam cups, they tasted the blend, pronounced it delicious, and proceeded to set up the campfire.

"Let's not forget the most important ingredient." Dart retreated back to the beached boats and pulled out their book-bags from school, emptying from each a year's worth of homework into the fire pit, squirting a generous amount of starter fluid onto the pile.

Lighting a match, he dropped it onto the stack, where it detonated with a satisfying, soft *whump*. They all settled back, watching flames consume the reams of spiral-bound notebooks, as Curt prepared to roll a joint.

"Well, this is it, guys." The cocktail was already working its way into Dart's brain. "We are now officially High School Freshman's."

"Yeah, 'cept I'll be going to Logan." Randy sulked.

"Enemies." Curt broke the seal of the tiny baggie. "Wow, this shit really reeks. Smells like that skunk weed that grows in the marsh."

"Maybe you got ripped off. Maybe that's what it is."

"Nah, can't be." He examined it against the firelight, pinching a small amount onto a Zig-Zag. "Looks totally different. Sticky, too."

"Man, it sure got dark fast." Dart searched the night. "Hey, does anybody think it's strange that our parents let us just take off and go camping for a whole weekend on the river?"

"No." Randy finished his drink. "Why?"

"I dunno'. Just wonder if it's, like, normal."

"I wouldn't know what normal is."

"Guess you got a point there, Rand."

"Hey, here's something." Curt finished twisting the joint, pointing it out to the darkened channel. "Anybody else think it's strange that on a super hot day like today, nobody's out on the river? I don't think I saw a single boat out the whole time."

"Yeah, now that *is* strange." Dart mixed another round of Slow Screws. "Why would you *not* want to be out here on a day like this?"

Curt lit the doobie, passed it around, and suddenly they were all coughing their lungs out, Randy nearly puking.

"Jesus, ..." Dart drew in a rattling breath. "...I don't know if that's really good or really bad."

Wheezing, Curt wiped watery eyes. "Afraid it's really good."

On his knees, Randy spat into the sand, gaping up in amazement. "Oh wow. Hey man, look at the fire."

"Ha!" The exclamation cost Dart pain. "Proof positive. It *is* really good."

A cicada drilled the night air from somewhere deep in the woods. They spent the next twenty minutes staring in fascination at the bonfire, listening to the thrumming of traffic on the highway from beyond the treeline. Randy finally sat back.

"Hey, you see on the news about the accident at Grandfather's Bluff last night?"

"Accident? ...no. What happened?"

"Guess three kids from High School got killed by a train. They're not saying who."

 "A train?"

"Yeah, a train."

"Fuck. Hope it's no one we know."

Curt shook his head. "Man, what a way to go."

"Sounded pretty bad."

"Shit… Hey, uh, do you guys, uh, …ah, never mind."

"Oh, come on." Randy scowled.

"Yeah, what is it?"

Dart toyed with his cup. "Do you remember the very first time that you really realized that you were going to die? That, like, you wouldn't live forever? That one day, just like everybody else, your life would end? You'd just be gone?"

A shocked silence followed, then Randy shivered.

"I try not to think about things like that."

"No." Curt sounded unsure.

"I was, what, …five or six? Couldn't sleep, so I was just lying there in the dark, thinking, when outtta' nowhere it just hit me. One day I would be dead. Would be nothing. Not even thought. It was like falling into a bottomless hole. Scared the shit outta' me. Still does."

Looking back earnestly, almost pleadingly, flames reflected in his eyes, Randy asked. "Dont'cha think you're going to heaven, Dart?"

"Heaven? Like in the bible? Like in your family's religion? Like God and the holy trinity versus the Devil? Good and evil? Like a bunch of guys thousands of years ago had all the answers to the universe that we're just now starting to find the questions to? Just can't believe in that stuff, Rand. Look at the way we treat the planet. We don't even understand the simplest things about nature, like how a virus lives, but we act like we know the big picture. And yeah, the devout will say, 'It's God speaking through us', but, you know, it's typical human ignorance and arrogance to assume that the maker of all creation made us in his image, and even gives a fuck about what each one of us is doing against all of eternity. Nah, …I think *we* created God, not the other way around."

The sky above suddenly erupted in brilliance. Veined talons of lightning exposed boiling banks of towering thunderheads, followed immediately by crackling explosions of thunder that rumbled and rolled off through the heavens.

"Think you might have pissed Him off."

"Holy shit!" Dart almost dropped his drink. "Did you *see* that?"

Curt whistled. "Those were some mean-looking clouds."

The initial display seemed to act as a triggering mechanism. The atmosphere abruptly came alive with a rapid salvo of bright purple flashes chased by a staccato cannonade of booming reports, each increasing in ferocity and intensity. The scorched smell of ozone filled the air.

They jumped to their feet.

Randy's voice was barely audible. "Is this real?"

"I'm seeing it too." Dart stared, hypnotized by the display of natural pyrotechnics.

A hissing sound from the fire behind them coincided with the painful pelting of a thousand tiny particulates.

"Hail!"

"Run away!"

"Book it, man!"

Snatching up the food and drink, they tore up the beach and dove for cover into the tent, it's canvas surface resonating drum-like with the torrent of tiny impacts. Giggling nervously, Curt lit the gas lantern, glow shifting from faint amber to bright white, filling the space.

"Man, that was freaky!" Randy regarded the surrounding walls, strobing with backlight. "Sure this thing is safe?"

Curt switched the cassette deck on, the equalizer's colored bars winking to life. "Man, we could ride a tornado out in this tent."

Dart settled back on his sleeping bag. "Not that we'll ever have to worry about that. Here, at least."

Choosing a tape from a small box, Curt pointed it. "Old Indian legend."

"Right."

"What's that?"

"You know that one, Rand."

"I don't think so."

Dart looked to Curt. "Chippewa, right?"

"Can't remember."

"Well, whoever, an Old Indian Legend says that tornados will never touch where three rivers meet."

"How they know?"

"I don't know, Rand, but they been around here a lot longer than us."

"But the Black joins the river a half-mile down from here."

"It's still in the vicinity."

"What's a tornado know of a vicinity?"

"God, I don't know Randy." Dart noticed that the hail had shifted to rain, a steady downpour, wind starting to pick up. "It's a legend."

Styx's 'Crystal Ball' played from the customized stereo, Tommy Shaw pleading in falsetto for the listener to tell him where he was going. Curt settled against one of the shivering walls mixing another round of drinks.

"So, are you and that Sara chick going steady now?"

"I don't know. Maybe. We made out."

Taking the cup from him, Dart felt a surreal dislocation sitting here, isolated in the tent. Just outside, the wind gusted though leaves with a tidal sound, rain striking the walls now from all directions.

"Get to second base yet?"

"Jeez Rand. A little, …uh, discretion maybe?"

He shrugged. "Well, she's got a great rack."

"Yeah." Dart smiled. "Something to look forward to."

A blinding, deafening detonation of light and sound filled the room, almost immediately sucked away with the wind, leaving them half-blind, ears ringing.

"Christ, that was close!" Dart tasted adrenaline.

"Yeah! Good one!" Curt laughed.

"You think it hit a tree? Think a tree might fall on us?"

"We're plenty far away from the trees, Rand."

"Shouldn't we go out and see?"

"I ain't going out in that." Curt held up the roach. "Only thing I'm gonna' do is finish this J, then this drink"

Dart shook his head. "Do you think that's a good idea?"

"The best! Jesus guys, would you mellow? I mean, we should be enjoying this, right? The end of school, and nature giving us the big show?"

"Yeah...yeah, you're right. Just a little jumpy from the weed."

"Just haven't had enough, is all."

They finished the remainder cautiously, smoking it right down to the last spark, *like true professionals*, thought Dart. He lay back, considerably more mellow now, contemplating the intersecting angles of the tent. The torrent outside seemed to have peaked, and was possibly even abating.

"Hey, you ever think, ...now that we're in High School and shit, like, what you might want to do for a living, after we're done?"

"Like, for the rest of our lives?"

"Yeah."

Sitting up, Randy's eyes were sleepy, swollen, and red. "Y'know, I always thought it would be cool to be a truck driver."

"You mean, driving semis cross-country? That shit?"

"Yeah, out on the highway, talkin' on the CB radio. Like that song." Holding an imaginary receiver up to his mouth, Randy squawked. "Breaker, breaker, one-nine. This here's the Rubber Duck."

Dart chuckled. "I suppose that's as noble calling as any."

Abandoning the mix altogether, Curt sipped from the bottle of gin, gasped. "Ahh! My old man, ...my old man says that this is a great time to join the Army. Ain't no wars now. Just serve your four years, get out; collect benefits for the rest of your life."

"Yeah, but a war could break out at any time."

"Chance you'd have to take."

"I don't know. That's pretty ballsy, Curt."

"Sounds pretty good to me."

"Couldn't do the Army myself."

"What *about* you. What do you want to do?'

"Been thinking about that. I don't know, ..."

"I know what you're gonna' be." Randy grabbed the bottle from Curt. "A big Hollywood movie maker."

"Yeah, …that one you made was really cool. The way you made those things move around."

"Well, I guess, …yeah, I'd really like to make films. But it's a lot more complicated than that. Not like you can just apply for the job."

"You'll figure it out. You're smart. You're creative."

"Yeah, …" Randy cringed at the taste of the gin. "You know how to draw. You can tell stories."

"Well, …thanks man." Dart was genuinely moved. "I appreciate that."

A low shuddering sound shook the ground.

"What do you think that was?"

"Probably just another one of those low-flying trucks."

Dart and Randy looked at each other, turned to Curt.

"Low-flying trucks?"

Curt smiled. "Did I just say that? Low-flying trucks?"

"Yeah!" Randy sniggered.

Curt did a sudden clumsy pirouette to the other side of the tent.

"Ha!" Dart clapped his hands.

"*Jesusfuckingchristididntdothatonpurpose*!" His eyes were wild.

"Huh?'

"*Thewallofthetentjustfuckenflippedmeoverhere*!" Curt was crying, hysterical.

"What?"

"*Wehavetogorightfuckingnow*!"

"You have to slow down, man, I can't understand you.'

Pointing to the doorway. "We have to go! Right! Fucking! Now!"

Ripping open the zipper, the door-flap snapped out into the night, and Curt dove through the opening, followed by the others. Dart had barely cleared the exit when the tent issued a great flapping crack, like the unfurling of a giant sail, and tore up into the sky. They stood in the lashing maelstrom, air gone suddenly very cool, dressed only in their cut-offs, staring against the onslaught of the driving rain at the leviathan funnel that stood over the river, boring into its very waters. Within it pulsed violent magnesium strobes, bolts reaching out from its base, licking at the churning wall cloud it hung from, in a relentless display. It advanced, touching the wooded tip of the peninsula, wrapping the canopy around itself, a terrible thrashing, crackling sound merging with the tornado's titanic heartbeat, the sound of a thousand locomotives.

Dart was instantly, utterly sober.

"*Let's move*! We have to get to the other side of the highway!"

They dashed up the beach, toward the highway, the rain actually driving upward now, into their noses and eyes. Cutting through the stand of cottonwoods, Dart felt a sharp pain as tearing gusts of wind lashed tops of the willows at their bodies. At the cyclone fence, Curt and Randy easily scaled up and over it. Dart, never a very good climber, struggled at the top, over the ragged row of wire twists, when a strong unbalancing gust shifted his weight.

He stared stunned as his palm was punctured by one of the barbs. Jerking the hand free, he slipped, dropping unmercifully down the other side onto the sandbur-infested boulders.

Sharp points of pain blossomed over his right side, but adrenaline drove him to stand and examine his injured hand in the stuttering lightstorm, a curious stuffing-like wad of what looked like gristle poking out from the wound, then he was off, loping laboriously up the rocks, cutting at his bare feet, feeling the sting of the sandburs embedded in his skin, following the diminishing forms of his friends over the rise of the deserted highway, the gale lifting, pushing him, nearly weightless over the median, claws of lightning and peals of thunder shredding the sky above, setting down on the opposite side to descend another bouldered slope, wind whistling and booming overhead, spotting the remarkable shelter of the deep-culvert that Curt and Randy were climbing into, air detonating as they helped him crawl into the whorled metal tube, barking shins against the ribbing, getting only a few feet in before a concussive blast of air turned him around, nearly pulling him back out, held by the human chain of Curt and Randy, the chamber resonating, ululating a deep, mournful note, din unearthly, reverberating in the very earth around them itself, and he was staring up into the eye of the vortex, a writhing, twisting whirlpool turned inside-out, choked with dancing, corkscrewing wires of lightning, and up, far beyond, burned silent stars against a tranquil patch of velvet night.

Then it was gone, the counter-rotation blasting him violently back inside against Curt and Randy, as the world grew opaque.

*　　*　　*　　*

They awoke to a cool, clear morning, huddled together for warmth in the culvert, embarrassed by the unconscious intimacy.

Dart's body burned with a constellation of small agonies, and he spent the time before leaving their shelter pulling out hundreds of the sharp burrs from wherever he could reach them. He was unsure of what to do about his wounded hand, the globule of fatty tissue still poking out of his palm. At least it had stopped bleeding, so he opted to protectively curl his fist around that which belonged inside of him, limping after his friends over the berm of the Interstate.

The sandbar was, predictably, a scene of utter devastation.

The cottonwoods had been smashed flat, churned into complex spiral patterns, older growth of the flanking peninsula faring little better. Birches, oaks, and maples stood naked, sheared of bark and branches, some snapped off at mid-point, others unearthed, lying flat to throw up great muddy crowns of roots, the beach covered in their debris of leaves and limbs. The two boats had been tossed far up the beach. They were still upright, flooded by rainwater to the transoms. The tent hung flaccidly from the upper boughs of a large surviving elm, bearing a scorched hole where the gas lantern had burned through, still presumably holding their clothes, provisions, sleeping bags, and what was left of Curt's stereo.

Dart dropped his aching body onto the damp sand. "Well, I got a new name for this place."

It was the first time anyone had spoken all morning.

From the main channel, out of the still, crisp morning air, came the sound of a motor, and something else.

"Look!" Curt pointed to the doppelganger of his own craft. It was skipping crazily over the waters of the Mississippi, charging out from behind the cove, dangerously fast, barely in control.

"Billy Ray." Randy whispered hoarsely.

"Lookit' the speed."

"The fucker's crazy." Dart watched, transfixed, as the craft pulled a wide, chopping turn, aligning its bow in with them, gradually throttling back. A stereo on board was broadcasting music, new to his ears, loud, aggressive, snarling vocals, something about 'God Save the Queen'. It approached, closing the distance, nosing up the embankment with a final push of the motor. It settled into silence along with the stereo.

Billy Ray rose from the rear seat, but it was a Billy Ray somehow transformed, head completely shaved, save for a bristling shock of dark hair that ran along the length of his skull, reminding Dart of early Indians he'd read about, the Mohicans. He was clad only in weathered cut-offs held together by stitches of safety pins, and worn brown working boots. His body was lean, rippling with muscles, a crude tattoo on one bicep of an encircled capital A, earring dangling from his left lobe, right nipple pierced. He traversed the length of the boat, dropping to the sand from the bow, regarding them with cool gray eyes.

"You River Rats look like you've had a hard night."

Randy stepped back. "How you know we River Rats?'

Snorting almost contemptuously, Billy Ray extracted a pack of Camel unfiltered from a pocket, tapped it twice on his wrist, and pulled a cigarette free, igniting it with the clink of a Zippo.

"I gotta' ask, how you get that thing so fast?" Curt hooked a thumb over his shoulder at his land-locked craft, and Billy Ray raised an eyebrow. "It's the same boat and motor as mine. I tried everything. Bored out the cylinders. Speed prop. Still don't move *nothin'* like yours."

Twin plumes of smoke rolled out Billy Ray's nostrils. "Did you take the governor off?"

Curt blinked, snapped his fingers. "The governor! Christ! Yes!"

Billy Ray turned to Dart. "Lookin' for someone. River Rat like you. Older. Name is Rip."

"Rip? What kind of name is that?"

"It's a name."

"Nah, never heard of a Rip."

He turned to the other two.

"You?"

"Woulda' remembered a Rip."

Randy shook his head.

"Weird." Scratching his chin, Billy Ray looked up and saw the tent. "Really weird. You guys into some kinda' alternative camping thing?"

"Storm." offered Dart.

"Yeah." Randy wilted to the sand. "That was way too intense. Just glad it's over."

Billy Ray laughed. "Over? Storm's not over, boys." He turned, pushed his boat into the shallows. "Real storm hasn't even fucking arrived."

Pausing briefly on the bow, he looked back at something down the beach. "Softshell? Huh, haven't seen one in years."

Dart, Curt, and Randy turned to watch the turtle, impeccably camouflaged, scuttle over the sand to the shoreline, where it slipped aerodynamically into the water.

Billy Ray pulled the motor to life, executed a tight power-turn, and tore through the center of the cove, stereo blaring, to meet the main channel, pulling out of sight around the peninsula beneath the Interstate Bridge. Dart was certain by the motor's wavering tone that Billy Ray was slaloming through the pylons, and for a brief moment he listened to the first wave of punk echo between solid and liquid, over the waters of the river, on the first day of a brand new summer.

Brian D Garrity

Acknowledgements

This was a project that evolved over a long period of time, frequently getting shelved for others, always somehow managing to drift back, and there are many people I am indebted to, so, profound apologies to those who have been overlooked.

First, thanks to Scott Addington [wherever you are] and all the crazy creatives at the Lighthouse Bay / Scooterville Building [RIP] for cultivating an atmosphere necessary to jump-start this thing, and to Christine Ziebarth and her encouragement at its inception, who sadly is not around to see its fruition. To Jodi Larson for her enthusiastic backing, and Heidi Arneson, for continued support and input, Cosmic Slop Radio for inspiration and their appreciation for all things '70's. The Linden Hills Library, where a large chunk of the manuscript was forged, and to the great people at the Ivy Building for the Arts.

Brian D Garrity

The author on the Mississippi River, 1978

About the author:

Brian D Garrity has held a variety of vocations, including artist, carpenter, musician, filmmaker, and photographer. Still Waters Run Deep is his first novel. He currently lives in Minneapolis.